W9-BKK-996

34311   02-25-16   26.95   B+T

CARRY ME

CARRY ME

a novel

Peter Behrens

Pantheon Books, New York

Library of Congress Cataloging-in-Publication Data
Behrens, Peter, [date]
Carry me : a novel / Peter Behrens.
pages ; cm
ISBN 978-1-101-87049-5 (hardcover : acid-free paper).
ISBN 978-1-101-87051-8 (eBook).
1. Man-woman relationships—Fiction.   2. Germany—
History—1933–1945—Fiction.   I. Title.
PR9199.3.B3769C37   2016   813'.54—dc23   2015022383

www.pantheonbooks.com

Jacket images: (top) *Manchester Daily Express*/SSP/ Getty Images; (bottom) RetroAtelier/Getty Images
Jacket design by Janet Hansen

Printed in the United States of America
First Edition

1 2 3 4 5 6 7 8 9

FOR BASHA AND HENRY

In dreams begin responsibility.

—W. B. YEATS

Daily Alta California (newspaper). San Francisco 1.8.1884. Lange Family Archive, 12 C-8-1884. Special Collections, McGill Library, McGill University, Montreal.

—

SHIPPING INTELLIGENCE

ARRIVED: GERMAN BARK *LILITH*, LANGE, 181 DAYS FROM HAMBURG; MDSE TO EPPINGER & CO. MEMORANDA PER *LILITH* — LEFT HAMBURG FEB 1, CROSSED THE EQUATOR IN THE ATLANTIC MARCH 9, ON W 25° 30', 23 DAYS OUT; FROM S. 45° HAD VERY HEAVY WEATHER; PASSED S. 50° IN THE ATLANTIC MAY 7; WAS 25 DAYS THENCE TO S. 50° IN THE PACIFIC; OFF THE CAPE, HAD STRONG NW GALES WHICH CONTINUED UP TO S. 33°; CROSSED THE EQUATOR IN THE PACIFIC, W. 109° 45'; CARRIED NE TRADES TO N. 29°; FROM THENCE TO PORT, MODERATE WEATHER.

THIS WILL BECOME THE STORY OF A YOUNG WOMAN, KARIN WEINBRENNER. Her story is not mine, but sometimes her story feels like the armature my life has wound itself around. I am telling it, so this story is also about me.

I was born 27 May 1909 on the Isle of Wight, in a house, Sanssouci, named after Frederick the Great's summer palace at Potsdam. I was baptized Hermann Lange but for most of my life have been called Billy.

Sanssouci still sits on a cliff overlooking the English Channel, which on a fair day spreads out below like blue butter. The house is now a small, expensive "boutique" hotel and no longer called Sanssouci. The management offers weekend-getaway packages for anxious Londoners who desire sea views, the scent of roses, and shadowy island lanes dripping with fuchsia.

Before the First World War the house belonged to Karin's father, Baron Hermann von Weinbrenner. He was a chemist and colorist and very rich: half the cotton shirts in the world were dyed with aniline colors he'd created. The kaiser had first given Weinbrenner his *von*, then raised him to the lowest rank of nobility after he married Karin's mother, daughter of an Irish peer.

Baron Hermann von Weinbrenner was the second Jewish member of the Royal Yacht Squadron at Cowes, on the Isle of Wight—Lord Rothschild was the first. Weinbrenner kept a pair of very fast gaff-rigged schooners, *Hermione* and *Hermione II*, and my father, Heinrich "Buck" Lange, was his racing skipper and trusted friend. Which is why my parents were living at Sanssouci and why I was born there.

Birthplaces, nationality—such details have consequences in this story.

My grandfather—also Heinrich Lange, but known in the family

as Captain Jack—was a professional sea captain out of Hamburg. The Lange family had been traders and merchants (mostly in the Baltic) for a couple of hundred years before Captain Jack persuaded a syndicate of uncles and cousins to speculate in the California grain trade. Which meant purchasing San Joaquin Valley wheat at Port Costa, on San Francisco Bay, and transporting the cargo to Europe aboard their own three-masted bark, *Lilith*, to sell on the Hamburg exchange.

Risky business.

After some very rough weather on her westward passage round Cape Horn, *Lilith* was one hundred and seventy-one days out of Hamburg and a thousand miles off Acapulco when my grandmother Constance, who was Irish, went into labor. A couple of hours later my father was born in the master's cabin, the delivery assisted by Captain Jack and by Joseph the Negro cook, who cried out, "Oh, the fine fellow! He is a bucko seaman!"

Christened Heinrich after his father and grandfather my father was known ever after as Buck.

Ten days later—six months out from Hamburg—*Lilith* dropped anchor at Yerba Buena Cove, and Heinrich/Buck was rowed ashore and registered as a loyal subject of the German emperor by Dr. Godeffroy, the consul at San Francisco.

The trouble starts there. Our story would have been quite different if, instead of being born on a German ship on the high seas, Buck had waited a few weeks to be born in a comfortable San Francisco hotel room.

Buck Lange an American citizen? How much simpler everything might have been.

But you can't operate on history that way. An American Buck might have joined the American Expeditionary Force in 1917. I can see him answering the call to colors. He'd have been shipped to France and killed in one of the ugly, costly battles the AEF fought in 1918—

I don't want to lose you over tedious genealogy and history that must be very dim to you. This is a story of real people who lived and died, about their times and what went wrong. I shall try to be honest even when it's apparent I am making things up, delivering scenes I couldn't have witnessed.

I know the truth in my bones. And that's what I shall give you.

I'll include documents—newspaper clippings, telegrams, even a film poster—from the Lange family archive, which McGill University has generously agreed to house. Calling it an *archive* is vainglorious. A few boxes on a library shelf are all it amounts to.

There are entries from Karin's journal, her *Kinds of Light* book. When I read them I hear her voice. Even when her entries are merely extracts from her reading, I still feel her mind at work in the process of selection.

You'll find letters here, from Karin, from others. I want you to hear the voices.

Otherwise they are all dead, aren't they? Otherwise, no one remembers.

><+>-O-<+><

Fast-forward, please, from San Francisco, 1884, to Germany, 1908, when Buck Lange, my sea-born father, is introduced to Eilín McDermott, my mother, at Walden, the von Weinbrenner estate outside Frankfurt.

Sanssouci was the baron's seaside villa, his dream of sea air, sunlight and Englishness, but Walden was his real home, his grounding. His ground.

Sailing season hadn't begun. Buck was in Germany to inspect plans for a brand-new racing yacht the baron had commissioned from the Townsend & Downey shipyard in New York City.

Eilín was living at Walden as lady secretary to Lady Maire, the baron's Irish wife, who had begun an extraordinary collection of medieval religious art. The baroness was unexpectedly pregnant and, at forty, very self-conscious of her condition.

The Weinbrenners' only child, a son, had died in infancy eleven years before.

My mother and father were almost the same age exactly, birthdays two days apart. Eilín was an Irish Catholic employed by an Irish Protestant aristocrat married to a German Jewish millionaire. After his landfall on the Barbary Coast, Buck's boyhood had been spent in Melbourne, Buenos Aires, and Hamburg. He'd done his military service in a regiment of Prussian cavalry and sailed round the world more than once.

My parents did share an Irish connection: her father and his mother were natives of the county Sligo and lived within a few miles of each other.

And at Walden, besieged by nineteenth-century furniture and stiff Wilhelmine formality, Eilín and Buck recognized a bold, light spirit in each other. They were both twentieth-century persons.

Karin would always envy me my parents, younger and more supple than her own. Eilín and Buck raised me in the life they made together. I lived inside my parents' marriage. The baron and Lady Maire never made room for Karin.

The day after they were introduced, my parents took a walk in the Walden woods. Buck wore tweeds. Eilín had on one of the elaborate hats of the Edwardian era, the size and shape of a small bathtub.

They were both tall. Her hair was honey-brown. She had full breasts, wide shoulders, and narrow hips. He'd lived all over the world, and his English could sound Australian, Irish, British, even American. He was also perfectly fluent in the dialect of a Hamburg Platt, the *Hochdeutsch* of a Hamburg shipowner.

Eilín hadn't lived anywhere but her father's house, the convent outside Dublin where she was educated, and the Weinbrenners' estate. Her accent was middle-class provincial Ireland. Her German was never much good.

After twenty minutes Buck stopped under a giant bare oak and asked Eilín to marry him. If she was willing, he said, he would arrange everything and meet her in London in two weeks. They could be married in London and live at Sanssouci. The Weinbrenners only used the house one month a year, during sailing season. The rest of the year it would be theirs: the baron had said so.

Eilín heard him out, then, without responding, turned and resumed striding along the forest path.

Buck was startled. He'd risked his dignity to make a proposal that had been ignored, even scorned. Dismayed and confused, he started after her, thinking he really ought to return to the house and leave her crashing through the woods like a hunted animal.

She wore a pale-blue dress. Her enormous hat kept getting snagged on leafless branches. It was early spring. Green shoots were just starting from a mat of brown oak leaves on the forest floor. Crusts of snow lingered in the shadows. Everything smelled of transhumance, rot, change.

Father Pursues Mother Through Hessian Woods, April 1908.

I can picture the scene as if it were captured in one of the (very few) family photographs—sepia toned, frail—that survive. Maybe *pursues* isn't accurate. For a gentleman to pursue a lady who has just turned down a sincere proposal of marriage would be clumsy, luckless, foolish. A gentleman does not chase a lady through a forest, even a small, superbly groomed German forest.

But if he's a man of spirit, he can't retreat to the house, either.

"Listen here," Buck called out. "What's the matter? Have I frightened you? Offended you?"

He was out of breath keeping up with her. Eilín walked purposefully. She was lithe. Even wearing the massive hat she could scamper along forest paths as quick and nimble as a deer.

"Won't you speak?"

He didn't want to admit to himself that she was fleeing from him.

And, in fact, she wasn't.

She stopped so abruptly he nearly crashed into her. "Oh no, I'm not frightened." She turned to face him.

"What is it then?" He was out of breath, and his dignity had been scrambled.

"I need to think. I think more clearly if I'm walking."

He continued to stare at her. She was rude, or perhaps just odd, and certainly beautiful.

"This hat! Not quite the thing, is it?"

Unpinning the magnificent hat, she removed it. Her hair was beautiful and thick, golden in certain lights, auburn in others. It was never cut, and always worn up, except when she went to bed.

"Well, I can't live at Sligo," she said. "I don't get on with my father."

"Who said anything about Sligo? We'll live at Sanssouci. I'll live with you anywhere."

"Is it nice there? Is it bright? Should I like it?"

"Well, yes, it is, rather. I expect you will. Beautiful gardens. The sea."

"I suppose I shall like it. When shall we do the thing, then?"

"Are you certain? Are you saying that you agree to marry me?"

"I knew the moment you came in the library yesterday. It's the details and effects one has to work through mentally."

She looked at him, her expression concerned and serious. She did have a wry sense of humor, my mother, but most of the time she was unnervingly straightforward. "I think we'll be very happy. As happy as married people are generally."

They were solitary people, and for the rest of their lives would rely on each other emotionally without much need of friends, except the Weinbrenners. The marriage never had trouble except when they were apart. Separations were a torment and destabilizing. Neither did well mentally without the other.

They were wed in London and went to live, as Buck had promised, at Sanssouci. Eleven months later I was born in the bedroom where Karin had been born the summer before. Ever since her son's death, Lady Maire had distrusted German doctors, which was why her daughter was born in England.

My parents asked the Weinbrenners to stand as my godparents, and they agreed and came over to London. I was baptized Hermann, after the baron. This was also the name of Karin's brother, buried at Walden.

Her parents did not bring Karin to London for my christening, but she was on the Isle of Wight the following summer. The Weinbrenners came out from Germany for August and settled into Sanssouci, and my parents and I shifted into a set of stuffy, eighteenth-century rooms above the bar at the Crab Inn, in Shanklin village.

While the Weinbrenners were in residence, my mother spent most afternoons up at the house, writing letters for the baroness, and I was looked after by a village girl, Miss Anne Hamilton. Hamilton usually had Karin in her charge as well and would push us into the village in a single pram. Once during that first summer Karin crept into the nursery while I was napping and poked at my eyes to test if I was real. I began wailing: real enough. Was she punished? Probably. A little girl born so late in their lives had been a shock and something of an embarrassment to her parents. They ought to have been grateful for another chance at parenthood, ought to have cherished Karin more than they did. But the baron had his aniline colors, his polo ponies, yachts, and great wealth; and Lady Maire had horses and hunting and medieval art. They mostly ignored their daughter.

Possibly my only real memory of Karin at Sanssouci—at the same time so sharp and so ungrounded, so full of sea noise and sea light that it seems a dream and not an entirely authentic memory—is the afternoon she tried to swim to America.

It was my third or fourth summer. Our nurse had brought us to the beach below the cliffs on a blazing blue afternoon. I was napping under a little shelter Hamilton had constructed out of napkins, sticks, and beach towels, and she must have dozed off, too. It was a shingle beach, with the lulling clatter of waves. I wasn't old enough to sea bathe— Hamilton would sometimes hold me and dabble me in up to my knees. But Karin had already learned to swim and must have seen her chance while our young nurse was dozing. Wading in against the small sharp waves, Karin plunged and started swimming offshore.

It's unusual enough that a child four or five years old would know how to swim. It's an extraordinary impulse in one that age to confront something as enormous and active as the sea without feeling the least intimidated. Karin was determined to enter that wild world and leave behind the calm and safety of shore.

Hamilton awoke after a few minutes, feeling dozy and heavy. She sat up and looked about. On a clear day in midsummer there was always a stun of yellow heat on the beach. I recall an unwholesome odor of potted-meat sandwiches and custard, wrapped in wax paper inside a wicker hamper.

No Karin in sight.

We always had that beach to ourselves. It was at the head of a small, tight cusp of a cove, seabirds whickering overhead. But the cove was open to the Channel. Hamilton scrambled to her feet and scanned the water. Leaving me under my little tent, she hurried along the shore to the foot of the cliff path, steps cut in rock, searching upward for a little girl in a white sundress, seeing only wheeling gulls.

Hamilton climbed a boulder, scanned seaward again, and made out a speck of white flotsam beyond the first break—Karin, in her bleached muslin sundress. By then she'd swallowed enough seawater to feel sick and was allowing tide and wave action to sway her back to the shore. Our nurse gave a yelp and dashed down to the water's edge. Not bothering about her boots and white stockings or the hem of her skirt, splashing through yellow surf, she grabbed Karin off the top of a wave, shook her, slapped her, and dragged her ashore where they collapsed in wet sand, both sobbing.

Wary of punishment herself, at first Hamilton didn't mention what had happened to any of the adults. I certainly wasn't old enough to inform anyone. But after the Weinbrenners went back to Germany, never to return—for this would have been the summer of 1913, and racing was canceled in '14 because of the European crisis—Anne Hamilton did tell my mother of the little German girl's wicked waywardness. What a fright it had given her, and the child had boldly insisted that she'd been swimming for America. Only the bitter-tasting sea hadn't wanted her and kept pushing her back.

"I told her it wasn't America it was only bloody old France that way! And if she turned up in France in a sopping wet frock with seaweed for hair, they'd call her a mermaid, the French would, and burn her at the stake."

1938

Letter. Addressed *Herr Billy Lange, Übersetzung Abteilung, IG Farben, Hauptsitz Frankfurt A.M.,* postmarked *Frankfurt A.M. 16.9.1938.* Lange Family Archive, 11 C-09-1938. Special Collections, McGill Library, McGill University, Montreal.

———

TRIERISCHEN GASSE 7*
16th September 1938

My dear Billy!

As your old schoolfellow I write in perfect honesty and sincerity. There is a matter I must bring to your attention. Your attitude to the national and racial developments in our Germany has never been made clear. Some fellows were discussing this yesterday and I will say they were sincerely troubled on your behalf. Your attitude is quite mystifying. We have reports that you claim you are not a German man.

Billy, old mate, let me say it's not a matter of what passport a fellow holds. It's that which is in his heart and his blood which counts. No more pettifoggery and bullshit please! Now you have come of age in Germany, a good German name, a handsome fellow of German blood, and you have a good position with the IG.

Believe me who wishes you the best. Our branch welcomes you. Consider. Join us in the struggle for a new world. Don't you think now is time you accept the proud national aspect and the duty of the German man?

Heil Hitler!
Günter

*My translation from German orig!—B.L. 9.2.88

Telegram, 4 Nov. 1938. Lange Family Archive, 11 C-11-1938. Special Collections, McGill Library, McGill University, Montreal.

——◆——

095 TELEGRAMM DEUTSCHE REICHSPOST

aus 2097 Berlin 04.11.1938

H. Lange IG Farben Hauptsitz Frankfurt A. M.

Billy Dear=Drastic News=Komm bitte

=K. vW +

A CLERK HAD DROPPED THE TELEGRAM ONTO MY DESK IN THE EXPORT
Sales Department, fifth floor, IG Farben headquarters, Frankfurt.
Karin was summoning me to Berlin.

I wondered what her "drastic news" could be. We were living in a
drastic period. Perhaps the emigration bureau where she assisted Jews
trying to flee Germany was finally being shut down.

It was five weeks since my last visit to Berlin. I slipped Karin's telegram into my briefcase and telephoned to reserve a seat on the next
morning's Berlin express. Then I rang my parents at Bad Homburg and
told them I was off for a hiking weekend in the Taunus.

I had always taken pains to conceal the current and depth of our
relationship from Buck and Eilín. They'd only have disapproved.
They'd have said in all kinds of ways that Karin von Weinbrenner was
too much for me.

Saturday morning I caught an FD express for Berlin. I intended to
persuade her it was time we both left Germany. If she would leave, then
I could, too. She was the only reason I hadn't.

A few weeks earlier, at the height of the Munich crisis, I'd received
the "friendly" note from my old schoolfellow Günter Krebs, now an SS
man. Günter had joined the party early, was one of the original sixteen
members of the first Schutzstaffel in the Gau Hessen-Nassau, and one
of the first men at my firm, IG Farben, to declare himself a Nazi.

Günter's note contained an implicit threat: if I stayed in Germany
I'd have to accept what the Nazified authorities already considered
my German nationality. And that meant military service in the rapidly
expanding *Heer* or arrest and a one-way trip to someplace like Dachau.

Karin, like me, held a British passport. Our parents had always seen to it that we maintained them. Our passports meant we didn't need exit visas to leave Germany.

So many were so desperate to flee that by then it seemed almost obscene that the pair of us had chosen not to.

But I couldn't leave without her. She called me her bodyguard.

She was living in Berlin, I was in Frankfurt, but by 1938 I was as close to her as I ever was in my life to any other person. I'll say that now. The sex we had was passionate but also, in a way, cool. It was like people taking a blood oath. Does that sound grim? Well, it wasn't. It was important, exciting, to be in bed together during those years when the ethical world of Germany was crumbling. But yes, it had a ritual aspect. Bed was wild but safe for both of us at a period when life in Germany (even for those carrying British passports) was becoming more and more precarious.

Karin was more German than I'd ever be. She was also, at least after the Nuremberg Laws, a Jew. She agreed that life in Germany was impossible, but she was unwilling to leave her father.

A British passport guaranteed the right to live and work in any of the Dominions. After receiving Günter's letter, I'd immediately written three of my best Canadian customers, and the day before Karin's telegram dropped on my desk I was offered a job in Vancouver, selling chlorophenolic compounds and petrochemicals to lumber mills deep in the Canadian forest. It sounded terribly far from Europe. And that was all right with me. I immediately booked two passages for New York aboard a Holland-America liner, the SS *Volendam*, sailing from Rotterdam in early December.

Going up to Berlin, I didn't know if I'd be able to persuade Karin to come to America, but I was determined to try.

My FD-Zug train arrived at the Anhalter Bahnhof at noon. I went straightaway to her office in a shabby building behind the Wertheim department store, on the Leipziger Platz. When she was fired from UFA after the film studio was commandeered by the Nazis, she'd first gone to work at the Zionist Agency in Berlin. After a few months she'd left them to join a small emigration bureau started by a lawyer, Stefan Koplin, also fired from UFA. "Kop" would help Jews go anywhere, not just to Palestine. He was an expert at bargaining for visas from South American embassies. Karin's specialty was calculating the "flight tax" that had to be paid before any exit permit was granted. The formula was insanely complex, and if the slightest error was made, exit permits were gleefully withheld. But Karin had her father's head for figures. She claimed she never made mistakes. Sometimes she even persuaded her father to help her Jews pay their flight tax. Herr Philipp Kaufman, the baron's lawyer, objected, saying it left Weinbrenner even more vulnerable to the regime, but the baron usually gave his daughter whatever she asked for, though he didn't approve of ordinary Jews leaving the country any more than he'd approved of the film stars and directors who were her friends quitting Berlin for Hollywood. To him they were all *Fahnenflüchtige:* deserters.

Baron von Weinbrenner told my father that if the Nazis wished *him* to leave they'd have to pick him up, carry him to the frontier, and physically throw him out, and still he would make his way back, because Germany was his country, not theirs.

Karin's office was listed as AUSWANDERUNGSBERATER in the lobby directory. Emigration consultants. I rode the elevator cage to the fifth floor, walked down a grimy corridor, and entered a room that had once been a leather shop. A half-dozen clerks sat with anxious clients at desks groaning with files. A program of Viennese music squawked from a radio. More files were stored in dozens of cartons stacked on the floor.

The previous summer a group of rabbinical students had invaded the office, furious that it remained open on the Jewish Sabbath. As a compromise Kop now shut the doors at 4:00 p.m. on Fridays, always with a herd of anxious clients who had to be pushed out the door. On Saturdays, however, they kept regular German office hours and stayed open until one o'clock.

The room had the harried, fretful atmosphere of a train station. Stale air, blue with cigarette smoke.

Kop waved at me from his desk. He was a young man, a brilliant lawyer, but overworked and overweight. In August he had lost his villa to the *Generalbauinspektorat* with zero compensation offered. He'd recently packed his wife and children off to Buenos Aires, but assured Karin he would not "abandon his post."

Karin had told me that before any application for an exit permit could be considered, the applicant had to list every item of personal property so the *Reichsfluchtsteuer* could be assessed.

"My Jews must pile up their goods, including the last pair of socks. Including the needles that darned the socks, Billy. Including the thread. Then if they drench the pile with kerosene, light it with a match, possibly the gentlemen of the *Finanzamt* will be satisfied. But perhaps not, perhaps you have forgotten to list those postage stamps your wife kept in the kitchen drawer, that spare can of motor oil in the boot of your car?

"I'll visit their mean apartments on Schweidnitzerstraße, Billy dear, I'll stop by their beautiful houses in Dahlem, I don't allow my Jews to overlook a single thing. I have them list the box of matches in their pocket. I feel the urge sometimes, I can hardly stifle it, I want to make them list their thoughts. 'Have you ideas, valuable or not, list on page seven, section three, *bitte*. Do you have desires, Jews? List. Do you have memories? *Aufzählen, bitte*. All the meals you have consumed. Every single one, *bitte*. Please write down the number of candles that no longer exist in Germany because you have lit them. List the volume of air sucked in since birth, in liters, please.'"

That Saturday she waved at me across the crowded room before turning her attention back to files on her desk, which also held an enormous gray typewriter and a Burroughs adding machine. She looked terribly thin. Whenever I came up to Berlin there was never much food in her apartment, maybe a packet of rye crusts, a scrap of butter, coffee. She'd stopped buying from the grocers on her street, ardent Nazis. Some days she consumed only apples, nuts, and black coffee.

I hadn't had anything to eat myself since buying a sausage roll at a stall at Frankfurt Hauptbahnhof. On our Berlin Saturdays, we usually had lunch at one of the cafés on Unter den Linden, then meandered through the city, wending our way back to her flat in Charlottenburg. An important newspaper editor—a party member—wanted that flat for his in-laws. Since late summer the threat of eviction had been hanging over Karin's Berlin existence. The building's *Hausmeister*, who was loyal to her, had warned that management was going to pitch her belongings out on the street one day.

"And then, I'll be a Wandering Jew," she said. "But not before."

I sat on a bench beside a man in a business suit tapping a malacca cane nervously against his alligator shoes. I watched Karin shuffling papers into a neat pile that she tied up with yellow string. Standing up, she put on her hat and started pulling on gloves. I headed for the elevator cage, and she met me there. We hardly spoke.

Coming together, especially in public, was usually like that for us. At first we needed silence.

She wore her gray-green Harris Tweed overcoat with a velvet collar, very smart. Waiting for the elevator, I could feel the vibration of the lift machinery and hear the rattle of the iron cage. She pouted her lips and applied fresh lipstick. At the Zionist agency, some of the people were radical socialists, some were very religious, but they'd all objected to her wearing lipstick. So of course she had responded with ever-more-flamboyant shades. And she'd worn sandals in summer and painted her toenails maroon.

We walked out into the bright, cold fall afternoon. I had my Taunus hiker's knapsack slung over one shoulder. Crowds seethed in and out of the great department stores. On Unter den Linden there was a chill wind. Patrons on the café terrace were swaddled in their overcoats. We ordered soup and venison and glasses of beer, and I handed her Günter Krebs's friendly little note and watched her face as she read it.

When she finished reading she looked up.

"I'm pregnant, dear Billy," she said.

THE NAVAL SPY

Hardboard notebook/journal. Holograph inside cover: *Arten von Licht Buch* [*Kinds of Light Book*], *Karin v Weinbrenner*. Unpaginated. In English and occ. German. Lange Family Archive, 11 C-12-1988. Special Collections, McGill Library, McGill University, Montreal.

—

Remembered light of summers at Shanklin on I of W)

Blues von cyan zu azur and greens are chief components. This is a complex light but soft. With the air which is tonic, my early scents of freedom. I only speak of summer, we only were there for summers. Not many, the war stopped us coming. This light, isle light, is actually quite changeable even in summer there is restlessness to it. When you suppose you know it white, heavy, blank, cool—the herring scent of the north, Wikingerluft—then the wind comes 'round, brokers the mist and the light sharpens and becomes focused and powerful. Clear. The rim appears on the horizon, floating—"why my dear, So ist Frankreich." The air in which I was born surrounded was a loving air. Saline briny tangy promising. Windows-banging light. Gusting 20 knots. A surround of excited light. A storm light. Suffusion. Powerful in the afternoons. Lay of sunlight across the garden at my Sanssouci and beyond it the navy sea . . .

KARIN AND HER PARENTS SPENT THE MONTH OF AUGUST ON THE ISLE. Each year, after the Weinbrenners returned to Germany, my parents and I would settle back into our beloved Sanssouci. The house wasn't handsome or old or very dignified, but it was an airy, lucky seaside villa. On clear days we could see the blue coast of France. Much later, during the war, Eilín and I listened to the rumble of guns from over there. There were gardens and a great spread of lawn and nothing to interfere with the sprawling, questing presence of the sea. We could watch ships entering and leaving Portsmouth Harbour.

Buck kept a pair of German naval binoculars close at hand. He wasn't interested in watching the great liners from Southampton or gray warships moving in and out of the naval base—only yachts, especially gaff-rigged racing schooners. The household was under instructions to sound an alert whenever a tall gaff rig was spotted. Buck had a professional interest in how efficiently a sailboat was handled, what speed she could make, in what sort of weather. Races were not casual affairs at the Royal Yacht Squadron. All skippers and crews were professionals, the only amateurs on board were owners and guests, and owners, if they hoped to win, never took the helm. There was always money riding on the race, private wagers breathlessly reported in London newspapers.

Baron Hermann Weinbrenner has wagered a thousand pounds that his Hermione II *will beat the Glaswegian biscuit manufacturer Mr. Beezlebub's* Snapcrack *on the annual Round the Island race.*

In blazers, white flannels, and yachting caps, the baron and the biscuit manufacturer would puff cigars on their respective decks while professional skippers like my father handled the boats.

My mother and I only went out on *Hermione* at the beginning and end of the season.

I'll offer you one hard blue day.

Everything blue: sea, sky. Eilín wearing a white dress and a cream flannel blazer, trimmed with blue ribbon. She is smiling, her teeth gleaming white in a face dark from the summer's worth of sun. She had never sailed before meeting my father. *The Irish are born with their backs to the sea*, my grandmother Con used to say.

But Con was herself an exception to the rule; and my mother was certainly another. Sailing delighted Eilín. I think my parents felt more free of care and worry on a good hard sail than any other time.

We're on *Hermione*, but the baron is not aboard, so it's July before his arrival, or September, after he's gone back to Germany. We're on a broad reach, boom sheeted way out. A helmsman must be at the wheel because Buck holds me in his arms. I sense pressure singing off canvas sails, that electric *thrum* of physical sound. My father wears a blue cap and blue blazer with gold buttons. At some point he must have brought me forward because I've a vision of our bow wave curling, its crest gleaming white like a bone between our schooner's teeth.

We'll go like this for hours, no one saying a word except the helmsman occasionally calling out "Jibe ho!" or "Hard a' lee!"

This is where my father longed to be all his life. Everything taut, tuned, everything perfect, weather fair. Everything alive and electric with spirit and speed. Everything *moving*.

▷─◆─○─◆─◁

When the baroness, Lady Maire, chose to visit her relations in London or Ireland, my mother was expected to manage the household and act as hostess to the baron's weekend parties, a role she did not enjoy.

Eilín wore white all summer, skin radiant, eyes blue as the sea on a fair day.

The baron had packs of guests down for Cowes Week, English and Germans. Hired coaches arrived from Ryde, disgorging blustery men in straw hats, with noxious cigars and mountains of leather baggage.

My mother would sit at one end of the dinner table and manage conversations between supercilious young aristocrats from the German embassy and millionaire yachtsmen from the British Midlands.

The guests were distracted by her Irish charm and her beauty, which allowed the baron—bored by dinner parties, even his own—to slip away whenever he chose, to his library, or to *Hermione*.

One night Weinbrenner elected to sleep aboard his yacht and left my mother to entertain twelve houseguests. It was Cowes Week, so August. It was nearly midnight when Eilín bid good night to the staff and left the gentlemen playing whist in the library, with whiskey and a plate of freshly cut sandwiches. She started back to the village and the Crab Inn, and one of the guests, Sir Ernest Dalton, slipped out of the house, caught up with her in a dark stretch of lane, and assaulted her.

I don't remember anyone telling me the story while I was growing up, nor do I remember a time when I wasn't aware that my mother had, once upon a time, been attacked by a man in the dark. I suppose I'd overheard my parents speaking of it. Perhaps they hadn't realized how much would sink in. While I was growing up, the story, dim in its details, was already embedded in my consciousness. I did not query my parents, for I felt guilty even knowing so much as I did. I held that knowledge furtively, like something stolen, something I really had no right to possess.

Except once, when I was nine years old—we were in Frankfurt, and I blurted out, "The man who hurt you, did you talk to him?"

"I did," she replied. "My mistake."

It was January 1919. Germany was in the last throes of her aborted revolution, and I'd just seen my first dead bodies on the street.

"Is that why he hurt you?"

"It was the devil in his own nature."

Almost sixty years later, Eilín did tell me exactly what happened. We were having tea at her cottage at Rosses Point in Sligo, reminiscing about sunny summers on the isle, when she unfurled the story. It was the last time I saw her alive—she died in her sleep a few weeks later.

Sir Ernest Dalton was a rich manufacturer of some homely houseware—table silver? Alarm clocks? Plumbing fixtures? Whatever he made, it made him one of the richest men in England.

Those island lanes were overgrown with fuchsia. He unlatched a metal gate and kept trying to push Eilín out into a field, one of the island's ancient meadows—chalky soil, grass wiry and rough. She struggled and fought and shouted for help. She broke away and fled across the grass but tripped and went down hard. She was lithe and quick, but Sir Ernest Dalton was bigger and stronger and twenty or thirty years older, bulky and wheezy. Then he was on top of her.

What I think of, because I don't wish to imagine the rest of it, is her white dress being wrecked and ruined on the wiry brown grass by that pig of a man who raped her.

He left her there and hurried back to Sanssouci, apparently.

She made her way to the Crab Inn. I was asleep, and Miss Anne Hamilton, my nurse, was stretched out on top of my parents' bed and asleep, too.

The innkeeper sent for the village policeman, who refused to do anything until my father had been informed and consulted. A messenger rowed out to *Hermione* on her mooring, and Buck was awakened and given some sort of garbled account. He and the baron rowed ashore and raced in a pony trap to Shanklin, where they heard the story from my mother, who had been bathed and put to bed but couldn't sleep.

The baron went to Sanssouci, roused all his guests, and ordered them to leave immediately in a coach he'd hired. Sir Ernest Dalton had already slipped away, probably to catch the dawn ferry at Ryde Pier, which connected to the early train leaving Southampton for Waterloo. Meanwhile, at the inn, a police inspector summoned from Newport asked my father what action he wished to pursue.

Buck wanted Sir Ernest Dalton prosecuted, convicted, and hanged. But my mother refused to be interviewed or provide any account to the authorities, even when a justice of the peace was summoned to her room. She had no interest in the processes of the law, perhaps because her father, an Irish barrister, had always been absorbed in law and politics to the exclusion of any real interest in the lives of his daughters. Eilín didn't care about the system of justice; she didn't care about the law's majesty; she wanted vengeance. *Eye for an eye, tooth for a tooth.* Her attacker had been the baron's guest, therefore punishment—vengeance—was the baron's responsibility.

I don't know where she learned this ancient code. It sounds like something out of *Beowulf.* But she still believed in it, sixty years later.

She had an interview with Hermann Weinbrenner in the library at Sanssouci the following day. The baron wept and told her he wanted to burn the house down to atone for the dishonor.

"You can't do that!" she said. "We'd have nowhere to live!"

She told him it was his responsibility to punish her attacker. She did not want my father involved in any way, in case there were consequences. *Blowback* would be the term now.

Karin's father was short, energetic, vital. He was by no means bloodthirsty, but he was direct, efficient, used to getting things done. His grandfather had been an old-clothes peddler in Breslau. His father founded the dyeworks that under the baron's leadership became Colora GmbH, which in the 1920s would merge with other chemical and pharmaceutical firms into the IG Farben cartel.

Through business connections in the West Midlands, contact was made with a Birmingham criminal gang. They were called . . . the Peaky Blinders. That's how my mother remembered the name, anyhow.

The Blinders set on Sir Ernest Dalton exactly one month after my mother was assaulted. She said they located him on a golf course and beat him with his clubs.

Then exactly one year to the day after the crime, the Peaky Blinders set upon Sir Ernest Dalton again. As soon as he recovered from the second assault he left England and went to live in Italy, where he died of cholera during the First World War.

How did that violence affect me? However they shrouded it from me, I knew something bad had happened. Can I isolate its effects from other violence I knew of or witnessed while I was a boy? If I had nightmares I don't remember them. Guilt? Yes. All my life I have felt guilty. Never protected my mother, you see.

Stating this so baldly makes it seem ridiculous.

▷·┼·◆▷·○·◁◆·┼·◁

You'd think she'd have been wary of the lanes, and hated the Isle of Wight, and wanted us to quit Sanssouci. But she didn't. Sanssouci remained our home, ours alone for eleven and a half months of the year. And we were always in the lanes between our house and the village, and farther afield. My parents enjoyed long walks in all sorts of weather, and I was set astride a little gray donkey, Whiz. Whiz was gentle and cooperative and didn't even need to be led. He just ambled along, and my father fed him lumps of sugar.

But I never expected the world outside our household, our little family, to be safe. I always assumed there would be lions out there, and sure enough, there were.

><+>-0-<+>-<

On the sunstruck Isle of Wight, the summer of 1914 was different than the others. By July, many yachtsmen could sniff the Balkan stew seething on the hob. Most of the foreign membership stayed home, in Berlin, Paris, St. Petersburg. Cowes Week remained on the RYS calendar, but the Weinbrenners stayed in Germany, where the baron had not spent a summer in twenty years.

It meant my parents and I didn't have to go into exile at the Crab Inn. That summer I had everything and everyone I wanted. Sunlight, seashells, and my parents. I was not much aware of time passing because there was no sense of anything changing, or being spoiled. The days flowed so smoothly they seem now, in memory, only one day, perfect, sunlit, calm. I used to hear my parents' calm voices after I was put down for my afternoon nap, while I watched sheer curtains dance in the wafts of an onshore breeze. That summer was entirely ours; we did not have to share it with the bristling baron and his cigars, late suppers, and packs of horrid houseguests. Buck did not have to race *Hermione* nor spend days and nights at the boatyard getting her ready to race. Instead he and Eilín worked together in the garden while I sat on the lawn watching them. Then he carried me on his shoulders down a steep, crooked path to the pebbled shingle below the cliffs, to dabble my toes in the sea.

Toward the end of July one of the elegant young men from the German embassy hurried down from London and took away *Hermione*'s logbook, which included ribald entries made by the kaiser, who had once or twice been a guest aboard her. Did the young diplomat warn my parents that they ought to clear out of England before the declaration of war?

I don't know.

All accounts insist there was sunny weather all over England the day the war began. On fair days the English Channel was dark blue, and white manes of foam blew off the tips of the waves. Following my afternoon nap my mother instructed Hamilton to take me into the village and buy ices at the shop. This was a rare treat.

Where was my father when Hamilton and I quit the house that afternoon? He might have been taking a nap himself or standing at the top of the cliff with his Leitz binoculars, looking out over the fair blue of the Channel. Cowes Week was on, but probably not so many yawls or racing schooners were out that afternoon, only battle-gray warships.

While Hamilton and I were enjoying our ice-cream treat at the village shop, a pair of policemen—one in uniform, one in plainclothes—arrived at Sanssouci, arrested Buck, and took him away.

I don't remember if my mother tried to explain his absence or if I wept or sulked or how I otherwise behaved. And I have no memory at all of the hours and days that followed, when she went up to London trying to learn what had happened to him and was met by official blankness and scorn. In the aftermath of my father's arrest as a German naval spy she must have been reeling, but I didn't notice. Or don't remember. It's as though a light was switched off, leaving me in the dark, and nothing of those days left any impression that has lasted, not even the darkness.

❧ 1938

On the café terrace on Unter den Linden, Karin was bent forward in her chair so that her face almost pressed against her knees. She wore an overcoat, hat, and woolen scarf, and the sounds she made were muffled. A few patrons glanced in our direction, but most didn't notice her weeping, or didn't want to.

The Saturday crowd streamed by on the sidewalk. It was Berlin as usual, pulsing, hectic, self-absorbed.

She suddenly sat up straight and dabbed her eyes with a handkerchief she took from her purse.

"I don't know why this monstrous thing has chosen to happen now," she said.

I touched her arm, but she wouldn't look at me, she faced the stream of passersby on Unter den Linden.

"I would consider getting rid of the thing, Billy, the bloody world doesn't need one more German. But then, my baby will be some sort of Jew, won't he? There's enough of Jews being kicked around, perhaps I'd better see him through. You'll stick by me won't you, Buffalo Billy?"

"What do you think?"

She smiled and went inside the café to wash her face.

When she returned I told her about the job offer from Vancouver, and the Dutch ship and the five-day crossing to New York.

"Vancouver, Canada. That's where we'll live. A city on the Pacific coast. We might get married in New York, buy a car, and drive across America. From the consulate in Köln we get tourist visas good for sixty days. I expect to pay about eight hundred marks for a reliable machine. We aim for California at first, then north for Canada."

Her eyes were shut, her face tilted to the bright, weak October sun. She was exhausted by her work, the dire responsibility of it.

"We'll drive south and west, toward the sun," I promised. "We'll cross *el llano*."

A river of citizens was flowing by. The typical Berlin mood of panic and rush with a salting of ruthlessness. The city always insisted on the *now*. Berlin couldn't bear delay. Hurry, hurry. That city had no patience, none. Old people stuttered along, leaning on their sticks. Sleek young people darted like fish against the current. Elegant ladies marched with fur stoles draped around their necks; uniformed messenger boys pumped along on bicycles; countrified soldier recruits looked lost; babies shouted from their prams.

"*El Llano Estacado.*"

I said the words just to hear them. Many, perhaps most, of the patrons on the terrace would have recognized that phrase. Because for our generation it was really an incantation.

El Llano Estacado, the Staked Plain, is an enormous mesa, a raised tableland flanked by red bluffs and sprawling over millions of acres from the Texas Panhandle into New Mexico. In Karl May's Winnetou novels, which Karin introduced me to when we were children, El Llano Estacado is the mystical hunting ground of the Mescalero Apache.

She shook her head. "My city won't eat me. I know my Berlin, Billy. She's a cross old bear, but I know her."

"You can't know what will happen."

She wouldn't look at me; she kept watching the passing crowd. She'd scarcely touched her venison. Patrons at the tables wore hats pulled low and scarves wrapped around their ears. The Berliners were unwilling to acknowledge the season for outdoor pleasure was nearly over. All the cafés would be drawing in their tables soon.

"I'm cold," she said at last. "Let's walk. Pay the bloody waiter, Billy."

>─◆>─०─<◆─◁

By the time we reached her flat in Charlottenburg it was dusk, not much light left in the sky.

Blue air of those Berlin autumn Saturdays. Cool and musky. November scented.

Oh, Christ.

She owned a collection of small Max Beckmann oils. Those paintings were always on the floor, propped against the walls, never hung.

She liked moving them about. Beckmann had been a medical orderly in the war; he'd served at the front. Everyone he painted, especially himself, looked as though they had been recently blown up by high explosives and hastily put back together.

The flat had hardly any furniture. Her little Naumann-Erika portable typewriter on its Bauhaus table. Her platform bed.

As was customary we went to bed immediately. White sheets, crisp and cool. We lay alongside each other, not touching at first. Then I took her hand. At first hand-holding, then kissing, then only gradually she let me touch her belly, shoulders, her small hard breasts. She moved my hand between her legs. Her cunt—if there is a better word, I don't know it—had something ripe to it, a seam ready to burst. She was always wet when I found her. She smelled of apple seed. I went into her as gently as possible, wary of the baby inside her now, even if it wasn't much more than a seed.

We slept, and the afternoon spun and changed to evening. I awoke next to her body radiating heat between the sheets. Fortune seemed very fragile. Feelings of happiness and plentitude brushed very close to feelings of dread. If she would not agree to leave Hitlerite Germany, what should I do? I couldn't bear the thought of our child born under the regime.

The air was cool. Before lying down we had shoved the big windows open wide. Now it was dark out, and neon reflections dashed against the white walls. Across the street leaves shimmered under yellow streetlight. I could hear the trams, the *Elektrische*, clashing, zinging along the Kurfürstendamm. Soon we would get up, draw a bath, lounge together in the tub, sharing the newspaper, reading aloud, laughing at its lies. We'd get dressed and go out and find a meal. We'd go dancing.

❧ HAMILTON

Holograph letter. *Eilín McDermott Lange to Constance O. Lange,* 4.8.1914, postmarked *Ryde, I of W, 4 Aug. 1914.* Lange Family Archive. C-08-1914. Special Collections, McGill Library, McGill University, Montreal.

—

"SANSSOUCI",
Shanklin, I. of Wight
4th August 1914

MRS C. LANGE
Wychwood
Calry,
Co. Sligo
Ireland

Dear Mother Lange,

I do not know how or if this will reach you, all mails to the Continent are stopped perhaps Ireland as well. This afternoon they have taken away my husband, your son . . . Buck is arrested. 2 policemen—PC Goon from the village with great black boots, helmet, and red face. And a weasel-faced Special Branch detective in a mackintosh, a Londoner. Buck is held tonight at the Royal Naval College Osborne House and most likely to be brought up to London but they wouldn't say when or where, I believe they didn't know. 'Sorry for your trouble, ma'am,' PC Goon mumbled. 'Order of the Home Secretary.' His patchy English decency made me want to scream. If they were savages I could fight them but it was our only dull kindly village policeman horrified yet delighted by his new powers, and the silent Londoner. Brutality just underneath.

Last week when we heard Germany and Russia were at war Buck said immediately—'That will do it for us because now France must go in so England as well' but we didn't really know what it would mean. A young man from the embassy, Count von Mueller-Hippmann, came down from London quite unexpected and asked Buck for the log-book from Hermione and a guest-book in which the Kaiser had written some foolish things when he dined here long ago. Mueller-Hippmann smiled and said, 'Our countries will soon be at war.' I felt a chill and knew he was right, however his way of speaking was very mild and kind, and we all felt sad knowing war must mean the end of our life at Sanssouci. He said hundreds of young Germans called up for the army were leaving England. Scenes at Charing Cross were frantic but most of these were young men in London by themselves working in as waiters, clerks, barbers & etc.

I told M-H it would go very hard on us to leave England and flee to Germany where we have never lived. Buck speaks German beautifully but he is really a stranger now to that country, this Island is where we have made our home. And Buck could hardly fight against England which he loves whilst his wife and son were living in England. M-H repeated the situation was a difficult one and that he was not qualified to give advice—then Buck took him in the trap to Ryde and the ferry.

That evening Buck went to the Crab Inn to see if there was any news and village boys jeered at him on the road saying he was a filthy Hun and a spy, etc. He recognized some from families we knew and were friendly with, and was very shaken. The next morning came the news—war with the German Empire—and a last telegram from the Baron asking Buck to watch over this house and the yacht but no word as to where the money would come from for Buck's salary, wages of the staff, or upkeep of the house and grounds, etc. As you know

we live on Buck's salary as captain & sailing master. The
arrangement gives us this house to live in as our own except
when the Baron will bring down a party in the summer.

Then Lord Ormonde the Commodore rang up and said—
as a fellow Irishman and sailor he was obliged to warn Buck he
must expect to be arrested as a <u>spy</u>, Special Branch men would
come to the house in a few hours, he must prepare himself, and
it was preposterous because everyone knew he wasn't a filthy
spy, but it would all come right soon enough.

All Buck could say was—Hermann must not see his father
taken by the police. I instructed Nurse to take him into the
village & the bathing beach and not return before teatime.
Then PC Goon and the detective arrived in a pony trap. I
had Buck's grip packed with his clothes, etc. only there wasn't
much time to think what he might need & no idea how long
he would be gone, or where—for all I know they are sending
him back to Germany. The detective would admit nothing only
that Buck was arrested by order the Home Secretary. They
hold him tonight at Osborne House. I will go there tomorrow
morning and try to see him. Hermann has had his bath, Nurse
reads bedtime stories, I shall go upstairs presently and kiss him
goodnight, he goes to sleep so quickly tired by the sea and sun
of these summer days. When he does ask where daddy is I shall
go to pieces. No—I won't. Thank God he is still a baby. Cook
caught me weeping in the pantry and said—it must blow over,
the trouble won't last, the Captain is really an Englishman, they
can't keep him for long. I hope she is right but she never has in
her life been off this I. of Wight so what can she know really . . .

I hope it is all panic, fright, excitement because of the decl.
of war which no one expected and when things settle down
the Home Sec'y must see it is wrong to take up a man who is
completely innocent.

I don't know what we shall live on. Buck's salary can't be
paid from Germany, and there is no more racing at Cowes.
We can't stay here without funds to keep up the house. If they
take Buck to the Tower of London I must find a way to be near

him. I can't think what else to do or write or think—I sit at this escritoire, windows open, wild green sea light and air, telling myself to make sense of what has happened to us by putting it down. If there is any sense to it, which I cannot see.

Yours with love,
Eilín

National Archives. Security Service MI5 file ref NS-1914.8KV 1-39.

—

THE METROPOLITAN POLICE

Interrogation Transcript
Date: August 11th 1914
Subject: Lange, Heinrich
Officer: Sir Basil Thomson, Asst. Comm. Metropolitan Police
Location: Sir Basil Thomson's room, Scotland Yard
Date of Arrest: August 4th Shanklin, I of Wight on advisement
    of Capt. V. Kell, Secret Service Bureau.

BT: What is your full name? Speak clearly please.

Subj: My name is Heinrich Lange.

BT: Your address please.

Subj: The house called *Sanssoucci*, Shanklin, the Isle of Wight. I
    am not a spy.

BT: If you are truthful things will go better for you here.

Subj: I am a sailing master. Skipper. Ask Lord Ormonde. Ask Sir
    Peter Belfrey.

BT: Who is your employer?

Subj: At present no one.

BT: Are you or do you claim to be a British subject?

Subj: No.

BT: Tell us your nationality please.

Subj: German. I'm a German.

BT: But you speak excellent English.

Subj: (groans)

BT: Where did you learn to speak English?

Subj: My mother. Look here.

BT: Where were you born?

Subj: I am not a spy.

BT: Where were you born? In America? Answer please.

Subj: I was born aboard my father's ship one thousand miles off Acapulco. I was registered for German nationality by the consul in San Francisco. My family, my father was from Hamburg. My mother is Irish. I don't have anything to tell you, I haven't any secrets, I don't know anything. I realize you have a job to do but you are wasting your time with me.

BT: Are you a reserve officer in the German army?

Subj: No.

BT: You have seen service in the German army.

Subj: Yes, I did my service at Potsdam when I was nineteen. The 1st Uhlan Guards. Cavalry.

BT: You are in the reserves, then.

Subj: I don't know, perhaps, I have not lived in Germany for years. I am not a spy. I was never an officer. I was in the ranks. Eighteen months service.

BT: Your mail has been intercepted.

Subj: (express surprise)

BT: So you see we are aware of your activities.

Subj: But there is nothing, I have done nothing, I am not a spy.

BT: Who pays your salary?

Subj: I have never done this. Nothing. This is a disgrace.

BT: The Baron Weinbrenner pays your salary. Is this correct?

Subj: I sail his yacht. I race it for him.

BT: You are in the employ of the German intelligence service. You have been their watchdog at Portsmouth these last four years.

Subj: Never. I have not.

BT: You make reports in invisible ink, we will have them out soon. We have intercepted letters.

Subj: No, there is nothing. How dare you read my letters.

BT: I advise you to think things through carefully. You are in a very dangerous spot.

Subj: Whatever your name is. I am a sailor. I observe the sailing yachts that is part of my job do you understand. There is no secret, ink, nothing. I am not watching battleships, believe me. I am the skipper of Weinbrenner's yacht *Hermione II*. Ask Lord Ormonde at the RYS and he will tell you this is the truth.

BT: They are holding you at the Tower of London, do you understand what this means? Do you know what is done with spies in time of war?

Subj: My wife is English. And my son.

BT: Your wife is Irish.

Subj: I would not spy. I don't care for the war. My son is English born.

BT: When we have examined your letters we shall have more to discuss. We know you are reporting to the German intelligence service. We know this. It would serve you well to make a clean breast of it now. Do you understand? There is nothing shameful in admitting your activities. You are a soldier of the German emperor, you were doing a soldier's duty. You are not a criminal and will not be treated as such. You are only a loyal subject and an honorable soldier. Of course we have our own men in Germany performing exactly the same sorts of duties you were performing here. So we understand your position perfectly. There is nothing wrong in what you have done only you see we cannot allow it to continue.

Subj: You do not.

BT: But you understand once war is declared everything changes. In wartime spies are always dealt with most severely. I want to be perfectly clear. I want to treat you as fairly as I would like to see our men treated but to a certain extent my hands are tied. The atmosphere is savage these days. If you could see what is written in the newspapers you would understand. I think we will be shooting spies before much longer.

Subj: I have done nothing.

BT: A loyal soldier is permitted to save his own life. The only way to save yourself is to speak honestly. What I would like from you—

Subj: I have nothing to say to you.

BT: What I would like to give you is a few quiet hours of solemn reflection. Think deeply about where you are. I understand your predicament perfectly and you have my sincere sympathy. But you must think about what we can do to save your life. The newspapers are howling for spies to be put to death. The newspapers are very important in this country. The newspapers say all spies must be shot. The government cannot ignore this. Your best chance is speak openly and answer all our questions. All the other men who are arrested have been doing their best to cooperate because they understand their lives are at stake. Now I want you to go back to your room and think and we shall have another chat soon.

I was "Hermann" until my father was arrested for a spy. Then Miss Anne Hamilton suggested to my mother that the name sounded "too German."

"'Hermann' will have people in the village seeing red, missus. No use saying it oughtn't, it just does. Isn't there another name you can pull out of the hat for him?"

It was Hamilton who started calling me Bill, after Buffalo Bill Cody. She had a program from Buffalo Bill's Wild West show, which her father had seen at Southampton. "Bill" became "Billy." And Billy Lange I have been ever since.

After they took my father away, first to Osborne House, then to the Tower of London, Eilín and I stayed on at Sanssouci, living like ghosts in a villa befuddled with fog, sea fog blowing through rooms where the Weinbrenners' massive furniture was shrouded now under white cotton sheets.

If my mother wasn't a Hun, she was Irish, which wasn't much better, as far as Shanklin village was concerned. Living in a house that belonged to a German baron—a house where the kaiser himself had once (before our time) spent a night—we were quite foreign enough to be shunned. After the Special Branch detective took Buck away, Sanssouci was no longer a living house, and certainly wasn't carefree. Autumn lawns grew shaggy and thick with small wildflowers. There was no money to pay the maid, cook, or gardener, so they departed, until Sanssouci, at last, held just the pair of us, Eilín and me. In some ways it was better then, quite magical, really. Most of the rooms were shut up. We lived between the library, the drawing room, and the kitchen. There was a gas fire in the drawing room. A massive iron range kept the kitchen warm, and there was a coal grate that made the library cozy, though coal was costly. As winter settled in, we shifted our beds down to the library. There were ship models, in glass cases, racing schooners. The kaiser's *Meteor V,* the baron's *Hermione.*

When we brought books down from the shelves, many volumes had their pages uncut. The baron owned an impressive English library, but he hadn't come to the island to spend his time reading. There was a bay window with a view of the sea and room for both of us on a very comforting window seat. The cushions were covered with a tapestry, rough and nubbly. We lay there and leafed through the baron's picture books and atlases. Sometimes there was cocoa.

The collection of atlases absorbed us for weeks. The first thing Eilín would look for when we opened any atlas was that point—N 20°56′ W 123°23′—where Buck was born. Sometimes the page "Mexico" was arranged generously enough to reach so far out into the empty blue, but usually it wasn't, and we'd find his birthplace on the Oceana page or in a spread of pages where the globe was sectioned like an orange and splayed out entire. When we found Buck's spot in an atlas or on a chart my mother would prick a tiny, discreet hole with the tip of a sharpened pencil. *In memoriam.* Next we'd search to locate my birthplace: in England, on the Isle of Wight, at the edge of Shanklin village, in this very house. I felt dizzy when she pricked the exact place on the correct atlas sheet. It seemed powerful somehow that we were lying on the window seat in the very house where I was born. When she pricked the map I could almost feel the pencil point's sharp little nudge. *Here you are.*

Here.

Here.

Here.

At that age I could put myself into a trance by repeating certain words. *Here* was one of my incantatory words. *I,* the first person singular, was another. *I,* repeated often enough and without distraction, would send me tumbling right down the rabbit hole. I suppose it represents a certain stage of development, the infant mind toying with its earliest, dazzling, sense of selfhood.

We're not the world, and the world isn't us.

We had barely enough money for food, fuel, and my mother's trips up to London, and none to spend on luxuries, but there was an enormous tin of Javanese cocoa in the larder, and in the library a humidor packed with Weinbrenner's special cigarettes which had the Walden crest (Irish shamrock intertwined with German cornflowers) embossed in gold on the paper tubes. In the evening after tucking me into my cot, Eilín used to sit in a leather club chair with her knees tucked up, smoking cigarettes, sipping cocoa, gazing at the fire. I enjoyed watching the firelight playing on her face, neck, shoulders, legs. She would know when I wasn't asleep, and after a while we'd start a conversation. Sometimes I wonder if these were dreams, and not real conversations at all, but they are grounded by the scent of tobacco smoke, firelight, and the delicious security I felt, being alone with my mother.

"I can't think where he is right now." Her voice was calm at night. During the day, she could sound harried; she often became impatient with my slowness, what she called my dreaminess. She was such a brisk person I must often have seemed that way to her.

"Daddy? Is it Daddy you mean?"

"Ah, little man, go to sleep, we're not to be talking now."

"But you've kept me awake."

"Have I?"

"I like to look at you."

"I'm nothing to look at these days. I'm less than nothing."

Some winter nights the sea wind would rattle and bang at the library windowpanes. My mother said it was the breath of the sea. The world was whirling so fast, she said, the wind was getting bold. "But we're not going to let it blow us down, Billy. The wind was your father's strong friend, always. Your father would taste the wind and know everything there was in it."

"He's a sailor."

"He's more than that."

"He's a captain."

"Captain and master. He'll come back to us one day. You'll see."

I didn't doubt that myself, except when she said it. Her statements of faith always sounded a bit . . . doubtful.

"Now put your head down and go to sleep, Billy."

I could never sleep merely from wanting to. And most nights I didn't even want to. I'd rather stay awake with her. I wanted to see her—see us both—through the long winter's dark, with sea wind smacking our villa like a gloved hand, rattling every piece of glass in the place. If the wind played out during the night, a few hours cold calm would leave a gray tongue of hoarfrost on the green, unkempt winter lawns.

We had no visitors except Hamilton, who came nearly every day. Her father was barman at the Crab Inn, her mother a harridan who took in laundry and forbade Hamilton to visit Sanssouci after my father's arrest. But she came anyway, because she loved and admired my mother, who had escaped her own irascible parent to make a life for herself on the Continent and marry a dashing sailor, even if he was now to be shot as a German spy. We had letters from my grandmother Con—Buck's mother—in Ireland, and from Eilín's sisters, my aunts Kate and Frances. None from Germany, of course. Nothing from Buck—he wasn't allowed to write. Eilín journeyed up to London every two weeks and attempted to see him but was never able to.

In the village they believed Buck had been condemned as a Hun spy and was awaiting execution in the Tower of London. If he hadn't already been shot.

Hamilton, who was fifteen, warned me to be prepared for bad news.

"The thing with bad news, when you hear it, is keep it inside, Billy. Hold it inside, don't let no one else see it, Billy, and be brave. That is what your father must expect from a brave boy."

"Will they chop off his head?"

"Ah, no. They shoot them nowadays."

She was our friend, but the rest of the village kept their distance. From their point of view we must have been something between criminals and actors in a melodrama. Eilín was very beautiful, after all, and I was very young, and I'm sure that for some of our neighbors our situation had an aura of romance, especially if Buck was executed.

The three of us took many walks along the dripping lanes. Hamilton had promised to marry a boy who was with her brother in the First Battalion of the Hampshire Regiment. The Hampshires had gone to France back in August. In those days I thought the soldiers were the luckiest fellows alive. My sense of what "the war" meant came from heroic paintings of the Battle of Waterloo reproduced in a folio in the library at Sanssouci. Lady Butler's *Scotland Forever,* depicting the gallant charge of the Scots Greys on magnificent pale horses, was my favorite.

I remember Hamilton saying she had "had it" with her soldier boy.

She was "fed up." She was "sick and tired." All these phrases were new and fresh. My ears pricked up as they always did whenever I sensed anger, restlessness, or impatience behind words.

"I don't miss men. I'm not unhappy they've cleared off. I want to clear off myself, I do. Go to London and see what I can make of it."

"There are plenty of men in London," my mother said calmly.

One of them being my father, lodged in the Tower.

"Oh, I don't hate men. My fellow said he would write, but of course he hasn't, not even a card. Perhaps he is dead. Shot through the heart."

"Don't say such things," my mother cautioned. She had Irish respect for the incantatory power of speech. One had to keep silent about the most important things and never mention whatever it was you most wanted, or most feared. The world was a twisting, scornful place with a dirty mind. And in London firing squads of soldiers were shooting men accused of spying, shooting them through the heart if they were lucky, through the brains or the eyes if they weren't. There was no telling where a stray bullet could go.

I missed Buck's hands, the strength in his arms, the timbre of his voice, his way of picking me up so easily, so casually, and blithely throwing me about. I loved tugging, punching, and wrestling with him; he knew exactly how much force I could handle without feeling overwhelmed. I missed the sense of motion radiating from an adult male: defiance of gravity. His tactile, physical playfulness gave me confidence in the world.

After he was taken away the world narrowed. We had cups of cocoa in the library, pinpricks on map sheets, my mother gazing into the coal fire, muddy walks with Hamilton.

Eilín did her best to keep my father alive and constantly in my mind. She told me his stories. Once, in the Marshall Islands Buck had been pursued by a man with a machete who sought to kill him for no other reason except that he had blond hair. My father had escaped by running into a Chinese shop where the shopkeeper brought out a Mauser pistol and shot the marauder dead.

Uncle Joseph, the Negro cook who attended Buck's birth, owned a tavern on the Deichstraße in Hamburg. When Captain Jack had gone down with his reefer in the South Atlantic, Joseph loaned his wife, my grandmother Con, three hundred and seventy-five Yankee dollars to live on while she waited for her widow's benefit to be paid. Those silver dollars were good as reichsmarks in the shops of Hamburg.

I'd heard the stories before, from my father, who enjoyed telling them. I knew Joseph had earned the dollars from the Yankee sailors in his tavern. I knew a reefer was a ship that carried frozen meat.

While Buck's life hung by a thread, I explored the island lanes with Hamilton, startling rabbits from hedges and pausing to stare at bulls in the fields. Hamilton would suddenly ask me, "What is your daddy doing at this moment?" as though she expected me to know.

As though it were perfectly rational that I should know.

So I'd make up stories of his doings, packing in as many details as I could.

"He is polishing his boots and eating a sandwich and putting brown sugar in his tea. He is looking out the window and watching the king. The king is getting out of his royal-blue state coach pulled by six horses."

"What color are the horses?"

"Oh, grays. Beautiful matched grays. Wonderful pullers. And Daddy has a pencil. He is making a drawing of the horses for me. He's very hungry for his tea. Crumpets and blackberry jam, honey and milk, hard-boiled eggs and ham sandwiches."

Hamilton liked to try on Eilín's clothes and especially her magnificent hats. Dread of going back to Ireland was preying on my mother's mind. The house at Strandhill, Sligo, where she'd grown up was *the red house*. Her father was a barrister who had married a fisherman's daughter from the island of Inishmor. After her mother died, Eilín had applied for the position of secretary to Lady Maire, Baroness von Weinbrenner, by answering the notice in the *Irish Times* with a letter written in three languages—English, German, and Irish. The German section was very short, and her sister Kate helped her with the Irish. Her application was successful, and Eilín left her father's house and went out to Germany.

On wild winter days while rain and wind knocked the house, we had our tea by the library fire, and my mother would tell Anne Hamilton and me all about leaving Ireland for the first time. Hamilton loved to hear it and sat enraptured.

"In those days, barefoot girls sold mussels and oysters on the streets of Dublin and the bridges over the Liffey. They had peculiar cries, like seabirds, I thought. Very haunting and beautiful, but they frightened me. I couldn't imagine myself barefoot and wearing a shawl and crying a basket of mussels in the city while people hurried past.

"I was too shy and wary to spend money on food, and by the time I boarded the steamer I'd not had a morsel in sixteen hours. A group of county Monaghan girls, going over to work in the woolen mills of Yorkshire, they were very kind and shared their food—mostly potatoes—and porter as well.

"They were very strong girls, real northerners. They smoked pipes and drank porter. One or two spoke the same sort of Irish as my own mother had, and I was nearly overcome to hear it, but that was really the only time I was sad to be leaving Ireland, and the feeling didn't last. I'd never taken drink before and was sick most of the way across. Then I caught a train across England to Hull, caught the steamer for Holland, then more trains. I was too frightened to speak to anyone, until a handsome student came into the carriage at Utrecht.

"His name was Peter, such fair skin he had, and black hair and jet-black eyes. Beautifully dressed all in gray, and his boots gleamed. We became great friends. We shared our food, and when it was time to change trains at Venlo he helped me through it or I certainly would have been lost. I fell in love with him. If you can call it love if it happens so quickly as that."

"You can," Hamilton assured her. "It does happen all the time, missus. Often on trains, especially in the war."

"Well, it wasn't war then, war was the furthest thing from our minds. In those days people thought there'd be no wars ever again, except perhaps in Ireland."

"Tell us about the singing," Hamilton encouraged.

"Well, he was scribbling for half an hour after Duisburg, before Köln. I was a bit hurt, I thought he was turning away, ignoring me."

"But he was writing the song!" said Anne Hamilton. "In German. He was."

"He was. Perhaps there's nothing sounds quite so strange and beautiful as a song sung in German by a young man with a fine voice."

"There can't be," Hamilton agreed.

"He was a tenor, pure as the air. He was getting off at Köln Hauptbahnhof. As the train was slowing up, he started getting down his things, then he shook hands with me. I was broken up, though trying not to show it. What a ridiculous idiotic elf, falling in love on the train to Germany! Suddenly I felt sick, frightened of everything, of how far I'd come. I didn't know a single soul in all Europe. I wished to scurry back to Ireland only I didn't have the money for it. Then he told me he'd composed a song in honor of my coming into Germany. He stood on the platform at the *Hauptbahnhof* and began singing. As the train started to move out he followed along, still singing."

"That's the most wonderful," Hamilton said. "That will never happen to me."

"You can't know," my mother told her. "You can't know what will happen. Things do change when you leave your own country.

"When I arrived at Frankfurt Hauptbahnhof, thirty-six hours out of Ireland, there was Lady Maire wearing a fur-trimmed cape and waiting impatiently on the platform, looking stern and awful. She was a daughter of the Earl of Tireragh, an Irish peer.

"She hadn't thought I'd be so young. 'I'm not,' I told her, 'only I am a bit tired.' We rode out to Walden in a motorcar, very noisy and smelly. She hardly said a word. I thought her very stiff. The Weinbrenners' estate is called Walden, and I thought it terribly strange and cold at first, not at all cheerful or welcoming. The baron was a famous polo player. Do you know what that is? You ride ponies and knock balls with a stick. He shouted at his ponies, and his guests and all the servants and me—though I never saw him treat an animal or a person unkindly. If you could stand being shouted at, he was all right.

"But Lady Maire—she was a queen on a playing card, very stiff. Only when she was with horses did another side show through. Graceful and gentle she was in the saddle. Didn't matter the horse—even a wild stallion—they all answered to her. Why, the baron would put her up on horses *he* was afraid to ride, and she would manage them beautifully.

"One night I was in the kitchen with the Swabian cook, weeping from homesickness, when the baroness found me. She took me by the hand and led me upstairs. She drew a bath, with lavender buds strewn in the water. While I sat in it she lit two cigarettes and handed me one. I'd never had a cigarette before, but I took it, of course.

"'You are missing old Ireland,' said Lady Maire to me, then she read aloud the poetry of Speranza, which is the pen name of Lady Jane Wilde, mother of Oscar, and Lady Maire's own cousin."

My mother could recite by heart:

> *My Country, wounded to the heart*
> *Could I but flash along thy soul*
> *Electric power to rive apart*
> *The thunder-clouds that round thee roll*

She loved Lady Maire. Starting in the 1920s they spent a dozen summers driving all over Europe—"Galicia to Galicia!" was my mother's gay description—at first in a Mercedes touring car driven by the baron's chauffeur, later in a little Ford that Eilín taught herself to drive. Together they tracked down most of what became the Weinbrenner Collection of medieval religious art. Fourteenth-century *Palmesels* in manor houses in Württemberg; fifteenth-century altarpieces in mountain churches of Asturias; priestly chasubles in Polish convents: some of the work was crude, some was masterful, all of it had the glow that objects only acquire after five or six hundred years of veneration. Along the way they were stranded, broken down, robbed, arrested, hospitalized with malaria, threatened, jailed more than once, and even stoned, in a Vlach village in northern Greece. They were stoic travelers. And by the time of Lady Maire's death they were more attached to each other than to their husbands or their children, though my mother would never have admitted this.

"I wish I could go out to Germany," Hamilton said. "If only it weren't for this horrid war."

She must have experienced the Isle of Wight as her own prison, the way certain people do with places that contain their youth. Did she ever escape? She was bold and rugged, and there were new opportunities for young women on account of the war. Later, up in London, we saw women bus conductors, and I used to imagine Hamilton traveling through the London hurly-burly in uniform, in command of her bus, putting up with no foolishness from soldiers on leave.

She rarely spent the night at Sanssouci, though my mother invited her to do so whenever the weather was nasty. When Hamilton did stay over, she slept on a pallet of rugs and pillows my mother arranged before the fire. But Anne Hamilton had no fear of island lanes, even in the wildest storms. She didn't mind walking after dark, and I think that she, like my mother, relished time alone. Hamilton was one of those people who can accept, even require, a certain amount of social intercourse but also need time to feast on their own thoughts. After putting on her boots (drying before the fire), her cloak, gloves, and carefully arranging her hat, she would shake hands with Eilín, shake hands with me, and start off for the village with a stick in her hand. In those days everyone in the country or the city carried a stick of one sort or another. Eilín would settle me into bed, then sit up alone, brooding and smoking cigarettes before the red glow of the fire.

><+>-0-<+><

The war felt very close. Standing on the cliffs, we watched steamers and ferries plowing across the Channel, carrying soldiers to France. On certain days, if the wind was right, Anne Hamilton and I believed we could hear the distant grumble of artillery barrage.

"Whatever happens, Billy, you must protect your mother. It's your duty."

So said Hamilton, more than once. It was wartime, and *duty*, *being brave*, *standing guard*, were familiar words and phrases.

"You're her soldier, like. Your duty, Billy, is to stand at arms, be prepared. For you're her soldier now."

My mother and I were ghosting it at Sanssouci because we had nowhere else to go. The obvious refuge was Ireland—county Sligo, where Buck's mother, Constance Lange, and Eilín's father, Joseph McDermott, both lived, though hardly aware of each other. However, so long as Buck was in the Tower facing a trial and the prospect of execution, my mother could not leave England.

She eked out what savings she had in her post-office account to buy necessities. She traveled up to London and tried to see government officials and lawyers, most of whom refused to meet her. While Eilín was in London, Hamilton settled into Sanssouci with me. She brought eggs and a loaf of brown bread, currant buns, blackberry and elderberry jam, once a freshly killed chicken. Our larders at Sanssouci were vast but empty. There was a wine cellar. We used to go down there and try to count the bottles, but we never reached the end.

We talked about the war. Hamilton's point was that my father was a soldier who had done his duty, and it was nasty and cruel of the first lord of the Admiralty, Mr. Winston Churchill, to lock him up in the Tower of London and shoot him.

At least they weren't going to chop off his head, which was what they'd done with Anne Boleyn. While we rambled the island's green, dripping lanes, Hamilton mimed holding a severed head on her hip as she sang,

> *Anne Boleyn walks the steps of the bloody Tower*
> *With her head tucked underneath her arm.*

Sometimes I was overcome with guilt and tears, knowing it was my job to save my father but not knowing how.

Hamilton said she was going to become a nursing sister once she turned sixteen.

"But I'll tell you, Billy my man, I don't intend to spend the duration scrubbing ward floors or emptying bedpans. I should like to be an officer. I should like to be a captain of nursing sisters. You've seen how sharp I am, not like the other girls in this village. I'd keep my uniform spotless. I'd have a white cap, sharply creased, crisp white apron, and my navy-blue nurse's cape fastened with silver chain and clasp. And I'll tell you this, Billy Lange: when the soldiers are wounded or killed—when the line breaks—if the trench is going to be overcome in a raid—it is the duty of the nurses to pick up the rifles and fight. I should like that. I wouldn't shirk. And you wouldn't neither, would you?"

I would not. However, I didn't see myself fighting in a nurse's uniform. I'd wear a soldier's khaki and one of the tin hats the troops were now being issued in France.

At night Hamilton and I slept together in the library in my mother's cot, which was bigger than mine. Hamilton wore a nightdress of unbleached linen, and her body's scent was soap and earth. The isle's winter floated around us in sea fog. Fog was silver, blue, and white. The grounds were green all winter, glowing, anxious green. Fuchsia grew dense in hedges, dripping tiny scarlet and pink petals on the skinny, wandering lanes. The gardens were wreckage, except for one neat plot from which mother and Hamilton and I took beets, carrots, and turnips all winter. Unmown grasses shook in waves as the wind swept through.

In London that autumn and winter there were trials and dawn executions of German naval spies. Of course no one told me. They had all been arrested on the first day of war. Eilín kept going up to London, traveling by coach to Ryde, steamer to Southampton, express train to Waterloo.

Then one afternoon in February Hamilton and I were shopping in the village when I saw my mother climb down from a charabanc just in from Ryde. Something about her seemed different. She wore a narrow gray skirt and jacket buttoned very snug against her trim, voluptuous figure. Her hat was pinned with waterproof cover against the winter wet. I pulled away from Hamilton and dashed across the road. I wanted to be with my mother, wanted to be as close as I could; I suppose what I really wanted was to climb back up inside her and hide from the rainy world. Funny how children know when things have changed, changed utterly. Even when she saw me running toward her, her face remained strangely expressionless. Probably she was still in shock. She was holding an umbrella, tightly furled, but still managed to hold her arms open wide, and I flew into them, then both of us were crying—that is my memory of it anyway. It's possible there had never been such a display of emotion in the rainy, tightly furled streets of Shanklin village. But we were foreigners, after all.

My father's life was spared. He was not to be tried as a spy. He was no longer threatened with execution. Perhaps it had been a matter of enough weeks passing and tempers cooling before the Special Branch detectives and MI5 men recognized that Buck Lange was exactly who he claimed to be: a racing skipper with a pair of excellent Leitz binoculars and a keen professional interest in how efficiently certain yachts were being sailed.

They weren't setting him free, however. He wasn't coming back to us. As a German male of military age, he was to be interned for the duration. In February 1915 my father was transported to Scotland and spent the rest of that winter aboard the hulk of an old ship moored in the Firth of Forth, with three hundred German and Austrian internees.

In September 1915 most of them were dispatched to an internment camp on the Isle of Man. But men with British wives, a category that included my father—Ireland was still British—were shipped south, to a camp that had been established at Alexandra Palace, a commercial exhibition hall on a windswept hill in north London.

Eilín said we must go to be near him. So we packed our belongings and left my birthplace, the green lanes, and the isle, and went up to London.

1938

THE DELPHI-PALAST STILL OFFERED A TEA DANCE ON SATURDAY AFTER-noons. Otto Kermbach's orchestra was rarely very interesting or stimulating, but the Delphi was only a five-minute walk from Karin's building on the Giesebrechtstraße. Kermbach's boys played commercial Viennese swing. Coy music, sweet as Viennese pastry, loaded with cream and chocolate.

In that bourgeois part of town the dance palaces were trying their hardest to adapt to the new Germany, which wasn't so new after five years. Managers and orchestra leaders were wary of the police, especially Sicherheitsdienst, SD, Himmler's secret policemen, who people believed were everywhere, even if they weren't. If anyone tried to jitterbug, Kermbach would have stopped his players immediately, herded everyone out, and closed and locked the doors. One Saturday we'd seen a uniformed SS man dancing with a pretty girl at the Delphi. We left immediately. But on my next visit to Berlin we went back.

Bed to bath to the tea dance at the Delphi-Palast: that was our Saturday afternoon ritual in Berlin, and we seemed to require ritual to ease us into the darkness and excitement of our Berlin evenings. The hottest Kansas City–style music was too much to absorb when emotions were still raw from sex. And anyway, that sort of playing could only be found late at night, and never in a sedate quarter like Charlottenburg.

So we started with Otto Kermbach's maudlin arrangements and moved on, searching out the Kansas City sound we really needed. And that particular night we were fortunate. We hit the right spots at the right time, each club smaller than the one before, at each one the riffing and jitterbugging fiercer, more sexual. Our last stop was a blind pig, an illegal venue. By day it was a car-repair shop in the suburb of Wedding. The concrete floor was greasy, there was an aroma of gasoline, and six young musicians took turns on extended solos that sounded to me like sharp signals of distrust for every aspect of the "Fatherland spirit" that was alive in our daytime Germany. The Kansas City sound, that 4/4 beat, was packed with disrespect; it embodied loathing for every aspect of the regime.

I had been studying faces in the crowd, trying to spot police informers, watchers, but finally gave it up, not caring.

The best jazz was hard and alive. Transformation—that's the business of music, is it not? Being with Karin Weinbrenner in a joint like that after midnight, I felt vulnerable and powerful all at once—proud of my daring, my sense for rhythm, my ear for the best playing, my beautiful, caustic jazz sensibility. To hear such intense music in such strange surroundings was like sucking down a draft of pure courage. Which can be toxic, like anything taken pure.

It was always a challenge to squeeze out everything there was of the night and still manage to get back to Charlottenburg before the trains and trams stopped running. Cabs were rare that late, and costly, and now I needed to save as much money as possible for America. Karin had no money. That night we were lucky; we managed to get most of the way back to Giesebrechtstraße before the U-Bahn shut down.

We were hustling the last blocks from Uhlandstraße in a downpour when Karin suddenly asked if I ever thought of our summer days at Sanssouci.

"Often!" The rain was really pelting.

"Light," she said. "That's what I remember. Nothing else do I want more of, Billy, except light. Not so often available in Germany. Quite precious, actually."

"Hence, *el llano*," I told her.

She stopped all of a sudden, so I had to as well. We had the street to ourselves. Trams had all returned to their barns for the night, no squealing of steel wheels from the Kurfürstendamm, no traffic rumble. All the windows in all the apartment blocks were black, and the street shone with rain. It was as though no one else were alive in that quarter of the city. We were both getting soaked to the bone.

She peered at me closely. "We're no longer children, Buffalo Billy. And aren't you talking about a dream, a childhood fantasy?"

"We'll see for ourselves," I promised her.

❊   MUSWELL HILL

Holograph letter. Addressed *Captain H Lange, Alexandra Palace Camp, London,* postmarked *Muswell Hill N10, 11:30 PM, 19 Dec 1915.* With addendum dated 12 Dec. 1955, initialed *E.McD.L* (Eilín McDermott Lange). Lange Family Archive, 12 C-12-1988. Special Collections, McGill Library, McGill University, Montreal.

19th Dec 1915

15 Dukes Avenue
Muswell Hill
London N10

Mein Liebster I am pressed very hard don't know that I can stand it. London smashes us, the boy has a cough now 3 weeks. You say—we must think of going to—Ireland! only it means my father's house. I cannot live with him—if you knew what passed between us you never wd suggest

When my poor mother was dying I returned only to comfort her she was so frightened poor little Mamaí—and my father a madman, embraced and kissed me most foul. So don't say that we ought go to him. I can't stand this I am in a box everything pressing—<u>why</u> did you leave us

Never Sent!—E.McD.L 12.12.1955

SOMETIMES A SHAFT OF SUN BROKE THROUGH THE LONDON SMOKE, PRO-
ducing rare silver light. Khaki soldiers were everywhere, and policemen
in blue. There were stabs of other colors, quick, violent, like bayonet
thrusts. The scarlet tabs and hatbands of staff officers. The grimy, daily
red of pillar-boxes and London buses. Eilín and I spent hours riding on
buses or waiting for them.

I was always protecting Eilín, or imagining myself protecting her.
On dirty London streets or riding buses, I stayed watchful and alert—
I imagined for her sake. Because the city frightened me, at least until I
got used to its growl.

London was thronged with men in khaki. At first I saw them as
threats, potential attackers, but soon I grew accustomed to the uniforms,
and after a while the men wearing them seemed ordinary enough.

Men interned at Alexandra Palace were permitted one family visit
per month. Twenty minutes. That was cruel, but at the start of the war
the English, like everyone else, forgot their decency. Or perhaps those
individuals with the most vindictive and primitive mentalities suddenly
found themselves at last in a position to give orders. Later on, when
decency came somewhat back into fashion, weekly visits became the
norm.

Ally Pally had a pretentious dome and enough size to dare call itself
a palace, but it was really just an unsuccessful indoor fairground, a Vic-
torian hulk on a hill, too big, too bleak, and too far from central London to be popular.

Now the perimeter was surrounded by barbed wire and patrolled by
armed guards.

Buck was penned up with two thousand German civilians, middle-
aged men who'd lived in England most of their lives. They ate rations of

soup and horsemeat and bread they baked themselves. No one starved, but internees died of pneumonia, of heart disease, and periodically men hanged themselves. Dozens of internees died during the influenza epidemic just after the armistice.

They all slept in the Great Hall: two thousand men, on plank beds, under army blankets, grunting, snoring, shouting out from nightmares.

For the rest of his life my father would sleep with all his bedroom windows open. It didn't matter how cold it was outside; the windows had to be open.

After the first winter the internees were allowed to stake out garden plots and raise vegetables. Some grew flowers. They argued bitterly over techniques of planting, weeding, fertilizing. There were envious rages, hatreds, seething sulks.

Ever after, Buck loathed gardens, especially formal, well-organized kitchen gardens. The sight of a neat *potager* made him anxious, even angry, and he'd make sneering comments about the gardeners and their "fanatic" desire to impose order on natural abundance.

Eilín and I settled into a lodging house on Dukes Avenue in Muswell Hill. The neighborhood was close to Ally Pally but miles from the suffragist tearoom on Oxford Street where she found work as a waitress.

When I started school she warned me not to mention that my father was a prisoner at Ally Pally, but the boys and girls all seemed to know. And they knew my German name, because our teacher barked "Lange, Hermann" on the first day, mocking me with a guttural Teutonic accent. My chief tormentor was a little boy named Albert Willspeed, and now I think of it, there is something odd and foreign—possibly German—about that name Willspeed, isn't there? *Vilspied?* That would make sense, if he himself was a little crypto-Hun. Maybe his father was in Ally Pally, too, or out on the Isle of Man.

Albert Willspeed, or Vilspied, never grew bored with the subject of my Germanness. I was *Herm the Germ*, the *nasty-basty Hun*. Sometimes he sounded almost cheerful about it, but the hectoring went on day after day. My father was a traitor. My father was to be shot by a firing squad, or hanged by the neck, and his dead body was going to be pitched into the river, because they would not bury a German rotter traitor in the earth of England.

That little boy was like a wolverine. He'd approach me in the school yard first thing and ask how my German sausage breakfast had tasted. He'd grab my satchel and spill my books. One of his cronies would crouch behind me, and I'd be toppled over his back with a shove. Once they had me down on the pavement, two or three would hold me while Albert hammered me with fierce punches. Sometimes he'd incite seven or eight others, girls and boys, to surround me, all screaming "German sausage! German sausage!" at the tops of their voices. They would lock arms so I couldn't break out of the circle. There was no question of aid or sympathy from teachers. I don't recall any teachers, except that one sallow woman who started it all by making fun of my German name.

A woman on the Quaker Emergency Committee had helped my mother find the job at Alan's Tea Rooms on Oxford Street. Alan's served only women, and the atmosphere was much less rowdy than an A.B.C. or a Lyons Corner House. But Oxford Street was almost an hour by bus and tube from Muswell Hill. Coming home one evening, Eilín had overheard a young woman on the bus speaking German to an older woman, then quite suddenly both women were set upon by a female passenger shouting at them, calling them filthy Huns and beating them with her rolled-up umbrella.

I was in the white-and-black kitchen of the lodging house when my mother reached home that day. I'd been helping the cook set mouse-traps. The cook was frightened of mice; I didn't mind them; rats unnerved us both.

I can still see Eilín perched on a stool near the stove, wearing her coat and hat and shivering while she described the helpless German ladies huddling down between the bus seats for protection.

"You never saw such a beastly thing. Like dogs fighting—only the Germans weren't fighting back; they couldn't. And everyone watching, with no one lifting a finger to help."

I think this was the first time I really saw my mother discomposed.

Oh, I wanted so badly to protect her.

"At last a soldier stepped up, an Ozzy"—an Australian soldier. "He got hold of the umbrella and broke it on his knee and pitched it down into the road!

"Oh Billy, Billy man." My mother sighed. "I know you'd do the same and so would your father."

"I would," I said, wishing to sound bold and brave. But I was near tears just from her telling, her dismay, the sense of a disordered London enveloping me.

Going up to Ally Pally on visiting days, we rode buses with other internee families. If they forgot themselves and started speaking German or Yiddish, Eilín would shush them. If they kept it up, we'd move as far away as possible. Sometimes we'd get off at the next stop.

But I began muttering secret, gobbledygook German to myself while walking to school along Muswell Hill Broadway. I couldn't speak a word of real German, but had no trouble generating guttural grunts and vowels that sounded, to me, defiant and subversive. Whispering ersatz German was like uttering a charm, allowing me to feel, in a small, secret way, untouchable. It was a carapace, protecting me.

One morning when Eilín was due at work in the West End, I had a bad cold. She was afraid to send me off to school because my teacher would probably send me home, and the cook, who sometimes "minded" me, was unavailable, having gone down to Somerset to visit her brother, whose son had been killed in France.

My mother decided I must spend the day with her at Alan's Tea Rooms, sitting at a table with my schoolbooks, pencils, and drawing paper.

We boarded her usual bus, but when the conductress came around, somehow Eilín hadn't brought enough money to pay both our fares.

This was unlike her. She'd been in a flurry getting me ready, hurrying me along. Maybe she'd left her little purse behind. Maybe she just did not have the cash to pay two fares.

We stood humiliated on the breezy, sooty rear platform while the conductress, who wasn't nearly so nice or pretty as Hamilton, scolded my mother. "You're off at the next stop, if you please! We aren't a charity!"

Eilín held on to a post to steady herself as the bus grumbled and rocked. She didn't argue. She just shut her eyes, and what frightened me was that she kept them shut as the bus trundled along, wheezing and smoking.

It seemed to me my mother was wishing herself away. She wanted to fly from the freezing, smelly bus and the rude conductress; from harridans with furled umbrellas; from boardinghouse lodgers and tearoom customers, Ally Pally guards and inmates. From everyone, including me.

Those old London General buses were brutally cold on winter mornings, no heaters and no window glass. The upper deck didn't even have a roof. Out on the rear platform, the swirling air tasted of black smut. We weren't permitted to take seats, and everyone was glaring at us. I was ashamed. My mother clutched the steel post and kept her eyes shut as we rocked and swayed. I could feel her shutting me out along with the rest of the world.

Then a young soldier stepped up. Even to me he looked young for a soldier. Pink face, khaki cap, puttees, brown boots. I bristled and knotted my fists—if anyone noticed, how ridiculous I must have seemed, how "cute" and how pathetic.

The soldier paid our fares.

The bus was slowing for the next stop. I sensed my mother poised and ready to jump off. But I wouldn't let her. I grabbed her hand, seized hold of the polished post, and hung on. I refused to allow her to jump down off the bus.

Meanwhile the conductress cranked out a pair of tickets and held them out with a sneer.

Had I not held on to her with all my strength, she'd have leaped off the bus. She'd have dodged into the sidewalk crowd and disappeared. *She'd have left me.* She might have regretted it a few moments later, but at that instant, if I'd let her go, she'd have disappeared into that blurred stretch of north London between Muswell Hill and Highgate.

Instead we climbed the twist of stairs to the top deck, which was open to the weather and truly, frightfully cold. The young soldier followed us and tried to make conversation, but Eilín was very cold to him. She'd been taught to refuse attentions from a stranger. Even kindness, or pity, or whatever it was.

We never spoke of what had almost happened. What was there to say? She hadn't left me, after all. We had made it through all right.

⊱──⊰

One Sunday a few weeks after we came up to London we went into Regent's Park to see the last roses and the autumn leaves. A demonstration trench had been excavated in the lawn to show civilians how their sons and husbands and brothers were living at the front. There were tangles of barbed wire curling on the grass, and thick breastworks of tawny sandbags. There was a wooden parapet for Tommies standing guard duty. Wooden duckboards lined the floor. It was very neat and dry. Signboards explained that the trench was cut in a zigzag so that if a portion were overrun, the enemy would not obtain a clear field of fire along the entire length.

The trench's narrowness, cleanliness, and depth appealed enormously. The London world was too wide open for me. In the school yard in Muswell Hill I felt exposed, vulnerable. The trench offered control and security. I was eager to climb down inside. There was a flight of steps at one end, built of pungent Canadian fir. I tugged Eilín's hand impatiently, but she didn't want to go down into it. I suppose she didn't want to risk getting her good shoes or her dress dirty. But she finally let me go, and I ran down the steps alone.

Tightness, enclosure, security, earth. Could it have been a grave I was really after? Part of me wanted to shut my life down, or at least become a spirit, not a schoolboy. Become invisible.

Cool earthen walls seven feet deep were sparingly braced with timbers. Burrows and notches had been scooped out of the walls—snug places where soldiers could nap, or shelter from bombardment. The trench might have been excavated by a very precise and skillful set of burrowing mammals—moles, badgers.

I felt untouchable in there so long as I remained perfectly still. A thrill of resonant safety. Is that why I remember so well the trench walls, carved sheer through layers of earth, with different colors to each stratum? The topmost was a fascinating tangle of yellow and white roots. Then came layers of black, brown, red, and gray earth and clay, with paler streaks—perhaps deposits of chalk or animal bones. It smelled of a different world, a cool, overwhelming earthiness.

My first tactile experience of *solitude*, a charged feeling, delicious, almost sexual in intensity.

⊱–◆◦◦–⊰

During our year in London I only saw my father a few times, right at the beginning. On my second or third visit he presented me with a model ship, a three-masted bark with her name—LILITH—scribed on her bow, and her homeport, HAMBURG, on her stern.

My mother told me much later that seeing me in the camp was very painful for him. He felt humiliated by his shabby clothes and squalid surroundings. It was difficult enough to endure her visits and feel the gulf opening between them. She seemed to be living at a different speed, breathing a different kind of air. Compared with the internees, their pallor and sleeplessness, my mother must have seemed feverishly exhilarated, rambunctious, and alive.

He couldn't see that war and separation were wearing her down as well.

And he hated that I should see him helpless. After the model-ship visit—which ended with all three of us in tears after I'd asked why he was afraid of the camp guards, who were all such old men—my mother began going alone to Ally Pally on visiting days. My father didn't wish to be a prisoner in my eyes. He thought my spirit would be stunted and I'd never make a success of life.

He and other prisoners tried constructing little tents or huts around their beds, in a feeble attempt to create some privacy. The camp authorities ordered these torn down.

Eilín's wages and tips from Alan's Tea Rooms were never enough to live on; we had to depend as well on the charity of the Quakers. Sometimes we found our dinner in a Quaker soup kitchen. My grandmother Con once sent us a ham from Ireland.

Then the matter of the stipend was settled. This was a small sum of money from the German government to be doled out every month to families of civilian internees. It would come via the Swiss embassy. It wouldn't be much, but it was something, and would be paid no matter where we lived. It would go a lot further if we weren't living in expensive London.

That was my father's argument. He was the only one in favor of us going to Ireland. My mother resisted. To her, Ireland meant her father, Joseph McDermott, with whom she had a fraught relationship.

My father said we might go to live at Wychwood, his mother's house at Sligo, only three or four miles from my McDermott grandfather's red villa at Strandhill. But Eilín had never met her mother-in-law, and Wychwood, though in Irish terms a "big house" owned by a family who for a hundred years had considered themselves gentry, was in famously poor condition, and undoubtedly cold and damp, as most "big houses" were. My mother thought it would be unhealthy for me.

When Eilín came down from Ally Pally hill, she was often frighteningly remote. She might reach out to embrace me—if she remembered. She didn't always remember. This was probably the period my parents were in disagreement over Sligo. My mother hated to be caught weeping or to be seen in any way as vulnerable. Eilín was forceful and competent, could even seem hard, but underneath she must have been close to despair. She always mastered it, but that didn't mean despair wasn't there, just below the surface and rising up especially during transitions, and in liminal spaces like train stations and ship quays.

We were riding aboard a London bus around this time when she remarked, "Daddy wishes us back into the bog."

I had no idea what she meant, but the phrase *back into the bog* has stayed with me.

By this time I had pretty much lost sight of my father as a person. He was a ghost.

Buck had convinced himself time would go by faster if the two of them didn't have to measure their lives from week to week, one visit to the next. Also it would be much cheaper, living at Sligo. Eilín wouldn't need to work as a waitress in a tea shop. Good food was plentiful in Ireland.

Twenty minutes together, only fingertips touching across a battered table in a visiting room with dozens of strangers doing exactly the same thing: such "visits" must have made it clear to my parents that the war was prying them apart, turning them into strangers. Years later she told me Buck spent three visits in a row talking about nothing but birds. No real intimacy was possible, so he'd given up trying. He'd reached a point where nothing outside the barbed wire had any weight for him. This was a symptom of what he called barbed-wire disease, and it made her furious, then ashamed of herself. It wasn't his fault. He was trapped in a crepuscular world of wheezing, snoring, complaining German and Austrian men. Given his sailor's sensitivity to sky, weather, breezes— the wide-open blue—he'd become obsessed with the careless, glamorous, wide-open lives of English birds.

I hated the jeering teachers at school and dreamed of drowning Albert Willspeed in the pond at Hampstead Heath. I might have tried if I'd ever come across him there. What should I do when he screamed and begged for help? Would I pull him out? I would never let an animal, even a duck, drown in the pond without attempting rescue. If I rescued scrawny, bleak little Albert I'd be a hero. Even though I'd pushed him in. Perhaps I'd win a Royal Life Saving medal.

><-><-0-<>-><

Eilín finally realized that our proximity (the boardinghouse was less than a mile from Ally Pally), rather than being a comfort, was torturing my father. He had dreams—nightmares—in which time was stopped. He told her during the worst periods he found himself noting and measuring each passing minute.

Barbed-wire disease.

So Eilín at last agreed we'd leave London for Ireland.

There'd be ham and fresh milk and potatoes in Ireland. We could collect the stipend there. Eilín hated our semi-communal life in the boardinghouse, hated sitting at the tea table with a dozen lodgers. There was a sickly Welsh preacher, Reverend Mr. Powell, always maneuvering to sit next to her. He had yellowed fingers and wore a ruby ring.

I took my tea downstairs with the others, but Eilín often carried a tray up to her room. No one else was permitted to do that; the housekeeper had a dread of crumbs and of mice—mice were an obsession in north London lodging houses. But the cook was fond of my mother so she was allowed to take her meals upstairs and alone.

In my mind Ireland was mixed up with the Isle of Wight. At first I was under the impression we were going home to Sanssouci, but as our time for departure grew nearer my confusion dissipated and it became clear "Ireland" was something quite different. However, I liked islands in principle. Ireland sounded a long way from Albert Willspeed, and that was good enough for me.

Going to Sligo would be like going to sleep until the war was over: that was what my parents hoped.

"The Irish aren't as angry," Eilín assured me, "they don't hate the Hun."

"We're not Huns."

"No one is, really. It's only what they say. You'll have a fresh start at school and a pony to ride."

The first payment of the stipend was delayed, so we were very low on funds during our last weeks in London. Wages and tips from Alan's Tea Rooms plus a few bob from the Quakers were all we had to live on. We used to count our money on a white chenille bedspread in our room. She never had paper notes, only coins—shillings, half sovereigns, the occasional crown. We washed the hoard by dumping the coins into a jug, pouring scalding water on them, adding a dollop of ammonia cleaning fluid, and stirring. We'd drain the water, then dump the mass of coins on a towel to dry. London money was filthy, she said. She preferred that I did the counting; she didn't like doing it.

What we had wasn't enough to pay our fare for Ireland, so most of our household goods and my father's handmade shoes had to go off to the pawnbroker, an elderly German Jew whose anarchist son was interned at Ally Pally. Eilín pawned her wedding band. Then we had enough for two tickets on the Irish boat-train.

Before we left London there was the zeppelin raid.

For me it started with a great noise in the streets—cheering that woke me up. I rolled out of bed and stumbled to the window. My mother was up a moment later, reaching for her woolen wrap, dazed and groggy—she worked so hard and slept so little and had to share her bed with me, a restless sleeper who thrashed and kicked most of the night.

I stood at the window clutching my ship *Lilith* and watching the fire in the sky. A British fighter had shot up the zep with incendiary bullets, and the airship was an enormous bag of fire, wafting from side to side and dripping fire in clots, like melted wax dripping from a candle. As soon as I realized it was a zep, I knew that all the crewmen aboard her would die; that was why we stared at the thing with such fascination. Then men began leaping from the ship, tiny bright specks, like glowing embers spat from a fire. Dots of orange death, plummeting to the ground.

The memory of that zeppelin night handles like a dream, and if my mother hadn't spoken of it up until the hour of her own death, I might believe that it was a dream. But it really happened, and we watched it.

That particular zep came to its end in a farmer's field at Potters Bar, Hertfordshire. By then all the crewmen had jumped to their deaths.

Burning aviators, clots of fire. The reeking night jar in our bedroom in Muswell Hill. Children skipping round me in a school yard, shouting taunts. My ship *Lilith*. London's winter cold and dark. The smell of ground sliced open in Regent's Park, my father's pale prisoner's face, his white hands on a table in the visiting hall. There it is. That was my war.

❧   1938

AT LAST WE TURNED UP HER LITTLE STREET. WE WERE EXHAUSTED FROM cold rain, from dancing, from Kansas City jubilation, from the long ride on the rackety late-night U-Bahn, and the long walk from Uhland-strasse in a downpour. We were jumpy from doubts, fears, dreams of America, the prospect of ourselves as parents.

As we hurried up the street I could see a heap on the sidewalk in front of her building. For a moment, I thought there'd been a car smash, then I recognized a typewriter perched haphazardly on top of a Bauhaus writing table.

All her goods, clothes, belongings, had been dumped on the side-walk. She didn't own much, but it still made a good-sized pile. Every-thing sodden.

"The paintings—"

"Don't bother!" she said. "The paintings are gone, I'm sure."

They were. Had they been destroyed as degenerate art, or had someone grabbed them on the sly, knowing they'd bring a good price in Amsterdam or Paris?

Her belongings heaped on the sidewalk in the rain—it was grue-some. Like staring at a bloody car wreck.

"Your job: find us a hotel room." She dragged out a leather suitcase from the pile and began throwing some wet clothes into it. "Tomor-row we'll go to Frankfurt. I'll go to America. I don't care about these fucking idiot things. My pile of shit! Except the paintings and they're not here. No, of course they are not. Well, forget them, forget them, what they are is what they've become. The loss is best managed by not talking about it."

She filled the suitcase and clipped it shut.

I saw my knapsack in the pile and extracted it.

"What about the rest—"

"Let them have it! If I could set the whole heap on fire, I would."

She'd lived in that building ten years. What had her neighbors, taking their poodles for evening promenades, thought when they saw her heap of things? Probably they'd scampered back up to their flats and locked and chained their doors.

All the cash in my wallet I spent on a cab to Unter den Linden and a room at the Hotel Adlon. I never had stayed in such a grand establishment before, but no one at the front desk asked if we were married, or if she was Jewish, and our room had a bathroom en suite. Karin bathed in the tub, and we fell asleep in the soft enormous bed.

✳ IRISH SEA

Holograph letter. Eilín McDermott Lange to Heinrich Lange ("Buck"), addressed *Capt H Lange, Alexandra Palace Camp, London N10*, post-marked *Sligo, 15 May 1916*. Lange Family Archive. 12 C-05-1916. Special Collections, McGill Library, McGill University, Montreal.

—

May 12th
STRANDHILL, SLIGO

Mein Liebster,

We are settled in the red house with father.

On the boat coming across Billy and I both were sick. I went out on deck and smelled the ground of Ireland. At Kingstown quay he had raging fever. Not knowing what else to do I begged a drayman to take us to the Loreto's where they might have a bed for him. The nuns bless them took us both in my old teacher Mother Power nursed him a week and it was scarlet fever but he is <u>completely recovered</u>. I did not write before as I wanted to wait until I could say your son is perfectly well: and now he is.

It was an odd sort of return to Ireland. Passing through Dublin we saw Sackville Street in ruins, buildings smashed, the Post Office a wreck, the city smelled of old fires. Billy has had too much war already. I don't want any more war for him. He still asks about the crew of the zep. Did they die—yes. Did they burn—yes. Did no one help them—don't know. Is hell like that—don't know.

Father is willing to keep us but his law practice is gone slack, none of the big landowners will use him now that he spends most of his time speaking against conscription. At Strandhill the subject of the war to be avoided at all costs or he will go on about the evils, conscripting poor Irishmen for English slaves, etc. The life of this house is entirely organized to his purposes & whims, the household run strictly according to his habits, my sisters are meek housecats, poor things. I may be unable to live in the same house as my Father, there it is. I tell myself, I must, for Billy's sake, but it may not be possible—my spirit shrivels here. Father feels the same about me, we are oil and water, he won't admit it. He is Great Britain to my Ireland. He the viceroy, me the seething rebel. Last night I put our situation to him like that (foolish, yes, but after a week of his lectures & commands & whims my head was reeling) and he thought I was making a joke of his republican faith, and insulting the sacred memory of the Fenian martyrs!! besides. I wasn't any honest rebel but I had a traitor's heart.

I said—That's what the British called those they shot, do you think I ought to be shot? He replied—it was no use talking to me as I couldn't talk sense.

And yet. And yet. The poor farmers in this part of the world think of him as their champion. Some of them, anyway. His little housemaid finds him very hard as an employer. He is determined to help the farmers and tenants win back what the ranchers have stolen and they love him for it but don't pay him hardly anything.

My sisters are very happy to have us and shower the boy with love & attention.

It's hard to think of now but when we were girls we all would go down to Strandhill on a sunny afternoon—father, poor little mother, and the 3 of us. Father would help us build our sandcastles. He'd take off his boots, swing us over tops of waves so our feet could dabble in the fizz. Now he is so hard and locked-up and difficult to know. Speeches and hatred crowd his head, he doesn't like to feel anything else.

I asked—When was the last time you were out on the strand?

He gave me a look as if I were talking nonsense.

I said—Organize a family party, all of us, take sandwiches and spend the day. You used to say S'hill is the most beautiful place in the world.

He shook his head as if I were talking Dutch and it was just noise to him.

I said—Don't you remember, rolling up your trousers and walking in the surf, we used to look at you so far off, such a tiny figure on the beach, we couldn't understand how you could ever be so small as that.

Father—I haven't time for that now.

He expects/wants Germany to win the war. He asks if you have organized a protest at A.P.? He says you ought to go on hunger strike. He is all for making martyrs. Don't you dare. Eat all the food you can, for your son's sake keep as strong as you can. One day the war will be over and he'll need his father. You must teach him about the wind, tides, stars, sailing close-hauled, shrouds, stays, tops'ls and all the lore I can't remember, he will learn to be a man in the world from your gentle ways & your sense of duty & purpose. My father is a patriot but isn't at home in the world. Thin and stalky—solitary as a heron. He writes ferocious letters to the Sligo Champion and I believe wishes he were at Kilmainham himself waiting to be shot—maybe he is weary of life and won't admit it. His anger—at the British, redmondites in parliament, cattle ranchers, recruiters, English landlords—is also directed at my sisters and the little maid and myself. Fury is his screen and behind it he hides. The only one he's mild with is: Billy.

On Thursday the boy and I did walk all the way to the old strand at Kilaspugrone, and I thought that wild wind would blow me away, old man, or blow me clean, at least, blow the London smut right out of me. Only it was a warm wind, warm and wet. There was two women far away gathering wrack in a cart, but not another soul, it seemed like the green end of the world.

I informed the boy I was going to remove my clothes to bathe in the sea and if my being naked made him uneasy he must walk a way down the strand toward the wrackers and not look back but I was his mother and this was the seashore where I'd bathed as a girl, these were my waves, and it was natural I should do so again.

He looked solemn, and said—But you should have brought your dipper.

—Well I haven't.

Then he said, he wasn't afraid, far from it, he would go in as well, only he wouldn't take off his clothes.

I said—The sea here is different than what you are accustomed to on our Isle—quite wild and big.

I can see, he said—but I'll be safe enough—you won't let anything happen to me.

He removed shoes and socks, his jumper and vest and walked down to the water's edge and began spinning stones into the backchat of waves just as my sisters and I used to do. I left my clothes under a few sticks and ran—straight into the waves.

The boy came in straight after me, throwing himself across the wave-tops, very bold . . . both of us screaming . . . for joy— I think. Feeling clean. Only wanting you.

I have twice gone out to Wychwood to your mother. The house is a ruin as you said it would be, very damp. She says there is plenty of room but most rooms are ruined—I don't know that your mother really sees what terrible condition the house is in. As far as I can tell she has no income whatsoever except very small rents from the few tenants that are willing to pay it. Her maid earns a few shillings selling eggs on market day and says that a few of the former tenants will leave bacon, apples, potatoes, milk, etc. at the 'big house' not out of any sense of obligation but out of pity. Many tenants in this part of the country have stopped paying the rent. If they do, the Sinn Feiners might cause trouble for them.

Your mother rides out every morning on her old hunter, 'Clip.' My father warns that a 'Shinner' might shoot her from behind a hedge one morning.

I must go to the post office to see if the stipend has come through.

There is war-work and wages at the mills in Derry so I may go up there, but I would have the Boy stay on here with my father & sisters, I don't want him in a dirty town like Derry, poor wee soul.

Ich liebe Dich,
E

I REMEMBER SMOKY CUPS OF TEA ON THE TRAIN FROM EUSTON STATION
and passageways crowded with soldiers in khaki. Windows in our third-
class carriage were unwashed and blurred the countryside with a dirty,
ugly fog. But while the train hammered across England and Wales, I
was absorbed by what was flowing on the other side of the glass: not the
countryside nor the towns, but the railway system itself. The ribbons of
steel rail on graded track bed. The elegant cuts, brickwork tunnels, stalwart iron bridges. The grassy, sinuous elegance of embankments and
the perfection of level grade fascinated me. It was as if the great work
had been done by gifted aliens. To carve a railway line through such
rolling and various country, through the hearts of densely clustered
cities and towns, and to keep the network alive and almost breathing
seemed to me so wonderful as to be nearly overpowering. I experienced
euphoria on that journey across England and Wales. As it turned out, I
was also incubating scarlet fever, which may have had something to do
with my exalted mental state.

The British railways struck me as one great *thing*. Before leaving
London I could not have imagined such a thing. Then I experienced it
as though it were one enormous, fantastic clockwork toy, or perhaps a
powerful animal, alive and uncaged, sprawling across hundreds of miles
of England and Wales.

It amazed me that people had built and could sustain such complexity. It made me feel deliriously proud of being human.

Some of this was fever coming on, also the emotional release I felt as
we sped farther and farther from the narrowness and terror of Muswell
Hill, my unpleasant schoolmates, and my barren, beaten-raw identity
as *Herm the Germ*.

In Ireland they would have to find something else to call me.

Eilín in those days wore her chestnut hair in a chignon that left the slender stalk of her neck exposed. We kept to ourselves on the train. She spoke to strangers only when she had to.

At Holyhead we boarded the steamer for Dublin. My maiden sea voyage, unless I count the little Isle of Wight steamer from Ryde to Southampton.

Crossing the Irish Sea with my mother does not compare with Buck's voyage in utero round the Horn, does it? Still, you must give us some credit for boldness. Or give it to her, anyway. Eilín, twenty-six, traveling with a seven-year-old son, and I doubt she had six extra shillings in her purse. We were sailing for Ireland to live out the war, if ever it would end. She had written her father asking for refuge and heard nothing back. After her mother's funeral she'd quit his house vowing never to return.

It was all a gamble.

Mother and Son. Promenade Deck, SS Hibernia. *Irish Sea, 1916.*

We had one bright hour out on the promenade deck before the fog closed in. I still feel her grip on my hand, squeezing hard. Her hair streaming in cold bright wind.

I suddenly was afraid she was going to climb the rail and leap into the sea.

But maybe she wasn't. Maybe it was a delusion, my delusion. Maybe it was the fever coming on.

Maybe what I really experienced on the steamer was the frightening, awe-inspiring sense we had been cut loose, were beyond sight of land, lost.

After all, what sort of woman, clutching the hand of her little boy, would actually consider climbing a ship's rail and leaping out into the Irish Sea?

What sort of woman would consider stepping off a London bus into crowds, into oblivion?

Only a woman penniless in wartime. Only a woman traveling into exile. Only a woman who suspects, from redness around his eyes and a croak in his voice, that her son has a life-threatening bout of scarlet fever coming on. Only a woman whose husband is a prisoner, whose father is a tyrant. Only a woman exhausted by life.

The promised stipend had yet to come through. None of the portents were good. It might have seemed to her, hatless and wind whipped on the promenade deck, that the only way she'd ever free herself from the humiliation of her situation was to climb over the rail and quickly, before anyone could interfere, jump.

Did she imagine wrapping arms around me and taking me with her into the next world?

It's possible she did, for a moment, and maybe that's what stopped her. Maybe she was prepared to end her own life but not mine. And if she took the jump alone, what would become of me? An orphanage? In Dublin? I'd be handed over to my grandfather Joseph McDermott. She didn't want her father raising her son.

It is April 1916. Most of her wardrobe has been pawned. She wears her best gray suit, the little jacket tightly buttoned at her waist. White blouse, black lisle stockings, boots. The hat she's left inside, on one of the benches in the third-class cabin, is another of the insane and gorgeous hats of the prewar period, big enough to bathe a good-sized baby in. She bought it to wear to summer parties on the lawn at the Royal Yacht Squadron. She has pawned her wedding band but kept the hat. Of course the ring brought more than the hat would have, but perhaps her need for the hat is greater. The hat identifies her, at least to herself, as a woman of boldness, spirit, and taste. Someone who from girlhood has grasped that life can, must, be an adventure. A fine, bold possession, not to be thrown away or wasted.

The ship slipped into a fog bank. Bright sunlight snapped off abruptly, as though someone had pressed a switch. We retreated to our bench in the third-class cabin, where I slept fitfully, my head in her lap.

And that evening Eilín McDermott Lange, with her son, Billy, aka Herm the Germ, dragged their (minimal) baggage down a slick gangway in the oyster light of Kingstown, Ireland. A homecoming, it was, but it may have felt like exile to her. On the quay she touched my shoulder, and there we stood, uncertainly poised at the limit of her native country, like children who have come a long way on a hot day to bathe in a cool pond but hesitate at the water's very edge, suddenly fearing what unseen creatures might be swimming and wriggling under the surface.

Everything I'm telling you is partly a dream, and so not to be trusted. But I do possess a freakishly accurate memory for dates. It was Saturday, April 22, 1916, when Eilín and I stepped down onto the quay. About six o'clock in the evening. Easter Saturday. All over the country, bands of Irish Volunteers were arguing whether to go ahead with their planned Rising on Easter Monday, but of course we didn't know that.

Right there on the bustling quay I fainted. I'd had enough of standing guard, and I went down like a stone. I had a raging fever and there was nothing for it but to get me under a roof as soon as possible and into a bed. A drayman was persuaded to take us, free of charge, to the Loreto Convent School, at Rathfarnham, where Eilín had once been a boarder. The nuns took us in, and we spent two weeks there, me isolated in the infirmary, while the Easter Rising played out in Dublin, with rebels occupying key buildings until the British Army moved in enough heavy artillery to blast them out and demolish a good chunk of central Dublin besides. I didn't hear the guns. A pink-faced nun fed and bathed me and kept an eye on my fever, which went dizzily up and down. I recall the scratchy comfort of a red-and-black Hudson's Bay blanket and a view from my sickroom window of rain clouds over the Dublin mountains.

Eilín must have been in touch with my grandmother Con, because as soon as I was strong enough to travel, an old admirer of Con's, Sir Charles Butler, came to fetch us and bring us to Amiens Street Station.

Charlie Butler was an Anglo-Irish squire, owner of a famous racing stable, Knockmealdown Stud. He had been a classmate of Oscar Wilde at Portora Royal School. He was a bowlegged, red-faced squireen with a white mustache, very jolly and kind, and it was my first ride in a motorcar. We ran straight through the heart of the city, past the General Post Office which the rebels had held for nearly a week. The GPO was now a shell, and O'Connell Street—Sackville Street, as it was then—was heaps of rubble. The rebel leaders were being held in Kilmainham Gaol. Charlie Butler said they were all to be shot, even the women.

Dublin in its wreckage bustled with horse carts and motors. I saw boys picking through mountains of fresh rubble and soldiers in khaki ignoring the boys. Rubble has an odor, not pleasant—dust and damp all at once, and a sweet, slippery smell like rotten bananas. Eilín feared my lungs would be inflamed by the dust and tied a handkerchief around my mouth and nose.

She'd tried to leave behind war's passions and hatred, yet here was her country's capital in ruins, with everyone talking of prisoners and executions.

Charlie Butler hired a porter to sling our baggage aboard the mail train for Sligo. We shook hands with Butler, and he handed me a sovereign, which startled me.

"Now, Billy, old blade, you've never yet met your grandmother, I suppose?"

"I haven't."

"Well, you're a lucky man, because you will. Your grandmama went round the Horn at nineteen with a baby in her belly, that being himself, your father."

"I know."

"When you see her, remember this: she likes a bold fellow. Likes a plunger. So you step up, bold as brass, kiss her the once, and say that's from you. Then another, and tell her that's from auld Charlie Butler to the handsomest woman in Ireland. Will you do it?"

"I will."

"Good man."

The sovereign meant a geometric increase in our funds, and Eilín made me hand it over as soon as we found our seats. On the journey we consumed the gorgeous picnic lunch Charlie Butler had provided in a wicker basket from his Kildare Street Club. After having eaten nothing for days except convent soup and dry toast, I was famished. At Muswell Hill, our boardinghouse rations tasted stale, mute, and tinny, and I understood that was the taste of war. But our feast aboard the Irish mail train—fresh ham sandwiches, biscuits, chocolate, even an orange to share, with lemonade for me and a bottle of porter for mother—was delicious, filling, and new.

Eilín hadn't sent a telegram ahead—didn't want to pay for it, I suppose, so there was no one to meet us when we got off at Sligo. Luckily, the stationmaster recognized her.

"You're the daughter of himself. You're the German."

"I'm not. But I'm married to the German." And she stared at him hard, daring him to call us a pair of Huns. He didn't. Instead he told a farmer who was collecting steel milk cans off the train to take us out to Strandhill in his jaunting car.

A couple of miles out, on the road to the sea, we drew up in front of a red villa. I saw an iron fence, a bricked stable yard to the side, and a small coach house peeking out from behind the main house, which had a tower in one corner. I hoped it signified a castle.

The red house really was just a suburban villa, built in the 1880s. My grandfather bought the house from the Pollexfens, W. B. Yeats's mother's family, and my mother and her two sisters grew up there. Eilín and her two younger sisters, Kate and Frances, had been packed off to school at the Loretos at Rathfarnham and only brought back to Strandhill when their mother was dying.

When he was a bachelor my grandfather had spent a summer learning Irish on the Irish-speaking island of Inishmor, where he seduced Noirín Flaherty, sixteen-year-old daughter of a fisherman. She wore an island woman's red cloak and cowhide slippers and had never slept a night anywhere but Inishmor until my grandfather, under violent threat from her brothers, married her and brought her to Sligo, where my mother was born seven and half months later.

Noirín never stopped mourning her island life, and died at Sligo when she was thirty-five, leaving Eilín and her two sisters motherless.

When she was very old, my mother insisted her father had never loved her mother; he'd only loved her beautiful Irish. He'd required Eilín and her sisters to speak Irish at home, even though Sligo was an English-speaking town.

In the jaunting car Eilín and I sat facing each other. She had pinned some sort of rubberized weatherproof material over her hat. I was getting soaked. I was gazing at the house, but my mother had her back to it and would not look around, even after the farmer had climbed down and was reaching for our baggage.

On the Strandhill Road in the rain, her independent life and her marriage must have seemed awfully distant, a life that had belonged to someone else.

Through dripping rain, I study her face under the tremendous hat. I'm not sure she's seeing me. She twists at the finger where her wedding band ought to be, but isn't. She wants back the life she founded on her voyage outward from Sligo, her position in Germany, her marriage. She misses the context and comradeship of marriage. She wants my father in her story, but he has unaccountably dropped from the narrative, or at least he's gone mute. He's watching birds flutter outside the barbed wire on Ally Pally hill. For a year she's passed through that wire on monthly, then weekly, visits. She's poured tea for prominent suffragists, waited on their tables, and attempted to persuade her son that the particles he saw sputtering in the night sky over north London were not, in fact, human beings on fire. She has washed up on the shore of her native country with a feverish boy and barely enough money for train fare. She has had to accept charity from her old schoolteachers.

Probably every damp mile out along the Strandhill Road there had been something to remind her that in this part of the world she'd never known what freedom was.

Silver rain. Green hedge. Blackness of wet road. Haunches of a bony old cart horse, soaked and glistening.

The red villa seemed magnificent to me. I was keen to meet my relations. I assumed they would adore me.

On her own she could have handled London. She'd returned only for my sake.

"Well, here we are," she said.

She sounded surprised, as if she couldn't quite believe what she had done. As if our journey had been a dream, and now we were waking up.

Our stipend would eventually arrive at the Sligo Post Office: two pounds seven shillings and fourpence, paid every month, for the duration of the war.

In another moment my two young aunts burst out of the house and made a great fuss over us, laughing, hugging, kissing. It was as much physical contact as I had ever had in my life. Meanwhile the farmer pulled our two bags inside and courteously refused the coin that Aunt Frances offered in payment.

"Oh, you must take it!" Frances cried.

"I cannot, no."

"You must!"

"I won't."

The farmer won that tussle and went off triumphantly *sans* shilling. Aunt Frances was black haired, blue eyed, the practical one who managed the housekeeping and did most of the cooking. At first I hoped she might be some sort of (very pretty) witch, always experimenting with recipes and medicaments, seething strange herbs in pots over the stove.

Aunt Kate, the youngest sister, loved fine things and intended to marry a rich man.

Soon we were all in the warm kitchen with a fire groaning in the nickel-plated range. They filled a copper tub with hot water, peeled off my wet clothes, put me in it. The little housemaid, Grainne, scrubbed me while the sisters chattered. Then we all had tea. I was wrapped in a blanket and settled in a chair close to the stove with a plate of scones smeared with butter and honey. A sepia-tinted, postcard-sized photograph of Eilín and Buck as newlyweds on the lawn at Sanssouci was passed around, and my aunts remarked how handsome he was, and what a wonderful house, and how unfair that poor Buck was locked up for being a German, which he couldn't help.

The controversy over the possibility of Irishmen being conscripted into the British Army was just beginning, and my grandfather was up in Fermanagh to deliver an anticonscription speech. He would travel all over the northwest for the next two and a half years, making speeches.

Kate was surprised to hear their father had not responded to Eilín's letter from London. She said he had certainly intended to write a letter inviting us, but it must have slipped his mind. "He's only gotten worse since the fight in Dublin. He made a Republican speech before the city council and might go to jail. He's not changed. He's all ideas and politics and caring for no one but himself, really."

We had supper in the chilly dining room. Leg of lamb and boiled potatoes. I couldn't eat the lamb, it was too strong, but I feasted on buttery potatoes sprinkled with salt and parsley. Afterward my mother and "the girls" settled back in the kitchen, drinking tea, while Grainne did the washing up. I was allowed to stay because the aunts were in love with me, and my bedroom was in the attic, a long way from the kitchen's bustle and warmth.

I felt surrounded and admired. The red villa was so much cozier and nicer than our boardinghouse in Muswell Hill.

The sisters were looking through Eilín's album of Sanssouci photographs when they heard their father entering the house.

"Go and greet him, Ellie. Bow and scrape to the chief, otherwise the pair of you will never get on."

My aunts wanted Eilín and my grandfather to get along. They wanted us to stay. They wanted a child in the house to break the mental siege of life with their demanding and lawless parent. I felt the depth of their affection and was already taking it as my due.

My mother went out to greet her father. The little maid Grainne hummed and grunted while scouring pots and pans.

A few minutes later the door swung open, and a very tall old man with streaming white hair stalked into the kitchen, followed by my mother. He wore a tweed ulster coat that smelled like a wet dog. Frances and Kate leaped to their feet and he kissed them. The soles of his boots made a crackle on the flagstones. Grainne was making a clatter with the pans. He kissed her.

That kiss infuriated my aunts and my mother. Even I sensed it. Grainne ignored him and kept on scouring. Standing barefoot on the kitchen flags she was quite small, and probably no more than sixteen or seventeen.

My grandfather stood before me saying something in a language I didn't understand. He switched to English. His voice was smooth, cogent, and musical.

"Are you the gentleman called Hermann Lange?"

Except for the schoolteacher at Muswell Hill, adults had always been my protectors. I wasn't shy with adults. It was other children I was wary of.

"I am. But that is not my real name."

"Isn't it? What, sir, is your real name?"

"I am Billy Lange, for the duration."

"Are you glad to be here, sir? Are these women treating you well?"

"They are."

He stared at me a moment longer, then he turned and left the kitchen. A few moments later the maid Grainne put away the last of the pans, dropped a quick curtsy to the three sisters, and followed him out. I fell asleep and was carried up to the attic bedroom I shared with Kate, next to the tiny garret where Grainne slept when she wasn't in my grandfather's bed.

☧ 1938

THE EFFICIENT LAUNDRY AT THE HOTEL ADLON DRIED AND FOLDED Karin's clothes, and the maid repacked everything in the surviving suitcase. It was Sunday morning, but Karin telephoned her partner Stefan Koplin first thing and arranged to meet him at their office. She wore a green suede jacket and a smart black-and-white frock made by her Berlin dressmaker, Lulu, an expatriate Parisienne with a trope for dazzling Japanese prints. Karin still wore her hair in a blunt, thick bob, with bangs nearly shrouding her eyes, a style that marked allegiance to the Berlin of the late 1920s.

She and Kop spent most of the day huddled over her desk, reviewing files, making notes, and telephoning all her Jews while I sat at another desk reading newspapers and doing crossword puzzles. Our train left at four o'clock, but she kept delaying: always one last file that needed to be discussed and annotated, one more telephone call that had to be made. I was starting to worry we'd never make the train. And I'd blown through all my cash, every last mark except for train fare, so where were we going to spend another night in Berlin? Certainly not at the Adlon. I was tapped out.

"Karin, we have to go."

"Yes, yes, another minute."

"Karin, we must go now!"

At last she stood up and shrugged on her coat. I lugged her suitcase into the rattletrap elevator and we rode down in creaky silence. Poor Koplin came with us.

Out on the street I shook hands with the fat little lawyer, then turned my attention to flagging down a taxi.

"Auf Wiedersehen, dear Kop!" Karin embraced him. "Please, please, dear man, watch out for yourself!"

"Never you mind about me!" Kop shouted as we were climbing into our taxi. "Keep your papers in order—that's all I say! All happiness in the New World!"

We arrived at the *Bahnhof* with about two minutes to spare, but she decided she must have a newspaper. An American newspaper.

"No longer can I read Nazi rubbish, all journalists in this damn country are utterly poltroons."

Of course foreign newspapers were no longer displayed on the racks at the train station and when she asked for a *Paris Herald* the newsagent took his time lifting a copy off a shelf behind him, then accepted her money with a snigger. Even the Berlin newsies had fallen sway to the regime.

Then she wanted to buy some fruit, but there wasn't time. It seemed to me she was trying to linger. And on the crowded platform, with her newspaper folded under her arm, she suddenly stopped cold.

"I cannot, Billy."

"Come on, our train leaves in a minute."

"I won't run away."

"You aren't."

We were speaking in English. People rushing to board were knocking past us.

"I am! People are drowning and I'm running away."

Anxious people were rushing by us; the loudspeaker was squawking arrivals, departures, and track changes.

Finally I just grabbed her arm.

"Let go of me!"

I ignored her. We struggled. She gave in, and I hustled us both along the platform, located our compartment, pushed her inside, then tossed our luggage into the overhead rack. I was angry, frightened, and sick feeling. I'd never ordered or forced her to do anything. As the train pulled out of the station, she was quietly weeping, but she fell asleep on my shoulder before we were even clear of the city's ugly outskirts.

We had the compartment to ourselves. I was relieved to be speeding west. I imagined the ride across Germany at night as the first stage of a journey that would end on the Pacific coast of Canada. I intended to withdraw all I could take out from my IG Farben pension fund and purchase as many dollars as I was allowed, but exchange rates weren't favorable. There'd be taxes and fines. To extract money from Germany was difficult. We'd be on a tight budget from now on.

It was a rattling second-class coach, the sort we called *ein Donnerbüchse*—a thunderbox. Wooden benches. Karin woke after a while and sat calmly leafing through her *Paris Herald*. Our relationship had always had the power of sex somewhere near its core. I'd always felt the pull of her body, the beauty of her bones, sweet curve of her ass, heat of her skin.

At Leipzig a pack of stalwart, sunburned young girls wearing the uniform of the Bund-Deutscher Mädel crowded into our compartment.

"Smells like a Jew in here!"

"French clothes and lipstick—she's no German!"

I wanted us to shift to another compartment, but Karin would not budge. She sat straight-backed, not saying a word, gazing at the leader of the troop, a buxom middle-aged woman who looked like a housewife and seemed flustered by her girls' behavior. She began shushing them. At last they opened their picnic baskets and, munching their wursts, cheese, and chocolate, ignored us for the rest of the trip.

Her partner, Stefan Koplin? For all his skill at arranging South American visas, he didn't get himself out in time. Kop died at Theresienstadt. Pneumonia. Winter of '41–'42.

❊ PRECIOUS GIRL

WYCHWOOD
May 13th 1916

SIR CHARLES BUTLER
Army & Navy Club
Pall Mall, London

Charley, a stor

My poor son remains a prisoner at the Alex. Palace. While you are in London Charley do go and see him and the warders will notice that he is <u>not</u> <u>without</u> friends. I can't help but think of poor OW and the Reading gaol which <u>wrecked</u> his health. What can you say of a country where the best men are in gaol? As for my daughter-in-law Eileen her plan is to stay with her father at Strandhill. I told her she might as well come to live at W'wood there is nothing but bedrooms and we have plenty of food, though the house is wet and the few meagre acres we still hold are neglected because so many of the men have gone into the army or are growing crops for the army. Getting in the hay will be a piece of work, so few hands available.

I don't know how we would get along, my daughter-in-law and myself, she is such a strong-minded little person.

For the moment they seem to have settled in with her father, an old fenian, Joseph McDermott, Esq.

The fight in Dublin is still all people talk about. E. says Sackville street is a wreck. No one hereabouts spoke for the rebels but day after day as we hear of executions the feeling changes. No one in Sligo had heard of James Connelly but when they had to put him in a chair to shoot him because he was unable to stand on account of his wounds!—he becomes a holy martyr. And Con Booth—the Baroness! Markievicz as she calls herself now, she was Madame M. when last I saw her—is to be shot. The Gore-Booth girls I always thought domineering & tiresome but I admit she has shown courage and spirit. If they shoot her it will cause a stir, the G-B family at Lissadell have been good landlords. E's father Jos. McDermott in a letter to the Champion writes of "the sickening thud that went through the heart of Ireland at the execution of each victim." This is correct. At first people called them fools, now the feeling is— they may be fools, only they acted for love of Ireland.

I hope you do find a war job, Charley, it's too bad for the country if they can't use an old campaigner in time of war. It's officers of your age who have the sand and will steady the young. Of course you are too old for active service, you must put that out of your mind my love, but there must be useful work for you, training troops as you said, or buying up horses for the cav., there was never a fellow with your eye for a horse Charley. Don't be shy but beard all friends & let them know you are looking for a place.

There is the news out of poor old Wychwood. Write and tell me you have seen my son.

Your old friend,
Con

THERE WAS A LIVE CURRENT OF FEELING BETWEEN GRAINNE AND MY grandfather. He looked at her as though he were famished and she were something to eat. And to her he was a great man, a sort of king. She took meticulous care of his clothes, brushing, sponging, pressing. She burnished his boots and ironed his snow-white collars. Once, I watched her tying a silk cravat around his neck, the purest moment of whatever was between them I ever witnessed. She had a sort of prideful glow, like an altar boy helping the priest into golden vestments.

The two aunts and my mother were furious at their father for carrying on with a skivvy. What complicated matters was that they couldn't help liking Grainne, an island girl from Achill. In her shyness and gaiety she reminded them of their mother. They were constantly trying to persuade Grainne to quit the red villa and find work somewhere else. I recall the maid sitting on a three-legged stool with my mother and her sisters berating her—Grainne was weeping. But she had nowhere else to go. Her parents were dead, and her brothers were in Scotland and Boston. Irish was her first language; her English wasn't strong. Skivvying at the red villa was her first paid job, and she was saving every penny for the fare to Boston even if the ships weren't sailing on account of the war. Grainne had only the vaguest notion where America was. I tried to explain, using my grandfather's *Cambridge Atlas*, but a map didn't mean much to her. She knew Boston and Sligo were each a considerable distance from her island of Achill, and that was all that mattered.

My grandfather paid her generously, even extravagantly, and Grainne was greedy for money and mad to save. She squirreled away every penny. And there wouldn't have been many positions open to an island girl who spoke better Irish than English and wasn't trained to the sort of manners that people who lived in towns like Sligo expected from servants.

Grainne used to play football with me on the cobblestones in the stable yard. My grandfather despised football as an English game, so we never played when he was at home. We didn't have a real football, only a pig's bladder my mother had gotten from a farmer. Grainne was always barefoot. She had a very powerful kick and was speedy and aggressive chasing the ball, laughing, hoisting her skirt to run faster. She fought for the ball relentlessly and never gave it up.

Aunt Frances did most of the cooking but Grainne lugged sticks, and turves of peat, and set all the fires, emptied the jakes, did the laundry, made the beds every morning, and cleaned our boots. A life of endless scouring, scrubbing, and washing up.

One evening she was showing me how to lay a fire in my grandfather's study when he came into the room and stood over us. He reached and touched the nape of her neck. For a second she froze, then went on with the work, giving the sticks and paper all her attention.

After he'd settled at his desk she demonstrated how to light a fire without wasting matches.

Grainne spoke a clear and beautiful form of Irish, the Achill Irish which has a good deal of Ulster in it, and my grandfather wanted his daughters to improve their Irish diction. But Grainne was very eager to polish up her English for America, and the young women always communicated in English when my grandfather was not at home.

Grainne had no overcoat, only a black shawl. She borrowed my aunt Kate's mackintosh because she hated the corner boys in town laughing at her as a "shawlie." Her only footwear was a pair of hand-sewn cowhide pampoots, more like slippers than shoes, which marked her as an island woman. So she preferred going barefoot. All of my aunts' shoes were too small for her.

"My feet is hard," she told my mother.

It was a rainy day, we were having tea in the kitchen, and Grainne was polishing the nickel plate on the stove. She liked to polish, liked to see the gleam; probably there had been little of it in her island cabin.

"I don't like those pampoots, they make me feel like an old woman. And I'm not, am I? I'm your Grainne, I'm your precious girl."

Like many native Irish speakers in those days, she spoke a form of English I would describe as "exalted."

"My feet is the real ground, and I shall only have the fine shoes in America."

She pronounced it *Amerikay*.

My grandfather offered Grainne to his daughters as a symbol of the comely and pure nation he wished Ireland to become, his mental Ireland. But he couldn't keep his hands off her. He wanted intimacy with the "real" Ireland. He may have felt he had a right to her.

He never tried to hide the affair—if you can call it that—from his daughters. Everything he did he believed in passionately, no matter who got hurt, but he must have known that if word got around that he was sleeping with a housemaid it would destroy his hope of a political career. Frances and Kate and my mother were too proud—or too ashamed—ever to let the secret outside the house.

My grandfather resented Grainne going shoeless into town. Shoeless on the western islands may have suggested a kind of purity; shoeless in town only meant you couldn't afford shoes. When he caught Grainne starting off to Sligo without shoes on her feet he would shout at her and she would tear up to her room in the attic, sobbing, then come down clomping in the hated pampoots, which she probably stashed in the hedge as soon as she was out of sight.

"Why does it matter so much that the girl wear shoes?" my mother said. She was the only one who dared question him.

"It's a disgrace to this house," he replied.

"Then buy her a decent pair of shoes!"

But he wouldn't. Maybe he figured she ought to spend some of her precious Boston savings to buy herself shoes.

There wasn't a lot of money to spare. My grandfather was a professional man, but his father had been a tenant, a cottier. The easiest way for a lawyer in that part of the world to make money was to represent the landed interest, then earn some sinecure from the Crown. He would not do that. He was a Republican, his clients were small farmers haggling over land, and Aunt Frances had to plead every week for the money to buy food to feed us all. But his precious girl Grainne had her wages every week. And there was always enough money to buy the special Scotch marmalade he liked, which was very expensive.

When the *Sligo Champion* referred to him as "the eminent barrister"

Grainne was the only one in the house to think of saving the newspaper, though she herself couldn't read. (It's slipcased in one of the boxes at McGill, but the newsprint has gone stiff and yellow and would probably crumble if anyone tried to look at it, but who ever would?)

Grainne assured me my grandfather was the most famous man in Ireland, which even at the time I knew was not the case. The leaders of the Easter Rising in Dublin were more famous. Outside the local law courts, who'd ever heard of Joseph McDermott, Esq., of Sligo?

In Sligo town one day, he saw Grainne smoking a cigarette and marched right up to her and tore it out of her mouth. Women smoking in public did not fit his ideal. No one could ever live up to his ideal of Irishness. But that evening when Grainne packed up her belongings and announced she was leaving the house, he burst into tears, pleaded with her to stay, and offered to marry her. My mother and aunts were aghast.

Grainne ignored the marriage offer, but stayed. She needed ten pounds for her fare to Boston, and something to land on.

My grandfather often told Grainne, and me, that America would be the ruin of her. He spoke scornfully of American emigrants. They were people to whom money mattered too much.

He gave me a penknife so that I could whittle sticks into spears and took me along on his rambles in the countryside. He knew the names of every field we crossed. Even the smallest field had an English name and an Irish one.

He would stop to speak to turf cutters and hay makers and men and women lifting the potatoes. People jabbed their thumbs to the west and mentioned Boston as casually as though it were the next town over, which for thousands of them it was.

I recall walking across a bog with my grandfather one afternoon. It is really the light I remember. We're crossing a shoulder bog, my grandfather Joseph McDermott and me. By then Eilín and I have been at the red villa two or three months, long enough for me to become accustomed to his ways. He frightens some people, but not me. With him, I am who I am. We're pacing out ground, measuring it by walking it. He wants to win a lawsuit on behalf of a client claiming ownership of the bog. I have only just absorbed the idea of landownership. Turf, heather, rocks, stunted trees—perhaps even the flicker of light and shadow across the land on such a breezy day—it all *belongs* to someone, exactly as my football belongs to me.

But my parents and I, we don't own land. Not an inch of it. The house Sanssouci was never ours. My mother had recently explained this fact. And we are never going back there, even when my father gets out of the Ally Pally, where they won't even allow him to build a hut for privacy. He doesn't own a piece of the Ally Pally, but the Ally Pally seems to own him. He was not born on any ground but aboard a sailing ship one thousand miles off the Pacific coast of Mexico. My mother was born in the red villa but seems unhappy there. She has been out to see my grandmother Con at Wychwood. The house is not in such bad shape, I've overheard her telling Aunt Kate.

"Some of it is tumbledown. Bits are rather grand. She needs help to make the hay."

As my grandfather and I cross the bog, light is coming in waves off the Atlantic, the sky is gray but luminous, one of those gray midsummer days in the northwest of Ireland when the west wind is warm and active and seems to carry the light. He wears a gold watch on a gold chain hooked to a button of his waistcoat. It must be June or July, because we meet a pair of turf cutters working a bank, not seeing them until we're almost upon them. My grandfather stops to talk to the men, and they seem happy to pause, putting down spades and lighting cigarettes, and that's all right, for my grandfather has nothing against the habit in men.

✳ 1938

When our train pulled into Frankfurt Hauptbahnhof, the mädel maidens were bickering over the tents and camping gear they would have to carry. Their leader looked fed up.

I walked Karin out to a rank of cabs. We hadn't cash to pay her cab fare out to Walden, her father's estate, so she offered a driver her earrings instead, which he accepted.

When Karin reached Walden that night, she found her father stretched out asleep on a sofa in his library. The other rooms were quite bare, and the only servant left on the place was Herta, widow of the baron's chauffeur, asleep on a cot in the kitchen. Karin made herself a nest of blankets in her old bedroom. Her four-poster bed had been stolen, along with most of the furniture in the house, her father's horses, and her mother's art collection.

I, meanwhile, walked the silent city of Frankfurt to my rooms near the Römer. After two years, my landlady had at last awarded me my own set of keys. I let myself into the house and tumbled into bed.

After work the next day I took a tram out to the resort town of Bad Homburg, where my parents were living in a once-grand hotel, the same establishment where the baron had been staying in 1895 when he was introduced to Lady Maire, who was touring the Continent with her parents.

Buck and Eilín had their room at a monthly rate, but they'd quickly learned how costly it was to live in a hotel. When the head housekeeper quit, the manager had offered my mother the position, and she took it. My father started working night-clerk shifts soon after.

They were in favor of my getting out of Germany, at least in theory. In practice, it would be a blow. I'd never shown them Günter Krebs's letter urging that I join him and his SS pals in the struggle for a new world. My father had a history with Günter Krebs, and I figured his letter would only frighten and dismay them.

Back in March, when it had looked like war over Czechoslovakia, my parents had talked about quitting Germany for Eire. But even if they could obtain exit visas—required, because Buck had only a German passport—Eire was desperately poor. And it was unclear what the free state would do with German nationals if it came to war. Probably intern them.

Buck believed he wouldn't survive another internment, and my mother and I agreed he probably wouldn't. So they'd made up their minds to stay in Germany come what may. My father assumed he was too old to be summoned back to the army.

The hotel elevator was a creaky monster. Their room was on the top floor. My mother was cleaning jewelry, and Buck lay on the bed looking at a copy of the London *Times*. The *Times* was pro-German, and Buck didn't like it, but read it when he found a copy, for lack of anything better. His favorite German newspapers, the *Vossische* and the *Frankfurter Zeitung*, had had their brains eaten out from the inside by Nazi bugs.

Their room was very small and, I would say, dingy, with a stale odor of dust and paint.

I informed them of my job offer from Vancouver. I hadn't formally resigned from IG Farben, but I had an appointment the following day to see my chief, Dr. Best.

"As it happens, Karin Weinbrenner will be crossing over as well," I said, trying for a casual tone. "We're sailing on the same ship, in fact."

Although I'd kept things hidden from them, for years I'd been trying to persuade myself my parents knew—they must know!—that I wasn't actually hiking in the Taunus on all those weekends away; that I was seeing Karin in Berlin.

I wanted to believe that people who knew us best had no difficulty imagining us together.

At the same time, in another corner of my brain, I knew my parents would be set against it. My mother would have been. She'd have predicted someone was going to get hurt.

"Karin Weinbrenner?" Buck sounded shocked. "Sailing for New York? But I saw her father only yesterday. He said nothing about it!"

"Good for her!" Eilín said. "Time she fled this horrid country. Her mother wanted her to leave years ago. I don't know how any of them stand it. If only the baron would see sense and go."

"You must look out for her, then," Buck said.

My mother sat straight-backed, hands folded in her lap.

"For her father's sake," my father continued, "her mother's memory, you watch out for that girl. We owe so much to the family."

He shook his head. He still seemed stunned.

"Resigning from the IG—I only hope you know what you're doing, Billy."

"I can't be caught in Germany, Dad, if there's a war."

"Of course he can't," Eilín said sharply.

"There won't be," my father insisted. "The generals won't allow it. If that fellow tries to start a war, they'll make short work of him."

Hitler was always *that fellow*. Buck would never say his name.

"Oh, Buck, of course he must go." My mother looked at me. "And when do you sail?"

"Two weeks tomorrow, from Rotterdam."

I had decided that I'd let them know about her pregnancy once we were safely across the water. Once we were married. I'd send a wire.

"Have you looked into exchange rates?" Buck asked. "Buying dollars, dreadfully expensive. Will they let you withdraw from your pension? How much can you take out of the country? What does Weinbrenner say, have you spoken to the baron? He'd have some good advice."

"Not yet."

"Do. Get his opinion on things, the man's a financial genius."

Sitting on the edge of their hotel bed, my parents looked old and tired. Helpless. I'd never seen them quite that way before.

My father suddenly reached out and clasped my hand with both of his.

Coming in late at night from escapades across the river, I always used to find Buck waiting up for me, in pajamas, slippers, and dressing gown. My father had difficulty sleeping unless he knew I was safely home. Without saying a word he used to wrap his arms around me and hold me close for a few moments. Then we could both go upstairs to our beds and sleep.

In that dispiriting hotel room, my father held my hand between his hands. Then Eilín reached out as well, and we were joined, and none of us could say a word.

My going away meant the end of us as a family, and we knew it.

❄ MICK

＊

June 20 1918

Today we were 4 women and 2 boys haymaking in the field known as <u>drom breek,</u> making the cockeens from hay cut last week. Open air and light. We had sandwiches and cold tea by the river and dozed in the high timothy while the boys hunted for frogs. Billy's 3rd summer haymaking and he can lift as much as anyone. His classmate Mick McClintock grandson of old Willy M'C. and has been haymaking since he could walk. The other haymakers were my daughter in law Eileen and her two sisters. Those 3 young women are a blessing to the house and I don't know if I could continue at Wychwood without them. I have dug myself into this country where I was born but haven't funds to stop the house falling down. Death's shadow often in my thinking. However—not dead yet. I can throw a cockeen as well as nearly anyone. I could dance all night if anyone would ask me to.

We build up the stacks seven–eight feet tall, weight the sugans with stones and throw them across, to hold the stack against the wind. Eileen heads them by raking loose hay off the top and we pack it on the sides.

June 23 1918

Sunday no haymaking. Weather stays fine, the hay was all turned yesterday in the Rath field, we can start there tomorrow making the cocks. Pat Lillis pulls the stacks to the haggard in his sled and declares it is the sweetest crop he has pulled off these meadows in years.

This afternoon my grandson's grandfather, the McDermott Himself, came to tea, and says it is now clear that the British armies are in full retreat in Flanders, the Germans will be in Paris any day, the French must sue for peace, the Germans will give them honorable terms, it is only bloodthirsty England that wants the war to go on. What about America? I said. Misguided! said he—America should never have come into the war at all, and then to have come in on the wrong side, he says it's the Jew bankers who have loaned out America's fortune to the British empire. And the King of England is ⅛ a Jew himself. Once England is finally smashed by Germany then Ireland will be free. So speaks Jos. McDermott, Esq.

June 24 1918

I hope and pray that Buck will settle his family in Ireland once the war is over and he is freed.

June 25 St John's Day

At Calry national school my grandson is surrounded by sacred hearts, plaster statues of dolled-up virgins, RC dogma. At home we don't say an apostate word not wishing to make his social position more difficult than it is. The McDermott sisters are unbelievers which is the one thing they share with their father though like him they must keep quiet about it. In this country no one is more hated than a non-believing Catholic. The papes will respect the wildest most bigoted Methodist preacher over one of their own who has dared wander from the flock. My grandson made his first Confession to the old bigot Father Griffin, took his First Communion from the hands of the same.

Billy and Eileen and the 2 girls attend Mass every week at St Patrick's, and on First Fridays and the other holy days of obligation they are expected to show up to Mass at the Cathedral. I'm at liberty to do as I like, no one cares if a protestant goes to church. Eileen is a free thinker but she keeps it down for Billy's sake.

Billy has been learning from Mick M'clintock the old Irish names for the Wychwood fields. Mick—shoeless urchin, cigarette dangling in his mouth—but has produced a beautiful map of the estate showing the path which the people here call the Mass walk and names of almost every corner, hill and field and what M says are the ruins of an old church, teampull a chlocaire.

July 1 1918

The last of the Triangle field is cut, turned, ready to be cocked.

My grandson and Mick M'clintock lie on in the sun studying their map of a forgotten path from Wychwood to a ruined church and I recall Jack and myself in a chandlery on the Diekstraße at Hamburg poring over charts—the South Atlantic, Straits of Magellan, Drake's Passage. The Mass path no longer visible (or I don't see it) but Mick swears it is there and Billy says the two of them have walked it, only there are occasionally buildings & cabins in the way, and a corner of our haggard. On the map Mick M has drawn the path crosses an orchard that I was always told was established by my great-great-great grandfather. Who owns this country?—this is our subject. The feet of mass pilgrims five hundred or a thousand years ago make what is considered locally to be a powerful claim.

July 16th 1918

We address our letters to Buck CAPTAIN HEINRICH LANGE Alexandra Palace Camp, London. Eileen says Buck don't like to be addressed as Captain unless he is aboard a vessel and has command but I think it must be good for him to be reminded of that life and perhaps eases the dreariness of his surroundings.

August 4th 1918

Jos. McDermott, Esq. comes to tea & admits the Germans are retreating and the war must end in a few days or weeks no side victorious all exhausted from the blood that has been spilt. There must be an election and sinn fein will fight every seat and it will be the birth of a new Ireland. He says the English must give in and let us have a government of our own, they won't have the stomach for the fight they must face if they don't. While he speaks his daughters watch him intently, faces hard and pale.

I heard from Mrs McCaffrey the butcher's wife the old man is sick in love with his housemaid another barefoot island girl just like his late wife, they say it's a miracle she's not produced a child.

Poring over charts, seeing ice castles, dreaming the Pacific, Jack and I once believed we were the artists of our fates. But we were only the medium, only the paint.

Aug 4th 1918

Four years since the decl. of War and Buck taken away.

AFTER WE SETTLED AT WYCHWOOD MY AUNTS KATE AND FRANCES USED to come out for the summers. They'd stay for weeks, helping with the hay. My grandmother Con taught me to ride, calling out instructions while I trotted round and round on my rugged little pony, Punch. At first I rode without a saddle; it was the best way to learn, she said. "Straight back, Billy!" Then she showed me how to harness and saddle Punch and adjust the stirrups myself.

"Keep light in the saddle! Rise! Rise! Toes up!"

I learned to feed and handle the pony in such a way that he never was irritated or shy. "Horses love the calm," my grandmother said. "Gentle, always. Hands, voice. They frighten easily."

Pat, one of her old tenants, set up a couple of jumps. Punch balked, and I nearly went over his head.

"It's a piece of fear you're jumping over," Con said. "Now gather him up, let him know there's no stopping, and see what it feels like."

It was like floating. Next day the jumps were set a little higher, and I wasn't scared anymore. There was no hunting, on account of the war, but my grandmother and I sometimes went out for the day, rode along the roads, and ate our lunch sitting in grassy verges with our backs against rough stone walls warmed by the sun.

"Buck never has seen this country," she said. "Your father has Ireland in his blood, but he's never seen it. He'll come out after the war's over. He's a lovely seat on a horse, your father, you'll be terribly proud."

At the National School, the teacher, Father Coughlin, wrote on the blackboard *an buachaill coigríche, the foreign boy*, and that was me. I had one friend at the school, Mick McClintock. He was a couple of years older. Frances said he was a *gurrier* and told my mother I deserved a friend who at least wore shoes, but my grandmother liked Mick. He smoked cigarettes whenever he could get them and took me on fishing expeditions—poaching, actually—which no one, not even my grandmother, knew about. He was impatient with people who couldn't put things together as fast as he could, or read situations as well.

One morning, clip-clopping ponies through Sligo town, heading for Rosses Point, we were stopped by a squad of policemen. Their armored car was blocking the road. A policeman had been shot dead at Ballina the day before, and they were in a wild mood.

In his saddlebags Mick had several bottles of his grandfather's poteen he was to deliver to customers on the Point. One of the policemen stepped forward and called out, "Where is your pa at this morning, we don't want to waste time looking for him."

Mick's father was supposed to be a big man in the Volunteers, though years later, in New York, Mick said he was merely a drunkard who sang rebel songs, and it was his grandfather, the poteen man, who'd taken the IRB oath and was a commander in the Volunteers.

The peeler was glaring at us. His holster was flapped open, and he held a blue revolver in his big white fist. I could smell liquor on him. The police had been joking with a pair of local girls as we came along. The policemen were laughing, but not the girls; they looked frightened.

The peeler raised his revolver and held it to the ear of Mick's pony. "Tell us where your old one's dug into or down goes the pony."

I couldn't bear to see him shoot the pony. I shut my eyes.

"I can't, because I don't know," I heard Mick say in a reasonable voice. "And when you shoot the pony he'll fall down and smash the bottles."

"What bottles are those?"

"Poteen, I suppose."

Silence. I could almost hear the policeman thinking.

"Give it over," he said, gruffly.

Mick reached into a saddlebag, extracted a bottle, and handed it over. The peeler uncorked it, sniffed, and took a taste.

"Give us the rest."

Mick obliged. The policeman holstered his revolver and soon had his arms full of whiskey bottles.

"There'll be a fine?" asked Mick.

"Aw, away with you."

I don't know if Mick got in trouble with his grandfather for handing over the poteen, but it was better than losing a pony or giving information to policemen. Mick knew how to handle himself. I never saw him flustered. Poaching was a risky business. Salmon were always owned by someone else. Keepers shot to kill. And a keeper shooting a poacher was common enough that it was used to cover up killings done for other reasons—politics or disputes over ownership of land.

The best poachers were men who knew the salmon runs and could "listen to the river," men intimately acquainted with the country. Mick said keepers were offered reward money by police to shoot and kill poachers who were Volunteers. The law might let the keeper go scot-free, but everyone would know who he was, and sooner or later he'd pay for his deeds.

I remember slipping out of the house at night without being caught, following Mick through glistening darkness, soft rain, slick mud, the scent of tide. I was eight or nine. Poachers didn't bother with elaborate tackle, it was too expensive, and graceful casts were dangerous, the zing and quiver of line would only call attention. We worked the banks of the Ballisodare River below the falls with carved and notched spears and nets.

"Poaching's a life-and-death business," Mick said. "Life for us ones, death for fish, that's the word. And keepers are rogues."

It wasn't sport he was after but the beautiful red meat of the salmon, which could be sold for a good bit of money.

Working the estuary that first night we had no luck. "No good. It's a boat we need, a currach," Mick finally admitted. "There was one of my grandfather's wee boats hidden along the shore, but she's rotted now, nothing lasts forever. We must try the upper stretch. Are you for it, Billy?"

"I am."

And I was, though also scared the whole time we were out in the dark: of keepers, rogues, of getting shot, scared even of the salmon, which Mick said were long as my arm and muscled by age and wisdom, with ferocious hooked jaws and teeth.

And the next week we did work the brisk narrows of the Ballisodare, a tiny river, no more than five miles long, from Collooney to the sea.

Mick stood out in the stream, clutching his lister, the fish spear, with its point whittled sharp, and I squatted on the bank, holding the net at the ready. Never had I experienced anything like it. Excepting Mick, no one in the world knew where I was. I wondered what my father would say if he knew. Surely he'd approve; he wouldn't be on the side of keepers, the rogues. My mother, aunts, and grandmother believed I was in bed, cozy, asleep. They took me for a little boy, but I was bold enough to be Mick's companion. I hadn't scampered when I saw those drunk policemen and their armored car. And now I was risking my life for a salmon.

I admired Mick McClintock, his grace, his knowledge. I was grateful that he accepted me as his friend.

It was cold. We had to keep quiet and still. Any noise that we made might rile and spook the fish. Mick was listening to the river streaming by his legs. He must have been nearly paralyzed with cold, but he was prepared to suffer—the poacher expected to pay for his catch.

And when first light was grainy in the sky, our fish did appear. Mick thrust the salmon through and lifted it out of the river, a big silver-green creature, twisting and flopping, spraying us both. "Quick now! Net the fellow before he's off!"

I splashed in. Our fish was so active and strong he was difficult to snag in the net, but I managed it. And our fish was one of hundreds— the little river was alive with their energy.

We waded ashore. "There it is." Mick said, addressing the salmon. "You must die but for the right reasons." He quickly killed and cleaned the fish, and we rode off with it, and the next day he sold it to the vicar in the Presbyterian church opposite the Roman Catholic cathedral in Sligo town.

⊱┈◦┈⊰

My grandmother Con was born at Wychwood. I never knew her father, my great-grandfather Hugh Ormsby, Baronet, who was a great-grandson of the second Earl of Tireragh, which meant Karin and I were distant cousins.

Sir Hugh fell off his horse and broke his neck before I was born. Country people didn't remember him fondly in Sligo—not a good landlord. During the two years my mother and I lived at Wychwood we heard lore of landlords assassinated, houses burned, blood feuds going back a couple of centuries or more. Con relished stories of ancient hatreds and reprisals, the mountain songs, the rebel songs, even if they were directed against her people. They allowed her to feel connected to the country. Northwest Ireland is not the most exciting place in the world, but the people have developed a habit of fantastic embroidery and lies to make it seem so, at least to themselves, and they fed my grandmother as much bloody folklore as she wanted.

My grandmother Con considered herself an aristocrat. She never had money to spare, but that was how she saw herself. An aristocrat was a person who didn't need care about ordinary things, like new clothes or paying bills or checking her bank balance. An aristocrat couldn't be expected to make her own bed, do her own laundry, or clean her own bathroom. She might set her own peat fire very neatly and light it with a single match, but she couldn't be expected to carry her own turves, nor should she be expected to wash up after dinner. An aristocrat cared for horses and books and dinner conversation with interesting people. An aristocrat paid attention to the sky and the weather and never listened to the wireless. An aristocrat might drive a car, but badly. Dogs and horses loved aristocrats. Aristocrats loved their children, who often misunderstood them.

On a fine soft day late in October, my mother, my aunt Kate, and I watched my grandmother gallop a point-to-point race in county Leitrim. Con rode a big stallion, Dan of the Mountains, which she'd been given to ride because no one else could manage him, and even the British Army horse purchasers didn't want him.

Con had warned my mother to put every penny she could on Dan of the Mountains to win. Eilín was no gambler, nor was my father. They both faced enough uncertainty in their lives and didn't wish to take more chances than absolutely required. But Eilín also believed my grandmother Con possessed a certain magic, a certain radiance. Call it luck. And she was a gallant rider of big, rough horses.

The Leitrim point-to-point was a small event, but in those days in that part of Ireland, people took seriously anything to do with horses. Bookmakers out from Sligo and Enniskillen stood on their boxes in a meadow, taking wagers. Eilín put eleven pounds and eleven shillings, our entire fortune, on Dan of the Mountains to win, and when the stallion galloped home first, we had the money we would need when the war ended a few days later and we had to rush back to London.

The guns stopped firing at eleven o'clock in the morning on November 11, 1918. Three days later Eilín and I were aboard the mail train for Dublin. If ever I said goodbye to my grandfather McDermott, I don't remember it. He died in Londonderry a year later, knocked down by a lorry outside the RIC barracks in Leckey Road. They gave him a grand Republican funeral at Sligo cathedral. Grainne had left for Boston by then.

✳ 1938

WHEN I INFORMED DR. ANTON BEST, MY CHIEF, THAT I INTENDED TO resign from IG Farben and emigrate to Canada, he sat back in his chair and gazed at me.

Signatory executives like Best—at IG Farben you never knew what they were thinking, unless they chose to tell you, and then you were never sure it was the whole truth.

Anton Best, as far as I knew, wasn't a party member. When he'd learned of my connection to the Baron von Weinbrenner, whose Colora GmbH was one of the founding companies of the IG Farbenindustrie cartel, he'd spoken respectfully.

"The old fellow, he knew his stuff. Probably has fifty patents to his name. Some of the colors he came up with—they'll never be topped. It's disgraceful, actually, the way he's been treated."

I'd been an IG Farben man for eight years. They'd treated me decently, but our department, export sales, had become a backwater after management began aligning its business strategy with the Nazi instinct for autarky. The directors were investing millions in programs for developing synthetic rubber—buna—and synthetic fuel and seemed no longer much interested in selling pharmaceuticals and dyestuffs to the rest of the world.

What they were doing, of course, was preparing for war.

I'd always had an excellent salary. Promotions came on schedule. The truth was, if you survived your first couple of years at IG Farben, they believed they owned you for life, and sometimes it was tempting to believe they did, but after that letter from Günter Krebs I knew I needed to take my life back before it was tossed into the future's bubbling black pot.

"If a war comes, holding a British passport, I should be in a very tough spot," I said.

Dr. Best hadn't invited me to sit down. IG executives at the signatory level never invited junior men to sit down.

"You needn't explain," he said.

"For a man in my position, it's an awkward situation."

"I understand perfectly. You needn't say more. Shall I date your termination effective the end of this week? Is that suitable?"

"Perfectly."

"You'll want to see the bookkeepers as regards your *Pensionskasse* and sort through all that."

He was a brilliant chemist, Dr. Best. Before joining IG Farben he'd been a professor at Marburg University. He held a number of patents himself.

In 1944 he was assigned to the IG plant at Auschwitz-Monowitz— I read this in a book after looking up his name in the index. I've often thumbed through indexes looking for names. For six months in 1944, Dr. A. Best oversaw methanol production at the Monowitz plant, which operated with slave labor. Then he became ill—the illness unspecified— and was sent back to Frankfurt.

"I'm actually surprised you have delayed until now," he said.

"Well, my parents are here. Rather difficult to leave them."

"Your parents are English aren't they? They ought to leave this country whilst they can. It won't get any easier for them here. Well, Godspeed, and *viel Glück*."

After work I went immediately to the travel bureau on the Zeil to confirm our passage on the Dutch liner.

"Well, my friend, you are lucky to have reserved two tickets, I'll tell you," the agent remarked. "I might have sold those three times over."

"Is that so?"

He was a young fellow, blond hair slicked down, wearing a sharply cut gray suit with a tiny party membership badge—red ring around crooked cross—pinned to his lapel.

"There's nothing left at the price you're paying! Every sailing from Le Havre, Rotterdam, Antwerp, Belgian—for New York, Montreal, Halifax, New Orleans—*ausverkauft*." Sold out. "I have Jews pleading for those ships. Paying through the nose, they are."

I asked to look at a railway timetable and checked train connections Frankfurt to Rotterdam while he dealt with a family of Jews whose house in Giessen had burned down. They were going for Madagascar via Lisbon, I overheard.

Probably their home had been torched by a gang of miscreants. That sort of thing was happening to Jews in rural districts of Hesse.

That railway timetable *Reichsbahn Kursbuch—Westdeutschland* handled like a pocket Bible, thick and soft, dense with small print, and stoked with information, all of it in some sort of code.

I was half listening to the agent scolding the Giessen Jews. "Once again, I must repeat: they will ask to see *all* documents before you are permitted to board!"

They looked to me like country people. The father and older son could have been livestock dealers or sold farm equipment. Maybe they'd owned a shoe shop or a grocery store.

I focused on the timetable. Frankfurt Hauptbahnhof to Mainz to Köln, across the Dutch frontier, change at Utrecht for Rotterdam.

It was time to get out.

Rotterdam–New York–Texas–Hollywood–Vancouver.

We'd be free, at last. Or safe, at least.

That was the plan.

⚜ THE DEPORTEES

Holograph letter. Signed *M v. Weinbrenner,* addressed *Mrs. H. Lange, Villa Moselle, 9 Dukes Avenue, London N10,* postmarked *Frankfurt am Main 28.12.1918.* Lange Family Archive, 12 C-12-1918. Special Collections, McGill Library, McGill University, Montreal.

HAUS WALDEN
Frankfurt am Main
Xmas Day 1918

My dear Eileen,

We were relieved to hear from you and pray Captain Lange will soon be released. The baron says—you must come out to Germany as soon as able to travel, there is the guest cottage—'Newport'—with plenty of room for you. This house has been a Home for wounded Officers since 1915, but we will have it back in our hands before long, and then you will come out here. People are starving in Germany. This morning our Cook reported seeing Crows hung in the butcher's window and a queue waiting to buy it. The baron had a slight wound two years ago otherwise we are well. More than I can say in this note, my dear girl—only you must come to Germany my dear we shall have a home ready for you all.

Affectionately,
M. v. Weinbrenner

Holograph letter. *Eilín McDermott Lange[?] to Heinrich Lange[?]*, undated, no envelope, no postmark. Lange Family Archive. 12 C-01-1919 Special Collections, McGill Library, McGill University, Montreal.

My dearest

I can't see it. The W's are grand people the bolsheviks must go after them and then what will happen with us . . . you ask for more than I can give, be calm you say but you've been asleep 4 years I have nothing more of calmness . . . this cold river this Germany is an iron trap, they hate us here, I feel it, B. has a horrid cough

I hear guns

I know Lady M will do her best I <u>know</u> but what is possible? I am [in?] despair this wet morn I confess

Your
E

ABOARD BARGE 'ST ANTONIUS'
on R. Rhine
Approaching Sankt Goar,
42 hrs 19 min out from R'dam
8:31
January 7th 1919

My dear wife,

Don't despair. Don't. Lady M is loyal to offer refuge at Walden. As to how I shall put bread in our mouths, all will become clear. A skipper once more—a groom or stableboy— I don't care. What matters is we three together & safe. I believe the boy will be all right, he is a strong fellow, so you are not to worry as you are doing. Right now I see him taking cocoa from kind Vrouw van Plaas and he really seems in excellent spirits, I think you will tear yourself to pieces if you worry over each cough. All right?

I understand worry. He needs warmer clothes for Germany. Yes. We will manage this—

Well we are nearing the end of our tiresome journey. I raise my eyes and look at you across the deck how wonderful you seem. Brave and true. I hope to be worthy of you.

I wish to know you better than I know how.

Good day to you, my brave, my lovely wife,

Your,
BUCK

THEY ARE NOT CONVERSING, ONLY SHARING A PARK BENCH, BUT THEY ARE obviously a couple, though my mother wears no wedding band. A bitter north London day. My father breathes steam in thin white puffs. He doesn't look strong, but he is very well turned out, in his cashmere overcoat, silk scarf, and gray homburg.

Buck had lost so much weight that none of his prewar clothes fit. A couple of days before his release my mother had brought his best suit to an internee tailor at Ally Pally, who made the necessary alterations.

In his pocket there is a letter from the Home Secretary ordering him to leave the United Kingdom. We are being deported to Germany.

My father hopes we may be allowed to go to Australia instead. He has made an application at Australia House on the Strand.

My mother's gray-gloved hand rests on my father's knee, and his hand covers hers. With his other hand he grips the silver knob of his walking stick, her wedding present to him. Where had it spent the war?

Their bodies are close but not touching.

The scene handles like a photograph in my mind. Does its stillness suggest domestic tranquillity, poise, companionship?

Unease, wariness, fear?

I'm not in the photograph; I hover just outside the frame, watching them, trying to decide where I fit in. Is there room for me on the park bench between my parents?

Should I move in a bit closer? He will look up and smile at me in a friendly way, but each smile costs him something, and I want him to save his strength. He is thirty-four.

Sitting on a park bench in London's gathering dark, my parents must have been wondering—*What next?*

Their son—believing himself their sentry, scout, guardian—wants them intact, safe. The night is damp, cold. Eilín dreads bringing Buck to our lodgings, on Dukes Avenue once more, where the corridors still stink of old soup and dirty carpets, and the lodgers might raise a fuss. Before Ally Pally he didn't have a German accent, but now he does. He's ever so much more German than he was in 1914.

Her feelings must be as tangled as those reels of barbed wire on Ally Pally hill. She doesn't know what to expect from her husband or what she has to give him.

They finally get up from the bench, it's just too cold to stay any longer, and she calls for the boy, who drifts nearer, and the three of them start walking out through the park's damp darkness. At the bus stop they wait in silence. When the bus arrives they climb aboard, she pays the conductor, and they find seats. She takes a packet of biscuits from her handbag and offers them to her husband and son. They each accept a biscuit, and then it seems they are all a bit happy; they have pulled something, a little pleasure, from the blackness and fog as the bus, lit up inside, trundles its route through north London.

⊢◄▹◦◂◃⊣

My parents needed to live again as husband and wife: one bedroom, one bed. At our lodgings on Dukes Avenue, I was dispatched to an attic room that had belonged to a scullery maid who went home to Ireland after her brother was killed in France on the last day of the war. Everything—iron bed, walls, floor, ceiling—was painted white. A rosary composed of white glass beads sat in a glinting huddle on the bureau. The atmosphere retained the musty scent of another person. I named the ghost Lily and brought offerings pilfered from the kitchen or from the other lodgers' rooms, which I left on the bureau: a piece of chocolate, an orange, an apple I cut into sections with a penknife I stole.

Of course I ended up eating the stuff myself. I relished the solitude at the top of the house. The only other person I ever saw up there was the new Irish kitchen maid who had the other attic bedroom and paid no attention to me. I liked to imagine my room was a forgotten place no one knew of, no one remembered, and no one would discover. My whole existence was secret—that was why I had to pilfer food from downstairs. In fact I barely existed—no one else could see me at all. I was the only one who knew there was a *me*. Mice scratched the walls and scampered across my blankets at night—I didn't care. My whole body resonated with a tight sense of well-being. Concealment was security.

Sliding out drawers of the bureau and using them for a ladder I could reach my one narrow window. The frame was sticky, but with the penknife I could pry it open, then crawl out onto the steep pitch of blue-black slates.

North London's night air was a stew of coal smoke and fog. Perched on the roof of the Villa Moselle, No. 9 Dukes Avenue, Muswell Hill, looking out across the glower of the city, I lit a cigarette from the flat tin of Sweet Aftons Mick had given me just before we left Sligo. I was nine years old, but in Ireland boys even younger smoked cigarettes whenever they could get them, or pipes made of clay.

I was glad my father was occupying what had been my half of my mother's bed; I did not begrudge him the warmth. I was relieved to have two parents again. Perhaps I would have resented him more had there not been those episodes when I'd sensed her pulling away from me, preparing to plunge. When, by emotional telepathy, I had just managed to pull her back.

I knew she needed my father. We both did.

>-+-◆>-○-◆+-◄

Australia turned us down, so it would have to be Germany, though my mother spoke only a bit of German and I none at all.

There were rich Lange cousins in Hamburg, but they had never forgiven Captain Jack for the disastrous gamble on the California grain trade, which had bankrupted the family firm. Buck insisted it was out of the question to expect help from them. He thought we must settle in a seaport—Bremerhafen, Kiel, even Hamburg—and he would try to find a position in the merchant marine.

He must have known he'd be competing with thousands of unemployed officers from the kaiser's beloved Imperial German Navy who had scuttled their ships at Scapa Flow rather than hand them over to the Royal Navy.

Buck's German accent came out when he was tired, which he often seemed to be, and it irritated my mother. So did certain sly habits he'd picked up at Ally Pally, such as carrying away food from the dinner table—crusts of bread, even scraps of meat—hidden in his pockets. And he never got out of bed before ten o'clock and took protracted afternoon naps. I think sleep had been his fortress in Ally Pally; he had trained himself to hide there from the killing boredom. But now my mother and I were his world, and he seemed to be hiding from us.

One morning he appeared at the breakfast table meticulously dressed but with silver stubble on his cheeks. At Ally Pally the prisoners didn't shave every day; they couldn't afford to wear out their precious razor blades.

My mother shot him a look of such cold fury. She hated seeing any traces of prisonerhood on him.

Waiting for his temporary passport to arrive, Buck spent afternoons sitting on benches in the London parks. Coal smoke and light rain. I can see him on a green bench on Hampstead Heath, wrapped in his overcoat, clutching his stick, and staring at . . . at what? Ducks in the pond? Green of wet grass blades? The freedom of hungry brown birds? He is too well dressed to be mistaken for a tramp or a shipwrecked sailor.

Eilín had gone back to the pawnshop where she'd left her wedding band. The old Jewish pawnbroker had scrupulously held on to it, so she was able to redeem the ring, and I watched her push it onto her finger. We rode the bus back to Muswell Hill to find an elegant linen envelope engraved with the Walden crest—shamrock and cornflowers entwined—in the letter basket.

It had a Deutsches Reich stamp.

This was the invitation from Karin's mother, Lady Maire, Baroness Weinbrenner.

My mother was thrilled and relieved. Later, on our journey up the Rhine, there would be moments when exhaustion and trepidation nearly overcame her—but she never had forgotten the kindness Lady Maire showed her as a young girl out of Ireland. If there was anywhere in Germany we could find a home, Eilín believed it must be at Walden.

And after he read Lady Maire's letter, my father persuaded himself that the baron must be planning to order a brand-new racing yacht, a replacement for *Hermione II*, probably to be built in America. She would need a skipper, and my father was the man for the job.

The Quakers would pay for our third-class tickets on the train to Hull and the steamer to Rotterdam. From there we would have to make our own way to Germany.

During those last, disorienting days in London, while Eilín was settling bills and packing everything we owned into a single trunk, my father sustained us with a vision of himself at the helm of a sharp new Yankee-built schooner dashing across Narragansett Bay, the crest of a bow wave gleaming like a bone between her teeth.

We should have been Americans.

>·+·•>·•·0·•<·+·<

A very old Quaker lady brought us to King's Cross in a horse cab. I stared out at traffic and whispered faux German under my breath. Ambulances were lined up outside the station, because weeks after the war ended they were still bringing home the worst cases from the military hospitals in France.

Whenever the Quaker spoke to Buck in German, he replied in English. He knew exactly how vulnerable we were.

"Auf Wiedersehen!" she cried as we were boarding the train, and I saw my mother flinch. The chilly, smoky concourse was crowded with Union Jacks and stretcher cases, and Germans were more hated than ever, I could feel it. I very nearly hated them myself.

>·+·•>·•·0·•<·+·<

Deported. What could that mean?

By then, I was accustomed to journeys. I felt safer traveling with both parents than with my mother alone. And my parents were safe as well, because we were all three together. All worry and strain, in fact, could rest with me. I would absorb all the things that threatened us, I would sop up the danger.

From King's Cross we traveled by train to Hull. January 1919. The Quaker lady had given Eilín a basket with potted-meat sandwiches, apples, hard-boiled eggs, chocolate, and a thermos flask of tea.

Buck sat in a corner of the railway carriage, legs crossed, reading his carefully folded *Times*.

There was a revolution on in Germany. Left-wing Spartacists were fighting it out with right-wing militia, the Freikorps. Street battles in Berlin, Munich, Bremen. Massacres.

"The country's in chaos," Buck said.

Chaos. A new word for me. Now I see that my notion of what was normal and ordinary included a strong measure of chaos, but no one had applied the word.

We all three longed to reconnect ourselves as a family.

⤙⬦⬥⬦⤙

From Hull we caught a little steamer, *Jervaulx Abbey*, across to Rotterdam, an overnight journey. Steerage passengers slept in berths stacked belowdecks, men separated from the women. Men's berths were stacked three high. I lay a few inches above my father. Poor ventilation and groaning men, did it remind him of the Ally Pally? But Buck was a sailor. Maybe it reassured him to be at sea. I wasn't a sailor and was horribly seasick. Everyone in steerage was, except my father. A stew of vomit slopped and slid on the steel deck. A couple of times Buck wrapped me up in both our overcoats and carried me up the companionway ladder and out onto the main deck.

Our little steamer was bouncing and riding across North Sea swells, and it was too cold to stay out there for more than a fresh minute; the cold was like a toxin. But while we could stand it, it was better outside than down below. There was liveliness and ferocity in the air. The grease of sea salt on deck, lit windows on the bridge—I felt part of something. But soon enough the cold became unbearable, and we slipped below again, never mind how foul it was down there.

He lifted me into my berth, but I couldn't sleep. Then I was sick, and sick again, and again, until there was nothing left, only black dribble that might have been blood and looked like Irish porter. After a while Buck would wrap me up again and carry me up the companionway ladder again. He was strong enough, my father, though he had been living on rations of horsemeat, cabbage, and tea for four years and toward the end of his imprisonment had stopped eating anything except potatoes the internees raised in their plots and the cups of fresh milk they were given once or twice a week.

I clung like a monkey to my father's back while he climbed up the companionway. Out on the main deck I could stand only if he stood behind me, hands on my shoulders, steadying me. I'd have blown away without my father.

In the murky dawn we steamed past concrete moles that smoothed the channel entrance to the harbor of Rotterdam, and the sea calmed, and I felt much better. *Jervaulx Abbey* pushed across the inner harbor and up to a quay. Lines were thrown, the whistle gave a hoot, and deckhands trundled out the gangway. I watched three Dutch customs men down on the quay, in white caps and gray uniforms, calmly puffing meerschaum pipes. After our febrile night at sea, I felt sharp and composed and wickedly hungry. Ready to absorb everything new while drawing as little attention to myself as possible.

The customs men told Buck all trains into Germany were stopped by a general strike. But we couldn't afford to stay on in Rotterdam, so he left us in a café near the Holland-America ticket bureau and went off to find a barge heading up the Waal for the Rhine with space for three passengers willing to travel rough.

Wintry air on the quays stank of coal smoke and bilge. In a dockworkers' canteen an enameled stove pumped out welcome heat, and my mother and I shared a bowl of coffee. The stevedores and waitresses were rosy and cheerful. We splurged, ate herrings and toasted rolls, and the waitress produced a blood orange for me, free of charge. My mother peeled it, and we saved a few sections for Buck, who was out prowling the quays and talking to the bargemen.

He came into the café and told us he'd found room for us on a barge headed upriver. He quickly swallowed his coffee, and a boy with a handcart trundled our trunk to the quay where our barge, *St. Antonius*, was taking on a cargo of barrels, crates, and sixty Dutch bicycles being shipped to Koblenz. There were burlap sacks of coffee beans in the hold and wheels of Gouda cheese wrapped in wax and gauze.

Kapitein van Plaas, the *St. Antonius*'s master, was a Dutchman with a blond beard. He and Vrouw van Plaas lived aboard with their black cat, Stocksi. He told us he was the son and grandson of barge captains and had been born on a barge on the Waal between Tiel and Nijmegen. We were given a snug little deck cabin. Eilín and Buck shared the narrow berth while I slept in a nest of empty burlap sacks, overcoats, and blankets on the floor.

It took most of the morning to finish loading, and then we backed off the quay. As *St. Antonius* chugged across the harbor and started up the complex tributaries of the Rhine, Vrouw van Plaas fed us mushroom soup and mashed potatoes with bacon and red cabbage.

The landscape of the Rhine delta is flat and wide, and the sky is larger than London's. The light is gray but soft, and fields are sodden and fiercely green, and the daylight felt more generous than wartime England's.

But I didn't spend a lot of time gazing at the Rembrandt sky. I ate delicious food, played with the barge's cat, and barely noticed the Dutch fields slipping past. At Rossum, Kapitein van Plaas had to tie up for mechanical repairs, which my father, who knew his way around a marine engine, assisted with. Afterward, the two of them sat in the wheelhouse, sipping Geneva gin from delftware cups.

When I was brought in to say good night, Buck put down his cup, held his arms open, then wrapped them around me and held me tightly so that I felt the rough graze of his cheeks, smelled fresh alcohol and the rich smoke of the *kapitein*'s pipe. I felt much safer on the *St. Antonius* than in London. I fell asleep quickly, lulled by the chug of the engine and the slap of current on the hull.

Heading up the Waal past Nijmegen we had driving sleet and mugs of hot cocoa, then skies cleared. We passed into Germany, and a band of soldiers boarded us at Duisburg. Stranded by the railway strike, they had commandeered a scow to bring them out on the river, and as soon as they came alongside *St. Antonius* they started scrambling aboard. Van Plaas didn't try to stop them. Probably he thought it would be dangerous to try. They were friendly enough, and his wife offered them bread and soup. They had given up their rifles somewhere but kept their coal-scuttle helmets, which dangled from their packs. The field-gray uniforms were faded and frayed. The soldiers sat on the foredeck amid the crates, bicycles, and casks, drinking apple brandy and playing cards. Buck spoke to them.

The soldiers told my father we were safer on the river than ashore. As *St. Antonius* was sliding past Köln, we heard peculiar stuttering noises. The soldiers said it was machine guns. Approaching the Hohenzollern Bridge, a sniper started firing at us. At first I thought the bullets snapping overhead were insects but there are no insects on the Rhine in winter. Buck quickly herded my mother and me down into the hold. The soldiers took cover behind barrels and crates and the stack of bicycles in the bow. A few moments later a soldier was shot in the brains—we heard the others yelling. Buck went up to see if he could help. As soon as we had passed Köln, the shooting ceased, and Eilín and I came topside. By then the other soldiers had laid out the dead man on deck, pushing aside barrels to make space. It wasn't that my parents were keen for me to see a dead soldier, but they couldn't prevent it; the barge was too small. The others had straightened his legs and placed his steel helmet on his head, covering the mortal wound. His field-gray overcoat was neatly buttoned, and his eyes were closed. His hands were demurely crossed. I saw that soldiers were accustomed to dealing quickly with their dead. A bloodstain had already seeped into the deck planks that Vrouw van Plaas was scrubbing with a holystone. At Koblenz the soldiers strapped their dead comrade onto a plank and carried him ashore, and more soldiers came aboard. They were unshaven and dirty and slept on the foredeck huddled in their overcoats or in the hold among sacks of Javanese coffee and wheels of cheese.

I noticed the whole way up the river that my parents mostly kept apart from each other. The three of us slept in our tiny cabin, but during the day my father enjoyed conversation with the *kapitein* in the wheelhouse while Eilín studied a little handbook of German grammar that Lady Maire had presented her years before. Once I watched Buck pass her a folded sheet of paper, and the next morning I saw her slip a piece of paper underneath his mug of coffee in the deckhouse. They were passing notes back and forth like schoolchildren! It seems an odd form of communication for husband and wife, but it was what they were used to. Letters had been their principal medium for four years.

When the river narrowed after Koblenz, its quickness reminded me of the Ballisodare, and I thought of poaching nights with Mick McClintock and missed him badly.

We encountered other barges. If there were children they usually waved at me. I'd had minimal contact with other children since Ireland and wasn't sure that I wanted any.

The current was quicker, sleeker, above Koblenz. Mick McClintock might have rigged some tackle and trolled this stretch of the Rhine. To Mick any quick river, even our little Garavogue on its tumble from Lake Innisfree to the sea, was a rich ribbon, a streak of promise, where sea trout or salmon might be hooked, speared, netted, or caught with bare hands. Poaching was dangerous, but so were most things worth doing, according to Mick.

I came on deck one morning, and there was a layer of white mist on the Rhine, very different than the dirty coal smoke at Düsseldorf and Köln. We were in a steep gorge, castle after castle looming over the river. Vrouw van Plaas wore a hooded red cloak and handed around cups of coffee, and Kapitein van Plaas offered my father the helm.

There was Buck, a skipper once again, even in his overcoat and pale-gray homburg, smiling and holding the barge against the current, much fiercer here than in the sluggish lower Rhine.

When we put in at Sankt Goar to discharge some cargo, a French officer trotted aboard with a squad of African troops, large men in blue greatcoats, legs wrapped in green puttees, rifles slung at their shoulders. The officer demanded certificates from Kapitein van Plaas, then tore them into shreds because they were not printed in French. The German soldiers, who had been playing cards in the hold, crowded up on deck and began to snarl at the African troops, who were ordered to fix bayonets, which they did very smartly. Eilín tried to pull me away, but I resisted; it was too interesting. Mist on the river was turning golden with the sun just peeking through. The German soldiers were prodded into the bow while a couple of Africans were sent below to search for contraband. The French officer examined Buck's papers. Our trunk was hauled out from our cabin, and the French officer ordered my mother to unlock it, then began rifling the contents while everyone stared. The first layers were my mother's white underwear—slips, camisoles, drawers—and he held up a pair of her silk drawers, intending, I suppose, to humiliate her in front of all the men. But she wasn't having it. In her convent French—learned from the nuns at Rathfarnham—she said, "If you are looking for presents for your dear mother, *mon capitaine*, you may help yourself to anything of mine."

That wiped the leer off his face. He ordered a couple of Africans to carry the trunk ashore while we were held aboard under guard. That trunk contained everything we owned except the clothes on our backs. Fifteen minutes later a couple of African soldiers brought it back to the quay, and two young German soldiers leaped down and hoisted it aboard. Then we cast off, the soldiers helping haul in our dock lines as *St. Antonius* fell out into the current.

My mother opened the trunk to see what had been stolen. A small chest of table silver, and an heirloom necklace and brooch Con gave my mother as a wedding present, had disappeared.

There was nothing to be done about it. My parents had been resigned to being robbed somewhere along the way. We were refugees, and it came with the territory, or the lack of one.

At Wiesbaden a few hours later we said goodbye to Kapitein van Plaas and his wife and disembarked.

"Auf Wiedersehen!" the soldiers cried, and this time my parents replied, "Auf Wiedersehen!" because it wasn't dangerous anymore to speak German.

꙳ 1938

KARIN RANG ME AT THE OFFICE AFTER I'D JUST HAD A MOST UNPLEASANT interview with a senior clerk at the IG Farben *Pensionskasse*. When I announced my intention to resign, he pretended at first not to understand. Impossible! Unthinkable! Dismaying! No one ever voluntarily left the IG.

After that he treated me brusquely, even rudely.

Good riddance to bad rubbish—he didn't say it, but that was his attitude.

"I know I'm not supposed to telephone you at work." Karin's warm-cool voice on the telephone line, this was something I was never able to get used to.

"It's all right."

"I've told my father."

"Yes?"

"I described your epic plan. It felt as if I were describing for him a film scenario. Not quite real. Ah, Billy, I don't know. Maybe I should be back in Berlin."

"Certainly not! This isn't the cinema—it's real. New York in three weeks. What does your father say?"

"He asks you to come out to Walden."

⊳·⊶·◦·⊷·⊲

I caught the tram across the river. I walked down the busy road from Niederrad village to Walden. The gate porter was long gone, but I dragged open one of the iron gates and slipped through.

For years Walden had been neglected. When I walked down the avenue that afternoon, tall weeds were sprouting through the gravel. The gardens hadn't been tended since 1936 and were a mess. The lawns had not been mown. A pad of leaves undulated in a foot or two of filthy water in the swimming pool, which had never been properly drained.

Instead of heading straight for the main house, I wandered the grounds for what I figured might be the last time. In the deserted stables, I caught a scent of horse, of neat's-foot oil, saddle soap, grain feed.

At least the hay had been cut recently. The meadow was clipped and sleek, the only section of the estate that still seemed to be managed, organized, cared for.

Newport, the shingle-style guest cottage that had been our refuge in 1919 and our home for many years after, stood off by itself in the Walden woods, one shutter loose and banging at the window of my old bedroom.

The baron's ancient red Mercedes and Lady Maire's black Ford were still parked inside the garage/coach house. A local Party boss had acquired title to the cars in 1936 but hadn't bothered taking them away.

A late-October afternoon in the flickering birch glades. Walden was a ghostland. I saw ghosts of beautiful horses, ghosts of my mother and father in their happiest days, even the ghost of my long-lost friend Mick asking questions, wanting to know all about the beautiful heiress *Karin von*.

It didn't matter whether or not she was emotionally prepared to leave Germany. It was time. And I would bring her to safety on the other side of the ocean. And we'd cross *el llano* to find our future on the other side.

I was operating out of an indecipherable mixture of training and instinct, like a well-trained gun dog, a retriever, trembling with eagerness to fetch the downed bird and carry it in his mouth softly, tenderly, without doing the slightest damage. It's his job. He's born for it.

Don't get in his way.

DON'T BE AFRAID

Arten von Licht Buch [Kinds of Light Book], Karin v Weinbrenner. Unpaginated. In English and occ. German. Lange Family Archive, 12 C-12-1988. Special Collections, McGill Library, McGill University, Montreal.

⌒

remembered light of wartime: Walden (1914–19)

the colors very STRONG: black/white/dark-spruce-green/ plenty of field gray uniforms/Red is bloody bandages. Our food is gray in war. Turnips, potatoes, porridge. All birds are killed for eating: sparrows, finches larks black crows with black feet. The officers with muddy yellow faces—have been gassed. Some wounds are purple. The nursing sister Zukermann wears pink says it is the most sensible shade, hides bloodstain scarlet would be better but—nursing sisters cannot wear scarlet!

—Father's Eisernem Kreuz, "W," black with silver edges, and ribbon white-red-black. Father's uniform: scarlet piping on field gray—he says to the tailor "Zu eng! Zu eng! Can't breathe!"

—It snows a great deal in the war.

—I lie on pillows on the rug in the library with tea reading "Sons of the Bear-Hunter" and "The Treasure of Silver Lake," thanks to the little Oberleutnant. After the war he says he will travel to the Llano for healing in the light. But—one of the graves they are digging—to be prepared, before the ground freezes too hard—will be, yes, for him.

—The little Oberleutnant's beautiful horse boots. Black, quality leather, supple, hardly worn. What is to be done?—polish them! polish them—he will wear them in seinem Grab!

Holograph letter. Signed *K. v. Weinbrenner,* addressed *Master Billy Lange Walden 60528 Frankfurt am Main Germany,* postmarked *Sherborne Dorset, 12 Nov. 1920.* Lange Family Archive, 12 C-11-1920. Special Collections, McGill Library, McGill University, Montreal.

SHERBORNE GIRLS SCHOOL
Sherborne, Dorset
11th November Armistice Day 1920

My dear young sir,
    If you truly are able to hit rabbit on the run then you are
a bowman as good as any apache of your age. Of course only
children hunt rabbits . . . when you are of an age—buffalo.
Still I am quite pleased with you. English boy at Walden with
his quite charmant parents & I at school with 209 unpleasant
English girls & neither of us quite "at home." There are
17 girls in this House. One Irish. You would not like them.
The stocky pink creature called Belinda Morgan-Grenville,
remarkably dreadful, big teeth, no poise, knocked my shins
with her hockey stick—twice. The second time I flue at her. Oh
terrible! Beastly foreigner bloody hun, "poor sport"! The Head
Girl of the School Rita Vanderheuven decides my punishment.
Part-Hollander, Vanderheuven she is not bad. Her I admire
actually. But now I am forbidden to leave school grounds—no
walks to the village shops—for 2 weeks. We walk to the vill. to

buy sweets, some . . . Zigaretten! Just before 11 o'clock the bells ring out—Two Minutes Silence. Is it possible to remember a german soldier here in english. Yes—it is. Leutnant Fröhlisch.

It is terrible how loud the Eng. girls are. Amusing sometimes. Read, read young sir. How does Winnetou? You may write me only in good german please.

Your sporting old friend,
K. v. Weinbrenner

Holograph letter. Signed *K. v. W*, addressed *Herr B. Lange Walden 60528 Frankfurt am Main Germany,* postmarked *Lausanne 11 Gare Exp, 11.11. 1925*. Lange Family Archive, 12 C-11-1925. Special Collections, McGill Library, McGill University, Montreal.

—

INSTITUT CHATEAU MONT-CHOISI
Lausanne Suisse
11ième Novembre 1925

Guillaume, mon frère

Positively gray skies EN SUISSE. mais dans mon rêve: EL LLANO ESTACADO. Would it not be grand, mon frère. Wouldn't it. These days suisse organized sombre orderly ne plus ultra. Why if my petit père were Madame Directrice he couldn't manage this establishment any more to his liking. Finishing School! We sleep on ironed sheets, we are exercised, nous sommes nourris, we study temperament, manners, pliér, household management of silver and linens. La révérence. No breeding done: otherwise the school operates like an excellent stable. Girls know the men they'll marry. I shall marry no one. The Hon. Jane Pitney has invited me to England at Christmas. If my Hon. Mother agrees I shall hunt with the Hon. Cottesmore in Jan.

Finishing School! Indeed! I shan't be finished, my Billy! After this swiss convent, or coven (not so bad really, but not so

good either) I shall go and live in Berlin. I shall take a flat in
Berlin. I shall be . . . unanswerable. Not finished either. Rather
I shall begin.

Thurs. last slipped away—to the Kino in town—Fantôme de
l'Opéra, American, superb, what a grip, watching such a picture
is like having an enormous dream—Alpträume—one staggers
into the street reeling, shaken, extraordinary sensations.
Nothing like the pictures, is there.

TODAY=Day of the dead. No 2 minutes silence in
Lausanne but this morning at 1100 all English girls stood
completely still. They froze like the upright dead.

Your only sister,
KvW

Arten von Licht Buch [Kinds of Light Book], Karin v Weinbrenner. Unpaginated. In English and German. Lange Family Archive, 11 C-12-1988. Special Collections, McGill Library, McGill University, Montreal.

A nocturnal ride across the desert which stretches itself out in the moonlight! How much I wish my dear readers could feel the majestic sensations which allow the human heart to swell higher and higher. However, the heart must be free from worry and from all that could oppress and constrain it . . . If only someone could give me a quill from which the right words would flow to describe the impression which such a nocturnal desert ride brings forth from a devout human heart!

Der Geist des Llano Estacado
_____
Karl May

—my transl!! kvw

Hollow cheeks, thin lips, gray clothes — the Germans resembled wolves, I thought, as our little suburban train puffed strenuously into Frankfurt Hauptbahnhof. A pair of beggars in ragged field-gray uniforms—one missing a leg—hectored a well-dressed couple stepping from a first-class compartment on our train. The gentleman was portly and wore a white silk scarf and a camel-hair overcoat draped nattily across his shoulders. The woman with him was much younger, slender, beautiful. I did not have enough German to interpret what the beggars were screaming, but from their twisted faces and the spit flying from their teeth the invective must have been passionate and foul, and the first-class couple scurried past them.

A porter wearing a blue smock and a row of medals was eager to hoist our trunk onto his barrow. Buck suddenly put out an arm to stop him and said to my mother, "My cigarette lighter! Did you see it? Have they stolen my lighter as well?"

I saw my mother was puzzled. Our table silver and an heirloom Irish necklace had been stolen from the trunk; why fuss over a lighter?

Buck opened the trunk and started digging frantically through layers of clothes, exposing everything, right there on the station platform. He was breathing in hoarse gasps. It scared me, because we were in Germany, land of the Hun.

"It doesn't matter!" my mother whispered through clenched teeth. Was Germany casting a spell over us? Would things only get more difficult from now on?

"Buck, Buck, forget the lighter, please, leave it for now, we mustn't delay."

He didn't respond. He was on his knees pawing through our mess of clothes. Germans hurrying for trains hurtled past. Young soldiers stared at us from under steel helmets. Crying whistles, hissing of air brakes, conductors yelping, the raw jabber of the German language— train stations were stews of anxiety as far as I was concerned; all train journeys had been versions of exile. I watched helplessly as my sweet father dug through layers of clothes like a dog after a bone. Eilín had packed everything so neatly; disorder frightened and dismayed her. The French inspectors at Sankt Goar had already smashed the lock and rifled through, and now Buck was tearing into it all over again. We'd been on German soil only a couple of hours, and already things were coming apart.

The porter, watching my father panting and scrabbling, kept shifting his expression between a grin and a disapproving scowl.

"Let it be, man!" Eilín whispered. "Buck, dear Buck, only let's get ourselves out of this place! We must, we must! Don't do this now—"

"Ah, so! Here it is! One thing they didn't steal!"

He'd come across his little lighter. It glinted in his hand. A slender, silver thing—I still have it. There's an inscription.

HERMIONE II
First Place
Round the Island
1913

All around us people were calling "Auf Wiedersehen!"—the first German phrase I grasped the meaning of and would remember. How many million *Auf Wiedersehen*s had been bawled and sobbed in Frankfurt Hauptbahnhof? The coal-smoky air was choked with *Auf Wiedersehen*, the impressive ironwork painted with it, the vaulting glass roof lacquered and smeared not only with pigeon shit but also with *Auf Wiedersehen*.

Buck flourished his lighter at us, snapped a small flame, then dropped it into his coat pocket. He didn't have any cigarettes left; he'd smoked his last English Player's aboard *St. Antonius* with van Plaas.

Eilín hastily repacked our trunk, and the porter heaved it onto his barrow and trundled off so fast we had to hurry to keep up with him. I was famished and shivering with cold. Germany seemed wide-awake, ferocious, the *Hauptbahnhof* was festooned with steam and shot with shafts of daylight that made my eyes tear. The people looked like beggars.

If there is a place on earth where I have felt most alive and also most stringently aware of death's certainty, it is on the platforms of Frankfurt Hauptbahnhof. My dreams are often set there. I'm dashing to catch a fast express to Berlin—an FD—or I'm waiting for a train to Utrecht and Rotterdam. I'm always alone. Even the pigeons murmur *Auf Wiedersehen, auf Wiedersehen* while I loiter on the platform, unsure of the schedule, unsure my information is correct, waiting without being certain there's anything worth waiting for.

►┼◄►─○─◄┼─◄

A big red Mercedes 28/95 stood fuming for us outside the *Hauptbahnhof.* The brilliant car seemed impatient and slightly terrifying—my first taste of life as it was lived anywhere near the Weinbrenners. A surly, one-eyed chauffeur strapped our trunk onto a running board, then sped us across a bridge over the river Main and through a run-down district called Sachsenhausen and another even-grittier suburb, Niederrad. Boys on the street had pinched faces and close-cropped hair, even shaved heads. Some of the girls, too, had heads shaved. Everyone I saw was spectrally thin, and the cart horses were bones and joints, with stringy manes. Solomon Dietz, the baron's chauffeur, wore a leather patch over his left eye and a front soldier's cap. He interrogated my father and blasted his horn at carts and wagons and any pedestrians who dared cross our path. They flinched and scuttled clear. My mother and I didn't understand a word, but the chauffeur's vehemence seemed to amuse my father.

Afterward he told us Solomon had demanded to know whether he was a socialist "because anyone who isn't has their head up their ass!"

A couple of miles south of the river, the Mercedes pulled up before an iron gate bearing the Walden crest. A porter dragged the gates open and saluted, and the big car thrust its way in. Gravel crunched and crackled under our tires. The avenue was flanked by what seemed to be a forest of spruce and birches, then by open meadows with paddocks and white rail fences. We passed a very large, very forbidding house and were brought straight to a wooden house, also large but much friendlier looking. Solomon cut the engine, jerked the hand brake, and cried, *"Newport!"*

We climbed out of the aggressive old Mercedes, all red paintwork and polished brass. The front door of the house was unlocked. The chauffeur and my father carried our trunk inside. Then Solomon shook hands with each of us, and I watched him crank-start the Mercedes. When it fired up, he gave me a clenched-fist salute, then climbed in and thundered away.

Newport was an eccentric, shingle-style New England "summer cottage" planted in the middle of a forest in Hesse. It had towers and cupolas and bay windows in a riot of planned spontaneity. It could have been in Northeast Harbor or Kennebunkport. In Germany, it was a displaced house for displaced persons, and its odd exuberance irritated certain people, Longo, for example, Karin's beau, who once remarked that Newport seemed a "flimsy" house. He preferred the stolid hunting-lodge atmosphere of the main house, though he also told Karin how "Jewish" it was of her grandfather, the dyestuff king from Breslau, to have built a hunting lodge in suburban countryside where there was nothing to shoot but rabbits.

Newport's American architect, Mr. Bailey Wemyss, was a young friend of Henry James. The baron had met Henry James taking a *kur* at Bad Homburg. The author introduced his architect friend, and the baron commissioned Newport soon after.

Buck liked Newport right away. Its Americanness was familiar and welcoming—he'd just about been born at San Francisco, after all. Eilín was delighted. Newport was airier, brighter, and far cleaner than anyplace we had lived since Sanssouci. As a guest cottage, closed up most of the year, it had been only lightly lived in. Everything seemed fresh and new. Rooms were paneled with cedar and other light woods, and in the afternoon sunlight they shone almost golden.

While Buck made his way to the main house for his interview with the baron, my mother began unpacking, and I explored. I was thinking about the Weinbrenners' son, Hermann, whom I'd been told was buried somewhere in the Walden forest. I'd been Hermann once, so long ago I could scarcely remember.

On the little train groaning up from Wiesbaden to Frankfurt—

there'd been barely enough coal to get up steam—I'd asked my mother if I was to be Hermann ever again. She looked at my father, who said he thought one name change was enough.

" 'Billy' is your name from now on, I should say."

My mother remarked that the baron would be disappointed. I'd originally been named for him, after all.

"Weinbrenner can call the boy Hermann if he chooses to," Buck replied. "But his name is Billy."

On the train from Wiesbaden my father had spoken English without seeming to care if anyone overheard. I think he felt at liberty for the first time in nearly five years and had decided he wasn't going to be interned inside or outside anyone's language. My German name, Hermann, was gone forever, like the things that disappeared from our trunk, or the white foam in the wake of a steamer crossing the North Sea.

I discovered a shed packed with firewood and helped my mother get a blaze going in the kitchen range, another in the library, and a third in the large bathroom upstairs. As we warmed the house, it seemed to creak and groan with satisfaction. The pantry drawers were crammed with monogrammed silverware, cupboards held stacks of dinner plates decorated with shamrocks and cornflowers. There were eiderdowns in the cedar closets, soft woolen blankets, and linen sheets.

It was not so large as my grandmother's house, but most of Wychwood had been falling down, and horses and pigs lived in some of it. At Newport, everything was swept, bright, shipshape, scented by balsam fir. When I ventured outside, the forest air carried a pungent evergreen fragrance. I wanted to scout the surroundings, orient myself. Footpaths and bridle paths were carpeted with pine needles.

I didn't see Karin at first. She wasn't hiding, exactly, only standing immobile in a stand of bare birches: "in plain sight" but absolutely still, so I didn't see her.

The quiet and the specter of those cold woods of Walden were exciting. Frankfurt's distant hum made the quiet seem a presence rather than an absence. I was stumbling along, eagerly and aimlessly, when something cut through the air a few inches in front of my eyebrows and smacked itself into a birch tree. The *zing-smack* was echoed by a hum, a vibration, as if the air, disturbed, required a moment to regain its composure.

I stared at the red-and-black shaft of an arrow at least twelve inches long, its point buried in the trunk of the birch tree. Black and white tail feathers. The shaft was still quivering.

"Guten Tag."

A girl stepped out onto the path.

Maybe if I'd been paying attention I'd have caught her scent sooner, but I was no woodsman, she was wrapped in wool, and the scent of winter woolens was so ordinary, so much the vernacular of daily existence, that it didn't stand out as a scent, even in those sharp woods. Everything in my life smelled of woolens: mittens, sweater, hat, coat, underclothes.

She stood in the path holding her beautiful (Apache) bow, made of mulberry wood, strung with sinew. A girl with brown hair in braids and pink cheeks. She wore a sailor's pea jacket, a skirt, woolen stockings, red boots, and a quiver of arrows slung at her shoulder on a rawhide string.

"You're the boy—Hermann." She eyed me. "Only that isn't your name anymore. You've caught another name, have you not? Something quite English, isn't it? George? Is it a George you've become, English boy?"

"No, it isn't."

"Alfred?"

"No."

"Tom?"

I shook my head.

"Well?"

I didn't want to give my name to her.

"Can't you manage it, boy? Introduce yourself properly. What a clumsy thing. Have you left your manners in the trenches?"

"I wasn't in the trenches."

"You weren't a front soldier?"

She was teasing me. I didn't like it. I held my tongue.

"Do you remember me at all?" she asked.

"I know who you are."

"Who, then?"

"The baron's daughter. Karin. We were born in the same room."

"Were we? Indeed. I'd quite forgotten. I am going away to school." Her voice was suddenly warmer, more humane. "To a boarding school of English girls, how do you like it?"

Her English was fluent but had a foreign ring, as though her thoughts had been framed in German before she nailed down English words to cover them.

They shan't much like you in England, I thought.

"They'll hate me for a Hun, I expect. Do you read? Have you read *Winnetou*?"

"I've read *The Jungle Book*. By Rudyard Kipling."

"Ah, so." She nodded. "Well, this is not bad. What do you know of Indians? Not Kipling's. The other sort, American Indians. Winnetou is chief of the Mescalero Apache. I think you might be a Red Indian. Do you know why?"

She was no taller than me, though almost a year older. Now that she was being nicer I couldn't dislike her so much. Something about her was like a bird, a hungry little bird, eager and quick.

She looked at me with a thoughtful expression. "Red Indians won't give their names away. They hold them quite *wertvolle*, just as you."

I gave in. "Billy. Billy is my name."

"Very good. You may read my Winnetou novels. Author: Karl May. They are on my shelf in my father's library. I'll tell him you have permissions to read. Karl May is a superb writer. I say they are the finest books ever written. What's it like in England? I barely can remember. Do you think they'll hate me?"

"I don't know. You're a German."

"I don't hate them, though the English ships have starved us, nearly. People down the road are eating crows. People eat their dogs and cats. I don't hate the English, though all the good Germans they've killed."

She stepped off the path and approached the tree where her arrow had stuck. With a sharp tug, she pulled it out and inspected the head before dropping it into the quiver.

"When strangers meet, they ought to smoke. That's the custom on El Llano Estacado."

El Llano Estacado. The first time I heard the phrase.

"But tobacco's rare these days. My father has cigars given him by an American general." Suddenly she held out the bow. "Here. Take it. Yours."

I didn't know what she meant. "No, it isn't."

"Yes. I hardly can carry it to boarding school, can I? Yours."

Stunned, I accepted the massive, sleek weapon, nearly five feet in length with a double curve. The smooth mulberry, stained with red ocher, was widest at the handle and tapered gracefully toward the ends.

Slipping the quiver off her shoulder, she held it out. "Arrows break, arrows fly off and don't come back. When you need more, one of the foresters here—Old Rudi, too old for the army—is quite good at making them. Now I'll show you the graves. You're to look after the graves until the men come back."

Without another word she started down the path, walking quickly.

I wasn't sure I wanted to see the graves. The daylight was fading, the air was getting colder, and I didn't want to get lost in the dark.

But I couldn't bear her thinking I was afraid, even though I was. So I slung the quiver of arrows on my shoulder and started after her, clutching the bow. My hands were cold; my eyes were leaking; my nose dripped. I was in fact on the cusp of the flu, the infamous influenza of 1918–19, which killed more people than the war. Maybe that's why that afternoon is so sharp in memory, why it feels inflicted: The stubborn scent of ground, though it was frozen hard. The weak but piercing daylight, the crackle of twigs, my own garbled breathing as I struggled to keep up. If I lost sight of her, I'd never catch up.

The woods broke open at a small grassy clearing. The stiff tufts of grass were winter yellow. Six metal crosses were arranged in precise formation—it was a cemetery. A soldiers' cemetery.

Karin stood facing a headstone that was set off on its own, away from the uniform iron crosses marking the other graves. I approached and stood beside her, quiver slung on my shoulder, clutching the Apache bow.

"All right, Billy. My brother."

The granite was scabbed with tawny lichen. The iron Fraktur letters on the stone were difficult to read in the dim light.

HIER RUHT IN FRIEDEN
Hermann
von Weinbrenner
7.9.96–2.2.97

"You come in here from time to time, Billy, do you accept?" Her expression was stern. "The old parents will never come out. So you must, from time to time—agreed? When it snows, brush the snow off. In spring you may put some simple flowers. There's nothing else to be done. He's dead, after all. But you shall come out? You won't forget?"

"No—yes—I will."

She looked around at the metal crosses marking the other graves. "These poor fellows were all soldiers. I knew them. Some were quite nice. That one—third in the first row, the little *Oberleutnant*, Fröhlisch—from him I first had the Winnetou novels. He gave me his own books, his mother brought them from Bavaria. We spoke quite often of El Llano Estacado."

She used the correct Spanish pronunciation: *yah-no.*

"He wished very much to cross *el llano* before he died, but he did not. Do you think he crosses it now? That would be nice, only I can't believe it. Fröhlisch as well taught me to play the piano. Ragtime! Do you play?"

"No."

"Do you do anything especially well?"

"I can ride."

"They've taken all the horses for the war," Karin said. "Except my mother's hunter. But my father will buy others, and the farrier shall find his way back from the front, and the saddlemaker and the vet. Only I shall be in England. Some of our old grooms showed up last week. One lost his arm. One was drunk. I must go now. I'm expected for tea."

Abruptly she started back the way we had come, following the path. I trailed her. The sky was cold blue, weak winter sun sinking fast through the trees. When we came to a place where two paths crossed, she pointed. "You go this way, I go that. Goodbye. Remember to do what you have promised."

"I'll remember."

"No snow on my brother. Flowers in spring. I hope you get enough to eat. In Germany we live on potatoes and turnips. No meat in ages. A scrap of bacon sometimes. My mother says there's plenty of food in England."

"Well, there is."

"Why can't they share it?" She scowled, then began walking away into the dark, the crisp dark of winter.

"Auf Wiedersehen!" I called.

"Auf Wiedersehen!" Her voice flew back at me, haunting and quite alone, like an owl winging deftly among the trees.

My father's interview with the baron took place in his library at Walden. It was a grand house, built by Karin's grandfather in the 1880s, in the craggy style of an East Prussian hunting lodge, except three or four times larger, with massive timbers, mounted heads of stags, and a dining hall that would have swallowed up a corps of Teutonic knights.

Karin's father believed Walden to be not only the largest but also the most beautiful house in Frankfurt, and when she was a girl he often reminded her how fortunate she was to grow up surrounded by one hundred and eighty four hectares of forest and meadow and artworks and beautiful horses. Whereas the children of Niederrad, just down the road, thought themselves fortunate just to have shoes on their feet and cabbages for supper.

In his library on the wintry afternoon of our first day in Germany, Hermann Weinbrenner proudly showed my father the Iron Crosses (second class and first class) kept in a leather box on his mahogany desk. The desk itself had once belonged to Admiral von Spee.

Then the little baron displayed his right hand, missing two fingers shot off at Courland, where his squadron of Garde-Reserve-Uhlanen had been in a cavalry skirmish. After recovering from the wound he wasn't permitted to return to the front and instead was ordered to supervise a team of chemists developing new poison gases at his dyeworks, Colora GmbH.

The baron had a passion for geography and cartography. He owned a collection of globes, atlases, and gazetteers, some quite ancient. He collected books on the history of organic chemistry, on German naval history, and the history of the Jews. Also Russian novels. He'd been a chemist, a businessman, a champion polo player, a yachtsman, and a soldier, but the library at Walden was where he felt most himself, with his Eiserne Kreuz in their leather box and his *Uhlanen* saber, its blade stamped IN TREUE FEST—*Loyalty Forever*—slung on the wall.

During the First World War, when Walden had been a rest home for wounded officers, the library was the one room in the main house reserved for use of the family. Karin spent hours in there alone, reading Winnetou stories.

The baron offered Buck a cigar from a box of Havanas an American general had given him. Weinbrenner started cursing the English sea lords, who'd commandeered his wonderful Yankee schooner *Hermione II* at the start of the war, and confiscated his English island house, Sanssouci, where we had once made our home.

"You must agree, Captain Lange, that house was without question the most beautiful, modern, and well-situated house on the Isle of Wight."

"It was a fine house."

"Why, English gentlemen—men whom I had considered my friends!—stood up on hind legs in the House of Commons and accused me of being a spymaster! It was poor you, my poor captain, whom they would shoot for a spy but it was me, Captain, whom they hated—the dastardly Hun who won their races too often! I tell you I shall never again enter the harbor of Cowes. I have no more taste for yachting. Bloody Englishmen and the Royal Yacht Squadron can go to hell!"

Buck's head spun. No yachting meant—no skipper's job. How then was he going to earn a living? We couldn't stay on as charity cases at Walden. And the Germany glimpsed between the *Hauptbahnhof* and Walden's iron gates looked savage and famished.

He was afraid my mother would decide to return to Ireland and take me with her and he'd never see either of us again.

"Of course, after this monstrous and wasteful tide of war, my complaints are petty and ridiculous even to myself," the baron remarked. "Now to the case of yourself, Captain, who has lost on my account four and a half years."

"There's many who've lost a good deal more," said Buck.

The baron struck a match and held it to my father's cigar. "No doubt. A business proposition I wish to make—and, by the way, is that not a fine smoke? The best since the war, do you agree?"

My father—reeling from disappointment but struggling not to show it—had nothing to say. He didn't really enjoy cigars.

"Captain Lange, my proposition." Hermann Weinbrenner enjoyed playing the role of bluff, shouting Prussian squire, but he could switch gears very quickly. And sitting down behind Admiral Spee's mahogany desk, he proceeded to offer Buck—the three of us—a new life.

"Here at Walden I intend to found a racing stable and stud. The best in Germany. In Europe, perhaps. In short, I wish you to be the manager of all: men, horses, breeding, training, racing. I intend to place the operation in your capable hands." The baron licked the tip of his own cigar and struck a match to light it. Then he smiled. "Do you accept?"

"You're not serious," my father said.

He thought Weinbrenner must be pulling his leg, and it made him angry.

Picking up his hat, he looked around for a place to put down his cigar. He couldn't bear being teased, even—especially—by his old benefactor.

You have to remember our vulnerable position, as deportees. And of course my father felt himself responsible for our poverty, our homelessness.

"Believe me, dear Captain, I can't make any such proposal without being utterly serious. If you agree, we start tomorrow."

Still holding his cigar—the approximate size of a baby's forearm—in one hand, hat in the other, Buck felt dizzy, as if he'd stood up too quickly. Though he'd never actually sat down.

"But why? How? Surely there are—"

"Dear Captain, you were undoubtedly the best horseman, the most instinctive, the most knowledgeable, of our *Uhlanen*. And that, my dear fellow, is saying something."

Buck had not thought of it for some time, but the fact was their relationship did go back to their days in the Uhlanen-Garde at the turn of the century, when Weinbrenner was the first Jewish (Reserve) officer in the history of the regiment, and Buck a young conscript with a reputation as a horse wizard, *Pferdezauberer*. The baron had known my father as a horseman before he knew him as a skipper.

And my father had known horses all his life. When Captain Jack was still a skipper in the Australian grain trade, Buck and Con lived in Melbourne, near the famous Flemington racetrack. At twelve my father was earning pocket money as an exercise rider. At fifteen he rode a horse called War God to a second-place finish in the Melbourne Cup.

In the *Uhlanen* Buck had been renowned for his uncanny skills as a horsebreaker and trainer of cavalry mounts. Even the rugged old instructor sergeants and veterinarians used to ask the raw recruit's advice, and that's when Hermann, Freiherr von Weinbrenner, who was in those days a famous polo player, as well as a reserve officer, first noticed him.

"Every aspect of your military career, not to mention our sailing days on the *Solent*, tells me you are exactly the racing manager I require."

"I don't know. Honestly, Baron . . ."

It was so different from what he'd expected. Abruptly, he sat down in one of the leather chairs. The cigar in his fist was smoldering fragrant silver smoke.

Cigars like that smelled of the jungle afire, he once told me, the jungle burning.

"And you are without a position at present, Captain, so I understand. Or so my wife believes. But perhaps she is misinformed?"

Suddenly my father was afraid that Weinbrenner was offering him the job out of charity. Making up a role for him, improvising. Was it merely a generous gesture of loyalty? Of gratitude? Of reparation? Was the racing stable and stud a moment's whim, and never a project the baron would commit himself to seriously?

But Weinbrenner was never one for gestures, generous or otherwise. He was above all a businessman.

"Let me make clear, my dear Captain Lange. I want you for one reason. I believe you will give me victories. I've seen you handle a race crew, dear Captain. I know what you can accomplish. And I shall rely on your instincts for bloodstock, for choosing our mares, breeding them, training up our offspring."

Karin once said her father loved mine because the baron was so accustomed to people wanting things from him, and Buck wanted so little. That wasn't entirely accurate: he wanted to win races. But the baron wanted victories even more and, as it turned out, he was more than willing to pay for them.

In the library that afternoon Buck listened to the baron outline his plan to make Walden the top racing stud in Europe. Before the war he had bred polo ponies and cavalry mounts at Walden, but his damaged hand could no longer grip a polo mallet, and his precious *Uhlanen* had been decimated on the eastern front and destroyed at Verdun. No more yachting, no more polo ponies, no cavalry horses—instead the baron intended to apply to the sport of kings the scientific and business methods that had made him one of the most successful colorists in history.

As general manager of Rennstall Walden, Buck Lange would be responsible for choosing breeding stock and overseeing the trainers, riders, grooms, and everyone else, with an excellent salary and a percentage of the winnings. For the greater glory of their Germany, they were going to breed, raise, and race the best bloodlines in Europe.

>→·+→·0·←+·←<

Our first dinner at Newport was exactly what Karin said it would be—turnips and potatoes. Buck and Eilín had a bottle of champagne from the baron's cellar, and I was offered a taste. That evening neither of my parents was able to muster much interest in my Apache bow.

We had all seen glowering, defeated Germany on our drive from the station, those gaunt faces and empty shopwindows, and half-dead nags pulling carts of junk. But now my father had a position, and during the afternoon Lady Maire had stopped at Newport to welcome my mother and ask her help organizing and cataloging the Walden art collection.

We had a future again.

While I handled my bow and inspected my beautiful, delicate arrows, I couldn't escape a feeling that I owed Karin a gift in exchange, but what did I have to offer a girl who had once started swimming for America?

There were twenty-two arrows in the quiver, striped red and black (the pigments came from Colora GmbH dyeworks). They were precisely feathered and had hammered-metal tips. The deerskin quiver smelled like a smoked ham, much more appetizing than the rude vegetables steaming on our table. The arrows were delicate, surprisingly frail, and the bow was the first thing I owned that wasn't a toy but an instrument shaped to accomplish certain specific business in the world—a machine, really. The baron had obtained an authentic Apache design from an ethnologist at Heidelberg University, and the same craftsman who made the ship models in his library had carved and steam-bent the bow for Karin. It had a draw weight of fifteen kilograms, and I would teach myself to hunt with it. In the winter of 1919 there was no game left on the estate, but the next year it started coming back—a few rabbits—and by then I had a good-enough aim and technique (the three-fingered Apache draw) to kill some of what I shot at.

While my parents sipped champagne from china teacups, toasting the future, I was worrying where I should keep my bow, keep it safe. I was afraid that if I didn't find the right spot for it, the bow would be ruined or smashed even before I learned to use it properly.

When my mother suggested I store my bow in the ugly brass barrel near the front door where umbrellas and walking sticks were kept—or, worse, toss it into the hall closet with our boots and overcoats—I felt physically sick. I didn't want my Apache bow mixed up with ordinary things.

I was nine years old. Yes, probably I was exhausted. Enough turmoil and dislocation had been thrown my way.

But in practically all cultures, powerful rituals and taboos govern the proper storage and keeping of weapons.

At last my father suggested that we take down a Dürer print above my bed and hang the bow in its place. It looked magnificent there, graceful and forceful, and it would be near at hand. I hung the quiver from the same picture hook, and suddenly my bedroom wasn't the barren bedroom of a deportee, a refugee, Herm the Germ, but the spartan lodge of a hunter and warrior.

Then I remembered the Sweet Afton cigarette tin Mick had presented when I left Sligo. There were even a few cigarettes left inside, dry, crumbly, a little bent, perhaps—but Karin had said tobacco was rare.

I threw on my coat and walked the gravel avenue to the main house with the Sweet Aftons tin in my pocket. I don't think my parents noticed me leave. My flu fever may have been coming on, for I wasn't at all cold.

I rapped a bronze knocker in the shape of a stag's head with antlers. No response. I rapped again. A servant poked her head out from one of the leaded windows above and said something in German. I repeated Karin's name a few times. The window shut.

When Karin opened the door, she had on a velvet dress, midnight blue, with white stockings. I held out the cigarette tin. Without hesitation, she took it.

"Well done. Now go home before you catch your death."

"Auf Wiedersehen."

"Auf Wiedersehen."

When I got back to Newport my parents were drinking champagne and washing up together. I brought in an armful of firewood, and they didn't ask where I'd been. They were excited and happy, chattering about plans. The war's bleakness was over with, and we were a real family living in a real house.

I was helping my father stoke the upstairs fireplace when we heard distant machine guns and an ominous *chunk-chunk-chunk*, which I soon learned to recognize as rapid mortar fire. I already knew the sound of machine guns from Köln; mortars were new to me. In English boys' magazines machine guns were always "chattering" or "barking," but the gas-driven discharge of a MG08, heard at a distance of a mile or more, sounded closer to a snarl. Any closer and the firing became distinctly staccato, like very rapid hammer blows, especially if the operator was experienced and wasn't running through his ammunition belts too quickly. An MG08 spewed a sharp, gassy reek, and if the firing was very close, I could smell the discharge.

>—◦—◦—◦—◦—◦—<

Newport cottage would never belong to us, but it was easy enough to pretend it did. Even its American gaucheness, its out-of-placeness, suited us well. Built entirely of wood, it would burn to the ground when a few incendiaries fell into the Walden forest during one of the thousand-bomber raids on Frankfurt in late '44.

A girl's pink cheeks and red boots. The graceful double curve of an Apache bow. A battered Sweet Aftons tin. Distant gunfire, pungence of balsam, winter sunlight filtered through evergreens. That's what I remember. Also the black scent of old, dead fires when my father and I knelt, crumpling parched newsprint from a stack of prewar *Frankfurter Zeitungen*, adding birchbark curlings, sticks, and beech logs, then lighting everything with the crack of a match, so that the scent of the dead fire flew away up the chimney, and in its place were the heat and light of a blaze crackling in the hearth of our own home in the heart of Germany.

⊷—❉—◦—❉—⊷

Lieber Leſer, weißt du, was das Wort Greenhorn bedeutet?

The Fraktur font wasn't easy to read, but I kept at it. I was determined to get my hands on the German language before starting school.
It was a matter of survival. Luckily, and thanks to Karin, I had the Winnetou novels of Karl May.

Dear reader! Do you know what the word "greenhorn" means?

I'd spent my first three weeks at Walden in bed with the flu. At last
the baron's physician, Dr. Solomon Lewin, told my mother I was well
enough to walk the snowy path through the woods from Newport to
the main house. Lady Maire had invited my mother to tea.

Of course I grew bored and restless while the ladies talked. After
eating my fill of buttered toast and cakes, I finally screwed up my courage and asked Lady Maire if I might explore the library.

Permission granted.

I found the books on their own shelf, where Karin had said they'd
be. The cover of the first Winnetou I pulled out had a Red Indian and
a frontiersman sharing a campfire with a pair of fine horses in the background. Both wore buckskins and carried sheathed knives and rifles.
Sitting down on the Persian rug, I cracked the book open.

A. FRÖLISCH

was inscribed on the flyleaf, in black ink, with a neat schoolboy hand.
I'd seen the *Oberleutnant*'s grave out in the woods.

FROHLISCH, AUGUST
Oblt 1.6.99–24.2.18
Königlich Bayerisches Infanterie

He was eighteen when he died. Had he known he was going to die?
His nose, cheek, and left ear had been smashed by machine-gun bullets.
He must have looked a horror, even wearing his metal mask, but for
Karin, who came of age surrounded by medieval imagery of tortured
saints and stigmata, his appearance wasn't so frightening.

"You might imagine the religious art my mother collects is her rebellion against her Protestant upbringing, or my Jewish father," Karin remarked, years later, on one of our café afternoons in Berlin. "But she is drawn to a work for the same reasons I am. She looks for the accurate and truthful picture of her world. That altarpiece, for example, the weeping women: this is a scene we witnessed at Walden many times during the war."

The piece she referred to was *The Lamentation*, which our mothers had discovered in a stable loft outside Segovia. It depicted five women with the lifeless body of their Christ just down from the cross. As an adolescent I'd watched a couple of grooms uncrate it at Walden, shocked to learn the baroness had paid two thousand marks for it, more than the price of the BMW R47 motorcycle I yearned for at the time.

"Oberleutnant Frölisch's mother and sisters came up from Bavaria in his last days," Karin said. "They washed his poor body themselves, and I watched them wrapping him in a shroud. This was *The Lamentation* exactly."

Frölisch had instructed his mother to bring his Winnetou books from Bavaria so he could give them to Karin. After he died she had stayed up alone, night after night in her father's library, in the house full of damaged men, slowly turning pages, absorbing the sunlight, piñon, and black powder smoke of Karl May's harsh, vivid world, where the Mescalero Apache chief called Winnetou rides a horse called Iltschi, the Wind, and roams *el llano*, a country May describes with surrealist passion.

Everything missing from our Germany—open space, unbounded distance, harsh sunlight, nobility of character—primed our longing for that space. The light of the High Plains became our dream light in German darkness. Our elders would take pleasure in reminding us that Karl May—*that charlatan!*—had never set foot in America when he wrote the Winnetou stories. But what did that matter? The world he offered was whole and round and easier to understand than our own.

That winter afternoon at Haus-Walden, I brought three Winnetou books back to Lady Maire's sitting room, and asked if I might borrow them.

She seemed surprised. "Wild West stories? But aren't they all in German? Do you read German, Billy?"

"Not yet, but I shall."

I would be starting school soon. I did not intend to be *an buachaill coigríche*, the foreign boy, all over again. I needed to learn German, and quickly.

That evening I took down an old Muret-Sanders dictionary, lugged it up to my bedroom, and began working my way through the Fraktur-printed pages of Oberleutnant Frölisch's *Winnetou, vol. 1*. It was hard going at first, but Karl May's Apache chief and his German blood brother, Old Shatterhand, spoke with the pure, clear syntax of heroes, and one of the lessons the book taught was that rites of passage are arduous. And Karin, scribbling in the margins, had translated some phrases into English, so with the help of the Muret-Sanders I started along the trail she'd marked, across El Llano Estacado and into the German language.

>·◆·○·◆·◁

February 1919. My mother and I caught a tram across the river Main one gray, raw afternoon. A soldier beggar wearing dark glasses boarded our tram and rattled his tin cup. The conductor seized him by the collar and was ready to throw him off, but passengers intervened. Others joined in, people were screaming at one another as the tram clanked across the Main bridge, and Eilín and I disembarked at the first stop on the city side. I was wearing an army greatcoat, heavy as lead. It belonged to the baron and had been altered for me.

The British naval blockade was over, but there was still very little in the shops, and beggars were on nearly every street corner.

Eilín and I had made a pact to speak German and only German during our excursion. She was eager to reconnect with Frankfurt, which had been her first foreign city. She wanted to show me her old haunts: the opera house, where Lady Maire had often taken her to hear Wagner; the medieval Römerberg; the Städel art museum.

During the last months of the war British aviators had dropped, or hurled, a few small bombs on Frankfurt, but the damage was minuscule. Frankfurt was still a medieval town of narrow streets lined with timbered buildings. The German revolution was playing out mostly in Berlin and Munich, but occasionally we saw lorries packed with soldiers careening through the streets. Some troops were loyal to the new

German republic, some weren't. They all wore tattered field gray, and it was hard to tell them apart.

We visited the opera house and the zoo, explored the Dom, peeked in the tiny windows of Goethe's house. I flung our last few English pennies into the fountain on the Römerberg. From there we intended to walk back across the bridge, look at pictures in the Städel Museum, and treat ourselves to an enormous tea before catching the tram back to Walden.

We were close to the bridge when we turned a corner and came upon the bodies. It's possible they'd been executed right there—although now I think of it, we'd not heard any shooting, so they could have been dumped off the back of a truck.

Half-a-dozen bodies strewn on the sidewalk. Men and women. Blood pooling on cement, thick, black, glinting.

Fresh blood is the reddest of reds, but it can seem black, viewed at a certain angle with a certain refraction of light.

A blood-soaked fawn overcoat. A homburg hat rolled into the gutter. Yellow soles of upturned shoes.

One of the reasons her parents were sending Karin to an English boarding school was so she'd be safe if the German revolution turned as bloody as the Russian.

Eilín grasped my arm and turned us about, and we walked away in a hurry. Even in those winter days of chaos the trams operated on schedule. I don't have any memory of getting home or describing to Buck what we'd seen. Maybe my mother didn't tell him, afraid he would retreat again behind his barbed wire.

I'm sure I spent that evening on El Llano Estacado, tracking the text inch by inch, working my way into Germany.

⊳·◆·○·◆·⊲

You could say that in Frankfurt—probably England and France, too—the dead were in charge. Millions were walking about the cities with memories of dead sons, fathers, husbands operating painfully on their minds.

One gray, fuming morning on the playground of our *Grundschule*, a boy named Günter Krebs—slight, fair haired, in short pants—began jeering at me.

Billy Billy Billy! Billy das verdammte Engländer!

I had been at the school a couple of weeks. Günter Krebs hadn't bothered me before, but with the dead in charge one never knew what to expect.

El Llano Estacado had become my refuge. The High Plains were wide and empty enough to consume all the things I was afraid of during those first weeks in Germany. A sunburned warrior, I walked to school in moccasins, sometimes armed with my Apache bow, sometimes carrying my magic rifle. Practically all my classmates were already under Winnetou's spell, and I didn't waste any time before letting them know that my father, Buck, had been born on a ship bound for Texas. That he carried a pair of pistols, Colt six-shooters, one in each pocket of his coat, and taught me to ride on a silver-tooled saddle won from a railroad man in a poker game in Santa Fe.

Boys respect the fathers of their friends. Not having one is a handicap in the power politics of the school yard. Many boys had lost fathers to the war machine; they'd been machine gunned, gassed, vaporized by artillery barrage. I'd been fatherless at Muswell Hill and Sligo, but now I had him back. Not only that, my father was the boss—*Geschäftsführer*—of the Walden stud. Enormous prestige.

Because I had an impressive father, because I could say *llano* in a Spanish accent that sounded to them "American," because I was prepared to describe galloping my rugged Indian pony across the plains (no black iron fences on *el llano*), my *Grundschule* classmates proved willing, even eager, to accept me.

Niederrad, the half suburb, half village where I went to school, seemed almost colorless. Everything in Niederrad was gray: streets, air, sky, the tattered *feldgrau* tunics worn by trench survivors who couldn't afford new clothes. The only place for village kids to play was in the streets: the iron gates at Walden with their cornflowers-and-shamrock crest had always been shut to neighborhood children. But I had the run of the estate and was allowed to invite friends to play there, so long as we did not bother the horses.

Over the coming summer, in the Walden woods, we would become Apache, Comanche, Taos comancheros, frontiersmen. We'd blaze trails, track renegades, plan ambushes. Make camp, light fires, send smoke signals. Paint our faces with pigment from sample bottles the baron brought home from the color laboratories at Colora GmbH.

My classmates, soon to be my comrades—Robert Briesewitz, Hans Fischer, Bernhard Färber, Anselm Schuster, Hermann Fleck, Hermann Metzger, Joseph Baumberg—were passionate for rituals. For codes of honor. We all wanted to carry ourselves as warriors. In the Walden woods we would press bloody thumbs together and swear brotherhood. But even then there were still a few, like Günter Krebs, to whom I would always be *der verdammte Engländer.*

A warrior must act boldly and ruthlessly against his enemies, and that wintry morning in the school yard while Günter was singing out his reedy little chant, *"Billy Billy Billy! Billy das verdammte Engländer!"* I lowered my head and charged him, running as fast as I could, butting him in the chest and knocking him down. And all the others all saw me do it.

Winded, Krebs sat on his ass and sobbed for breath while my warrior brothers gathered around, taunting him. Taunting *him*, not *me*. For once I happened to be in the right place at the right time. I was a frontiersman, priest of the right cult, willing to make use of all the spurious associations my classmates wanted to attach to me.

During those first weeks at school in grim Niederrad I *was* the Wild West, and that was all the breathing room I needed. When the bell rang we trooped inside, boys patting me on the back, patting my shoulders, smiling at me.

My tribe.

The Winnetou cult faded as we grew older but it never died out. I'm certain some of my classmates, Indian braves and plainsmen to the last, were carrying copies of *Winnetou* in their haversacks on the frozen steppe twenty years later when they attacked and were attacked, when they killed and when they perished.

><

My father selected the animals—Hesperide, Festino, Henry of Navarre—that became the foundation of the famous Walden stud. Banned from England and Ireland himself, he pored over the registry books and bloodlines and chose the mares and stallions Weinbrenner would buy at Doncaster, Newmarket, and Kildare. By the end of our first year in Germany Buck was managing a staff of twenty trainers, grooms, and exercise riders. There was a veterinarian, a farrier, a saddler, each with his pack of journeymen and apprentices. In late summer, crews of peasants came from the hills to mow the meadows and make tons of Walden hay.

In March 1920, the ridiculous Kapp Putsch played out mostly in Berlin. For us *Grundschule* boys it meant no class for two or three days. I remember lying in bed at night and hearing occasional rifle shots from across the river, and longing for a rifle like Old Shatterhand's *Henrystutzen*, which could fire twenty-five rounds without reloading.

The German government refused to pay war reparations, and French troops briefly occupied Frankfurt in April. Our schoolmaster insisted we ignore them. We were to act as though they were invisible. But they existed, whether we acknowledged them or not; a squad of *képis* besieged on the Schillerplatz opened fire one day, killing five civilians, and my classmates wept from sheer hatred of the French. Ten-year-olds sobbed bitterly, while friends gathered round to console them. Boys hated so powerfully they couldn't speak, only howl.

I'll give you one day. Twenty-one months after the armistice. Summer of our first Walden-bred colts and fillies.

Walden. August 11, 1920. Early morning.

Everything quiet, peaceful. Slanted light. Dew steaming from grass.

A pair of grooms saddle a pair of young horses for the first time.

With only a snaffle bit, saddles are put on, and the two lightest riders on the place—myself and Karin Weinbrenner—are each given a leg up.

Karin was home from England on summer vacation. For the first two days she'd spoken only English to me. Since then, only German.

"Deutsch ist die richtige Sprache des Waldes," she insisted. German is the language of the forest.

She'd wanted to know if I'd been hunting with the Apache bow. She'd quizzed me on Winnetou lore.

"Was ist der Name von Winnetous Pferd?" Name of Winnetou's horse?

"Iltschi."

"Old Shatterhand's?"

"Hatatitla."

"Und was bedeutet das?" Meaning?

"*Es bedeutet Blitz.*" It means "Lightning."

August 11, 1920. Early morning, high summer. Insects chirping in the woods. I'm eleven years old and a horseman.

The day will be fiercely hot, but isn't yet. Karin and I wear matching fawn breeches, pale-blue cotton shirts, and mahogany-top boots made by the Belgian boot maker in Frankfurt. My father and mother, and the baron and Lady Maire, are watching.

My father's method of breaking young horses is *not* breaking them. Once we're aboard, the horses are merely led about under our weight, a groom with a leading rein on each side. Our job is to stay calm and steady, to communicate poise and confidence to the young animals. We mustn't do anything to spook them, or my father's curriculum of training will be upset, and the young racehorses might never reach their potential, might never be as good as they could be.

I don't intend to disappoint my father, and I don't. The exercise goes admirably. After fifteen minutes, we both slip down, and the grooms take over. Our horses are led back to the stable, where they'll be rubbed down and fed. Since they have been handled and taught obedience from the time they were foaled, this is all the breaking they will need. After two or three more walkabouts, always in the cool of early morning, professional riders will start taking them out alone, and after a month they'll be ridden in company, like other horses. Before they go off to be raced they'll gallop the Walden track, twenty-five-hundred meters straightway, with a regulation starting gate, so when they go to real racetracks for the first time they'll see nothing unusual to spook them.

We're asked to join the Weinbrenners at breakfast. My mother and Lady Maire are walking up the gravel avenue, arm in arm. My father and the baron compare notes on their young horses. And I'm enjoying the crisp crackle of my boot soles on gravel, while eavesdropping on a quarrel between Karin and her mother, who's insisting that Karin change out of riding clothes before joining us at breakfast.

"But I don't want to change, why must I? Billy isn't changing."

"Go and do as I say. And brush your hair and for once remember to wash your hands."

Karin ran ahead.

I loved my riding clothes. The feel of well-made horse boots on the leg was like nothing else. I felt lithe and powerful.

"More willful than ever!" I heard Lady Maire tell my mother. "I wonder if a French convent school might not be the best thing. During the war things were awkward here, such horrors, and I never could get a proper English governess, only a Viennese puppet who flirted with the officers. Karin's schooling has been irregular. I blame myself."

"She'll come round," my mother said.

"It's the Jewish blood. She's awfully like her father."

In the breakfast room we helped ourselves to eggs, ham, jellied meat. There were cheeses, basket of fresh rolls, silver pots of marmalade, and delicious strawberry jam. Coffee in a silver pitcher, fresh cream, cold milk. Champagne for the grown-ups. The breakfast room at Walden had more light, gleam, and spirit than anyplace else in the house except the library.

I was greedily stuffing down rolls slathered with strawberry jam when Karin slipped in and began helping herself from the buffet. She wore dowdy English schoolgirl clothes: a middy blouse, navy-blue skirt, red leather summer sandals. Her hair was an unkempt mop, chestnut with streaks of strawberry blonde.

The grown-ups were discussing which horse belonging to whom would take that year's Grand International d'Ostend. I saw Lady Maire throw an exasperated glance at her daughter. Karin ignored her mother and sat down and ate with gusto. The grown-ups were still talking racing when she finished and got up without saying a word and left.

><+♦>-0-<♦+<

Even for me it's hard to believe a person such as Lady Maire existed in my lifetime. Karin's mother's aristocratic chill, her stiff sense of duty, and her awesome reserve seem as historically remote as one of the carved saints she gathered, with my mother's help, from every corner of Europe.

Yet she was a real person. Her interests were Catholicism, though she had been raised an Irish Protestant; medieval art; and horses. She was much easier with horses than people. She knew how to handle horses, she was able to sense their moods, she always knew what they needed.

When Karin was small, she was desperate for physical contact with her mother. She told me it was like a terrible thirst, driving and intense, with an edge of panic. In the stables she used to watch her mother currying her old hunter Paddy with tender and meticulous care. Later, in the drawing room—the baroness rarely visited the nursery—she'd crawl into her mother's lap and plead to have her hair brushed. Lady Maire would dutifully start brushing, but Karin always could sense her distaste for such an intimate act. It was as if she had used up her affection on the son who had died and there was nothing left for Karin.

Her mother quickly tired of hair-brushing and would push her away. "There you are. Very pretty. Go and have Nanny tie you a ribbon."

And she'd use that same hairbrush to spank Karin when she was naughty.

She spoke softly to horses, but I can still hear her Anglo-Irish voice braying across the lawns, admonishing Karin for one infraction or another. A tonal blend of Wilhelmine-era *Hochdeutsch* with the innate bossiness of Anglo-Ireland, her voice rubbed practically everyone the wrong way.

"My mother is afraid no one will listen to her," Karin once remarked. "She believes it. So it becomes true."

One afternoon I watched Karin ferociously sweep snow from her brother's headstone. She used a broom made of twigs bunched and bound to a stick.

Her little brother had died in his first winter.

"So typical that my parents couldn't keep their damned great house warm enough for a little boy."

Karin could sound very bitter.

Lady Maire's tomb is in a little neighborhood church she endowed in a working-class section of Niederrad. The last time I visited, the whole structure seemed to cower under the screams of jets taking off and landing at Frankfurt Airport. All that survives of her art collection are a crucifix and altarpiece in the Niederrad chapel, both Istrian, fifteenth century; a half-dozen pieces at the Cloisters; the Stations of the Cross at the Getty in Los Angeles; and some chalices and chasubles at the Walters Art Museum in Baltimore. It's likely there are more pieces in private collections whose owners don't know their provenance or don't wish to acknowledge it.

Karin's mother could ride just about anything, or that's how it seemed to me, as an observant youngster around the stables. She communicated easily with horses and stayed out of touch with her daughter.

Karin was an accomplished rider, but Lady Maire was a superb horsewoman. There is something infuriating about a parent who can't be surpassed, but Karin kept trying. She was sixteen the first time she broke her shoulder, hunting in Shropshire with the Ludlow, a notoriously difficult country. Later that winter she was up and hunting again—she always would have something to prove.

Lady Maire had spent her childhood in ice-cold big houses in northwest Ireland. "If you wish to understand my mother's character," Karin once remarked, "you want to know that she comes from the hills. From the away of the away. They left her alone in one beastly damp house or another. Her only friends were housemaids and horses."

When Karin was in Berlin she used to insist she'd never for a second felt at home at Walden. "Impossible there, Billy. Too much money, too many ghosts, too much gloom."

"Wonderful horses, though."

"Yes," she'd agreed, "such wonderful horses, and one always dreamed to gallop away."

If you don't count the afternoon she set off swimming for America, Karin ran away for the first time during the war, when she was nine: creeping into the stables at dawn, saddling her favorite pony, and cantering off for the Taunus hills, where she hoped to persuade a peasant family to adopt her. Her mother dispatched little Oberleutnant Fröhlisch to bring her back. He caught up with her on the Sachsenhausen road and led her home. He told her he was sorry to do it—and she believed him. He said all persons ought to have the right to run away.

August 1920. Summer of the first Walden-bred racehorses. A few hours after that breakfast.

Solid heat of early afternoon. White sky. Humid.

Karin and I are standing at her brother's grave. All around us, the Walden woods, bleating and snapping with insect life.

Under what pretext had we come there? Can't remember. Maybe I'd encountered her on the bridle path, collecting berries. She could always get me to follow her.

I'm still wearing my riding habit. I didn't want to take those clothes off. My beautiful boots.

She's in her dowdy English-schoolgirl outfit.

Kicking off her red English sandals, she pulls off her schoolgirl straw hat with its striped ribbon, drops it on the grass. Then she starts pulling her white middy blouse over her head.

"*Fürchte dich nicht.*" Don't be afraid. Her voice muffled as she struggles with her blouse.

She keeps dropping her things on the grass. Undershirt. Navy-blue skirt. Bloomers.

"*Nehmen Sie Ihre vlothes, Billy, bitte.*" Take off your clothes, please.

I stand frozen.

Lying down on the grass, she stretches out, naked, eyes squeezed shut, her body narrow and white as a freshly peeled stick. I watch her fingers digging into the turf, as if the world is spinning like a centrifuge, and she has to hold on tight or be spun off.

The cemetery is the only grassy opening on the Walden estate that's not meadow or paddock or pasture.

"*Du musst keine Angst haben, Billy.*" Don't be afraid.

I feel torpid, mentally slow. I pull off my boots and start unbuttoning my blue shirt. This is no game, but the most serious thing I've ever contemplated or been asked to do. Drowning Albert Willspeed in the Hampstead ponds might have been as serious, but I'd been too fearful of the consequences to try, and anyway the opportunity had never presented itself.

I pull off my blue shirt, vest, breeches, and drawers and lie next to her on the prickly August grass. She reaches for my hand and gives it a squeeze. The sun's light and heat is spinning me, disordering my thoughts, and I feel the ground ripple and heave. I keep my eyes shut.

The experience is tantalizing, thrilling, and upsetting, without being exactly sexual.

After a while I can hear her breathing deeply. Has she fallen asleep? Suddenly she sits up.

"I'm losing my head," she says.

I open my eyes. She scrambles to her feet. So I do as well.

"Aha! *Schau dich mal an*, Billy." Look at you.

I was a skinny kid. I was self-conscious about it but there was nothing to do about it, I couldn't possibly eat more than I already did.

"You're taller since last year," she says. "You'll be a tall one like your beautiful father. Who wants to be small like my little pa? He'd rather have been grenadier than *Uhlan*, but you need to stand over six feet in socks to be accepted into that regiment. *Bist du stark*, Billy?"

Are you strong?

I knew boys stronger. But I was stronger than some.

"I am."

"Enough to carry me? Come. *Versuchen wir es.*" Let's try it. "I wish you to carry me around this place one time."

"What for?"

She touches my shoulder, like an experienced rider touching the horse before throwing her leg over.

"I just want you to."

"But why?"

"I don't know. Come, I'm not so much to carry. Come." Then she gives a little skip, and I catch her legs, and suddenly she's in my arms.

"Carry me. Just carry me. Carry me like I'm your child."

"Where?"

She doesn't answer. So I carry her around the perimeter of the grassy cemetery, neither of us saying a word.

Weird scene, I agree. Inchoate desire, at least on my part. That doesn't mean not real.

Prickly grass underfoot, both of us naked. Don't ask where I got the strength. But from that time forward I would be her faithful steed. Her warhorse.

"That's enough. Now please to put me down."

As soon as I do so, she turns her back, starts pulling on her clothes. She seems embarrassed all of a sudden.

"You don't have to look at me. Get dressed, Billy. Hurry! Before someone comes along."

And I am embarrassed, too, and hurriedly begin to dress.

"You won't tell anyone." She sounds anxious. "You won't tell my mother, yes? Promise you will not."

"Yes. No. I promise."

"Swear it on the heart."

"I swear it."

"Not a word to anyone, Billy."

"Not a word."

We walk up the bridle path without speaking until we come to the cross where our paths part.

"I know you I can trust. Goodbye, Billy." She offers her hand and looks me in the eye as we shake. Her eyes pale gray.

She returned to England a few days later, and I don't believe I saw her again until the following summer.

In 1922, right-wing nationalists assassinated Germany's foreign minister, Walter Rathenau, while he was being driven to work. He was a Jew. On his visits to Walden Lady Maire always tried in vain to get him up on a horse. Rathenau had recruited the baron to the committee negotiating war reparations with the Allies, a dangerous assignment for Weinbrenner, because it made him, too, a target. All Germany hated reparations.

One bitter-cold morning in the autumn after the Rathenau assassination, we boys were standing on the steps at school waiting for the doors to open when Günter Krebs announced that Germany had lost the war because of a bet the Frankfurt Jews made with the Jews of London.

We were stamping our feet against the cold, impatient for the bell to ring and the doors to swing open so we could shove our way inside.

"You see, fellows, they each wagered on the other country to win. Each tribe figured they could fix the fight! Yids are utterly ruthless."

Günter's father was a lawyer who became an important city official after the NSDAP took power.

It wasn't much warmer inside our school than out. Strikes and political demonstrations against the French occupation of the Ruhr meant frequent shortages of coal. On days when the furnace wasn't being fed we were permitted to wear overcoats and scarves in the classroom, even gloves and hats.

"Our tribe of Jews caused the defeat of Germany and collected millions of pounds in reward. They were able to stab in the back the best army the world had ever seen."

"That's a load of trash!" Kracauer, one of three Jews in our class, spoke up. "My old man served at the front. All he collected was a packet of metal in his legs. You're a *Pappnase*, Krebs."

False nose, liar.

Kracauer was smaller than Günter Krebs and, at that time, considerably more popular. He was a good athlete. His parents owned a shop that sold handsome leather luggage. Most of us carried our schoolbooks slung on a strap but Kracauer had a smart leather briefcase with brass fittings.

"One of the tribe," Günter jeered. "A Yid is hardly likely to bleat the truth."

Günter was tall for his age, but, like many children who'd survived near-famine during the last months of the war, he was quite scrawny. His teeth were crooked and brown.

"And you've the brains of a headless chicken!" Kracauer replied.

The doors swung open. We stampeded inside and that was the end of that particular debate.

We used to play football in the road after school. The ball belonged to Weinberg, richest boy in the school. Footballs were expensive. Weinberg was chauffeured to school every morning in his father's red Mercedes.

One afternoon—it was raining, rain was freezing on the road, but we were still playing—Kracauer gave Weinberg's leather ball a good hard kick and smacked Günter Krebs in the head so hard that he sat down in the middle of the road and began weeping, a stream of snot flowing from his nose.

Kracauer had been trying to boot in a goal; he hadn't meant to knock Günter for a loop. We were embarrassed by Krebs's display, which seemed babyish to us. A couple of boys began helping him to his feet. Then all of a sudden Günter, windmilling his fists, launched at Kracauer. "Yid! Yid! Bloody cheater!"

Streaming snot and tears, swinging wildly, Günter obviously wasn't much of brawler.

Kracauer backed away, laughing, refusing to engage. Then a horn sounded—Weinberg's limousine pulled up. Weinberg grabbed his football, and he and his pals, including Kracauer, piled into the red limo and drove off, and Krebs was left there, sobbing and coughing. A couple of boys stood with him, but I started for home. This vulnerability of his embarrassed me. I always wanted to get away.

Then there was the famous upset in the river.

Rowing was a German-schoolboy passion. Many of us already belonged to junior clubs. Rowing sweeps on the river Main on a cold May afternoon, Günter got his oar tangled with some others, which upset his boat's rhythm, and a moment later it turned into the current and spilled, dumping the crew into the river.

The current wasn't much—the boys swam ashore pushing their boat—but they were soaked and furious and blamed Günter for the upset. When he began hoisting himself onto the float, his crewmates kept pushing him back into the water. They wouldn't let him climb out. He panicked and began shouting for help.

I thought it pretty cruel, but it wasn't my boat, or my crew.

A policeman looking down from the bridge blew his whistle, and the boys finally let Günter drag himself out. He must have swallowed a good deal of water, and he missed school for a week.

It was after that that Kracauer, in English class, first started calling Günter Krebs "Ducky." The name stuck, perhaps because Günter had such a distinctive gait, walking with his toes pointed out. Like a duck, he waddled.

Years later in the Translation Department at IG Farben, men were still calling him Ducky.

Three Jews in our class: Kracauer, Weinberg, and Koch. Koch was a Hungarian, timid, bespectacled, and brilliant at math, who never said a word to anyone. He was murdered at Auschwitz. Weinberg's father owned one of the department stores. Weinberg *fils* was generous and not at all stuck up. If he saw classmates walking to school in the morning, or waiting for trams, he always had the chauffeur pull over and gave them a lift. At school there'd be a dozen boys packed into the Mercedes, shouting and wrestling as they piled out, an uproarious mob. Even Günter Krebs accepted lifts in Weinberg's Mercedes.

><+>-0-<+><

Karin came home for a few weeks every summer. In 1923 the baron had a swimming pool and tennis court built for her at Walden, and I was enlisted as her tennis partner. Lady Maire had my mother order tennis flannels for me, and Karin told her which racket to buy.

Karin preferred to play very early in the morning, before the day got too hot. My father would rouse me, I'd pull on my whites, stumble out of the house, grab my bicycle from the shed, and pedal hard to the tennis court. She was always there first, impatiently banging balls off the backboard. "What is the matter with you, Billy Lange, can't you ever get here on time?"

After tennis we would go swimming and lie in the sun discussing Karl May or other writers, if she felt like talking.

No one at her boarding school cared for Winnetou. The English girls preferred reading magazines about American film stars.

I lay on the chaise longue, a skinny boy, undeveloped, brown from summer, and watched Karin Weinbrenner swim lengths of the pool. It occurred to me that my confusion, stupor, might mean I was in love with her. And this was an astounding revelation. I didn't wish to be in love. Not with her, not with anyone. I had other things to do. I preferred the raucous company of schoolfellows, my tribe. I certainly didn't need to be in love with a girl.

She pulled herself out of the pool, picked up her towel, and that was when we both heard the scream.

My first thought was *Horse down, broken leg.* In the spring a colt had gone down with a shattered foreleg, and my father shot him. He allowed me to watch, and I stood with a somber bunch of grooms, trainers, and stableboys as Buck held the Browning pistol to the colt's forehead, took aim along the spine, and pulled the trigger. That was how death was delivered: quickly. *"Den Gnadenschuss geben,"* the men called it. The mercy shot. Death in an instant.

More screams, but now recognizably human, German, and female.

Then a batch of furious masculine shouting.

"That's Solomon and Herta, winding up," Karin said. She was drying herself with a towel. "He's beating her again, the cur."

The brick garage/coach house where the chauffeur Solomon Dietz and his Sorb wife, Herta, lived was across the lawn and down the avenue a little way. The one-eyed chauffeur was one of the few Walden employees who did not report to my father. Solomon was like an ogre out of a German folktale, rude and surly to everyone. He was a veteran front soldier, a Jew, and an active member of the Reichsbanner, the Social Democrat street fighters' organization. Solomon Dietz considered himself the baron's bodyguard and always kept a Browning pistol tucked under the front seat of the Mercedes.

"That man's not all right in the head," Lady Maire had cautioned my mother. "The war has scrambled him up. Do be careful."

More screams and shouting.

"Aren't you going to do something, Billy?" Karin said.

My father tried to have as little to do with Solomon as possible. Me? What could I do? I was a boy. Solomon was a man.

"Well then," Karin remarked, "if you won't, I must."

Wrapping the towel around her bathing costume Karin picked up her tennis racket in its press and started for the coach house. I caught her scent—chlorine and a trace of eau de cologne. Her father had recently given her a bottle of eau de cologne, to which her mother had objected.

Of course I had to follow. Had to demonstrate pluck. Though I didn't feel plucky. I was barefoot and wearing a bathing costume. My tennis shoes were in the cabana—no time to put them on.

Karin was already climbing up the rickety outside staircase that led to the chauffeur's apartment above the garage.

Another scream. By the time I reached the bottom of the stairs, she was pounding the door with her fist.

She looked down at me and grinned. "What if they're in bed together?"

Her skin was brown with summer, freckled across the nose and cheeks. Her teeth were white. Her thick, rough chestnut hair was bluntly cut and streaked red and golden by sun.

I started upstairs. Another shout, a blow, another scream.

"What say you, Billy Lange? Perhaps they are in bed having fun."

"It doesn't sound like fun."

Standing next to her, again I smelled her scent. She pounded the door with her fist. *"Herta? Was ist das Problem? Was ist los dadrinnen?"*

She tried the door, and it opened.

The chauffeur's apartment was like a hut in some peasant village on the steppe, floor and walls painted bright red lacquer and decorated with painted wildflowers. Solomon stood with his back to the kitchen sink and his forearm crooked around Herta's throat. His eye patch was askew and the hollow of his empty eye socket was purple, like a bruise.

"Lass sie gehen, du Verbrecher!" Karin ordered him.

Instead of releasing his wife, Solomon tightened his choke hold. She flailed her arms and made croaking sounds. Stepping forward, Karin struck Solomon with her tennis racket, banging at his neck and shoulders until he had to let Herta go. Gasping and coughing, Herta tried to seize the racket from Karin.

"No, no, Herta!" Karin warned.

"Du Bastard! Ich schneide dir deinen Schwarz ab!" Herta lunged for a kitchen knife but Karin swung the tennis racket and knocked the knife off the table along with a bottle of schnapps which smashed on the floor.

Karin started pushing Herta toward the door. The husband and wife were screaming curses at each other. The room smelled of schnapps. Karin got Herta out the door and began forcing her down the steps. Herta kept trying to start back up, but Karin wouldn't let her. I was afraid Solomon would come out after us but he didn't appear.

At the bottom of the stairs Herta was kissing our hands. Maybe she was drunk.

"That brute will murder her one day," Karin said. "My father must get rid of him. Come along, Herta."

I watched them going along the birch-lined avenue that led to the main house, Karin in her bathing costume with her white towel wrapped around her waist.

Her father, of course, was never going to fire his ultra-loyal, very well-armed chauffeur-bodyguard, not after Walter Rathenau had been murdered in his car on his way to work.

Herta turned down the baron's offer of a train ticket to Berlin, excellent references and enough money to get a room of her own, and returned to the apartment above the coach house in time to fix her husband's lunch.

><>-O-<>-<

The newspapers had printed a "death list" found in the pocket of Rathenau's assassin, with Hermann Weinbrenner's name on it. After that, my father and Solomon—and occasionally the baron—would walk deep into the Walden woods to take weekly target practice. The chauffeur had begged my father to accept a Belgian Browning pistol and practice shooting so that he could help defend the baron from reactionaries.

Buck insisted they go as far from the stables as possible because he didn't want to spook the mares. The men blasted at paper targets pinned to tree stumps. I was a better marksman than any of them—but a good bow, once you know how to use it, is always more accurate than a pistol.

Then my father decided I might as well learn to use a pistol and showed me how to load a magazine and slide it into the butt of the Browning. Those nine-millimeter cartridges were shiny little dead-weights, cold and greasy to the touch. He demonstrated flipping off the thumb safety and drawing back the slide, then handed the weapon to me.

"Fire when ready!"

The pistol had a strong kick, and I emptied my first magazine without hitting the target once. But over the summer my aim improved. The pistols spat out brass cartridges which it was my job to collect from the forest floor.

Just before she returned to school I taught Karin to shoot. We used my father's Browning. He approved, and so did the baron. Walter Rathenau's blood had spilled over everything, or at least over the lives of rich Frankfurt Jews. It was nearly five years since the end of the war, and the baron was about to publish the first volume of his memoirs. No one reads his *Lebenserinnerungen U. Politische Denkwürdigkeiten* these days, but the books touched a raw nerve in Germany of the 1920s. Using official documents, including Foreign Office telegrams, Weinbrenner argued that Germany had been chiefly responsible for the world war and that it was bunglers in Berlin, including the kaiser, who brought about the *debacle* of August 1914.

After the first volume appeared the right-wing papers began referring to Karin's father as *der verräterische Judenbaron*—the Jewish traitor baron—and then the nationalists really got him in their sights.

An automatic pistol is no marksman's weapon, but Karin's aim improved very quickly. Something about gunfire seemed to calm her instead of flustering her, which is how it usually affects people who aren't accustomed to it. At first we shot at paper targets and pieces of old crockery, but that didn't satisfy her. She said she wanted something "human" to shoot at.

"Something with a scent of human, at least."

Returning to the main house, she came back with an armful of her own dresses. It made me uneasy when she began draping them over tree branches.

"All right, dear Billy, let's load and fire."

"Are you sure?"

"Silly old frocks. Let's make use of them."

"You could give them away."

"Of course, of course, I could," she said impatiently. "I'll give away plenty, give away everything, but these I want to shoot. Come, dear Billy, please hand me the pistol and show me again how to load it."

I loaded and reloaded, and we took turns firing at her things. Sometimes a bullet took a dress down, whipped it to the ground, like a bird killed in midflight. Sometimes bullets tore through the fabric but left the dress hanging, fluttering from the impact. Karin was calm and steady and shot very well for a beginner. Afterward she gave me the pistol to clean, and we shook hands, and the next morning she started back to England.

She had one more year at boarding school, then her parents packed her off to a finishing school at Lausanne.

※ 1938

"Billy! *hier bitte!*"

I was wandering the Walden grounds, floating on a weird mood of nostalgia and self-importance, when I encountered Karin on the bridle path.

In her narrow slippers and her fitted Harris Tweed overcoat she looked very sleek and *mondän*, very Berlin, very out of place. Her mother had crammed the estate with medieval iconography, her father bred the fastest thoroughbreds in Europe, her brother was buried in a clearing with six young soldiers from the war—but Karin had always insisted she felt more herself in other places.

"Whatever have you been doing with yourself, Billy? I watched you coming up the drive an hour ago!"

"Oh, just wandering. Trying to get my fill."

I reminded her we had an appointment at the American consulate in Köln in two days—Kop had made it for us. We needed our passports stamped with tourist visas so that we could drive across the United States.

She linked arms with me. "I regret my Berlin," she said.

"There's nothing for you there these days."

But I knew I'd miss Berlin, too. Weekends in the metropolis had always left me humming like an electrified wire. We'd never had more than two or three days together, I'd always wanted more, but what we had seemed enough for her. I possessed her physically, but on every occasion she possessed far more of me.

She said, "Whatever fails you, Billy, you miss the most."

We started back toward the house. I was not looking forward to the interview with her father. Almost everything he owned had been looted by the regime, and now I was stealing his daughter.

When I was a boy, and she offered them to me, I had taken in the Winnetou stories as delicious fantasy. Until one afternoon when I was ten or eleven, leafing through a North American atlas, *Ortsverzeichnis von Nordamerika*, in the baron's library. That's when I saw the words

L L A N O   E S T A C A D O

strewn across an otherwise empty map of West Texas and eastern New Mexico and realized that the landscape of Winnetou actually *existed*. For me, this was a great, wonderful shock—like finding God listed in the Frankfurt telephone directory.

But Karin had always understood *el llano* was real space. She'd started collecting books and scholarly articles when she was a girl. She read everything she could get her hands on having to do with that country.

"The point of *el llano*, Billy," she remarked, one morning in Charlottenburg, "is that this is the world we should much prefer. It's bare and clean. There's nothing infected. Out on *el llano* one might climb on a horse and ride for days with the sun and the wind. That's salvation, if you ask me."

After five years of Hitler's Germany, the idea of crossing *el llano* together seemed to offer—I won't say salvation, but cleansing. Caustic sunlight and dry desert heat, to burn the drag of history from our wings.

The bridle path was unkempt, with overhanging branches that might have knocked an unwary rider from the saddle. But no one rode the Walden bridle paths anymore. The horses were gone; so were the foresters. Maybe they were all working in IG Farben plants, synthesizing airplane fuel or buna rubber. Maybe they'd all been scooped up by the army.

Walden was never a handsome house, and with the brown leaves of November blowing helter-skelter across the shaggy, untended lawns it looked gloomier than ever.

"He's waiting to see you in the library."

Karin ran upstairs before I thought to ask if she'd told her father she was pregnant.

When I entered the library the little baron was sitting behind Admiral Spee's enormous mahogany desk, which for some reason the city had left behind when it expropriated the rest of the furnishings.

Baron Hermann von Weinbrenner sat with hunched shoulders, like a windblown little hawk perched on a wire. He'd once seemed ageless: brown and tough as a walnut. After his wife's death he started losing weight. Now he seemed meager and frail.

"America at last!" he croaked. *"Hurra!"*

His bookshelves were stripped bare but for his collection on Jewish history and philosophy. I suppose the dealers who helped themselves to the rest of his books had not dared express any interest in those. And there was also the shelf of Karin's old Winnetou books, popular editions, probably too battered and common to interest the bookmen.

"We really must get out, sir."

"Good for you! I'm delighted to learn you've taken matters into your hands."

"It's time."

"Of course it is."

"I'm sorry."

"For what are you sorry?"

The library had been his aerie, locus of his power. It was where he'd offered my father a new career, and all three of us a new life. It was where he'd written the memoirs that made him such a target, *der verräterische Judenbaron.*

When I was a boy, his library seemed the most powerful room in the world.

"I'm sorry to be taking Karin so far away."

"I'm not sorry! Berlin's a dreadful place, worse than ever, I hear. America—your father's American born, is he not?"

"Not exactly."

"I expect to see you back in Germany after this bunch of petit-bourgeois finaglers, Rasputins, and champagne salesmen go to the wall. They can't last much longer, the generals have had a bellyful of the corporal and are getting ready to shit him out. Anyway, they can't bother me anymore. From me they already have everything. I recognize it's quite time that my daughter flew from this increasingly filthy cage, however. I wish I could write a good-sized check to send her off with, but I can't."

"I have a job waiting in Canada."

"Yes, yes, good for you. When I was a young man, I imagined going out to Canada. Some did. One of these days the army's going to knock that fellow off his perch, you know. The Germans won't stand him much longer. You'll see. The army will put him up against the wall, and then—who knows? Who'll heal Germany? The old kaiser? Well, I loved him in his day, but he was an absolute nincompoop. Not wicked, mind you, but he was never master of himself, and he was terribly angry at his poor English mother. Not such a good combination for Germany."

"We have your blessing, then?"

"My blessing?" He shrugged. "You want that? From an old Jew? It isn't worth anything. But if you want it, take it. My blessing? Ha! A bank draft on Mr. Morgan's bank would serve you better! At one time I could have managed it. Not now. Yes. Care for my daughter. Care for each other. Don't forget your people in Germany."

THE DANUBIAN ODDBALL

Lady Maire acquired her Ford in the spring of 1927. The baron's chauffeur, Solomon Dietz, taught my mother to drive and to perform maintenance and small repairs. The women were planning a summer motor trip through Spain.

On previous expeditions Solomon had driven them in the Mercedes, but he'd been thrown in jail the summer before after brawling with French army recruits at Avignon, and Lady Maire had made up her mind to do without him. So she bought the black Ford, and my mother practiced her driving on hilly roads in the Taunus.

My grandmother Con was due to arrive at Walden a few days before Lady Maire and my mother left for Spain. Aunt Kate, who'd married a rich grazier, kept an eye on things at Wychwood and had written to say there was now more sky than slate in the roof of the house. In her opinion, Con couldn't possibly last another season there.

Buck wrote inviting his mother to come to live with us at Newport cottage. To his surprise Con accepted the invitation. He arranged that she travel out to Germany in the company of a famous mare, Lovely Morn, that had belonged to her old friend Sir Charles Butler of the Knockmealdown Stud, county Galway. Charlie Butler was dead, and his stable was being sold off at Tattersalls. My father had seen Lovely Morn win the Grand International d'Ostende. He wanted her for a broodmare, and the baron had wired an offer straight to Knockmealdown, which was accepted.

Con hadn't left county Sligo in years, and Buck was concerned that the journey by train to Dublin, steamer to Liverpool, train across England to Hull, steamer to Rotterdam, and train to Frankfurt via Köln might be too much for her. So he'd asked if Charlie Butler's groom, who was bringing the mare to Germany, might keep an eye on my grandmother as well.

The three traveled together, and on a shiny August morning Eilín drove us to Frankfurt Hauptbahnhof in the Ford to meet them. Karin and her beau Longo came with us. One-eyed Solomon followed, driving the horse van.

After Lausanne Karin had spent part of a year in Paris before her parents agreed to her living in Berlin with an allowance, quite unsupervised. My parents were surprised. According to my mother, Karin was "running wild" in Berlin. Twice we'd heard she was engaged, but both engagements had been broken off.

Longo was her latest beau and, from the Walden point of view, her first acceptable suitor.

Cycling past the tennis court at dawn early one morning, I'd heard a ball slapping against a backboard. Karin was alone, hitting vigorous forehands and backhands. She wore a sleeveless black evening dress. She was barefoot. When she saw me, she waved her racket.

"How are you, old Billy?" she called.

I stopped my bike. "Hello, Karin."

"Are you growing up all right? You're quite handsome, you know. Are you going to become a horseman like your lovely father?"

She was spending only a couple of weeks at Walden. Berlin was supposed to be stifling in summer, and no doubt she missed the Walden horses, the swimming pool, the scents of balsam and sweet hay. Lady Maire rode her hunter to early morning Mass at the Catholic church in Niederrad, and I'd seen Karin with her a couple of times, mother and daughter clip-clopping along the gray village streets. Karin would have been nineteen, just.

"Much too young to be off by herself in a wicked city like Berlin!" my mother said.

"I don't think I'll ever be that much of a rider," I told Karin. "Unless I find a horse like Hatatitla. If I do I'll steal her and strike out across *el llano*."

"Good for you! I'll come with you, Billy! Across *el llano* together."

She didn't mean anything by it, wasn't even flirting, just tossing a light line across the gap—in experience, in worldliness—that separated us. Or that's what I told myself then.

After a stunned moment, I pedaled away. I had a job that summer as an office boy for the baron's lawyer, Herr Kaufman, and was in the habit of stopping at a Parisian-style café on the Friedberger Landstraße to sip café au lait and read *Le Figaro*, the *Daily Telegraph*, or the *Paris Herald Tribune*. Reading foreign newspapers made me feel like myself, or the man I wanted to be. I didn't feel like myself at Kaufman's. My father had set up that arrangement. He had hopes I would choose the law for a career, but that was never going to happen. I didn't know who I was, but sipping a café au lait and reading the *Paris Herald*, I was at least trying to get into character, like an out-of-work actor auditioning for a role.

›—‹◊›—○—‹◊›—‹

Oberleutnant Fröhlisch had taught Karin to play ragtime during the war. And Longo actually was a decent player; he and Karin did a lively four-handed "Saint Louis Blues." They listened to jazz records in her father's library late at night and danced the shimmy. They'd roll up the rug and push the windows open wide, and I could hear the nervous music floating across the lawn along with their laughter.

Sometimes late at night Karin played Chopin with the windows flung open. Once I lay out on the cold grass and imagined she was playing those nocturnes for me.

Longo's real name was Paul von Müller-Languedoc. He got on well with everyone. The Weinbrenners were relieved he wasn't a wild Berlin bohemian.

My mother was applying salve to his saber scar when Longo announced he was going to marry Karin Weinbrenner when she "settled down."

"Karin is a yearling, the yearlings are always crazy. You can break them or let them run. I shall let our beautiful Karin run. And when she has run herself out, I shall marry her."

Longo had acquired his scar, his *Schmiss*, at Heidelberg, where he was studying law. Ritualized sword fighting—the *Mensur*—was a big deal for students in fraternal *Brüderschaften*. For those too young to have fought in the war, the *Mensur* was a slice of savagery they could have for their very own.

Longo's *Schmiss* was on his left temple, running from the corner of his mouth almost to his ear. A *Schmiss* was supposed to be proof of a manly and fearless character. Even my middle-class schoolmates at the Klinger-Oberrealschule in Frankfurt, aiming to be businessmen or engineers, could hardly wait to join a university *Korps* of some sort. We heard stories of young men cutting themselves with razors to simulate saber scars.

Longo's scar was fresh and raw. It wasn't healing neatly. Sometimes young men disturbed the healing process deliberately; they wanted scars as ugly as possible. Karin called it the bug—"What is that horrid bug doing on your pretty face, Longo?"

He was proud of his *Schmiss*, and I think it annoyed him that Karin didn't seem impressed.

>-⟶-○-⟨⟶-⟨

When we reached the train yards that morning we were told the wagon with the Irish mare had been detached and pushed onto a siding.

As my father and I approached the wagon, a young man leaped down. He had on a suit of tweed, with a cap, and a silk scarf around his neck, and horse boots. A cigarette hung at his lips, but he tossed it away before shaking hands with my father.

"Have you traveled well?" Buck asked.

"I have," the groom replied. "And herself as well, for a country girl." Then he grinned at me. "Any salmon running hereabouts?"

And that was when I recognized my Sligo companion-in-arms, Mick McClintock.

Later I learned that it was my grandmother who told Charlie Butler to hire Mick for a stableboy. He'd worked his way up to the position of head groom at Knockmealdown and had been handling Lovely Mare since she was foaled.

My father understood the angst caused by uprooting and dislocation, and he believed animals were vulnerable to that sorrow as well. That was why he'd asked that a Knockmealdown groom accompany Lovely Morn on the journey. Mick McClintock was actually leaving Ireland for good—he was emigrating to America—but it had been arranged that he would see the mare settled at Walden first. In exchange, the baron was paying Mick's passage from Bremerhafen to New York.

We shook hands. Mick McClintock had the strong grip of a point-to-point rider, accustomed to holding horses to stone fences and wild country. He was medium height and leathery. I was tall, frail, and frequently stumbled over my own large feet. The boyhood we'd shared at Sligo seemed remote.

Mick's brown tweeds were rough and horsey. I wore plus fours and a schoolboy's white blouse with a necktie. I wasn't allowed to go anywhere in my father's company unless I wore a necktie: it was one of Buck's iron laws. Over the years he'd grown increasingly obsessive about attire. The baron, the richest man in Frankfurt, might wear the same ragged green-and-blue polo jersey day after day, but English worsted suits, crisp collars, and a pale-gray homburg on his head were essential to my father's sense of himself. If he wasn't wearing one of the elegant suits made by his English tailor in Hamburg, perhaps he feared he'd be mistaken for a prisoner or a deportee. Tweeds, brogans, and a soft-collared shirt were just acceptable for a Sunday walk in the Taunus hills, but that was as dishabille as you'd ever see Buck Lange. And he spent at least an hour and a half every week polishing his boots. Not only his, my mother's and mine as well. This adds up to three days per year. And that's a month out of each decade, polishing boots.

In some ways his imprisonment never did end.

In my gawky regalia I felt like a schoolboy next to Mick. His handsome clothes and the raffish way he wore them, his Sweet Afton cigarettes, the confident manner in which he addressed my father, one horseman to another . . . Mick McClintock was a person out of another country. And I don't mean Ireland, but a territory I'd imagined though not yet visited, the unclaimed region of experience, savoir faire, knowledge.

I'd never seen Longo shake hands with grooms or exercise riders at Walden, but that morning he shook hands with Mick. Longo was impressed by anything authentically English, and "Irish" was just a more intense form of Englishness as far as he was concerned. Longo was a snob, but he could sense that Mick McClintock wasn't going to be a groom for the rest of his life.

"Well, aren't you something wild!"

I looked up to see my grandmother Con standing in the door of the train wagon, with all the powerful eccentricity I remembered from Sligo still attached to her. She was tall and rangy and brown in the face as all Irish country people seemed to be. Her tweed suit had bits of hay and straw stuck to it, but she had the radiance of a powerful person, strong willed and physically striking, though she was in her seventies by then.

I would have liked to be wild, but wasn't. When I wasn't sipping my *bol* of café au lait and looking at foreign newspapers, I ran Herr Kaufman's messages, sorted the post, emptied the wastebaskets, and flirted meekly with the lawyer's youngest secretary, name of Heidi. Every now and then Kaufman handed me a contract to proofread. The work of a lawyer seemed to mostly involve reading and rereading paragraphs of High German legalese until they began to blur, until they achieved perfect meaninglessness and read like a transcription of monkey chatter.

I was eighteen. Women were not real to me. Even Karin. Not then. I wasn't even a practical enough or normal enough adolescent to fantasize having sex. In my most daring fantasies she and I were riding across boundless open country together, Texas or New Mexico, under wide blue sky.

That morning in the Frankfurt freight yards, I had to listen to Longo pointing out all Lovely Morn's qualities to Karin while Mick led the nervous, whickering mare down the ramp.

"See, from the size of the nostrils you can tell her volume of air intake, it means she has the raw ability, the heart power, so she can run. Ears alert, see them twitching, and bright eyes—it means she has a good brain, she knows how we are watching her. Broad chest, yes. Good hips, yes, cannon bones not very long, big feet—this hints that your mare is a wonderful runner."

Longo knew horses, I have to admit. Lovely Morn *was* a beauty. She would be a great success at Walden. At least two of her foals, Desmond and Herald, were Deutsche Derby winners.

While Longo was showing off his equine knowledge, Buck was helping his mother down from the horse wagon. Con had insisted on traveling in the windowless wagon after Duisburg, so that Mick, who'd never been out of Ireland before, could take her seat in a second-class carriage and see something of Germany.

"Oh, Buck, my own!" my grandmother crooned. "A beautiful man you are."

They'd not seen each other in nearly twenty years. Buck *was* beautiful then. He had the gift of becoming more slender each year. He took only a single glass of Rhine wine or beer in the evening while looking at the *Vossische Zeitung*, or reading the baron's memoirs. He rode every day, and on Sundays we often went hiking in the Taunus. We ate well, fresh food, some of it grown right there on the estate. The famous Walden pears were a staple for us.

My Irish grandmother, on the other hand, looked . . . unique, and gallant, but poor. As in destitute. A piece of the lining drooped from the hem of her tweed skirt, her stockings were all wrinkles, her brogues were cracked and ancient. At Wychwood she had been lady of the manor, even if the manor was falling down, but she had come out of Ireland with only a suitcase, an ancient leather baggage my father strapped to the Ford's running board while Mick coaxed the anxious mare into the horse van, and Solomon stood glowering and puffing one of the baron's cigars. The chauffeur distrusted horses.

Mick was going to ride in the horse van with Solomon. Karin, Longo, and my grandmother crowded into the backseat of the Ford. My parents and I squeezed into the front seat, with Eilín at the wheel and me in the middle, gearshift between my legs. The canvas top was up to give us some protection from the noon sun. The seats were button-tufted black leather and there was a not-unpleasant aroma of steel, engine lubricant, and horse. My mother set the advance and kicked the starter button. The engine rattled to life.

Eilín was just shifting into gear when Karin in the backseat said, "Hold up, please, Frau Lange."

I twisted around to see her opening her door. She was climbing out.

"I shall catch a ride in the van," she said, "and leave you a bit more room!"

Longo started to protest, but she ignored him and shut the door. I watched her approach the cab of the horse van and say something to Mick in the passenger seat. He jumped down and helped her climb in. Then Mick got back in himself, shut the door, and gave us a thumbs-up. Eilín let out the Ford's clutch, Longo sighed, and with a jerk and sputter we all set off for Walden.

I don't know how thoroughly my parents had discussed Con coming to live with us. She had given birth to the *bucko seaman* one thousand miles off the Pacific coast of Mexico, brought him ashore to the Barbary Coast of San Francisco, and made agreeable if chaotic childhood homes for him at Melbourne and Hamburg. But they'd spent most of their adult lives in different countries, writing letters back and forth. They weren't familiar with each other, whereas my mother and I, after our time at Wychwood during the war, thought we understood Con pretty well. She was poetic and romantic and disorganized and enjoyed spending money she didn't have. She liked to gamble. She could be supercilious, snobbish. We knew she had no interest in housekeeping and was not fastidious in her personal habits. She smoked cigarettes while reading in bed and more than once had fallen asleep and set the mattress on fire.

Con had Anglo-Irishness, horsemanship, and hunting in common with Karin's mother, and maybe that was what drew Karin to Con, especially as Con radiated a warmth the baroness lacked. When Karin was at Walden she and my grandmother occasionally had tea in Con's upstairs sitting room. And they often rode the bridle paths together.

My grandmother borrowed money. From Karin. Small amounts, which Con bet on horses. She loved to gamble but never would bet against a Walden runner—that was a matter of principle with her. When she was flush she sometimes took Karin into Frankfurt and repaid her with extravagant lunches.

My father, Buck, was a most-meticulous, punctilious person. He structured his days with routines and rituals. My father was aware of the speed of life, how life seems to beg all questions and deliver no answers. Four and a half years had been taken from him and not given back. I think he still felt *empty* sometimes, and he had learned to use ritual and routine to get himself through those spells.

Routines and schedules were irritations to my grandmother Con, who had trouble with numbers and never could keep track of time. Buck was born at sea because she'd completely miscalculated her due date.

Con often went days without sitting down to a meal. She never ate breakfast, and breakfast was one of my father's rituals. Every morning he ate an orange and a slice of rye toast with bitter marmalade, but without butter, which he despised. He drank two small cups of black coffee. At the breakfast table he looked at the *Frankfurter Zeitung* and didn't like to share it with me, though if there'd been an important football match the day before he might tear off the sports page, carefully, and hand it over.

Still, it wouldn't have surprised anyone to learn Buck was his mother's son. They had the same rangy height and broad shoulders. They dressed in ways that illustrated their personalities so perfectly that their clothes seemed like costumes. The baron once remarked to my mother, "Your Buck is so well tailored that looking at him brings tears to my eyes." Con's tweeds were startling. Where in remotest Donegal did she find those weaves, so hairy and intense, always with a line of unexpected color—scarlet, chrome yellow—shot through the pattern?

Buck and Con did share a love of hats. He wore a dove-gray Homburg with a black two-inch band. She preferred velvet sombreros.

Con had her suite—bedroom, bathroom, sitting room, each with its own fireplace—on the second floor of our Newport cottage. It was cold up there in the winter, hardly luxurious, but more comfortable than Wychwood, where toward the end she had been living almost out in the open.

After my grandmother settled in at Newport, her chaos engorged the second floor. At first Buck tried to organize and manage her affairs, which only irritated her. He sorted her mail, looking out for bills that he'd have to pay anyway. He gave her money to buy clothes and disallowed an extra telephone line she had ordered, as it was ridiculously expensive and she chiefly wanted it so that she could call her bookmaker at Frankie's English Bar, across the river, and place bets. The disorder in her rooms upset him deeply, until he at last took my mother's advice and stopped going upstairs. Twice a week our charwoman was dispatched to clean and tidy my grandmother's apartment. Con offered the woman tea and cigarettes, practiced speaking German with her, and tipped her extravagantly.

Every now and then Con had a check from her brother, who lived on his farm in the Happy Valley, in British East Africa; but she depended on the allowance my father provided. He had set up an account for her at the local bank. If a teller refused to let her withdraw money she didn't have, she would storm into the bank manager's office and insult him. She usually wanted the cash to bet on a horse. In Frankfurt she used a Polish bookmaker, Willy Chopdelau, who kept his own table at Frankie's and gave odds for all the English and Irish races.

I remember my father's dismay whenever he heard of my grandmother's quarrels at the bank, usually in an acerbic note from the bank manager.

"How can she want to spend money she does not have?"

"She's your mother, my dear," Eilín would say.

But his mother's ways, I think, remained a mystery to Buck. They understood horses better than they understood each other. Buck would always know to the penny what he had in the bank. He kept a dozen perfectly sharpened Faber pencils lined up on his desk like a rank of little yellow soldiers, and made strenuous inquiries if one went missing. He hated to gamble, and when he learned his mother had put four hundred reichsmarks—real money, probably loaned by Karin—on Graf Isolani to win the Deutsche Derby, he flinched in real pain, though of course she'd told him only after her horse had galloped home a winner. Walden didn't have a derby runner that year, otherwise my grandmother would have put her money on the Walden horse as a matter of principle, whether or not she liked its chances.

⊱─◈─○─◈─⊰

When my mother and I lived at Wychwood the McClintocks had long since stopped paying rent to my grandmother and insisted they owned the patchwork of tiny fields where they grazed scraggly sheep, made hay, cut turf, and lifted lumper potatoes. However, Con got along well enough with the tribe, apart from occasional feuds. Wychwood was one of the few big houses in that part of the world not torched during the War of Independence. Con believed she'd been spared on account of the McClintocks' putting in a good word with local Volunteers, but Mick told me that no one ever considered the house worth burning as it was already a ruin.

During his stay at Walden he was given a room above the horse stalls. After Lovely Morn was rested and feeding well, it was time to show her off.

My father didn't like to run horses, especially broodmares, in the full heat of a summer's day. So it was early morning, just after dawn, when we gathered around the paddock and watched Mick leading her out.

Lovely Morn was big even by Irish standards, nearly seventeen hands, and spirited. But she came out calm and easy with Mick, even with all the strangers about. You could see she trusted people; she had been handled well. No matter their bloodline, badly raised thorough-breds waste so much spirit in fussing and worrying that they rarely realize their potential.

Karin stood at the rail, holding a little leather crop, looking like a dangerous angel in her summer riding habit of pale-blue blouse, white breeches, and mahogany-top English boots. Longo, whom her parents considered Karin's all-but-official fiancé, was probably still in bed. He and Karin had been staying out late at parties.

As Mick put Lovely Morn through her paces on the longe line I could see he was terribly proud of her. A good groom feels kinship with his horse, and from the light, immaculate way Mick handled her and the way she responded, I could tell they both felt this.

"Very nice, very nice," the baron said to Mick. "But what do you say, sir? I think perhaps we see her on the run. The saddle's up for a reason, I suppose."

"Sure enough," Mick replied. When we were boys in Ireland he hadn't owned a pair of shoes, but at Walden he seemed entirely confi-dent and at ease, a horseman who knew his business.

The first hay had just been cut, so the turf was sleek. Mick was wear-ing horse boots and must have intended to be up himself, but I saw Karin speak to her father, who said something to Mick, and the next moment Mick was giving Karin a leg up without looking very happy about it. She was so fine and light he nearly tossed her over the mare's back—I saw her laugh at his apology. While he shortened the stirrup straps she was settling herself and communicating to the mare, via the telepathy real riders share with their mounts, that she, Karin, was in charge now, that the mare was perfectly safe in her hands, and that she would be careful, diligent, and wise enough for both of them. (It flows through the hands, this communication, the hands, and the voice.)

Mick held the bridle, waiting for Karin's nod. The moment he let go, the mare launched her thoroughbred spring and flew down the track cut into the woods, where we lost sight of them.

It is one of those scenes I have retained in its roundness all my life: cool-blue light of the summer dawn, scent of trees, of tobacco smoke. My father's stopwatch ticking. My father saying a word to the baron, the baron's bark of laughter.

Almost too soon we heard the faintest tremor of hoofbeats. Then Karin and the mare were coming out of the woods at a gallop.

She would have been no weight at all on a horse like that, nothing but a pair of hands.

They took another turn, then Karin slowed the mare down and began walking her out. By then the baron and my father had started back toward the main house where they would take coffee together.

Karin slipped down off the mare and handed the reins to Mick. The sun was flaring through the woods, and the trainers, grooms, and stable hands had gone off to their day's work. The grass was steaming dew, and I watched Mick and Karin walk the mare back to her stable. Karin was speaking with animation, her face glowing like a child's.

Was I envious? Of course. But we'd hardly exchanged a word all summer. She was a year older and living in the great city of Berlin. Mick was a professional horseman and on his way to America. I cycled off to my café au lait and foreign newspapers, telling myself the sooner I started a career of my own, the better.

That morning I began considering Herr Kaufman's youngest secretary, Heidi, as a travel companion, though I wasn't convinced such *ein gesundes* Fräulein would be willing to take on the emptiness of the American High Plains. Blonde and pretty, Heidi spoke not a word of English and every Saturday eagerly rode the bus back to her family's swine farm at Schwalbach in the Taunus.

After work I passed by the BMW showroom and paused to gaze at the motorcycles in the window. Easy to imagine one of these machines as the up-to-date version of Old Shatterhand's magnificent horse, Lightning. What a thrilling idea, to set off across El Llano Estacado riding such a beast. With a sidecar fitted on, there was certainly room for a girl.

The cinema was the only place that could possibly suit my heightened mood, so from the motorcycle shop I went on to catch the new Gary Cooper picture, *Nevada*. Coop played an outlaw hired to protect a rich rancher's daughter from the band of outlaws aiming to kidnap her. I could imagine myself gunning down a gang of criminals for the sake of a girl. I'd help her into my sidecar, gun my engine, and we'd zoom together across a landscape of light.

><+>+0+<+>+<

My mother invited Mick to have dinner with us. She liked the Sligo in him, the curl in his voice. She'd been sounding more Sligo herself since Mick and my grandmother had arrived.

Afterward he and I took an evening stroll around the paddocks. On summer evenings horses were always turned out of the stalls, and it was enjoyable to see the long-legged colts frisking.

Mick offered me a Sweet Afton. He said Walden was the grandest horse establishment he'd ever seen. The only thing that came close was the National Stud at Kildare, which was falling apart "like everything in Ireland. But I'm not going back to Ireland, Billy."

"You're emigrating."

"I am. Going for America, like most of them from our old Calry National. Except them that went for England, and one fella that got himself murdered by the Tans."

"Do you remember, the peelers, in the road?"

"'Down goes the pony'?"

"I thought he would shoot."

"Do you know what would suit me, Billy Lange? Taking that girl across with me. I'd say the two of us might make a start together in New York."

It startled me. "She's other fish to fry."

Mick smiled. "Ah, you mean that tall drink of water, Longo von Himself? But is he really in the running? I wouldn't be so sure. The fellow does have money, I suppose."

"He's not as rich as she is."

"I've lived twenty years without being knocked over by a woman. And here I am with a passage for America, one foot on the boat, and now there's a girl in old Germany I won't be forgetting. Ah, man, it is cruel."

He was smiling. He didn't seem too distraught.

"What'll you do in New York?" I asked. I didn't want to talk anymore about Karin.

"Try to get on the police, I suppose. Dream of your Karin von, that's what. She was something, up on the mare, was she not? Light as a bird. Jesus."

The rest of that week I didn't see much of Mick. Once or twice I caught a glimpse of him in the paddock or on the yearling track, and Karin was there as well. She wore blue cotton shirts that summer and breeches and mahogany-top boots the same as mine, which I'd outgrown.

One evening when I came home from the lawyer's office I saw Mick sitting on a rail. I went over to him and stood holding my bicycle while we watched Karin gallop out of the woods.

"There you are, Billy boy." Mick sighed. "There's something beautiful and fast. I'm afraid your Karin von has me beat."

Watching yearlings run is as close as I ever have come to feeling music in my soul. That's putting it in a very German way, isn't it? It's the beauty of the thing itself, their bright eyes and bright coats, the drumbeat of hooves, the squeaks and snorts of young thoroughbreds breathing hard. Creak of saddle leather. Spurts of red dust rising from the turf.

After all, it's not only the chance of winning a pile that brings people to the track, it's the hard beauty of the thing, and this was something we understood at Walden. Maybe those two, Mick and Karin, had little in common but love of horses. But that's not insignificant. Like having an ear for melody, or a sense of rhythm, a feeling for horses connects you in all kinds of ways to others who share it.

Longo wasn't a bad rider. He'd show jumped at quite an advanced level before giving it up to practice law. But horses to him were just expensive machines, more or less like his Mercedes. Pieces of action, not living beings.

Karin made Longo get up awfully early for tennis. One morning, cycling past the clay court on my way to work, I saw him miss a return. Perhaps it cost him the set, because he started cursing and banging his racket on the clay. I kept cycling, but I didn't mind seeing Longo lose his sangfroid.

That evening I visited Mick in his room above the stable and was shocked to find Karin sitting on his bed, an old army cot. A lot of gear and trappings around the Walden stables were war surplus. Trainers and exercise riders wore army horse boots; military saddles and tack were used on walking-out horses. Some grooms still wore their field-gray tunics.

Karin smiled. "Hello, Billy." She was perched at the foot of the bed. Mick was sitting at the other end, knees drawn up.

Was she annoyed at my intrusion? Probably. But she didn't show it. We were old friends, after all. Her legs were bare and brown, no stockings, nor shoes. Her feet were dirty. She wore an evening dress, loose on her slight figure and at the same time revealing. The sort of dress, I thought, the goddess Diana might have worn.

Her mother would have been stunned if she'd known Karin was in the stable quarters, visiting a groom.

"Billy's a wise lad," said Mick. "Billy knows a horse from a donkey."

Karin was looking at me. "He does."

"We've been down some lanes together, have we not, Billy?" Mick said.

"We have," I agreed. "Stealing salmon."

"And that old peeler who was after shooting the pony. Worse than the Tans, those lads. Billy's your man," Mick said to Karin. "You may rely on old Billy there, he's got the stuff, he won't let you down."

"Your Mick is leaving," she told me. "I've asked him not to, but he says he must."

I was confused. Everyone knew Mick was going for America.

"He's emigrating," I said.

"He is," Mick said. "Sick of mucking stables. Can't find a place for himself, this side of the water. Wants a piece of America. Crossing over to see what he can get."

"I'd go with you," she said.

He laughed. She was smiling. But I knew she was serious.

"Flatbush, Brooklyn," Mick told her. "Uncle Jer's a sergeant on the New York police. He's offered me a bed. But he's got six kids, or seven."

"We needn't stay with Uncle Jer." She was smiling and her voice was light.

It had been a warm day. A scent that was sweet hay, horse dung, and old dry timbers rose from the stalls below. Were they going to run off to America? Together? Could two people not much older than myself take their lives in their hands that way?

A car horn broke the stillness aggressively. I recognized the sound of Longo's Mercedes. Longo and Karin were going off for the evening, that explained why she was dressed as Diana.

Without another word she got up and left. We listened to her run lightly down the wooden staircase.

Mick raised a finger to his lips. "Don't say a word, Billy. You weren't here. Didn't see nor hear anything, right?"

"If you say so."

"Let's go for a walkabout and a smoke."

><+>-0-<>+<

Longo wasn't getting the attention he thought he deserved. That probably explains everything that happened. He was too much of a snob to believe Karin could be seriously interested in a groom, but he was certainly irritated by the hours she spent on horseback with Mick that week. That's where the idea of the excursion originated. Longo wanted to get Karin into the front seat of his powerful Mercedes car and out on the roads where she'd be much more in his hands.

Longo needed people to be fascinated with him. Unusually for a German, he'd gone to school in the United States—two years at Choate—while his father worked at Morgan's bank in New York. Longo spoke excellent American English. Like me, he enjoyed westerns. He was a Gary Cooper fan. We went to the cinema together a few times. He insisted on paying for my ticket.

He could be charming and lively, though the grooms weren't fond of him and neither was my father. Longo shouted at the horses and used the crop too much.

There were grains and streaks of kindness and empathy in Longo's character. Along with charm and money and beautiful clothes, he had a natural warmth and liveliness, which explained his large circle of friends.

His scheme had been to go off with Karin alone in his car, but Lady Maire would not hear of it. My being included in the party made it acceptable. An eighteen-year-old boy could hardly be considered a proper chaperone, but from Lady Maire's point of view I was my parents' son, so my trustworthiness and devotion to the Weinbrenners' good name was taken for granted.

Her grasp of human relations was flawed. I'm sure Karin knew the truth, which was that, as far as I was concerned, she could do anything she wanted. I would accept any number of saber cuts much deeper than Longo's before I'd ever betray Karin, to her mother or anyone else.

Our original itinerary included Sankt Goar, the Lorelei, and lunch at a castle belonging to Longo's relatives. But after he had a telegram from one of his *Korpsbrüder*, Longo decided we must aim for Heidelberg instead. He was proud of his membership in the Korps-Rhenania and wanted to show Karin off to his friends.

Having the stable manager's son along was tiresome but necessary. When Karin said she'd invited the Irish groom as well, Longo gave an impatient snort. "The groom? Invite the bloody groom? Whatever for?"

"To show him more of our beautiful Germany. Don't be such a snob, Longo."

The excursion was set for Saturday. I worked at Kaufman's law office until noon, when they would pick me up in the Mercedes.

Longo's Mercedes was an S-Class, the young person's Mercedes. The rich young person's Mercedes: an open tourer with four bucket seats, a supercharged engine, and a top speed of one hundred thirty kilometers per hour. Painted battleship gray, she had straightforward lines and wasn't overladen with chrome, as Mercedes cars were a decade later, when they became the chosen steeds of the major criminals.

They picked me up outside Kaufman's office in a small street off the Römerberg. The top was down. Karin and Longo had the bucket seats in front; I joined Mick in back. Longo had removed the bandage from his *Schmiss*. Perhaps the scar had healed enough, or maybe he was impatient to display it to his *Korpsbrüder*. Karin made fun of it, but probably many young men in her circle wore scars from the *Mensur*. She moved in a more aristocratic crowd than her parents. The baron's houseguests were typically scientists or businessmen, many of them Jews. I don't know if the baron considered himself Jewish at that time. In Breslau he'd been baptized a Lutheran. At Walden they celebrated Christmas, Easter, All Souls' Day, and I never heard anything about Yom Kippur or Passover. Maybe it wasn't an either/or question for him. At the house, his wife's Christian iconography was everywhere, but he wasn't religious. He was German. Perhaps he felt Jewish sometimes, but most of the time it seemed irrelevant. It was only after his "treasonous" memoirs were published that the right-wing press started referring to him as a Jew.

Karin, for her part, knew a lot of rich young people from conservative families. She was young, beautiful in an unexpected way, and the granddaughter of an Irish peer, who also held an English title and a seat in the House of Lords. Some of the grandees inviting her to weekend house parties at castles on the Rhine or hunting estates in East Prussia probably whispered horrid things about her father. Maybe they were counting her fortune, plotting their sons would marry her to save their rotten old houses. Probably they were impressed that she would ride their biggest, roughest horses. Karin and her father were much more German than I was, though some people would never consider them such, no matter their horsemanship or their courage.

Longo liked going fast. We ate sandwiches in the car and stopped only once, at a creamery, deep in the countryside. Karin ran inside and came out with a bottle of cold milk, which we all shared. There wasn't much point trying to talk at one hundred twenty kilometers per hour with the top down and the supercharger whining. Anyhow, talk wasn't needed. I felt supercharged with emotion. It was all I could do not to spill this out in the form of tears, but I wasn't sad. I felt extraordinarily happy in the company of these three, quite without my usual baggage of self-conscious unease.

The road was lined with beech trees. We sped down canyons of greenery. Above the flapping leaves, pure blue sky. I'd not often been in such a motorcar, never in one driven so fast, with a young woman in the front seat turning to offer me a bottle of cold, fresh milk and her smile. I experienced for the first time the tranquillity and poise that most of my life have been accessible only in liminal space, at speed, on highways across open country, occasionally in airports. The pure air of transition.

After the caustic wash of highway speed, Heidelberg's tight streets felt claustrophobic. Longo drove us straight to the home of his cherished *Korps*, on the Hauptstraße. The Rhenanenhaus was a pile from the late-Wilhelmian period, nothing modern about it but nothing charming or ancient, either. The ground floor was stuccoed. Steel bars were fastened over the windows. To passersby on the street, it offered the cold, verging on brutal, stare of the official class of Germany. A stonework relief over the door had something of the florid flair of a cuirassier's brass helmet. The upper stories were more urbane. But it was a fraternity house with the *Gestalt* of a fortress.

Korps-Rhenania was the control center of Longo's value system at that time. Membership in all those *Korps* was for life. *Korpsbrüder* and their old-boy networks, the *Alte Herren*, believed themselves a privileged elect. The Rhenanians were Longo's family, until he turned traitor on them too.

There was a drawing room on the ground floor where visitors were received, and this is where Longo brought us. The hallway and the rooms we passed were paneled in a dark wood. Everything shone. The house was oddly dark and bright at once. Like the main house at Walden it was lacquered with an atmosphere of privilege but more than a little uncomfortable. We sat on dark, carved chairs. A flunky served us coffee and stale cakes.

"Longo, old chap," Karin said, "you've brought us all this way in your wonderful motorcar, but aren't you going to show us the heart of the house? We want to see how you really live here. These rooms are a bit dreary, my dear. A bit grim, aren't they? Let's go up to your room and have our coffee there. Aren't you going to show us your precious boudoir?"

"No women allowed upstairs, of course."

"How sad."

"Not at all. The spirit of brotherhood within a *Korpshaus*, my dear Karin, is something a woman will never understand."

"Can't you break the rules for once? Only a little?"

"You don't know what you're asking, Karin. Of course I can't."

Usually Longo was a good sport about her teasing but it was clear that, in the *Korpshaus* anything less than reverence very much annoyed him.

"It would be against my honor to do so," he continued. "It would be a violation. Don't you feel the spirit of this place? It is quite ineffable and, at the same time, solid as rock. Everything we have as Rhenanianer is built on the spirit of honesty and straightforwardness. It's not a matter of rules for us, it's a matter of honor."

Karin smiled, but I could tell she was irritated by Longo's tone, quite unlike his usual easygoing, man-of-the-world demeanor. "Why ever did you bring me here, dear Longo, if it wasn't to visit your boudoir?"

Just then a couple of blond *Korpsbrüder* entered the room. Longo leaped to his feet and began introducing them to Karin and, somewhat offhandedly, to Mick and to me. It seemed to me Longo was flustered.

The young men were being very cool with us, even with Karin. One of them, Hugo von-something, had been Longo's *Füchsmajor,* or "sponsor," when Longo was a "fox," which was what they called new members of the *Korps.*

The *Brüder* had just returned from a visit to England, and both wore atrociously wide, cream-colored Oxford "bags," along with fresh, raw haircuts, and saber scars on their left cheeks. I knew from their accents and their self-confidence they were rich. They ignored the three of us and started talking to Longo about England, what an unpleasant country it was.

"English trains are so filthy!" I remember the sneer on blond Hugo's lips as he spoke. "The people unkempt! In London these days you hardly ever see such a thing as the English gentleman! And the women! The English race is dying out: it's true. When you're there it is hard to believe that London is the capital of an empire, that's all I can say, because it doesn't have anything of greatness. No, not a bit. The English are great no longer."

"We played some wonderful tennis, though," the other blond remarked.

"Games!" sneered Hugo. "It's all the English do well. They are corrupt and lazy and really the first-class coaches are disgusting."

"You fellows won't know anything about England until you've rid-

den to hounds in a good country like Northamptonshire or Shropshire."
Karin was refusing to be ignored. "People tell you Northamptonshire is
the best hunting country, but that's only because the railway timetables
make it easy to get to, whereas it's bloody difficult getting to Shropshire
on time. I should say the Ludlow is a jolly good hunt and as rough as
any, but I had no luck with my horses, ever. I was asked to stay at Attingham, which is a very damp house, but Lord Berwick was such a great
friend of my grandfather's I couldn't refuse, do you know Attingham?
No? It's not a great house, but big enough, only one can become a bit
fed up with England and English weekends after a while, I must say. The
food's never much good; there is something a bit too frugal and cold and
ridiculous. Were you at the Savoy? It's my favorite hotel in the world."

The *Korpsbrüder* were smirking. They'd identified exactly who Karin
was, the noisy daughter of the filthy rich Jewish baron, the traitor.

Longo was looking increasingly uncomfortable. He was still only
a fox as far as the Rhenanians were concerned. Underneath his skin,
underneath his scar, he must have been afraid of his *Korpsbrüder*. They
controlled so much that he wanted.

Karin went on, undimmed. "Oxford is amusing for a while. But I
must say, the undergraduates, such sad young men, they don't seem as
manly as the German youth."

It was embarrassing.

"But whenever I'm in England, I never for so much as a second
forget about the war, do you agree? I broke my damned shoulder hunting in Shropshire, it wasn't my fault at all, really, the horse was a shyer,
everyone thinks they must give the timid horse to the girl. Do you
hunt? Only it's no good, riding a weak horse like that, I'd be much better on a thruster. When I was out at the Bismarcks' place last month
they gave me a half-broke gelding to ride, a big black fellow, probably
seventeen hands, and we had some fun. Of course it wasn't hunting
season, but they are all mad for tennis, the Bismarcks."

The *Korpsbrüder* nodded their heads at the same time and exchanged
a quick glance. They were impressed despite themselves. How I hated
them. I was furious at Longo for having brought us there and at Karin
for displaying such vulnerability.

"Do you play tennis? You look so elegant in your flannels. We'll
organize a tennis afternoon at Walden. Poor Longo is getting awfully

tired that I'm beating him again and again; his forehand is mighty, but his backhand is nothing to be proud of—"

I couldn't listen anymore. Getting to my feet, I announced Mick and I were going to take a look around the town.

Karin threw a glance at us. Did she want us to rescue her? Were we abandoning her to the German wolves?

She laughed. "Well, go on, then, dear Billy, go on, we certainly don't want to keep you."

Turning her back, she resumed conversation with the blond pair. Whose narrow bodies, I must admit, were bending toward her. It wasn't just famous old names she was strewing before them. She was the sun in the room. Her energy, her heat, were winning them.

Longo looked relieved. With a friendly smile he suggested to Mick we all meet up later at a famous old student tavern, the Red Ox Inn. "We'll have a glass of beer and a bite to eat before starting back. Now you boys take a good look around our old town. You're in the heart of Germany here. We'll see you at the Red Ox, say around seven."

As we were leaving, Karin threw another glance at Mick, and for a second I hoped she was about to abandon the *Korpsbrüder* and come along with us, *den beiden Iren*. But she didn't. She was where she most wanted to be, a German among Germans. We were dismissed.

><+>-○-<+><

It was warm and close in Heidelberg. I could smell the river as we hiked up to the ruined castle. We sat on a wall overlooking the town and smoked cigarettes. I started telling Mick my idea of heading out across El Llano Estacado aboard the motorcycle I'd seen in the BMW showroom in Frankfurt.

"And once you get across, Billy, what then?"

"You sound like my father."

Buck was worried because I hadn't fixed on a profession. My mother said the problem of my future was keeping him awake at night. If the law wasn't what I wanted, then we ought to ask the baron about finding me a place at IG Farben when I graduated. With headquarters in Frankfurt, IG Farbenindustrie was the largest corporation in Europe, fourth largest in the world, and the baron had a seat on the board of supervising directors.

My father wanted iron security for me because his life had been improvised, scattered, even reckless. Born out of sight of land. A jockey at fifteen. A cavalryman. An ex-prisoner. A man whose two careers—racing yachts in the English Channel and raising thoroughbred horses for the highest levels of European competition—were all about risk, chance, beating the odds.

The west wall of my bedroom at Newport was covered with oil company road maps, courtesy of the U.S. consul at Köln. I'd pinned the states in sequence and traced a route in blue pencil from New York to California that dipped south to cross El Llano Estacado. That blue line floated over me as I slept and was the first thing my eyes fixed on when I awoke. Sometimes it seemed a skeleton, the bones of a dream. Sometimes a skeleton key, unlocking a life I couldn't even imagine yet.

The afternoon was too hot and close to inspire us to take in the sights of Heidelberg. Neither of us had any interest in being tourists. I could feel a thunderstorm starting to build. The azure sky was foaming over with gray. The air was thick, with scarcely a breeze, even along the Neckar.

That was where we met the two girls, Lilly and Coco.

They were from Strasbourg and a bit older than us. Speaking Alsatian dialect, they told us they'd been working in vineyards up the Rhine and along the Mosel.

It was Mick's idea that we treat the girls to beer at the café near the train station. Lilly told us her father was the deputy mayor of Strasbourg. Coco said her father was a famous general killed in the war. When I asked which side he had fought on, she laughed, and it dawned on me that we weren't meant to believe their stories.

The girls went inside the station to use the restroom. Mick said, "I'd say ten marks each, Billy, and no more."

"What for?"

"They're brassers, Billy. Whores."

"Of course. Yes. Certainly." But it hadn't occurred to me. I thought of prostitutes as heavy, scarred wretches like the women on the Kaiserstraße in Frankfurt. Lilly and Coco were small, sunburned, cheerful. "Are we going to sleep with them?"

"We're going to fuck them, Billy my man, once we've settled on a price."

There was no way to back out of the situation without seeming like a schoolboy. Not that Mick would have said anything; he wasn't interested in making people feel small. And when I was with him I was always bolder and older, more satisfied with my own life. So I knew I was going to follow him again, though I felt anxious about it.

When the girls came out of the station lugging one suitcase between them, Mick handled negotiations with Coco. He didn't speak French or Alsatian, but that transaction is a straightforward one, and they had no trouble understanding each other.

The girls didn't have a room in Heidelberg; they were passing through. Coco suggested we hike up into the woods above the town where they had spent the night sleeping rough. Mick and I took turns carrying their suitcase as we climbed back up the hill toward the ruined castle. The girls led us off the road and down a path through woods to a grassy clearing where they had slept. Opening their suitcase, each took out a little gray blanket. We hadn't discussed who was going with whom, though we'd settled on twenty marks for the two of us. Coco took the money. I was nervous, tense, and wasn't sure I wanted to go through with it, but the redhead, Lilly, hooked her arm in mine. Chattering gaily like a little French Alsatian bird she led me down the steep path to another grassy spot. I helped spread out and smooth her blanket. She wore a yellow dress bought in Köln, which she was proud of. I agreed with her that it was *vraiment gentille*. She hated her boots, which were falling apart, the soles worn thin and starting to separate. Did she wear underclothes of any sort? I don't remember. The sex was over pretty quickly, as you can imagine. Her breasts were soft but her nipples were hard. Afterward, it was stunning to be lying there with my hand cupping a woman's bush and the sun warm on my back. I dozed. It began to rain lightly and I sat up, not knowing where I was for a moment. Lilly, wriggling into her dress, smiled at me. I looked down at the red-tiled roofs of Heidelberg squeezed into that narrow cleft of a valley with the Neckar running through. The rain came down all of a sudden in a thick silver drench. It was warm. We were both soaked in an instant. A wonderful rain.

We bought the girls coffee and cakes at the station café, then Mick heaved their suitcase aboard a third-class coach, and as the train wheezed from the platform they leaned out the window waving and blowing kisses at us.

"That was charming," Mick remarked. "However, Billy Lange, from the looks of you, we both could stand a bath and a curry before we see the vons."

We were disheveled. Mick solved the problem by charming our way into a guesthouse where the landlady agreed to dry our clothes on her kitchen hob and press our suits while charging us two marks to share an enormous tub, where we sat soaking at opposite ends, smoking, and sipping tumblers of cherry brandy. We did not discuss our experiences with the girls, Mick somehow making it clear that to compare notes on that subject was unmanly. Instead we talked of horses and of Mick's uncle Jer in Flatbush, Brooklyn.

"I'll want a bed for a night or two, no more," Mick told me. "There's a fellow Jer knows who can steer me to getting on the police. It won't happen overnight. There's an examination. It might be I do stable work at first. There's plenty of Irish at the horse tracks."

"Do you think Karin meant it? About going with you?" Lolling in the hot bath, smoking and sipping cherry brandy, I felt manly and nonchalant.

"Jesus," said Mick. "You must leave off that subject."

"I wish she'd come with us instead of hanging on to Longo's pals."

"Your Karin von don't know what she wants." He blew out a stream of cigarette smoke. "Can you see a girl like that on the run with a fellow like me? No money, nothing behind me. Girls like her are expensive, I would say."

"Have you known girls like her?"

"No. No. She's one of a kind, your Karin von."

"But you won't let her come with you to America."

"I tell you what, let's drop the subject. It would end badly, Billy boy, it surely must."

The evening—close, gray, shot with weird bullets of light—was gathering to another downpour as we came out of the guesthouse. We were clean, our clothes in good order. I wondered if Lilly could replace Karin in my fantasy life. Could I imagine Lilly traveling across Texas at fantastic speed?

At the Red Ox we found Karin and Longo drinking beer in one of the snugs. The student tavern was dark and smelled of smoke and yeast and hops. In the next nook, a table of American students bawled drinking songs in execrable German.

"We're awfully glad to see you boys, aren't we, Longo?" Karin said. "It's been a perfectly wonderful day. We went punting on the river and got soaked. Longo's not nearly so good an oarsman as you'd think. Not so good as he ought to be. Really it was rather a disappointing performance, Longo."

She was angry about something, I could tell right away. Something had upset her.

"Don't be silly, Karin, it was perfectly fine, and you looked beautiful in the rain."

The waiter brought tankards of beer for Mick and me, and Longo ordered *Jägerschnitzel* for all of us.

"Longo has tickets to hear a perfectly dreadful little man speak at the Stadthalle," Karin said. "Dear Longo says it's time I opened my eyes to the eternal truths of Germany. What do you think, Mick McClintock? Are my eyes open?"

She looked straight at Mick who was raising a tankard to his lips.

"They are," he replied. "Very much so."

"Here's my idea," Longo said. "Herr Hitler is scheduled to speak at the Stadthalle at eight o'clock but probably won't get there until nine at the earliest. I have got my hands on four tickets. The fellows say it could be amusing. My father heard him speak last year at the Atlantic Hotel in Hamburg."

Was that the first time I heard of Herr Hitler? He was not a famous figure yet, not outside Bavaria anyway. He was still banned from public speaking in most of Germany—in the state of Prussia, for example, which included Frankfurt.

"Tell them what your father called him, Longo dear," Karin said.

"Dear Karin," Longo said patiently, "if you don't wish us to go, that's the end of it, we shan't."

"It's not what I want or don't want, it's that *you* want to take me. That's what I find so fascinating."

"But I'm not insisting."

"Only because it is not in your power to insist, Longo dear."

"Fine!" He spoke in sharp, rapid German. "We'll go straight back to Walden, that's all. And you may ride your wonderful Irish horses, win your tennis matches, and allow your papa's great pile of money to keep you out of the world. And anything you don't like, that you don't wish to see, you can offer it money and hope it will go away. Fine! The rest of us may be curious, we may wish to know our country better, our Germany. But that is that. We will leave."

It shocked me to hear him use that tone with her.

Karin spoke English. "Your Germany, Longo? Tell them what your father called the Hitler clown. *Your* Germany?"

"*Die Donaustaaten Kuriosität.*" Longo shrugged.

"'The Danubian Curiosity,'" Karin translated.

"My father doesn't like Austrians," Longo said, with another shrug. "Northerners hate southerners, Protestants hate Catholics, all the Germans have such idiotic complaints. We refuse to understand we are one nation after all."

"*Die Donaustaaten Kuriosität*, it actually means: 'from Austria, the strange,'" Karin said. "The Strange One. In American they should say, perhaps, 'the oddball.' The Danubian Oddball."

"Very funny." Longo was getting fed up. Probably the attitude of his *Korpsbrüder* when first meeting her had surprised him; though considering who her father was, Longo should have seen that coming. But Longo wasn't used to resistance or to people disapproving his choices.

"Easy to dismiss a fellow whose accent isn't as nice as yours." The morning's ride in the open car had reddened Longo's *Schmiss*. "My father, however, also said, 'There is something there.' This Hitler was a front soldier. He hates the Bolsheviks. He speaks, and plain folk understand him even with *ein Donauakzent*. And he is lively entertainment, say my *Korpsbrüder*. I have tickets to the hall for four. We can go or not, as you like, Karin."

"He's a Jew baiter," Karin said.

"He was a front soldier and hates the Reds. I think we must hear him for ourselves. My dear Karin, it is time you knew your Germany a little better. Anyway you've never before claimed to love the Jews."

"Don't be an ass, Longo. I am a Jew," she said.

"Your old fellow may be a Jew." Longo smiled. "But you, my dear girl, are a German."

"Anyway, Herr Hitler is not my Germany."

"How do you know, until you hear what he has to say?"

Our *Jägerschnitzel* arrived. They were crisp and excellent. I was famished. The others, too: we wolfed our food. Normally I would have been intensely aware of Karin's nearness, her scent, of everything she said, but I was lost in memories of the afternoon's encounter in the woods. Could I arrange to see Lilly again? How much did a train ticket to Strasbourg cost?

Longo ordered more beer. The atmosphere in the tavern was rambunctious. Students and tourists crowded the heavy old beer tables, singing.

Karin began teasing Longo about his *Schmiss*. The scars of his *Verbindungbrüder* were bigger than his. Did they compare scars? And whose really was biggest?

Away from the Rhenanenhaus, Longo was his debonaire self, able to laugh at Karin's sallies. Someone, somewhere, was playing a piano badly. Suddenly Longo left the table, and Karin slid along the bench until she was next to Mick. I didn't pay much attention, I kept seeing Lily in thick silver rain, tilting her face to the sky, laughing as raindrops dribbled off her chin.

Someone was playing "Anybody See My Gal" and I recognized Longo's harsh touch at the piano, pounding out his beloved ragtime. Mick and Karin were in urgent conversation, but I couldn't hear a word. I closed my eyes and saw a motorcycle speeding across horizontal yellow plains toward a range of red mountains crisp against the sky.

She was holding Mick's hand between hers like it was something precious.

Longo started into "Ain't She Sweet."

━━◆━◆━○━◆━◆━

Fringe politicians delivering speeches in hired halls were a dime a dozen. Who bothered keeping track? Radio wasn't widespread. My parents didn't own a set. The newspapers my father took—the *F-Zeit* and the *Vossische*—would not have paid much attention to a rabble-rouser from the uncivilized Deep South of Germany or, even worse, Austria. Anyway, I only saw the football and the racing pages.

We ate our *Jägerschnitzel*, drank down our tankards of beer, and went off to see the elephant.

Karin was flushed and seemed excited but not drunk. She must have been aware that Longo, Mick, and I were entranced with her.

As we walked past the formations of rugged, often astonishingly ugly youths wearing brown shirts and red-and-white armbands with the weird, jagged black cross, we were mostly concerned with ourselves, each of us with sex, love, loneliness probably foremost in our minds.

And the militant atmosphere in the streets wasn't unfamiliar. All political parties had paramilitaries, uniformed tribes of fighters. This was the world we'd come of age in. Squads of NSDAP toughs might have been overgrown Boy Scouts for all they spooked us, and Mick probably viewed them as just one more strange German tendency, like preferring Pilsner to porter. Like riding through a summer day in a top-down Mercedes at eighty miles per hour, or making love to Alsatian girls in the steep woods between the castle and the town.

Along the Hauptstraße we were joined by Longo's two *Korpsbrüder*, the languid sunburned blonds, Hugo and Willy. Instead of their flamboyant Oxford bags they wore regular trousers, and open-necked shirts, perhaps to fit in better with the crowd. Longo fell back to chat with them. Karin linked arms with Mick. We passed more squads of uniformed youth, some carrying rubber truncheons. There were also ordinary citizens and tourists curious to see what was causing such a fuss on a sticky summer evening that smelled like rank thunder.

It was nearly nine o'clock. The Danubian Oddball was already an hour late, but from the excitement outside the Stadthalle it seemed he was expected at any moment. A tiny girl clutched a bouquet of flowers and was guarded by a woman who wore the traditional hat with red balls of the Black Forest. A pair of beefy brownshirts were sizing people up at the door. Longo linked arms with Karin, who was still linked with Mick, and the three of them swept inside together. I was about to follow when a flurry rippled through the crowd and I turned around and saw a big open Mercedes four-door—a *breezer* we called them, all black, much more massive and powerful than Longo's S-Class—drawing up. Behind it another Mercedes, just the same. A squad of very rugged, sunburned brownshirts leaped from the second car and began shoving bystanders aside and linking arms to clear a path. I was practically in the doorway and one of them pushed me roughly.

A man wearing an ordinary brown trench coat over an ordinary blue suit climbed out of the first Mercedes. The brownshirts began thrusting out a stiff-armed salute, chanting "Heil! Heil! Heil!"

He returned the salute—wearily, I thought. Of course it was Hitler, but he looked unremarkable, he could have been the owner of a stationery store or a minor official from the town hall. Dark hair cropped very close on the sides, military-style, and the toothbrush mustache. The little girl was led forward by her mother to offer her bouquet. Hitler patted the blonde head but did not accept the flowers. Shooting his shirt cuffs he began to stroll almost languidly along the pathway cleared by his bodyguard. He seemed to have no difficulty ignoring the tumult surrounding him, the salutes, the yelping, the general male hysteria. The mob of acolytes was pressing against the linked arms of Hitler's bodyguards, trying to get as near him as possible, and the bodyguards were huffing and grunting and straining to hold them back, you could read the effort on their red faces. As for Hitler, it was as if he were taking a stroll in the garden all alone. He simply ignored everything, and sauntered inside the hall.

The chain of linked arms broke down, an excited mob rushed the door, and I was swept along with them.

The hall was packed. Did we stand or were we sitting on benches? I can't remember. A cloud of cigarette smoke floated above everyone. Bats flickered in the rafters.

I watched those bats a good portion of the evening because after the hysteria provoked by Hitler's arrival, his speech was for the most part dull. It was difficult to hear, for one thing. The problem wasn't the Austrian accent, he had already trained that out of himself. His German was neutral, perhaps with the slightest tinge of Bavarian. But there were upward of a thousand crammed into the old hall, and more spilling out onto the outside steps, and no sound system other than the speaker's vocal cords. So it took an effort to speak and a greater effort to hear him because at first he spoke so softly and hesitantly. We were all straining to listen.

Soon after he began came the first references to Jews as *bloodsuckers. Aliens. War profiteers.* Such language was not unusual. There were boys at Klinger-Oberrealschule, and a couple of teachers, who spoke that way.

Some writers say Hitler possessed powers of nearly magical enchantment which allowed him to enthrall ordinary, decent Germans. I don't know how many ordinary, decent Germans were in the Stadthalle that night, they were mostly boys in brown shirts, and the slack-jawed bruisers around me looked as bored as I felt. After the first ten minutes or so I gave up trying to listen. I tuned Herr Hitler out, watched bats fluttering around the rafters, scanned the crowd for my companions, and daydreamed exciting sex with Lilly.

Hitler spoke for at least an hour. During most of that time he seemed disconnected from the crowd, which was becoming restless. He still had a way to go as a speaker. Or maybe he was just tired that evening. Even the early tirade against the Jews sounded pro forma. Only toward the end of his speech did he begin stirring up the hall, letting passion in.

He used a trick: he began repeating the word *Deutschland* until almost every sentence contained a *Deutschland*, pronounced ever more raucously and harshly, until even the drowsiest brownshirts caught the rhythm. *Deutschland. Deutschland!* They were opening their throats, stomping their boots and howling along with him. Then, abruptly, he stopped.

While the howls crashed over him he stood at attention, arms at his sides, a blissful expression on his face, as if the hysteria he'd summoned from the crowd was a miracle cure for him. He allowed himself to soak it up for a few more moments. Then he nodded precisely, like an engineer pleased with his work, and moved briskly off the platform. His personal protection squad flanked him and they moved for the exit in a scrum, while the audience simpered and moaned.

As soon as their führer had left the hall, the brownshirts began streaming for the door, and I was pulled along in the undertow. Outside, the pair of big Mercedes were already pulling away and the crowd was seething with something like anger. I caught sight of Karin and Mick and Longo, who was shaking hands with his *Korpsbrüder*. I began making my way toward my friends. Clutching Mick's arm, Karin looked pale and slight, the day's color gone from her cheeks.

"Let's get away," Mick was saying. "I don't much like the smell of this."

Hearing English spoken, a pair of brownshirt boys wearing buckled leather shoulder-straps turned to stare at us. The night smelled clogged, unclean—the summer rankness of the Neckar, the crowd of overheated men and restless, frantic boys. How much did I take in, how much did I miss? My first sex, my first Hitler—I was struck, dazed. I am aware from the history books that Jews were attacked and beaten in Heidelberg that night. We all sensed the blood anger in those rancorous uniformed boys. Karin looked as if she'd seen a ghost; perhaps she had.

After his farewells to his *Korpsbrüder* Longo reached for Karin's other hand, brought it to his lips, kissed it. A repulsive gesture, really, at that point, but she didn't react. What had he been thinking? Was it sadism, bringing her to hear Hitler? Or could Longo sense what was coming? Maybe he felt it in his German bones, maybe he was trying to warn her.

"*Lasst uns gehen!*" Longo said. Let's go.

When we were past the last squad of brownshirts, back in student territory, Longo spoke English. "The man is a villain. Crude. Don't think I don't see it."

Mick had placed his tweed jacket over Karin's shoulders. It was raining hard by then.

The Mercedes was in a garage close by the Rhenanenhaus. The garage attendant and Longo and I worked together to unfold the top and snap it down to cover us for the journey home.

"What a wonderful day," Karin said. She was wearing Mick's jacket and shivering. "What an interesting talk. What lively companions you have, Longo. Where do you keep *your* little uniform?"

"Don't speak of it, Karin. And please do not mention it to your father. Those brutes are hardly companions of mine."

Longo probably was wary of the baron, at that time still a powerful figure. We drove back to Walden through slashing rain. I don't remember conversation, just lighting cigarettes, and the desolate outskirts of Niederrad: darkened shops and wet pavement glistening. It was after midnight when the Mercedes rolled through the iron gates. Longo drew up outside the main house to let Karin out under the porte cochere. She got out without a word and ran inside.

Longo departed early the next morning. When I told my father we had attended an NSDAP rally he was furious, not just with Longo but with me.

"What were you thinking of, bringing the young lady there? Bad enough that you show up yourself, but you had no business exposing the Weinbrenners' daughter to such trash. Really, Billy, I'm disappointed by such a failure of judgment."

But I don't see how I could have stopped Longo from bringing Karin to the Stadthalle. All sorts of speakers—KPD, SDP, nationalists—ranted in hired halls every night all over Germany. Herr Hitler was a nobody. But it was no use making excuses to my father. I had never seen him so annoyed.

Many years later, in February 1945, I came across Longo in one of our POW cages in the western Netherlands. He didn't remember me at first. During the standard POW interrogation, without revealing my identity, I asked him when he had joined the Nazi party.

"Nineteen twenty-eight."

The year after our Heidelberg excursion. It didn't make him a veteran Nazi, one of the "old fighters," but it would have meant a respectably low number on his membership card.

He complimented me on my German, and that was when I told him I'd come of age at Walden, son of the manager of Baron Weinbrenner's racing stable.

He peered at me closely, then his face broke into a grin. "Ah so! Billy!" He reached across the interview table and clapped me on the shoulder. "My old comrade! I remember you *well*! Ah, those happy days at Walden!"

I asked him what Karin had thought of his decision to join the party.

"I never told Karin, of course." He smiled, shaking his head. "That little girl had a temper. She would have spat in my face!"

Longo had always understood himself to be a cheerful bon vivant, a cosmopolitan, scion of a proud family. After departing Walden in his Mercedes he didn't show up again until the following summer when a new crop of yearlings was being trained to the track. After that he was an occasional weekend guest. He rode well. He brought cases of excellent wines. I don't think her parents would have been displeased had he asked to marry Karin; all grown-ups at Walden were keen for Karin to "settle down," and Longo with his excellent family, his law degree, and his good looks was thought a "good catch." But by then she had met Anna von Rabou and started working at the famous UFA studio. Her parents could not understand what in the world she was doing there. It made no sense to them that a daughter of theirs would choose to spend her time with a mob of actors and writers.

When I interviewed Longo at the POW camp he didn't really have much to say about Karin, or about anything except the war. His recent experiences as a tank commander in Normandy were very fresh in his mind. He described a couple of dismaying episodes in a disconcertingly lighthearted manner, but many POWs I interviewed told their most horrifying stories in a similar tone.

Karin once remarked that Longo was like the façade of an elegant, old-fashioned building with nothing behind it. "He was like the false streets they keep at Warner's and MGM."

During his interrogation Longo described how one of his men had brutally and needlessly executed two Canadian prisoners. Such things were terrible for discipline, but after weeks of combat he'd been losing control of his young soldiers. "You must rely on discipline and training but those break down after a while and soldiers in a killing field become frightened, hunted beasts. *Mein lieber Freund* Billy, do you remember the Weinbrenners' chauffeur? The one-eyed Solomon?"

"Yes. Of course."

I felt sorry for Longo, and still I loathed him. He must have sensed it.

"Believe me or not, Billy, after what happened to the chauffeur, and to the baron's lawyer, what was his name—Kaufman—I felt quite ashamed of having joined the party."

"Did you tear up your card?"

"Ah, but it wasn't so simple. I was in Berlin, you know. I had a government post. My father was no party man, far from it, but he had been able to fix that job for me. To quit the party then would have put not only me but my father in jeopardy."

"I see."

"I stopped visiting the Weinbrenners long before the chauffeur was killed, but not for the reason you think. I couldn't have done anything to help them, you see. I wasn't in a strong position at work. There were people in the ministry who didn't like me, didn't believe I was on the team, which I wasn't. I'd only have made the baron's situation more precarious by interfering. The best I could do was to stay away."

When I asked if he remembered our outing to Heidelberg, he shook his head. He said he had no memory of taking Karin Weinbrenner to hear Hitler at the Stadthalle.

Was he lying to himself, or just lying, or had he really forgotten? I don't know.

>⎯◦⎯⦁⎯◦⎯◦⎯◦⎯<

The fact was, a few days after we saw Herr Hitler, Karin fell ill and was taken by her mother to the Burghölzli Clinic at the University of Zurich. My mother said Karin had suffered a "nervous breakdown"— the first time I heard that phrase.

My father was certain it was the encounter with "that fellow" and his entourage that was to blame. "She's a sensitive creature, Karin, a thoroughbred. The trash those people speak, it's disgusting. There ought to be a law."

❧   1938

Eleven days before the ss *Volendam* was due to sail from Rotterdam, a Polish Jewish boy shot a German diplomat in Paris. Pogroms organized by the regime broke out all over Germany. Shops were smashed; Jews were assaulted, sometimes killed. Reichskristallnacht, they called it afterward: Night of Crystal, Night of Broken Glass. It was worse in urbane, civilized Frankfurt than in many places.

Six party rascals in a hijacked beer truck smashed down the iron gates at Walden and broke into the house. The only people staying there were Karin, her father, and Herta, widow of the chauffeur.

There wasn't much left to plunder at Walden. Using drapery cord, the *Sturmtruppen* tied Karin and her father to chairs in the library and forced Herta to lead them down to the wine cellar.

She recognized two of them—local boys, classmates of mine from *Grundschule*, members of the Winnetou tribe, who'd played in the Walden woods and cadged snacks from the kitchen.

All the baron's wine had been "auctioned" off, with only bosses from party headquarters of Hesse allowed to bid. The wine cellar was empty, and this annoyed the invaders. They stormed through the house looking for hidden Jewish treasure, taking breaks to suck beer from barrels on their hijacked truck. When they stumbled back into the library they were so drunk they could hardly stand. They shouted at the baron that he'd be executed on the spot unless he showed them where he'd buried his gold.

He shook his head. "No buried gold here, lads. If you want to help yourself to my property, by all means, go ahead, but you'll find most of it's in the basement at the Städel. They've picked me clean to the bone."

These young men had probably never heard of the Städel Museum, even though it was on their (south) side of the river. Niederrad folk didn't go to art museums. Maybe they thought he was making fun of them. They gathered around him wolfishly and began abusing him, demanding he lead them to his hoard of buried gold. What rich old Jew did not have a hoard of buried gold?

Tied to a chair Karin was forced to watch these imbeciles torment her father. The young men were strange and wild. One of them politely offered to fetch her a glass of water; another offered a cigarette. Meanwhile, their companions were dumping her father's collection of Hebrew books and manuscripts into the fire.

At last the baron agreed to lead them to his buried treasure. His lip was cut and blood had run down his chin and throat. Perhaps he just couldn't stand those fellows polluting his home any longer. Maybe he planned to lead them on a wild-goose chase through the Walden woods, ending at the little cemetery where his son was buried with the soldiers from the war. Perhaps he figured they were going to kill him anyway and he didn't wish to be murdered in front of his daughter.

They were stupid enough, or drunk enough, to let him go into a cloakroom off the front hall to retrieve his coat and hat. His *Uhlanen* saber was in a dim corner, hanging on the same hook as his old army greatcoat. He dropped the coat on the floor, drew the blade from its sheath, and came out wielding it: seven hundred and fifty-two millimeters of honed steel. Weyersberg craftsmanship, always kept in superb condition. IN TREUE FEST stamped on the blade. *Loyalty Forever.*

I think what Karin's father really wanted was to die fighting them.

❄ ANNA

Arten von Licht Buch [Kinds of Light Book], *Karin v Weinbrenner*. Unpaginated. In English and occ. German. Lange Family Archive, 11 C-12-1988. Special Collections, McGill Library, McGill University, Montreal.

—Anna von Rabou. Famous old Prussia name. She laughs about this but I see is also—proud. Married to Fred Scheps but for all purposes she remains: Anna v Rabou

—the first afternoon cold blue fall aroma of roasting chestnuts and schnapps I am introduced to AvR on the k'damm she asks 'are you one of us?' and (so I think) she means a kommunist but—no! she despises KPD.

Me—'I'm not certain what you mean so you had better explain if you want me to respond'.

AvR—'Are you a producer or a parasite? Do you produce to feed the soul of the human race or are you one of these young women whose decadent lives we encounter in the pages of Tempo?'

Me—'well I shall have to think about that. I'll let you know.'

Her boldness makes me angry but there is something there and she won't let me go.

—she is beloved by all persons high and low at the UFA.

—very handsome and self-assured but not interested in being 'the great lady'. She says 'my people not grand aristo, not by any means, but der niederer Adel—country gentry?—very proud, rather poor, nothing as grand as you wealthy jews'

—she needs to work and says everyone needs to work for the feeding of their spirit we all have the instinct to contribute something and it is important to recognize and act upon it otherwise our lives have no value and it is though we never lived at all.

Advertisement. In *Film-kurier Nummer 1472 12. ausgabe 101 vom 15. Oktober 1930 (Mittwoch)*. Lange Family Archive, C 12 10-1930. Special Collections, McGill Library, McGill University, Montreal.

—◆—

LIEBLING DER GÖTTER

Darstellar: Emil Jannings, Renate Müller und
Olga Tschechowa

Regisseur: Hanns Schwarz

Produzent: Erich Prommer

Drehbuch: Hans Müller, K. Weinbrenner

Musik: Willy Schmidt-Gentner

Fotografische Leitung Konstantin Irmen-Tschet
Günther Rittau

Herausgeber: Willy Zeyn

Studio: Universum Film AG

Verteilt Durch: Universum Film AG

Premierenstag: 13 Oktober 1930

Movie Poster. Lange Family Archive, 12 HL-8-1932. Special Collections, McGill Library, McGill University, Montreal.

DIE TÄNZERIN VON SANS SOUCI

mit Otto Gebühr

und Lil Dagover § Rosa Valetti

Produktionsleiter Gabriel Levy

Drehbuch Hans Behrendt § K. Weinbrenner

Ein UFA Film

Die 6. Woche

Im UFA Theater Kurfürstendamm Berlin

Arten von Licht Buch [Kinds of Light Book], Karin v Weinbrenner. Unpaginated. In English and occ. German. Lange Family Archive, 11 C-12-1988. Special Collections, McGill Library, McGill University, Montreal.

scene: young Karin With wise Anna

Her light is strong & is the mother I never had obviously

She feeds cast & crew. Her delight in this

A: 'The writer is a telegraph wire carrying current between the picture (the pictures, meaning a sequence of images) the director imagines in his mind—and the story an audience can absorb. The total effect on the audience of a film is result of these (images, story) in combination.'

A: 'The film will happen like a dream does in the dark.'

A: 'Bild und Erzählung. Images and story. To absorb a film utterly different process than to read a book. More like a dream.'

Really the writer makes the picture by making the story.

A: 'Some directors really only want to paint (with light and shadow—images) not interested to tell a story.' Here she speaks (perhaps?) of F. Scheps her husband.

She has no envy she believes she is great

A: 'Pictures will grow'

A: 'Wagner always'

As a woman at Neubabelsberg she creates herself 'Sie sind die Arbeit, die Sie tun' You are the work you do!

Arten von Licht Buch [Kinds of Light Book], Karin v Weinbrenner. Unpaginated. In English and occ. German. Lange Family Archive, 11 C-12-1988. Special Collections, McGill Library, McGill University, Montreal.

———

Karl Mays "Winnetou", Ideas for film treatment

The university student fights the mensur, takes his scar, it does not satisfy him. He comes into America, seeking adventure. On the streets of New York confronting robbers we see this man likes to fight. His name now: Old Shatterhand. Too many people for him. West he must go.

The railroad, controlled only by greed, pushes west. Hero accepts employment otherwise he will starve. His job: promising whiskey & blankets to Indians who sign away their ground. Only on el llano estacado, hunting ground of the Mescalero Apaches, he encounters a resolute foe, chief of Mescaleros, Winnetou. Combat they engage. Knives. Surprise: the former student Korpsbruder is a swordsman, their match is even. As they struggle to the death, a brown bear charges. They must fight the bear or each other. The bear is killed. From this moment they will be brothers.

Adventures as they seek to defeat the Comanche and are victorious.

Sickening slaughter. Corrupt railroad boss invites Winnetou to a 'feast' to celebrate his 'victory' over Comanche. W eats poison. Dies.

Shatterhand dares enter camp of Comanche warriors where he faces death but a wise chief listens. Shatterhand leads Apache and Comanche to attack the railroad camp. Victory. They name him their war chief. He has located his destiny. He will take an Indian bride. A new race is born.

Arten von Licht Buch [Kinds of Light Book], *Karin v Weinbrenner*. Unpaginated. In English and occ. German. Lange Family Archive, 11 C-12-1988. Special Collections, McGill Library, McGill University, Montreal.

⟞

AR: 'art is unity'!!

But,

K:(Art is destruction too isn't it)!?

AR has no patience for Max Beckmann. 'degenerate vision'

AR: 'Wir sind Deutsche Juden. Wir teilen den gleichen Raum, aber wir sind nicht gleich' which I will translate as 'Germans and jews share the space only they are not the same people'

AR admires 'a german spirit' that she will not define because 'indefinable' only one feels it.

AR holds one, and one feels quite safe

Beautiful care, the hungry carpenters, the electrician, cast and crew she feeds, she gives extra food to bring home to their family

of Dr. Goebbels she says: wicked but brilliant understanding the strange soul of an artist

Ich nehme mir vor, dass ich sie nicht wiedersehen werde—

I resolve: I shall not speak of her again.

So far as I am concerned. Elle est morte.

KARIN WAS BACK AT WALDEN FOR A FEW WEEKS IN THE SPRING OF 1928. The New York stock market hadn't crashed yet but the German economy was falling apart, though the Weinbrenners didn't appear to notice. The baron was still buying broodmares in England, Ireland, and Belgium. Lady Maire and my mother were planning that summer's expedition, to Portugal.

I'd graduated from high school but hadn't been able to line up any sort of job except the two afternoons a week I still put in as file clerk and translator for the lawyer, Kaufman. I didn't cross paths with Karin until I met her walking along the gravel drive one afternoon as I was pedaling home from Kaufman's on my ridiculous bicycle. I knew she'd been ill, but she looked strong and rosy. She wore her riding habit.

"Hello, old Billy."

"Hello, Karin." Dismounting, I walked beside her, pushing my bike. She was silent.

"Going for a ride?" I said, finally.

"I am."

It seemed so long ago when we'd first met in the Walden woods, that raw and ferocious first winter after the war; that season of blood and beggars.

As an unemployed person, I felt life passing me by. I'd missed the bus somehow. I wanted to engage passionately with life, but I was only a tall, skinny, underemployed youth pushing a bicycle.

"Will you come hacking with me?" she said suddenly.

"Really? Wouldn't you'd rather go alone? Shall I?"

"You must come along."

"Are you sure?"

"Of course."

So I pedaled to Newport, changed hastily, pulled on a pair of my father's boots. By the time I reached the stable she'd saddled two horses: her mother's hunter, Paddy, and Prince Hal, the walking-out horse my father usually rode.

"Does Prince Hal suit you?"

"Perfectly," I said.

I followed her down the bridle path. She reached to open a gate so that we could canter across a meadow. We stayed out an hour, and didn't speak the whole time, just enjoyed the thrilling thump of hooves, squeak of saddle leather, our gallant horses breathing hard.

When we finally returned to the stable we looked after the animals ourselves without troubling the grooms. We stripped off saddles and tack, rubbed the horses down, fed them, watered them, and turned them out in the paddock. It was wonderful to be working alongside her. She knew how to behave around horses. Not every rider does.

Still, she seemed different. Quieter than the rackety girl in the fast car speeding to Heidelberg. I hadn't noticed it during our gallop. Our horses hadn't been ridden much lately and were in high spirits. But in the quiet of the stable, I noticed. She seemed more self-possessed. Or detached.

When we said goodbye she reached out to shake hands with me.

"Good luck, old Billy, it's good to see you. Such an old soul you are."

Somehow shaking hands didn't feel right—it just didn't. It dismayed me, in fact. Though I had no right to expect anything else.

"Actually," I blurted out, "I'm young and an idiot! Spend all my time lying in bed listening to jazz! Haven't a proper job or any direction in life. My father's fed up with my uselessness and so am I."

She smiled. "Don't let the old ones frighten you. I'm sure you'll find your way."

She headed back to the big house, and I didn't see her again before she returned to her Berlin, roaring Berlin, Berlin of the late twenties, city of nightclubs, cabarets, and parties, a city I glimpsed only in the startling pages of tabloid newspapers.

⊱┈◈┈◦┈◈┈⊰

Never was Karin the riotous bohemian her mother imagined her to be. If she liked to live intensely, even wildly, there was also something austere to her character. It came up more after Zurich, perhaps, but had always been there—the silence of the spruce forest, the little girl ranging snowy paths with her Apache bow.

She would sometimes go for days without leaving her flat, which was in the Charlottenburg district.

Later, when we were spending weekends together in Berlin, she often used to talk about earlier phases of her life in the city. It wasn't that she was trying to make me jealous or feel I'd missed important things—though I was, and I had. I believe her intention was to force our intimacy, which had been put off for so long, force it so it would blossom quickly, make up for lost time.

She was a solitary, Karin. You wouldn't know it to look at her, but she was.

"Billy, in those days, I never was lonely. Days without speaking one word, answering to no one—excellent! What could be better? Always the tram noise, traffic floating up from the street, and voices from the café across the road. That was all right, that was the background, the structure of the city. One was not required to participate."

For a while she'd even stopped paying her telephone bill and her line had been cut off, which irritated her parents. Her father provided her an allowance, not an extravagant one, and she started buying pictures. Max Beckmann taught at the Städelschule in Frankfurt, but she first encountered his paintings in Berlin.

The earliest sound films, the talkies, were just coming out. She became a devotee of the cinema. The afternoon she met Anna Rabou, she had just seen—heard!—Pabst's *Westfront 1918*, an antiwar picture set on the western front.

Emerging into the city after taking in a powerful picture was always a disorienting experience. "What a shock, to suddenly be walking·the same old boulevards in the same old crowd—while mentally I'm still with a dying front soldier—or an Apache warrior, or a Texas outlaw about to be hanged! At such times I feel weightless, and horribly seasick, Billy, and terrific excitement, all at once. I want someplace to go, someplace jolly, noisy, fierce! A loud café, and a chocolate, because in such moods I become maudlin and *contretemps* if I take a schnapps or whiskey, I'll end up lurching off by myself for another wallow in solitary."

It was at a fashionable café on the Kurfürstendamm, the sort of bril-

liant Berlin "scene" she usually avoided, that she first met Anna von
Rabou, who was sharing a table with a girl Karin recognized from Lausanne, Marie-Therese von Zeiten.

At finishing school Zeiten, the youngest daughter of a Prussian general, had declared herself a Communist. She and Anna Rabou were
cousins, but family was the only real connection between them. They
certainly weren't close politically, and Anna was fifteen years older.

It was chilly on the terrace. Marie Zeiten wore a fur stole bundled
about her shoulders. She invited Karin to join them. Anna von Rabou
offered her an English cigarette and ordered her a hot chocolate.
Anna was one of those people who effortlessly can command a waiter's
attention.

While they sipped their drinks and smoked cigarettes—at that time
still bold behavior for women of their class, in a public place—along
the Kurfürstendamm came a parade of Reichsbanner: war veterans in
uniform, marching up the most bourgeois boulevard in the city.

The Social Democrat Reichsbanner was only one of the party mili-
tias of that period. They fought street battles with the Communists'
RFB, the right-wing Stahlhelm, and the Nazi *Sturmtruppen*. In their
ranks that day were a couple of dozen veterans blinded or crippled in
the war. When Karin saw that many well-heeled patrons on the café
terrace were literally turning their backs and refusing to look at the
marching men, it dismayed her. "Why can't they look at these fellows?
They were heroes, now they go hungry. Why turn from the truth?
What's the use of that?"

"What's the truth, Miss Weinbrenner?" Anna asked.

Karin was surprised by the intense way Anna was looking at her.
Looking right into her, it seemed.

"Are you one of us?" Anna demanded.

Karin laughed. "I'm not certain what you mean, so you had better
explain if you want me to respond."

"Are you a producer or a parasite, Miss Weinbrenner? Do you produce good work to feed the soul of the human race or are you one of
these young women whose decadent lives we encounter in the pages of
Tempo?"

"Well, I shall have to think about that." Karin was flustered, and annoyed, but also intrigued. She wasn't used to being challenged by people. "I'll let you know."

Anna had gray eyes. Nowhere near pretty, but striking. She'd grown up shooting stags and riding big horses on her family's estate in the Mark Brandenburg. Her father had died of a heart attack on the first day of the war in 1914. Like a lot of Prussian daughters, she was mostly self-educated, but she could read Greek and Latin, and had swum naked in Lake Constance with the American lyric poet Edna St. Vincent Millay. She smoked, heavily, always English cigarettes, Senior Service, and took whiskey in her coffee, even at breakfast. Slouching in her café chair, studying Karin through quick clouds of cigarette smoke, her manner was languid, even rude. But that was the style, the manner, of women of her class. When she wanted to, Anna could move like an aristocratic panther, and Karin told me she was a better horsewoman than even Lady Maire.

"Do tell me something true, Miss Weinbrenner."

It seemed to Karin that if any truth was in her reach, it was contained in certain scenes witnessed at Walden during the war. She'd been a little girl then, but she remembered certain scenes very vividly and had never shared them with anyone.

Karin began telling Anna about young officers soon to be sent back to the front, stripping off their gray tunics and shirts to sun themselves on the Walden lawns. Rows of white bodies glinting on green grass, like trout freshly pulled from a stream. She described the one-armed cavalryman she'd watched struggling to mount a spirited horse and bursting into tears when he couldn't manage it. She described the baron's unexpected homecoming in the middle of the night, in the middle of the war, the dressings on his hand soaked in brown blood, more blood crusted on his uniform, smelling awful. She described a wheelchair race organized by nursing sisters, a young officer wailing and beating his head and fists on the grass after he had lost.

When Karin fell silent Anna reached over, took her gloved hand, and kissed it. An unusual—bizarre—gesture between women, especially old-line Prussian gentry like Anna von Rabou. "Thank you, Miss Weinbrenner, for your gifts, your beautiful, terrible, painful gifts of the war."

Later Karin witnessed Anna provoking others to spill memory, and came to understand this was how Anna Rabou as a writer operated in the world. Bored by anecdotes, Anna was interested only in fragments, raw shards of memory: material details: textures, light, scent. She was interested in her interviewees' powers of recall, not of reflection. She didn't want memories that had already been assembled into anecdotes and assigned meaning. She wanted raw snapshots of a scene—mise-en-scène—not "story" about what had happened. Anna absorbed other people's basic sensory impressions of a scene and by infusing these with dialogue and fitting them into a dramatic arc, she forced them into her own novels, plays, and films.

She was married to Fred Scheps, the most famous film director in Germany. Stories about them ran in the illustrated papers: a glamorous Berlin pair. Rabou had established her fame with her novels and had just started writing screenplays for the talkies at the Universum Film AG lot at Neubabelsberg in Potsdam, just outside Berlin. The famous UFA.

Even in those days it was apparent that the talking pictures were more than a technological advance, more than compounds of light and electromagnetic signal on reels of chemically treated film. Talking pictures possessed powers like magic did, or like our dreams.

But no one outside the business knew anything about how such pictures were actually put together. When Karin confessed she had not the slightest idea of how a film like *Westfront 1918* was made, or what it was made of, Anna insisted she must come out to Neubabelsberg to see the process for herself.

"Filmmaking isn't hocus-pocus, Miss Weinbrenner. It's like building motor cars, or making a soufflé. Skilled, industrious people work together, everyone doing his bit. A picture comes first, yes, from the brain of a writer but that is like saying the soufflé comes from the hen. Yes, ultimately it does, but so what? There is more to cookery than egg production. But come out and see for yourself, Miss Weinbrenner. Take the S-Bahn out to Neubabelsberg, or a car if you have one at your disposal. I'll give you lunch. You'll light the place up. Will you come? You must give me your word of honor."

From photographs I've seen, Rabou at that period dressed in a style all her own: severely tailored dresses, Javanese scarves, a felt hat like a helmet. It was all about line and form with her. The one time I met her, the impression was severe, elegant, and somehow classical, though it was hard to imagine anyone in the classical world, or in any other period had ever dressed quite the way she did.

Later, after the Nazi takeover, she would pose in whipcord breeches and English riding boots, a cigarette in one hand, a little whip in the other.

The Reichsbanner parade passed. Normal traffic resumed on the boulevard, and soon a great blue Mercedes drew up at the curb, the driver honking impatiently. Karin recognized silver-haired Fred Scheps.

(Scheps was another under the *llano* spell. He read *Winnetou* as a schoolboy in Vienna.)

Anna kissed her cousin Zeiten, then shook hands with Karin and made her promise to come out to the studio the next day. Karin surprised herself by swearing she would.

▷┼◈▹─○─◃┼◁

UFA had lost a lot of money on Fred Scheps's penultimate silent picture *Urbanos*, with its cast of thousands and old-fashioned melodramatic acting. The old silent-film studio at Templehof had been abandoned, and UFA relocated to Neubabelsberg, where they built four enormous soundstages joined in one giant cruciform building, the Tonkreuz—the cross of sound—which became a symbol of German moviemaking.

When she went out to the lot, Karin found to her dismay that Anna Rabou had arranged a screen test. Karin had zero interest in being a performer, and her looks weren't the kind that made sense on film, at least films of that era. But on the sets that day she encountered dozens of purposeful, very skilled people—set carpenters, costume designers, actors—working toward a common goal. The beehive atmosphere was exhilarating. For weeks she'd been living a monastic existence in the middle of the Berlin delirium, and now she was ready for excitement and companionship. She was keen to learn, eager to develop her powers as a writer.

One of the first things Anna Rabou had done at the studio was organize a canteen. No one at UFA was paid very much, so healthy delicious food was one of the great boons of working there. She sometimes worked in the canteen herself, baking enormous loaves of rye bread and preparing her own recipes for leek soup and lentil stew. Everyone on the lot—producers, directors, grips, stars, extras—ate at Anna's canteen. No one went hungry, and everyone was treated exactly the same. She loaned money to all sorts of people at UFA without expecting repayment.

Everyone at UFA loved to see Anna Rabou ladling out homemade soup while discussing the latest draft of a script with its producer and making sure actors and crew—anyone who had something to say—were included in the discussion. Anna believed in new German technologies in optics, sound, and film chemistry and in making new kinds of art possible. And she believed successful films worked the same way German opera did, especially Wagner, where magical nonsense was handled with such magnificent seriousness that it transcended itself and became intimate, human, and piercing.

When Anna offered Karin a job as her secretary, Karin surprised herself by accepting it. She was drawn to the purposeful energy and bustle on the studio lot. Her periods of silence and withdrawal were almost always followed by periods of high energy, sociability, connection. Later in the decade, our weekends in Berlin incorporated those polarities: daylight hours were spent quietly, calmly, often reading in bed, but at night we roved the electric city, neon Berlin, riding trams and trains to venues in distant suburbs, seeking out our raucous Kansas City jazz, dancing until dawn.

Before sound, film scripts had been lists of scenes and locations, brief character profiles, along with a few lines of dialogue that might be put up on cards. But sound films demanded lines that fit an actor's mouth and sounded natural when spoken. Anna Rabou was one of the pioneers writing real dialogue for real actors to speak and vast audiences to hear.

In her first days on the lot Karin merely typed out Anna's pages, using a studio typewriter with a three-colored ribbon: red for camerawork, black for action, dialogue in blue. When Anna felt blocked by problems of structure, they talked through stories together. They developed scenes and came up with dialogue by acting them out in Rabou's office. It was great fun.

It was the period when Karin started keeping the *Arten von Licht* notebook, which survives. It means *Kinds of Light*. Sometimes she is trying to imagine herself as a camera and writes about varieties of light, which is all a camera sees when it looks at the world. She also used the notebook to practice her written English. And she had a habit of copying in extracts from her wide reading about *el llano*.

The UFA studio was a film factory. Anna Rabou couldn't keep up with the demand for scenarios, and within a couple of weeks Karin was writing her own dialogue for scenes sometimes shot the following day. The pictures were mostly costume dramas set in royal courts of the eighteenth or nineteenth century, a genre unaccountably popular in Germany in those earliest days of sound. They weren't classics of cinema, but she was a young woman learning the new language of film, and learning quickly.

⊱─━─◦─◈─━─⊰

Karin had begun a career. I, meanwhile, was still without a job.

I'd earned top marks at school. I had my Abitur, but I didn't see how my parents could support me for three or four more years while I studied law at university. Anyway, I didn't wish to become a lawyer.

In Frankfurt it wasn't a good season for job hunting. Every week thousands were losing their jobs. I applied at dozens of firms and didn't get a single interview.

There was radio by then, and a jazz program late at night. Music of speed, music of dreams. I heard Louis Armstrong for the first time in my bedroom at Newport. Swing was just starting, and many of the popular tunes were from Broadway shows. I'd lie in bed listening to Hoagy Carmichael's "Georgia on My Mind," Bix Beiderbecke on coronet. During the empty days I felt immobilized, frozen, stuck, helpless. Late at night, jazz broke loneliness in half and made it almost inspiring. The music was everything to me.

I still put in two afternoons a week at Kaufman's law office, translating documents mostly concerning apparently endless legal battles with His Majesty's government over property expropriated from the baron in 1914, including his sailboat *Hermione II* and his house Sanssouci. I was paid very little. Kaufman really felt I ought to be working gratis and grateful for the experience.

Fed up with my passivity, my father at last approached Hermann Weinbrenner and asked for his advice. The next day I was summoned to the library where I found the little baron, brown as a walnut, sitting behind his wonderful naval desk.

"Ah so, dear Billy! Enter! Enter!"

He smiled brightly. I was groomed and polished—my father had seen to that—and the baron was alert to every detail. He was always absorbing new information, updating his own ideas and opinions—and he had opinions on everything.

"Well, my dear Billy, here is some news. Your interview has been arranged with Dr. Ziegler of IG Farben's Translation Department. By the way, that is an excellent suit; you are as debonair as your father, I am pleased to see. Very much the English gentleman. I'm sure quite successful with the ladies."

"Well, not exactly."

My romance with Kaufman's junior secretary Heidi had culminated in a bout of kissing at the cinema when I took her to see Gary Cooper as the Llano Kid, a young bandit with a price on his head, in *The Texan*. I'd spent one rainy Saturday at a muddy farm up in the Taunus, paying my respects to her family. After an enormous lunch I persuaded Heidi to take a walk in the woods with me. She said her mother thought I didn't seem very "strong."

"What does that mean?"

"She says perhaps you cannot do the work of a man."

"Utterly ridiculous."

"She means the work of a farmer. Your bones aren't heavy enough."

It was clear to me that Heidi's parents' opinions mattered a good deal to her, and shortly thereafter she left Kaufman's to marry a young swine farmer from her village. The lawyer's new secretary, Frau Fleck, was an older woman who viewed me, unfairly, as a spoiled, idle, rich boy. I was spoiled and idle, but not rich.

"We Germans, Billy, relish a sense of belonging!"

The baron popped out of his chair and came around the massive desk. Slight and wiry, bristling with energy and drive, Karin's father wasn't fiery, exactly—he was too cool minded and rational—but I never saw him carefree or relaxed. And he never could sit still.

That afternoon he wore a green-and-blue-striped polo jersey and a pair of riding breeches. The narrow Vandyke beard on his chin was clipped very close. His brown eyes were lit with intelligence and, I would say, wariness. The animal he most resembled was a fox: clever, resourceful, nimble.

"Billy!" He was peering up at me, smiling.

I was seven or eight inches taller. Probably I had not been quite real to him before, just a boy on the estate, even though I was his godson and namesake.

"In August 1914, Billy, the Uhlanen-Garde were the finest soldiers, the finest body of men, in the world. Do you know what was the quality they possessed above all that allowed them to be such excellent troops?"

"Courage?"

"Loyalty! A *Uhlan* was ready to die for the honor of the regiment. You cannot ask more than that of a man. Billy, I am pleased to have arranged your interview with Dr. Anton Ziegler. But you'll have to win the position on your own merits. He won't have you on my say-so. IG Farben cannot take in every booby who wants a place merely because one of the directors happens to be the booby's godfather. I'm not saying you're a booby, you understand. But as to whether you've a head for business, how should I know? I'm sure you have your father's pristine character, but do you also have his drive? In short: you'll have to stand up on your own legs and convince Anton Ziegler you've the makings of an IG man."

"Thank you, sir. I'll do my best."

"Billy! My point is that men seeking to join an organization, I don't care if it's the priesthood, a regiment, or a business firm, must be prepared to offer total loyalty. Any organization of human beings that can't command such loyalty is crippled and pathetic. And a man who doesn't feel that he belongs to something larger and greater than himself sooner or later simply gives up the struggle of life. He succumbs. You see it all around us these days, millions without work and, eventually, without hope. If you join an organization you had better be able to believe you work for a higher good, something bigger than yourself, or you'll never find it in yourself to make the sacrifices required. In short, you must be willing to bleed. That is the spirit of the *Uhlanen* of August 1914. It wasn't that they had the best mounts or the first pick of conscripts. What made them great was the unquenchable spirit of loyalty."

I had heard my father remark that the *Uhlans* of 1914 were almost to a man dead by Christmas, but I didn't reflect on that.

"Thank you, sir."

"Good luck, Billy!" His grip was fierce and quick. "I only wish you'd kept your good Deutsche 'Hermann,' instead of English 'Billy'!"

⤚⤙⤛⤜⤝⤞

The next day I went off on the trams to the IG plant at Hoechst, where I was interviewed by Dr. Ziegler, who wore a soft, collared shirt and a brown Brooks Brothers suit, very relaxed by the standards of German business attire. He had just returned from four years at an IG subsidiary's plant on the Hudson River in upstate New York.

"I only want men with perfect marks from school," Dr. Ziegler said. "Without much office experience, so no bad habits. If we take you on, you'd be on my 'flying squad,' principally working out of headquarters but traveling wherever needed. Some translation is very technical. Your background in organic chemistry is weak. There are technical courses which you'll be expected to take. We also write and translate speeches for directors and signatories and prepare strategic summaries of developments abroad. Do you have any politics, Billy Lange?"

"Well . . ."

"An English liberal, yes? I don't give a damn. Keep your opinions to yourself, that's what the work demands. Believe it or not, we've Nazis and KPD working in the same office. We are a business, nothing else. Understand?"

"Completely."

"So, no colorful armbands. No lapel pins, no 'worker' caps, no uniforms. No party newspapers on your desk. To read the *Times* of London is required. The *Manchester Guardian* is acceptable. The *Daily Worker*, never. If you belong to a political party here or in England I suggest you quit."

"I don't."

"Excellent." He handed me a copy of the British *Journal of Industrial and Engineering Chemistry* with one article bookmarked. "Go find yourself a desk and translate this. No errors, please."

It was hard going, but not so difficult as the prevarications and legalese I was used to at Kaufman's. The translation still took most of the day and Dr. Ziegler evaluated my work while I stood before his desk. Finally he nodded and told me I would be taken on at the rank of commercial clerk, on a probationary basis, with a weekly salary of eighty marks. At the time, perhaps twenty dollars, and a very decent salary for a young fellow.

My parents were overjoyed.

Our office was in the process of relocating from the plant at Hoechst to the brand-new IG headquarters in the West-End, the largest office building in Europe, unlike anything else in sleepy old medieval Frankfurt. Weinbrenner had been on the committee that chose the site and the architect. It was intended to be a steel-and-concrete symbol of Germany's commercial and scientific manpower, and it was. Headquarters was all about the present and the future; it had nothing to do with the ruinous past, which made sense for a country whose nightmares stank of trench rot and mustard gas. The new building was bold and exciting, a new start for Germany. Our offices were streamlined and sleek, with beautiful wood paneling and rich woolen carpeting that absorbed sound. A dozen paternoster elevators operated silently and endlessly, like vertical conveyor belts, with telephone booth–sized cubicles that a person stepped into to be carried up or down.

Every morning it gave me a thrill to report for work.

Since the start of the worldwide depression IG had been letting people go, so my new colleagues were surprised, and annoyed, when I showed up. They were anxious about their own careers—what was Dr. Ziegler doing hiring an English boy? Everyone at IG was anxious almost all the time. Anxiety was an operating principle there. The atmosphere was wide-awake, tense, competitive. Every corner of the biggest office building in Europe was filled with bright young men. If you weren't bright and willing to work fanatically long hours, they wouldn't keep you. Anyone let go had good reason to believe he'd never find another job. There were plenty of suicides in Frankfurt in those days. If your work was satisfactory, they gave you more responsibility with less supervision. Your salary was regularly raised without anyone saying a word about it. When they stopped raising your pay, that was when you had to worry.

The only fellow who took time to show me the ropes was Günter Krebs, my old schoolmate. I hadn't forgotten his bullying at *Grundschule*, but he took care to introduce me to everyone in our department, from higher-ups to secretaries. The other fellows could be shockingly rude to the female secretaries, but Günter treated them with respect and was popular with them. His mother had been a secretary, he told me.

He invited me to sit with him at lunch. When I mentioned that the *Paris Trib* was my favorite newspaper, he nodded and said it was wise to keep up with English and American newspapers. It was more than acceptable in the Translation Department to be seen reading newspapers at one's desk, he said, so long as they were the correct newspaper. "Not trash, mind you, not the *Daily Mirror*, but the *Times* or your *Herald Tribune*."

Günter warned me that Dr. Ziegler liked to see clean desks at the end of the day. "If you are assigned a project, you'd better complete it before you think of going home. If it means working all night, so be it. We've all done our share of those. Ziegler—a smart fellow, to be sure. Doctorate in chemistry from Freiburg. Lots of brains around here. No tolerance for mistakes. That's fine, pressure is good, keeps us on our toes. Dr. Ziegler can be a bear, but he looks out for his boys. If you can stand the pace of the work, who knows, your next post could be overseas. I went to Warsaw with the boss last month. We had some jolly good dinners, all on the expense account, of course. He likes sidecars—brandy, Cointreau, lemon juice, lots of ice. Not bad."

Everyone else in the Translation Department was standoffish on principle, the principle being to dislike new people. Even my old classmate Robert Briesewitz didn't bother being friendly at first, and he'd been one of my original Apache tribe, in the Walden woods.

Krebs invited me to see the new Gary Cooper film playing at the Harmonie, in Sachsenhausen, across the river. As we walked to the tram stop he asked if my father had been in the war. His father, a lawyer in civilian life, had spent his military career "pushing a pencil," drafting contracts between the army and suppliers. "My old fellow was never wounded. Five years in the army and not a scratch."

"That was lucky."

"You think so? I'm not so sure. An honorable wound, that can set you up for life."

Günter's mother was a Frenchwoman. He admitted that he'd spoken French before he spoke German. He laughed when he mentioned boys on his street calling him a *Parlewuh* and a *Froschschenkelfresser* during the war, slang their fathers brought back from the front.

"I don't blame them really. Kids can't abide anything outside their own realm of experience. It's natural. And those Frenchies marching in here after the armistice, the black fellows? What a disgrace. Peace with honor? What pig shit. They were rubbing our noses in defeat. Listen, old fellow, we ought to plan a hiking weekend. You'll find a lot of men in the department who are oarsmen, or pretend to be, but there's not much hiking spirit. But for me, you know, growing up in this god-awful city, going out in the mountains with a knapsack makes me feel really a German."

He was tall and slightly pear shaped. Ungainly. Not exactly ugly, but not handsome. His flat hair was yellow-blond. His chin was small. He walked like . . . a duck. His manner could be haughty and dismissive, but there was also in him a friendliness, an eagerness to connect to people.

On our way to the cinema we passed the BMW showroom and paused to have a look through the window. I pointed out a couple of machines and mentioned my old ambition of riding a motorcycle across El Llano Estacado.

"There really is such a place?" He was stunned. "Karl May didn't make it up?"

"No, *el llano* is real. Look it up in a good atlas, you'll see."

"Well, well, my friend Billy." He clapped me on the shoulder. "I think this is a marvelous plan of yours. I quite approve. You should hold to it. Buy your motorbike and strike off across El Llano Estacado. Wouldn't Old Shatterhand be pleased!"

"Unlikely. Don't see how. I'm not about to give up my job."

"When the other kids would call me frogeater, I would go home, tuck myself in, and read Karl May. Used to see myself roaming *el llano* but I never dreamed there was such a place, so never looked into it. And now you say there is—that's wonderful. I hope you get out there, old fellow. Remember to send me a postcard, will you?"

"Certainly."

The Gary Cooper film at the Harmonie was *City Streets*, dubbed in German. Sylvia Sydney was female lead. Afterward Krebs insisted we stop in at a historic old *Apfelweinwirtschaft* where he said he knew the proprietor. He ordered broiled pork for both of us—it really was pretty good. We were on our second jug of *Apfelwein* when he pulled out his

NSDAP membership card to show me. "Really I ought to wear the lapel pin, only it would count against me at work. It's really shameful. Dr. Ziegler has been for too long in America. He's out of touch with the moral crisis of Germany."

It surprised me that an IG Farben man, likable and good-natured if a bit odd, was also an NSDAP man. But I didn't want to get into it with Krebs.

"What did you think of the film?" I asked.

"Why, Billy, do you admire Gary Cooper? Because I find this film quite disgusting."

"Really?"

"For certain. A decent young man dragged down by his awful Jew of a girlfriend and her criminal father. Yet the young man is taken to be a hero—because he is loyal to her? In fact he is a degraded criminal of the worst type."

"Sylvia Sidney? How do you know she's Jewish?"

"Come on. You can smell a Jewess like that certainly."

"In the movies?"

"You merely have to look at her nose."

"I thought she was good-looking."

"That's how they work."

"Who?"

"A Jewish-seductress type. Vavavoom. Look. The character your Cooper plays, the Kid; he is perfectly Aryan. The Kid may even have a chance of making a contribution to the general welfare of society; instead he chooses loyalty to his awful Jewess. And the story wants us to believe he is a hero because of this? No. No. Never.

"The most disgusting thing of Hollywood, all run by Jews, is that Cooper himself, the actual fellow, I would say is the perfect Aryan. He is the ideal of our racial type. And yet in the mongrel society of Hollywood he has to play swine, utter swine. I only wish we had more like the real Gary Cooper at work here in Germany, here at the IG, and fewer rancid little Polish Jewboys. Some mornings I am almost sick to my stomach, the florid stink that Kracauer slime brings to our office. The cologne they wear, it's disgusting. I can't see why Ziegler tolerates it. But this is excellent cider, Billy—have some more. The best *Apfelwein* in the world is here in Frankfurt. No one else makes it so purely as we *Hessen* do."

We were speaking in German. Günter had good French, on account of his French mother, but his English was not strong.

He reached over to fill my glass from the *Bembel*, the cider jug. I found his anti-Semitism embarrassing. It was in poor taste, so creaky and old-fashioned, totally out of line with the crisp, modern spirit at our headquarters. I told myself *he'd* be embarrassed in the morning when he woke up with a headache. His rant was surely a case of the apple cider doing the talking.

After we said good night, I watched him hurrying to catch his tram. He didn't run gracefully—more an uncollected gallop than a sprint. His arms and legs weren't working together, I thought he was going to fall flat on his face. But he made the tram, just, and turned and waved enthusiastically. I think he lived with his mother in a flat way out on the Bockenheimer Landstraße.

>─◆─○─◆─◆

I started off handling files of correspondence from IG Farben subsidiaries in Britain, Canada, Australia, and the States. When it came to dyes, paints, synthetics, pharmaceuticals, fuels, and fertilizers, we owned the patents, we had developed the most-advanced processes, we were the leaders of the world. It was fun to be the English voice of such a power.

My father still took the *F-Zeit* and the *Vossische*, newspapers that paid as little attention as possible to the radical parties, but like everyone else we had a radio, and by now everyone knew who the Nazis were. There were brownshirt parades each week in Frankfurt, but, absorbed in the bright aniline excitement of working at IG Farben, I paid little attention. My Conoco road maps were still pinned up in my bedroom at Newport, but they had become invisible. I could no longer see them.

My first months at IG vanquished my depression, if that was what it was, but those days of aimlessness had left a scar. I'd suffered a spell of barbed-wire disease, tasted a bit of nothingness. Now, holding on to a job, having a career, meant something it had not before. I suppose you could say I was growing up.

✳ 1938

As soon as the savages sped off in their stolen beer truck, Karin rang my father at the hotel in Bad Homburg. I had no telephone in my rooms. Buck was on duty at the front desk, where he was reading Kessler's biography of Walther Rathenau. He summoned a janitor to take over and awakened my mother. On their way out to Walden they stopped at my lodgings. My father rapped on my door, and when I opened it my landlady stood behind him, wringing her hands. Buck wouldn't say much in front of her, only that "we are wanted across the river."

I dressed and hurried out to my parents waiting in a taxi. I recognized their driver, a young fellow called Otto Stahl, formerly an exercise rider at Walden—wry face a bit like a monkey's, always with a hand-rolled cigarette dangling from his lips.

"Saddle up, old pal!" Otto cried. He had a Kölsch accent—streetwise, smart-alecky, and tough. "Apache on the warpath! Everyone called inside the stockade. Saddle up and let's ride!"

As we drove quickly through deserted streets my father told me the baron had been assaulted and left for dead. Karin was unharmed physically but probably in shock.

I absorbed the news and peered out the window. In the *gemütlichen* glow of Frankfurt's cozy old-fashioned streetlamps there was nothing much to be seen. The latest pogrom had spent itself, apparently. The fire brigade had soaked out the flames, hooligans were swilling cider in warm taverns or asleep in their beds, a few dozen Jewish men were on their way to Dachau and Sachsenhausen. In another couple of hours municipal workers would be hard at it with brooms and shovels, sweeping up broken glass.

I'm not saying I had insight into the future. The present was bad enough. Who could imagine extermination camps? Thousand-bomber raids? Not me. Not Buffalo Billy.

From my road maps I knew that, just south of the Canadian River and a few miles north of Amarillo, a highway climbed steep red bluffs up onto an enormous tabletop mesa that the explorer Coronado had named El Llano Estacado, the Staked Plain, or the Palisaded Plain— exactly what he meant is unclear. It's possible he was referring to the bluffs which, seen from the approaches, resemble a fortress wall, a "pal- isade." Or maybe he was referring to the stalky yucca stems that sprout on the plains, or stakes the Comanche used to mark trails across that vast, featureless landscape.

Shutting my eyes I imagined the pair of us speeding across the hori- zontal yellow of those plains. More than ever we needed a span of emp- tiness, sunlight, and caustic highway speed. We would cross *el llano* to cauterize ourselves. And on the other side (California? Vancouver?), we'd reorganize ourselves, establish new connections to life, become different people. Become Americans or Canadians.

Escapism? Of course it was. Escapism was for realists in Frankfurt then. Escapists saw things plain.

><->--o--<-><

The iron gates of Walden with their crests of the shamrock and corn- flowers had been broken off their hinges and lay flat on the road. Otto stopped the taxi and I helped him drag the wreckage out of our way.

When Karin let us into the house her father was still sprawled on the floor in the front hall, not dead but not conscious, either, pulse very weak. She'd covered him with a blanket and cleaned and bandaged the gouges on his scalp. The attackers had broken the hilt off his saber and left the weapon in pieces on the floor. Herta's wails echoed from the wine cellar.

"She sounds like a banshee!" my mother said.

"She won't come upstairs, she's too frightened," Karin admitted.

"That's doing no good at all," Eilín said sharply. "She'll have to stop that."

Karin herself seemed weirdly calm. I don't know what I expected. Fury? She was cocooned in shock. We needed to get her father up off the floor where he was stuck in the glue of his own blood. Buck had the idea of using a folding metal card table for a stretcher. It took all of us to lift him as gently as possible. With Karin and my mother supporting his legs and feet we just managed to carry him into the library where we laid him on his sofa bed.

My mother telephoned Dr. Lewin, who lived in an apartment building just off the Boerne-Platz. Lewin said the synagogue on the Boerne-Platz was burning: he could see the flames. She begged him to come out to Walden but he said he was wary of going out whilst packs of hooligans who looked like off-duty policemen were still roaming his part of town.

Lewin had tickets for himself, his wife, and their two children on a French liner sailing from Le Havre for Havana in two days, but he finally agreed to come out to Walden after my mother promised to send Otto to pick him up.

Herta's howls from the cellar were dispiriting, the sound of the fear we all felt. I noticed my father's hands trembling when he lit his cigarette with the little silver lighter he'd once ransacked our trunk to find.

Karin went down to the cellar to persuade Herta to come upstairs. Karin seemed more composed than any of us.

I don't think anyone imagined her father would survive. He'd been in a coma for two hours by then, with possibly a fractured skull as well as a concussion, and maybe a broken hip as well. His blood was lacquered over flagstones in the front hall. His pulse barely registered. My mother tried smelling salts but he remained comatose, his breathing shallow and hoarse.

The house was cold. While we waited for the doctor my father and I brought in armloads of firewood.

"Do you think they'll come back, the *Sturmtruppen*? A return visit?" Buck asked.

"I don't know, Dad. Possibly."

"Your mother wanted us to go for Australia in 1919," he said. "But they wouldn't let me in."

He was shaken. He'd never been a person to waste time moaning over what might have been. Anyone who bred thoroughbreds for a living knew that life raced only one way around the oval, and as fast as possible. Buck had understood better than most: the only way to live is at forward speed. A racehorse opens its heart and *runs*.

We built up blazes in the library fireplace and the kitchen. I wondered if Dr. Lewin would make it out to Walden. Traveling across the city, even in a taxi, he'd be taking his life in his hands. There might be wolf packs roaming the town, and they might decide to stop a lone taxi, drag out a Jewish passenger, beat him up, pitch him in the river Main.

However, the taxi arrived with Dr. Lewin safe and sound. After an examination he confirmed the baron had a fractured hip, a fractured skull, and remained in a coma. The hip required immediate surgery, but Lewin reminded us that as a Jew he was no longer permitted to do surgery at any hospital in Frankfurt, and in any case he was leaving for Cuba with his family and couldn't delay their departure. He promised to make some calls to Aryan colleagues.

While my parents were out in the kitchen consoling Herta, I overheard Dr. Lewin describe to Karin the correct procedure for injecting morphine.

"If and when your father wakes up he will no doubt feel excruciating pain. This will be hard for him to bear and worse I would think for you. Hence, opiates."

He said he'd be leaving a box containing syringes of various sizes, needles, and four sixty-milliliter bottles of morphia.

"If the pain becomes too much, my dear, a dose of sixty milliliters, understand? That's one entire bottle. Fill the large syringe and push it in all at once, quickly. Within a few minutes your father's respiratory system will no longer be functioning. He'll be unconscious, he won't suffer. Sixty mills. All at once. Understand?"

She nodded, but she hadn't slept in nearly twenty-four hours, and I couldn't tell if she really grasped what Dr. Lewin was telling her.

What was in store for her father but more humiliation? If he'd been a racehorse Buck would have led him to the edge of the woods, pressed the pistol barrel to the forehead, aimed the bullet along the spine, and fired.

That would have been the right thing to do, without question.

That would have been mercy.

☩ FRANKIE'S ENGLISH BAR

Postcard. Unsigned, *"Tonkreuz-UFA-Neuebabelsberg"* [Soundstage UFA studio, Neuebabelsberg], addressed *Herr Billy Lange, Frankfurt A. M., Übersetzung Abteilung IG Farben Hauptsitz,* postmarked *Berlin 17.7.1931.* Holograph inscription quoting Rilke. Lange Family Archive, 11 C-12-1988. Special Collections, McGill Library, McGill University, Montreal.

Auch ich stehe still und voll tiefen Vertrauens vor den Toren dieser Einsamkeit, weil ich für die höchste Aufgabe einer Verbindung zweier Menschen diese halte: dass einer dem andern seine Einsamkeit bewache—Rilke

I tell you this is the highest bond between two people: that each protects the solitude of the other.

my trans.!—BL Sept 3rd 1988
in Toronto

THE TELEPHONE CALL CAME THROUGH THE SWITCHBOARD. MY GRAND-mother Con was on the line.

"Is something the matter, Granny? Are you all right?"

I could hear a lot of uproar. I was irritated. We were not supposed to receive personal phone calls at work. But Dr. Ziegler was in Lisbon, the other fellows had gone home, and I was eating an orange and reading the novel going around the office that month, Pearl Buck's *The Good Earth*.

"Dear Billy, I'm at Frankie's."

To my father's dismay, my grandmother had become a regular at Frankie's English Bar, where she gambled on horses and enjoyed champagne cocktails with her horsey friends, most of them elderly. Willie Chopdelau, the bookmaker, had two telephone lines at Frankie's and took bets on all the Irish and English racing.

"Would you come around, Billy? There's a debt of honor. I'm a bit short."

Con's "debts of honor" were always gambling debts.

"How much?"

"My dear, I had one hundred marks on Cockpen for the derby, but April the Fifth has come in. Such a bore when the favorite takes it. Awfully slow field this year. Dear Willy let me have the go but now I find I'm forty marks short."

I was tempted to tell her to call my father but knew it would dishearten him to have to pluck his mother out of a nightclub. I was irritated because I relished the rare calm of the office in the evening, when I could read novels in peace.

Ziegler was an impressive chief. Despite his American suits and soft collars, his manner was rather fierce and formal. He was hard-driving, and hated sloppy work, but he looked out for "his boys" when it came to transfers and promotions.

Everyone in the Translation Department at IG Farben was young. My close friends were Robert Briesewitz, who'd warmed up after his initial coolness, and Ernest Mack, another member of the tribe of Walden Apache, who'd earned his doctorate in organic chemistry. Ernest and Robert loved jazz. Ernest had a fabulous collection of discs and Robert played the trumpet.

Translations was a recognized training ground for future *Prokuristen*, executives. We certainly thought of ourselves as an elite. In our department everyone expected promotions and overseas postings. An IG sales office had just been opened in China, our biggest export market for dyestuffs, and we figured one or two positions at Shanghai must go to fellows from the department. *The Good Earth* had just been published in America and England, one of our fellows had brought a copy back from New York, and Pearl Buck's novel was spinning a sort of Chinese magic for us. The peasant Wang Lung's mystic feeling for the soil moved me. The irony was that he loved the soil so much it became a terrible, all-consuming lust that ruined him, broke his family, and turned his sons against him.

We all wanted China, but there was no point putting oneself forward as a candidate. At IG Farben you were told what your next post would be; you didn't dare ask for it.

However, I was thinking about China a lot. What should I do if word came down from the sixth floor that I was transferred to the Shanghai bureau? Shanghai was a blank page. China meant opportunity. Salary. An expense allowance. I could write my own story there.

But men sent to China or South America were expected to stay on those posts for years, even spend the rest of their careers overseas.

Early in the summer Karin had spent a week at Walden while her mother was recuperating from her first cancer surgery, but I rarely got a chance to speak to her. Once or twice she'd waved from sporting roadsters with Berlin registrations, going very fast along the gravel drive.

"Too fast!" Buck complained, concerned as always for the safety of his horses.

I could imagine posting letters to Karin from exotic Shanghai. But what would I say in them? I hated to think of her marrying some fellow with a sports car.

Meanwhile I had to settle up with my grandmother's bookie. Picking up my hat, I rode the lift down and caught a tram to Frankie's. It was raining hard, the streets were gloomy and slick. Frankfurt didn't have much nightlife, unless you counted parades, marches, and riots, NSDAP *Sturmtruppen* exchanging shots with KPD gunmen, both of those brawling with uniformed squads from the Reichsbanner.

I was soaked by the time I reached Frankie's, in a narrow street not far from Goethe's house, next to a musical-instrument shop. The entrance was looked after by a doorman, Brutus, supposed to be a White Russian prince. He also dealt in hashish, and wristwatches and car parts, probably stolen.

After midnight drunken SA men sometimes gathered on the sidewalk across the street and yowled insults at patrons coming out of Frankie's wearing "decadent" gowns and evening clothes. Since the NSDAP victory in the spring, when the party had taken the biggest percentage of votes in the Reichstag elections, *Sturmtruppen* had been haranguing people dressed in styles they didn't approve of, especially anyone they imagined looked Jewish. Sometimes the Schutzpolizei intervened. Usually they didn't.

In Dr. Ziegler's Translation Department we considered ourselves cosmopolitan sophisticates. Ordering a martini or manhattan at Frankie's was as cosmopolitan and sophisticated as things got in Frankfurt. But the place was too expensive to be our regular hangout, and the SA goons lurking outside with their rubber truncheons and dog-whips targeted special abuse and threats at young fellows un-German enough to prefer handmade English shoes to jackboots, manhattan cocktails to cider in some smoky hole of *Apfelweinwirtschaft.*

Frankie's was one long narrow slot of a room with a polished mahogany bar along its length. Leather banquettes lined the wall opposite. There were also *tables à deux* and a small dance floor and usually a jazz band that started playing after eleven o'clock.

Even in the blaze of German summer it was cool in Frankie's, the atmosphere scented by ice, polished glass, liquor. Bottles and champagne buckets sparkled in the mirrors behind the bar. The air itself seemed polished. The tiny kitchen opened at midnight, and a young Siamese cook prepared the only two dishes on the menu: Frankie's Irish stew or scrambled eggs and bacon. Eddy Morrison, the owner, was a tough customer from East Belfast who always wore a dinner jacket with satin lapels that somehow didn't make him look any less a bruiser. He'd been shot in the neck on the Somme in 1916, and I could see the scar peeking over his stiff collar. Morrison had spent some time in New York and San Francisco before opening Charlie's American Bar in Paris a week after Lindbergh landed in France. He once told me he'd sent a telegram offering Lindy partnership in the bar.

"I doubt he ever was offered a better business opportunity. But not a word back. Head in the clouds, I'd say."

Eddy had arrived in Germany after some trouble with the Paris police. He bet heavily on the horses, and I believe my grandmother offered him tips on Walden runners. He called me Charles or Charlie, he said, because I reminded him of Lindbergh.

I could see my grandmother seated in a banquette, playing cards with Karin Weinbrenner. I hadn't seen Karin in months.

While she was with her parents at Walden she'd often been less well-turned-out than you might expect of a person of her background. A button or two missing from a blouse; a front soldier's *feldgrau* great-coat thrown over her shoulders, instead of an elegant wrap. Jodhpurs instead of afternoon dresses. Such reckless dishabille certainly annoyed her mother, but she had set the style for a pack of young women, and for a while all the golden young things in Frankfurt had dressed *à la Karin:* belted overcoats with belts untied, blouses radically unbuttoned. Old jodhpurs with woolen jumpers and mahogany-top horse boots. Most girls had bobbed their hair, but Karin's bob was always blunt and rough, as though cropped with a pair of fetlock shears. Her chestnut hair was so thick and lustrous that even in its wreckage it was beautiful.

I've never felt at ease unless I am well dressed. All my life I've paid more attention to clothes than a real gentleman ought to. It's insecurity, plainly. Uncertain social standing: my parents didn't own the house where I was born.

That night at Frankie's she wore a black sheath dress with a string of pearls falling down her chest. Her neck and shoulders were white. She looked sleek, sophisticated, urbane—*Very Berlin*, I thought, though her hair was its usual thick, alluring tangle. I'd never been to Berlin. I had been to Paris on a business trip, however. And I was scheduled to fly to Birmingham with Dr. Ziegler in a couple of weeks: my first airplane trip. And I was pondering Shanghai. All in all, despite certain misgivings, I was pleased with myself, with what I was beginning to think of as my *career*, with the silk neckties I'd bought on the rue de Rivoli. I was beginning to feel quite accomplished, experienced. A man of the world. An IG man.

You are aware that people at IG Farben did discreditable things once the directors got in bed with the NSDAP. You know they offered a significant amount of financial support to Hitler in 1933. They expected profits from the conquest of Europe. Thousands slaved in the IG Farben plants at Auschwitz, producing synthetic rubber and fuel. You know Zyklon-B, the gas used to kill off unproductive slaves at the factories and millions more in the death camps, was originally an IG product marketed as insecticide.

In the early thirties, I was *proud* to be an IG Farben man.

"Hello, Billy." Karin seemed older and somehow less complicated than I remembered, but even more attractive.

"Hello, Karin."

I lingered by the table without sitting down, no longer feeling quite so self-assured. They were both focused on their cards.

If I were a wristwatch, she was a magnet. Coming close to her disordered my sense of time.

"Dear Billy," my grandmother said, "do go and see Mr. Chopdelau."

The bookie Willy Chopdelau sat at his banquette with his money box and his pair of telephones. He was a Pole, muscular and young, always dressed in horsey tweeds. He was sipping a glass of milk and reading the *F-Zeit*. He seemed satisfied to take my check for forty marks. We spoke French.

"What's outside, Charlie?" he asked.

"Raining. Buckets."

"Dear fellow, any SA goons?"

"Not tonight."

"I like rain, Charles," said Willy. "It makes things clean."

There weren't many customers at the bar. It was still early and

Frankie's drew a late-night crowd. I ordered a glass of beer. I'd rather have had a cocktail, but cocktails were expensive.

Karin smiled across the room at me. My grandmother was expertly shuffling the deck. It looked as though they would be playing another hand. I watched Con deal the cards briskly. As soon as the hand was played I intended to hire a taxi so we might all three ride out to Walden together. I never took taxis myself, too expensive, but my grandmother disliked trams and took taxis everywhere, whether she had funds or not, and I doubted Karin had ever taken a tram.

The hand was played out, and Karin lost. As I approached their table my grandmother was putting money into her purse.

"Put Constance in a cab, Billy," Karin said. "She's taken every last penny. Then do come back and buy me a drink. I should like to hear what you've been up to."

Drinks at Frankie's with Karin von? Amazing. A stunning new height of sophistication had been reached.

"Good night, my dear," Con said, kissing Karin's cheek. "Don't talk to strange men."

"I shan't say a word to anyone but your terribly handsome grandson."

My grandmother held my arm as we left the bar. "They don't get on, she and her mother," Con remarked.

"They never have."

"Her mother's people in Ireland were known for cold blood. I didn't get on with my parents, either. But I married Captain Jack, and a few months later we set off for California. Didn't tell him I was pregnant until we were off Brazil. Couldn't bear being left behind—oh, your grandfather never liked being stuck to a place, the great thing for him was to move! Had we not met I'd have married Charlie Butler. My parents were terribly keen for me to marry poor Charlie, but I wanted my bold German sailor. Your grandfather had the vital spark! Oh, my dear, he most certainly did."

There was no mention of my paying off her bookie—or, rather, of her paying back her grandson.

There were always a couple of taxis waiting outside Frankie's, at least until the SA goons spooked the drivers away. I helped my grandmother into one.

"Thank you, dear boy. Never bet the favorite. Not much fun. Even when you win—not much fun at all."

I watched her cab rattle away. The rain had stopped. Gray cobblestones glistened. No NSDAP men in sight. Going back inside the bar, I felt bold and strong. Felt the jangle of my life's admittedly thin history trailing behind me like a string of medals. The Louisiana Seven (jazz boys from Duisburg and Köln) were warming up: discordant squeaks, throttles, the rattle of drums. I was a man of experience and substance, a man of the world, and Karin Weinbrenner was waiting for me in her buttoned-leather banquette.

She smiled as I slid in beside her. A waiter hovered. Karin asked for another martini just like the last, and I ordered the same. In Frankfurt a martini, if you could get one, was customarily served in an old-fashioned glass, on the rocks. One-third vermouth, and no olive. But Karin preferred a few drops of vermouth per ounce of gin, stirred with ice, strained into a chilled martini glass, and served with an olive. In Berlin these were known as clear-colds.

Rescuing my grandmother from a gambling debt, paying off her bookie—for me, this had been potentially an embarrassing situation, but Karin seemed not to notice. While we waited for our drinks she asked for a cigarette. I shook two from a pack, stuck them both in my mouth, and lit them. Another height of sophistication was reached.

"Where do you get those?" she said.

I was smoking Sweet Aftons. They cost a bit more than the German brands—*Ecksteins, Mokris, Attikahs*—and there was only one tobacconist in Frankfurt that carried them. I thought they were distinctive and made me seem less ordinary than my peers.

"They're Irish. I get them at Rothstein's shop."

"Billy Lange, Billy Lange." Karin smiled. "I don't know you at all, do I? What an interesting necktie that is. Are you at university now? You're not a fighting man, I see."

I reminded her I'd joined the Translation Department of IG Farben. No one on Dr. Ziegler's flying squad wore a *Schmiss*. Anyone with a saber scar would be laughed out of headquarters. Krebs was the only Nazi in our office, and he had to be discreet because Dr. Ziegler certainly was no party man.

Though there were two Jews in translation, Kracauer and Roth-bart, Krebs knew he must keep his politics and racial opinions out of the office; he loathed Kracauer, who was probably responsible for the spreading of Günter's old nickname, Ducky, around IG.

Flying-squad esprit de corps was intense. At a period when jobs were scarce, my position in the ultra-modern firm IG Farben made me feel special. Lucky. Worldly. Smart. In our department we used as much American or English slang as we could get away with. We called Dr. Ziegler "Chief" or sometimes "Boss," informality unimaginable in other branches or departments. We wore fedora hats with brims snapped down, like Chicago gangsters. Our crisp striped shirts were ordered from Jermyn Street, London. More than anything, we despised German shoes. Only English handmade shoes would do for us.

I hoped all this sartorial style might disguise how out of my depth I actually felt, sitting in a banquette at Frankie's English Bar, having drinks with Karin Weinbrenner.

I knew what I *ought* to do, were China offered: get the vaccinations, purchase the tropical suits, say goodbye to the parents, and leave.

I didn't know if I'd actually be able leave *her*.

Years before, after target shooting in the woods, she'd asked me to bury her shot-up dresses. She didn't want her mother finding them. I'd fetched a spade and done as she asked, and there was something melancholy about it, like burying a dead bird, a robin the cat had pounced on. I'd kept one of the dresses for a while. A red dress with a bullet hole. My mother found it and looked at me strangely. She didn't say anything but took it away, and I never laid eyes on it again.

I gave Karin another Sweet Afton and snapped us both a light. The waiter was fetching our drinks. The bookie Willie Chopdelau was having a mild argument with a friend of my grandmother's—Istvan, a penniless Hungarian count. The count also owed Willie money. Most of my grandmother's friends in Frankfurt were in debt to the bookmaker, and most of them were some version of Istvan—old chancers who carried themselves like military men and liked to bet on horses.

Karin was quiet. That was fine with me. Being in her company for the first time as an adult was enough. We didn't need talk. Being with her always gave me some purchase on who I was myself. After the initial disturbance she caused I could always see myself more clearly.

"This is a cozy sort of place," she said. "In Berlin, things are more brutal. One's own thoughts won't let one think. In Berlin my mind is chasing itself. How are you these days?"

I let her know I was off to England in a few days, on a flying visit with Dr. Ziegler. And there was a possibility of Shanghai, I told her. If I was offered that post, I didn't know what I should do.

"Ah, Billy, my blood brother, surely China's too far."

The waiter arrived with our drinks. My first clear-cold. The sharp infusion of gin was a bit breathtaking. Or maybe it was her calling me blood brother that spun my head a little.

"Do you know what's up on my bedroom wall, Karin?"

"Don't tell me you've become an art collector."

"Road maps. States of America. When I was in school I pinned them up in a sequence, east to west, and traced the route that crosses El Llano Estacado."

She shook out two more Sweet Aftons, put them both between her lips, lit them, and gave one to me. "When do you leave?"

"Have you ever looked again at the Winnetou stories, Karin? They don't bear up. They really are quite ridiculous."

"They worked on our dreams."

"One doesn't find answers with a road map, Karin."

"Really?"

"It would take money, for one thing," I said. "And blue sky is just— blue sky. In real Texas, there are sharecroppers. Actually, peasants. They can't get enough money for cotton they raise. Can't afford shoes. Dress in rags. They're starving. I read about them in the *Paris Trib*."

"We don't have to inhabit our historical situation, Billy. You don't have to become whatever it is they are training you to become, a Frankfurt businessman. Old Shatterhand, you recall, was working for the railroad when first he met Winnetou. He soon gave that up."

I'll cross el llano *if you'll come with me.*

I very nearly said those words, very nearly cast off my pose of sophistication, my very thin worldliness, my wonderful career.

Instead I ordered another round of drinks, then worried whether I had enough cash in my wallet to pay for them.

"It's quite reassuring to see you, my old Billy. You're looking very debonair."

I was mentally adding up the cost of drinks, trying to figure out how many marks were in my billfold without having to pull it out and check.

"Are you meeting someone?" she asked. "A girl? You have your plans for the evening."

"No. I don't."

She put a finger to her lips. "A secret, all right? I'm not staying at Walden. I keep a little flat on the Eschenheimer. My pied-à-terre. The parents, they aren't aware, they'd only be hurt. You won't tell?"

"No. Of course not."

"One needs to dodge out of Berlin from time to time."

"Yes, but—shouldn't you see your mother? She's not been well."

"I should, yes."

Drinks arrived.

"Do you know Berlin, Billy?"

"Not really."

"This time I left in rather a hurry. There was a man in my flat—he wouldn't leave. Couldn't stand it anymore. One of us had to go. To tell you the truth, he frightened me. So I left."

"It's not Longo, is it? Can't you throw him out?"

A few months earlier I'd encountered Longo crossing the lobby at IG headquarters. He seemed impressed that I was an IG man and gave me his card. He had a government post in Berlin.

She laughed. "No, not Longo. Much simpler if it were. It was always easy to get poor Longo to do whatever I wanted. Never had a problem with Longo, my dear. No. This fellow is a friend of Marie Zeiten—"

"Who's that?"

"—I met this fellow at a cocktail party at Zeiten's. Hardly spoke to him, then suddenly he turns up at my flat. He keeps saying he is a dangerous man. He won't leave. It was becoming tedious. I finally had to get away, so while he was in the bath I threw a few things in an overnight case and dashed off to catch the train for good old Frankfurt."

"You left him in your Berlin flat?"

"I left him some money. Enough to get to Paris at least. He has a pistol."

"A pistol?"

"It's a good thing I've learned to pack quickly. Who really needs more than two dresses, two pairs of shoes?"

"Inform your *Hausmeister.* Inform the police! Have him arrested."

"Well, I feel sorry for him. I'll go back in a day or two. I expect by then he'll have cleared out. I came here straight from the *Hauptbahnhof.* Left my train case in the ladies' room."

"Who is he? Some sort of criminal?" In those days the tabloid papers were blazing with stories about killers for hire in Berlin and drug dealers.

"A Russian. I don't know that he has anywhere else to go."

It sounded the sort of thing that only happened in films. I had seen her name flash past in the credits on UFA films like *Liebling der Götter—Darling of the Gods*—and knew that she "wrote" films even if I wasn't clear how they could be written.

I wondered if she was teasing me, making it all up.

"What type of pistol?"

"A funny little Russian thing. His precious Tokareva. He says he is a dangerous man, but I think he means he is a man in danger. His German is far from perfect."

"I'll go back to Berlin with you," I told her. "I'll see him off."

It was gin talking. I was a junior commercial clerk in the Translation Department at IG Farben, wearing a natty Paris tie, discussing Russians and Tokareva pistols with the most surprising young woman in Frankfurt. I hadn't the slightest idea how to handle a Russian armed with a pistol. And I had to report to work in the morning.

By then the Louisiana Seven were swooping and diving through "Back Home Again in Indiana." I owned a collection of records and, like a million other young men, practiced dance steps with footprint maps I ordered through the mail. Everyone danced a fox-trot in those days, though there were a hundred different fox-trots.

Karin sipped her clear-cold. "He can't return to Russia because he's gotten on the wrong side of people there. He says he can't ask the KPD for help, they'll bundle him straight back to Moscow. And if I tell Anna about him, she'll want to call the police."

"Anna?"

"Anna Rabou. Anna *von* Rabou."

"The writer?"

"Anna hates the KPD. She didn't want me going to Marie's. No, I've left him enough to get himself to Paris. I can work here."

"What will you tell your parents?"

"Oh, they won't know I'm here. I don't go out to Walden. Too much fuss. Too many questions. My little place here is extravagant, but. You won't mention seeing me, not to anyone, Billy, not to your parents, who would inform mine, certainly. Dear Con has sworn silence."

"No. Of course I won't. No."

"Are you still my blood brother, Billy Lange?"

"I am. Yes."

Russians, pistols, Paris, little flats on the Eschenheimer Anlage. Spending an evening in her company was like hearing sounds pitched far above my normal range.

She smiled. "Billy Lange, you have become exactly the man I hoped. It's so nice when people come up to expectations. Won't you ask me to dance?"

Dancing while holding her was nothing like practicing the fox-trot on my footprint map. Her scent was everywhere. I wasn't a bad dancer, either. That pleased her.

It was nearly three o'clock in the morning when we left Frankie's after a breakfast of scrambled eggs, bacon, and coffee. The rain had stopped. The sky was dark blue and starry.

"Filthy Jews! Bloodsuckers!"

A pair of stormtroopers, uniformed and jackbooted, stood on the curb opposite, hands on hips and bawling at us while Brutus the doorman whistled up the last late-night cab.

"Leeches! Bloodsuckers! Whore! Whore! Jew whore!"

She was shivering as we climbed into the car. People in Frankfurt liked to tell one another that the NSDAP imported bumpkins from remote parts of the countryside but I knew they could just as well have been city boys. We passed the BMW showroom, its window lit, a motorcycle gleaming inside like a projectile of pure speed, just waiting to be launched. I was due back at the office in a few hours. I'd spent practically all my cash on drinks. Luckily, Eddy Morrison, like my grandmother's bookmaker, had also been willing to take my check— I hoped there were funds sufficient to cover it. In my pocket I had just enough for the taxi to Karin's apartment house on the Eschenheimer Anlage but not for my fare across the river and home. Frankfurt trams didn't start running before 6:00 a.m. so I faced a long walk back to

Walden, where I'd just have time to bathe, change, gulp a cup of coffee, and deal with my parents' questions before starting back to the West-End.

We stared out our separate windows, watching our dark town slip by. We weren't far enough from the animal howls yet. I remembered those bodies dumped on the pavement in 1919. Overcoats, spilled hats, black blood, and the tram running on time, taking us back out to Walden.

I lit two Sweet Aftons. She accepted hers without a word and the cab turned onto the Eschenheimer and a minute later braked in front of her building, an impressive white pile. I told the driver to wait.

"No," she said, "he must go. You must come up with me, Billy. We throw open the French doors and watch the sun come up. I wish to feel the sun, quite desperately."

The building's elderly *Hausmeister*, uniformed like a grenadier, was dozing sitting up on a stone bench as we crossed the lobby to the iron lift. Her apartment occupied the third floor. The door was unlocked. She pushed it open and I followed her inside.

Her parents never did learn about that flat. A bare white room with an exalted ceiling, that's what I remember. The bathroom was tiles and a huge tub. I glimpsed a corner of a stark platform bed through the half-open door of her bedroom.

Furniture was a bore, she used to say, furniture sucked in the light and gave nothing back, and in a room it was only the light that mattered.

In the tiny kitchen I watched her fill a kettle and set it to boil. We hadn't spoken since getting out of the taxi. Maybe we both were still hearing Nazi catcalls reverberating in our brains.

I didn't know what was expected of me.

"Perhaps I should leave."

"No. Please don't." Setting down the kettle she came over and kissed me. A quick, dry, quite startling kiss on the lips. "We're not going to sleep together, not tonight, are we, but I don't want you to leave, Billy. Do you remember that brilliant afternoon when you carried me?"

"Yes."

"Don't look embarrassed, it was nothing wrong. Will you stay for a bit? Billy, I require your company. We'll sit together and watch the dawn come in. Please."

"Of course."

She disappeared into the bedroom. When the kettle whistled, I made tea in a sleek silver teapot, also from the Bauhaus. A streamlined Marianne Brandt design, its bare shape seemed to speak the language of speed. *Hurry. Quick. Fast. Now.*

She came out wearing a Scotch plaid dressing gown over her night-dress. She had washed her face; her skin was pale, shining. I watched her close her eyes and breathe in the fragrance of the tea. She put the tea things on a tray and I carried it out to the big white room.

Karin tugged open a pair of French doors and I smelled rain on the trees in the *Palmengarten* across the road. The air was cool, damp, fresh. She fetched two Moroccan cushions for us to sit on, then poured tea. I sat awkwardly on my cushion, unsure what to do with my legs. She sat in what I later came to know as the lotus position: legs crossed, back straight. Light filled the sky, slowly.

Karen Weinbrenner was a young woman impatient for the light of day; she made herself watch for it and wait. For her it was meaningful to be awake at dawn, and almost always she was. Inching, glowering dawn over Germany, skies that resembled a bruise slowly filling.

"Tell me who you are, Billy Lange. Tell me who you are actually. Do you seek adventure? Do you turn pages to see what comes next? Do you like thin air? Isn't it cold up there? Have you crashed, ever? Are you barnstorming? What is it like to go walking out on a wing? Might you have room for a passenger?"

Abruptly she stopped talking. None of it had made much sense, but I didn't say anything for a while. I let the quiet settle. Those howling boys outside Frankie's were still with us. We needed silence to establish ourselves in the present, in the safety.

She began humming. Tunelessly, like the hum of wind on fence wire.

There was tension in the room, as if we were on the High Plains and a twister was spinning toward us; a black sky was about to explode. I could still hear the *Sturmtruppen* and so could she.

"Billy?"

"Yes?"

"Tell me a story, old man. I need a story, I'm fresh out. Spin me a tale, old fellow. Put me in the picture."

I wanted to calm her, reassure her. Not knowing what else to do

I began reciting the story of my father's birth one thousand miles off the Pacific coast of Mexico. I described his first landfall on the Barbary Coast, brought ashore in a gig boat after the bark *Lilith* had dropped anchor in Yerba Buena Cove.

I told her about visiting my father when he was a prisoner, then not seeing him again for years. I invited her to smell a cold, dirty breeze from the upper deck of a London bus in winter, and see aviators cast from a burning zeppelin like red embers spat from a fire. I described crossing the Irish Sea with my mother and my fear that she was going to jump in. I walked across the boglands in company with my grandfather McDermott, who happened to be sleeping with his pretty housemaid, and galloped ponies with Mick McClintock, and poached a salmon from the Ballisodare River, and aboard a Rhine barge a young soldier was shot in the head.

If a person was made of anything, it seemed to me I was made of those stories.

What I was after, I suppose, was intimacy. Light filled slowly into the room. The sleek teapot grew cold. She sat calmly, and after a while I calmed too. We sat for some minutes in that silence. I never had felt such connection to another person.

I realized the best thing to do was get up, collect my hat and leave before the streetcars began jangling up and down the Eschenheimer. So I did. I left without saying goodbye. She was poised, calm, her breathing was steady, she was composed in the light, she was smiling.

⊱────⊰

There wasn't time to go home. I could have a washup at the office before reporting for work. At a café on the Grunebergweg I had coffee and a roll.

At my desk in the Translation Department I felt replete with joy. I telephoned my parents and told them I'd been working all night on a special assignment. It may have been the first lie I told them. They had been worried, but such hours were not so uncommon in Dr. Ziegler's department, and it wasn't yet the era when, if people didn't show up, one's first thought was that something monstrous had happened to them.

"You wear the same tie as yesterday, *liebster* Billy," Günter Krebs remarked at lunch. "The same shirt as well. I think you have been not sleeping at home. You have been playing the cat-and-mouse. Have you caught yourself a mouse, dear Billy?"

I felt exhausted and mature, but as the day wore on I found myself brooding about the Russian, whoever he was, with his Tokareva pistol. After work, instead of catching my usual tram, I walked down the Eschenheimer and asked the old *Hausmeister* to ring the buzzer for Karin's apartment.

"No use!" he barked. "No one at home! The young lady has gone away."

By the time I reached home I was shaky from exhaustion, and worried. I needed advice from someone but didn't dare say a word about Karin's Russian to my father, who would feel it his duty to inform the baron, as my mother would certainly have told Lady Maire.

I had another sleepless night, worrying about Karin and the Russian and the pistol. Heading to work the next morning, not knowing what else to do, I stopped at Rothstein's Tobacco Shop and rang up Longo's office in Berlin.

I wasn't fond of Longo, but he was an old friend of Karin. And he was in Berlin where, according to his card, he worked in the Civil Law and Procedure Division of the Ministry of Justice.

A secretary answered the phone and told me sternly that Herr Dr. von Müller-Languedoc was never available before eleven o'clock.

At lunchtime I quit the office with a pocketful of coins, found another cigar shop with a telephone, and called his office once more. This time I got past the secretary. When I told Longo that I was calling on Karin's behalf, he snorted.

"Well, my good fellow, I'm not seeing much of *her* these days."

It was true that I hadn't seen him at Walden lately, but Karin had hardly been at Walden, either.

I said Karin might be in some sort of trouble.

"A *Schlampe* like that little Karin is made for trouble. She drags trouble around with her like a cat dragging around a fish head."

He spoke harshly, the way he used to speak to the grooms and stableboys. I suppose it's how he thought of me, as a stableboy.

"At that cesspool called UFA, they do nothing but stir trouble and mischief. Always it stinks. Her old man's the same. Making trouble everywhere."

I thought it a peculiar way to speak of a family that had always been hospitable to him.

"They stir up trouble, this tribe of caterwauling Jews, then try to blame their woes on us. I'm sick to death, let me tell you. They've ruined nearly everything decent and honorable in Germany. And now they squeal. It's time something was done about it."

Suddenly I wanted to get off the phone. It had been a mistake to call him.

"Tell me, is it the so-called baron who has put you up to call me?" Longo said. "It's most improper to make such calls here; we have important work and I can't be bothered about the Weinbrenners and whatever scrape Karin has gotten herself into. All right? Goodbye."

He hung up. I felt dizzy. The conversation had literally taken my breath away. Whatever had been human in Longo seemed absent. It had been like trying to speak to a sick machine. By then he had been a party member for four years. He must have feared his past association with the Jewish traitor baron would be used against him.

I checked the railway timetable. There was an express, an FD-Zug at 1709 that got into Berlin before midnight. It was expensive—those super-express trains only offered first or second class—but I had no choice, my conscience wouldn't release me. If the fellow was still in her apartment, that was where the danger was. Of course I hadn't a clue where in the Charlottenburg quarter she lived, and I couldn't ask her parents.

Our office had street directories of every city in Germany. I slipped out the Berlin volume. It was subdivided by district and in Charlottenburg—Aha!—I found *v. Weinbrenner, K.* living at Giesebrechtstraße 5. I studied the Berlin street plan. My train would arrive at the Anhalter Bahnhof. Either the U-Bahn to Uhlandstrasse or a tram up the Kurfürstendamm would bring me very close.

A few minutes later the mailroom clerk dropped a postcard on my desk. On the front of the card was a photograph of the Tonkreuz soundstage at the UFA studio in Neuebabelsberg. It was unsigned, but I knew it was from her. On the back she had written a line from Rilke, not from a poem but from one of his letters.

So she was safe and wouldn't need me or want me there. She was safe. I dropped my idiotic plan to ride to the rescue. Instead I went home and lay awake for a long time, thinking of her.

Later that month Solomon Dietz drove her parents up to Berlin to see officials about an art museum Lady Maire intended to build on the estate. Karin invited her parents to a "cocktail" at her Charlottenburg flat and Lady Maire told my mother they found their daughter's rooms packed with noisy, oddly dressed people and left as soon as they could.

1938

MY PARENTS HAD TO GET BACK TO BAD HOMBURG, AND OTTO TOOK THEM and Dr. Lewin back across the river in his taxi. Karin went upstairs to take a nap on the pile of rugs and blankets in her old bedroom.

Late that afternoon—it was an early dark, *feldgrauer* November—Herta was in the kitchen baking bread and I was alone in the library when the old man startled me by suddenly muttering, moaning, and twitching his limbs.

The first signs of life he'd shown since the attack. I'd always assumed he wasn't going to make it, so when he started to groan and sputter I thought it was his death rattle. He certainly looked like someone in extremis. I hoped he was. I wanted him to die. We had to get to Rotterdam. Our ship was sailing in a few days. Before we left I wanted to bury the old man in the cemetery with his son.

His blue eyes snapped open, and he lay there blinking and moaning. Herta came in just then, saw him, and shouted for Karin, who came running downstairs.

Half an hour later they had the old man sitting up, swallowing broth Herta made and Karin spooned into him.

"There you are, Daddy, take a little bit at a time. We're going to get you better."

Her father was clinging to a very dim level of consciousness, barely able to open his lips, and I'd never seen her behave with such tenderness. I think she had all kinds of wild feelings kept in reserve through her childhood and now, with her mother dead and her father dying, those feelings were running around like children released from school.

A few minutes later Hermann, Freiherr von Weinbrenner, was vomiting and shitting with such devastating violence it seemed as if he were literally pouring his guts out.

We changed the sheets. He screeched when we tried to lift him. I used my necktie as a tourniquet to bind his arm, and Karin took a breath and plunged the needle, delivering the first injection, fifteen milliliters. His skin, gray as tallow. The whites of his eyes were stained with yellow.

The shot stunned him within a few minutes, but three hours later he was awake again, or at least conscious, and in pain—writhing and twisting. The pain was like a snake in his body, restlessly coiling and uncoiling. Karin had for some reason started a Mozart serenade on the turntable. Herta and I struggled to hold his arm while Karin stabbed at it, trying to hit a vein. She was weeping without making a sound, dripping tears while "Eine kleine Nachtsmusik" pranced deliriously through the room. At last she struck a vein and pushed the dose in far too quickly. Within a few seconds her father's eyes rolled back in his head.

"Oh my Christ, Billy, I've killed him."

We listened, I was hoping she had—but he kept breathing, hoarsely. He sounded like a bus grunting up the slope of Muswell Hill under wartime sky, carrying my mother and me.

We arranged rugs and blankets for our bed on the library floor. In the middle of the night her father swam back into consciousness. His moaning and thrashing awakened us, and I held him down while she delivered another shot in his arm.

❧ KLINGER SCHOOL

Arten von Licht Buch [*Kinds of Light Book*], *Karin v Weinbrenner.* Unpaginated. In English and occ. German. Lange Family Archive, 11 C-12-1988. Special Collections, McGill Library, McGill University, Montreal.

━━━

Spread before you a map of prairie-land, and I shall point out the tract of territory known as the "Llano Estacado" or Staked Plain. It must be a map of modern time, based on the latest explorations; else you will have some difficulty comprehending the limits assigned to this singular, and yet almost unexplored district of country.

—Mayne Reid, The Lone Ranch, 1871

VON PAPEN AND HIS CIRCLE INVITED THE DANUBIAN ODDBALL TO BECOME chancellor in January 1933. My father insisted the Germans would not tolerate the scoundrel for long. Such a shocking appointment could not stand. *That fellow* was a dupe, a simpleton. The reactionary politicians were using him to eliminate socialists and liberals they feared. But the generals would never submit to such a monkey whose insane program must lead to disastrous war.

That fellow would be gone after a couple of weeks. A month at most.

Buck's analysis sounded sensible enough; it just didn't bear any relationship to what was happening.

Immediately after Hitler's appointment Günter Krebs started sporting his party membership pin on his lapel. This was against the code at IG Farben, but no one admonished him. Then one Friday he reported for work kitted out in a black SS uniform. Dr. Ziegler cast dark looks in his direction, but Günter ignored our chief and patiently explained the meanings of his various insignia and informed anyone who'd listen that his rank as SS *Untersturmführer* more or less corresponded to second-lieutenant rank in the army.

"You look like an undertaker in fancy dress!" my pal Ernst Mack told him.

"And you don't show real pride as a German!" Gunter replied. "You fellows, with your cosmopolitan spirit, are seriously ill! But things will change."

The following Monday he wore an ordinary business suit, but a precedent had been established, and from then on he appeared in his SS regalia at least one day each week.

And the "Horst Wessel Lied" had become the national anthem. At a joint meeting with the export sales staff, sheets printed with lyrics had been handed round, and everyone, including Kracauer, the last Jewish member of our department, had to stand up and sing:

> *For the last time, the call to arms is sounded!*
> *For the fight, we all stand prepared!*
> *Soon Hitler's banners will fly over all streets.*
> *The time of bondage will last but a little while now!*

One afternoon Dr. Ziegler stopped by my desk to congratulate me for a précis of economic news I'd prepared from the American financial press.

"The work was well done, Lange, though I don't know if they are in a mood to read it upstairs."

"I can't help that."

"How well do you think the 'Horst Wessel Lied' will translate?" His tone was sardonic.

"Not very well."

"I wouldn't think so. No one quite understands us Germans. I'm not sure I do myself. I've just authorized Kracauer's transfer to the Montevideo sales office. At least he won't have to sing 'Horst Wessel' anymore."

A few weeks later—February 27, 1933—the Reichstag burned. The morning after, newspapers and the radio were insisting the fire had been set by Bolsheviks plotting a putsch. Even my father's favorite read, the liberal and respected *Vossische Zeitung*, warned the situation presented a clear danger to the state and nation. A roundup of suspects was ordered. All of a sudden SA men were acting as auxiliary police. On my way to work I saw their brownshirt squads reeling through the streets in commandeered lorries.

That morning was sleeting and gray. At eleven o'clock all of us in the Translation Department were summoned to a meeting in one of the sleek conference rooms on the sixth floor. The sixth was where signatory executives had their aeries. We took seats around a magnificent African mahogany conference table. From the expansive windows there were wide views of the city and the black river. Waitresses went around pouring coffee into porcelain cups bearing the IG logo in gold.

We were aggressive young fellows. We thought a lot of ourselves.

Each of us spoke two languages at least, and we referred to workers in other branches of IG Farben as "the drones." We were a noisy bunch, but that morning we waited in silence. Most of us had never set foot on the sixth floor before. We didn't know who'd be addressing us—it wasn't even clear who'd called the meeting. Our chief, Dr. Ziegler, hadn't shown up. Where the hell was he?

As minutes crept by and no one senior appeared, the tension expanded, the room pressurized. Could all this have something to do with what was going on outside, the truckloads of SA toughs rolling about the city; the smoldering ruin of the Reichstag in Berlin? And where was our much-admired chief?

Counting heads, I realized the only one from our department missing, apart from Dr. Ziegler, was Günter Krebs.

During the last few weeks Dr. Ziegler had been spending a lot of his time either visiting the plant at Hoechst or shut up in his office, his door guarded by his gorgeous Jewish secretary, Fräulein Reffe. Since getting to see the chief was so difficult, certain fellows in the department had started bringing their questions and work problems to—Günter Krebs. We were like a ship with the first mate beginning to take over command from the captain without anything being said about it. Weird. We were used to a clear hierarchy, so this kink in the chain of command was troubling. Ducky Krebs wasn't competent to be a first mate; with his skills level, he was barely a deckhand. His authority derived solely from his black uniform. The atmosphere at IG had changed the moment Hitler had been appointed chancellor. One suddenly overheard *Heil Hitler* greetings being barked around the lobby in the morning. NSDAP pins sprouted on the lapels of senior executives, well-dressed men with *Prokurist* status whom I only saw when they were crossing the lobby in the morning and stepping into the paternoster elevators that lifted them noiselessly, elegantly to their sixth floor.

"The army of the black?" Kracauer had sneered, when Günter first showed up in SS regalia. "What's wrong with the old *feldgrau*? That's no uniform you're wearing, Ducky, it's a costume, and you don't even know the difference."

I missed Kracauer's derisive tongue. Kracauer had kept Ducky in his place. He wouldn't let Günter get away so easily with newfound authority based upon silver Death's Head collar buttons.

The door of the conference room opened soundlessly, and two men entered. I recognized Dr. Schiller, *Prokurist*, the signatory executive in charge of Western Hemisphere export sales, supposedly a brilliant chemist. Schiller was a perfect IG Farben man, tall and slender, with a beautifully cut gray suit and a big head. In fact he looked like a well-dressed university professor. He was wearing a gold wristwatch on a brown leather strap, the thinnest watch I'd ever seen, no thicker than a five-mark coin.

The second man I didn't recognize. He was younger than Dr. Schiller, fatter, and wore a rumpled suit of reddish tweed. He looked harried and clutched a sheaf of files under his arm.

The pressure in the room increased. I could hear crows yapping outside. Without sitting down Dr. Schiller placed both hands on the conference table and looked around at us.

"I'm sorry to keep you away from your important work. There are a few matters that need clearing up. Is everyone here? Krebs isn't? Well, Untersturmführer Krebs has important business to attend.

"First things first. Dr. Ziegler is no longer of the Translation Department. He is no longer with the IG. This is a closed matter, and I am not at liberty to discuss it further. As of now, you serve under a new chief—Dr. Winnacker." Schiller glanced at the fat man, who gave a little bow. "Dr. Winnacker is an esteemed scientist and a linguist and a good German, though he's spent far too much time in South America, from my point of view. Anyway, now he is a headquarters man and your chief. It's your responsibility to inform him of your current projects and in all ways to help him take up the reins of his work. Understood? Yes? Good.

"Second—and this statement is being read out in our offices and plants around the country, indeed around the world this morning."

He read from a piece of paper in his hand.

" 'Given the very difficult situation our führer faces as he confronts the Bolshevik element, the board of directors of the IG Farbenindustrie affirms to its staff and to the German *Volk* that Adolf Hitler, the National Socialist Party, and the German nation are essentially one, that the recent and refreshing change in leadership has our absolute support, as do all measures our führer takes to maintain the integrity and dignity of the German people.' "

Dr. Schiller looked around the room. I couldn't tell if he believed what he was saying. He was an executive trained to put force into his words whether or not he believed them, an executive for whom belief wasn't essential. He found himself pushed out of IG three years later, and his pension severely cut, after some indiscreet words at a reception at the American embassy.

There was nothing for the rest of us to do but nod stupidly. The meeting was adjourned and we crept back to our department. Dr. Winnacker settled into Dr. Ziegler's room, and that was that. Fräulien Reffe looked unhappy, but she wasn't going to discuss what had happened.

━━━━○━━━

On my way home I paused outside at the BMW showroom and peered in at their latest motorcycle, the R11.

Passion in metal, that's what I was thinking. A thousand parts all working together. A piece of speed. A promise. Distance. Transcendence. That wicked, low-slung machine had over me something of the power that Lady Maire's altarpieces, *Palmesels*, and chalices must have had over the faithful.

A salesman, a fellow about my own age, came out while I was staring at the bike.

"A beautiful machine, isn't it?" the salesman remarked. "But let me ask. I've seen you here often enough. Are you shopping or dreaming?"

"Are BMW spare parts available in America? Out in the western parts? Texas? New Mexico?"

On that sleeting Frankfurt evening I just needed to hear myself say those bright sunny words. *Texas. New. Mexico.*

"No idea!" the salesman replied, with a cheerful smile. "Can't say! But let me make some inquiries. I'm sure I can find out!"

━━━━○━━━

I was at work the next morning when Herta, the chauffeur's wife, approached my father in the stables at Walden. She was distraught. Her husband Solomon had gone out the evening before to drink beer at the Reichsbanner clubhouse in Niederrad and hadn't returned. She was afraid he'd been taken into custody by SA auxiliaries.

Solomon was a loudmouth and a brawler and very proud of his membership in the Reichsbanner. Herta was too frightened to go to the clubhouse. Everyone had seen the *Sturmtruppen* uproarious and drunk, rushing back and forth across the river in stolen trucks. Everyone had listened to the radio announcer insisting that "nests of Communists" were being "wiped out" in retaliation for setting the Reichstag on fire.

Herta pleaded with my father to do something. Solomon was a Jew who worked for the Jewish traitor baron and that was enough to make him a target if he happened to be in the wrong place at the wrong time. A Reichsbanner drinking club the night after the Reichstag fire was certainly that.

The baron and Lady Maire were visiting her family in England. The baroness was riding to hounds on her brother's estate in Northamptonshire.

Herta wept while my parents discussed what should be done. Buck made up his mind to visit Solomon's club, which was a storefront in Niederrad, and make inquiries. It was possible Solomon had been arrested. "Arrested" was at that point the worst outcome my parents permitted themselves to imagine. For them, "arrested" was bad enough. After Buck's arrest in 1914 they had lost control of their own lives for four and a half years. His arrest had cost them a fundamental sense of security, a sense of owning their lives.

Maybe up until the Reichstag fire it had not been unreasonable to assume that life in Germany would gradually find its way back to normal—but my reasonable parents still didn't realize that things were actually moving in the opposite direction.

Buck planned to check at the club, then, if necessary, go to the local police station and offer a statement testifying to Solomon's character, employment, and war record. If the chauffeur was charged with an offense—and not just sleeping off the aftereffects of a brawl—my father would call in the baron's lawyer, Kaufman, and hand matters over to him.

While all this was going on I was at my desk in the Translation Department, where the mood was unsettled. Not only had Dr. Ziegler disappeared, but Günter Krebs hadn't shown up for work since before the Reichstag fire. There was a rumor going around that Ducky had demanded a week's leave to deal with "party responsibilities" and that this preposterous request had been granted by our new chief, Dr. Winnacker.

Was it now acceptable at IG Farbenindustrie to be openly Nazi?

The question took courage to ask. Perhaps that was why Dr. Winnacker seemed to be dodging it and hiding in his office.

Meanwhile, on the other side of the river Main, my father, Buck, set off on foot for the center of Niederrad. That dingy neighborhood lay between Walden and Frankfurt city proper and had the atmosphere of a down-at-heel Hessian village. It hadn't shown much improvement since 1919. People kept chickens and pigs and milk cows. There were as many horse carts as cars on the road.

Buck headed straight for the clubhouse of the Reichsbanner on Schwanheimerstraße where he found a wreck: windows smashed, door battered down. There had been some sort of bonfire lit inside. It had been put out by then, but when he walked through, the walls were blackened and the air greasy from smoke. Everything was smashed and broken.

No passerby would say anything about what had happened. People averted their eyes and walked past the place quickly. Finally a clerk at the newsagents' across the street told my father the club had been raided by SA auxiliary police, which meant stormtroopers with white armbands and Mauser rifles. They'd arrested the Reichsbanner men, loaded them in the back of a truck, and driven off.

My father asked the newsagent if he had any idea where prisoners were being held. The man just pressed his lips together and ignored Buck until he turned and left the shop.

He was perplexed, annoyed, and, understandably, frightened. He wanted to go back to Walden, work with his beloved yearlings, forget the stench of burned rooms. He always had disliked Solomon Dietz. But Herta had a right to know what had happened to her man.

Buck decided to go to the Schutzpolizei. If Solomon was under arrest, the local police station was most likely where he would be held, wasn't it?

At the police station the *Oberwachtmeister* insisted his cells held no prisoners. If auxiliaries arrested the Reichsbanner, then it was auxiliaries who were most likely detaining them. He himself knew nothing whatsoever about the matter.

"Detaining them where?"

"You would be wise, Herr Lange, to let the matter drop. The fellow will undoubtedly turn up, sooner or later."

"But, really, where do you imagine he is held? And are they treating him badly?"

"If you want to pursue the matter officially," the cop said, "you'll have to approach the central police office on the Römer. But it would be a waste of time, because they won't know, either."

Buck couldn't face Herta without bringing home any news. So he caught a tram across the bridge and headed for the Schutzpolizei headquarters. He saw lorries and cars packed with SA hurtling through the streets. Shops owned by Jews had their windows smashed. There was broken glass everywhere.

At the police station, Buck asked for any information on *Dietz, Solomon*, a chauffeur employed by the Baron Hermann von Weinbrenner. Last seen at the Reichsbanner club, in Niederrad.

"The Jewish baron, eh?" The *Wachtmeister* grimaced. "Come back tomorrow."

"But do you have him or not? Is he being held?" Buck was by no means confrontational, but he could be stubborn. "If so, what is the charge? I must inform his wife."

"How should I know? No one tells me anything."

"Well, isn't it your job to know?"

"Don't tell me my fucking job," the policeman replied. "Anyway, what are you, English?"

"I must establish this man's whereabouts, it's for the sake of his wife. She's extremely upset, as you can imagine. If you have any idea—"

"Do you know the Klinger-Oberrealschule?"

"My son was a scholar there."

"Well, a little bird told me there's some funny stuff going on in the basement of the Klinger-Oberrealschule. One of their 'wild camps.' I shouldn't poke my nose in it, if I were you. Now get out of here, mister, and leave me in peace. I've had a hell of a bloody day, I'll tell you that!"

Stunned, feeling as though he were all of a sudden living in a strange city, my father went into a café on the Römer and ordered a cup of coffee, most unusual for him. He disliked spending money in cafés.

The afternoon papers screamed about a Communist conspiracy, a network of arsonists under orders to burn down the structures of civilized life in Germany. There was a telephone at the back of the café, and Buck rang me at the office, the only time I can remember either of my parents doing so.

"The *Wachtmeister* said something about goings-on at your old school. In the basement. A wild camp—have you any idea what that means?"

"No."

"Ah so, Billy, this is fools' business. Do you think Dietz can be in serious trouble? Can he be mixed up in this putsch?"

By then most people had swallowed the line that the Reichstag fire had been set by Communists as part of a putsch. The crazy Dutchman who'd been arrested was certifiably a Communist. Dr. Goebbels, the propaganda chief, was playing the story perfectly.

"Ought I go up there, to your old school? What do you think? Should I send off a telegram to the baron?"

Had my father ever before asked me for advice? I don't believe he had.

We both still were under the impression that Hermann, Freiherr von Weinbrenner, commanded influence in Frankfurt. Hadn't the university granted him the title of *Ehrensenator,* "honorary senator," on his sixtieth birthday? Hadn't the city of Frankfurt given him a silver plaque and named him *Ehrenbürgerwürde,* "honored citizen"? As far as I knew he still had his seat on IG Farben's supervisory board of directors. When he wasn't attending horse races in Belgium or yearling sales in England, he spent a lot of time going over architectural plans for the art museum Lady Maire wanted to build. The main house was crowded to overflowing with altarpieces from Italy and the Low Countries, *Palmesels* from all over Germany, calvaires from Brittany, devotional statuary from every corner of Christendom, cases of chalices and Mass hardware in beaten gold. There were cases stacked with priestly chasubles of Flemish cloth that somehow had survived the centuries. Lady Maire was determined to build a museum on the Walden grounds to properly house and display her collection. As she got weaker from cancer and the regime grew stronger, she only grew more passionate about this.

The baron hated the notion of a museum sprouting up at Walden and attracting visitors. So did my father. They didn't want their horses disturbed. And they didn't want to give up any of the stables or a single hectare of hay meadow. If there was to be a museum, the site would have to be carved out of the Walden woods. But cutting down trees was a complex matter in Germany, requiring applications to be submitted to municipal, regional, and state authorities, supplemented by negotiations with contradictory bureaucrats. Lady Maire's museum project wasn't moving forward quickly. My mother complained bitterly about this—they were denying a very ill woman her most cherished dream. But the delay was probably fine with the baron and with my father.

"I could send a telegram to England, but I don't know what he could do," Buck mused. "Weinbrenner has troubles of his own these days."

There was a pause while he lit a cigarette. When he spoke again, he sounded weary.

"Honestly, Billy, I'm worried. I don't like the sound of this wild camp. The longer they hold our fellow, the worse it will be for him."

Another pause. I wondered if our connection had been dropped. Or had we been disconnected by the office switchboard? Was someone listening in?

"Dad? Still there?"

"Right here. Only thinking. I would describe the woman, his wife, Herta, as getting near the hysterical stage when I left."

"I don't really have time to talk now, Dad."

"Of course, she's a Sorb. They're emotional. But he's Jewish, as well as a Reichsbanner. If they're holding him . . . do you hear me, Billy? If they are holding him—brownshirts, I mean—I don't suppose they'll be treating him with . . . with kid gloves. Oh no. Au contraire."

The quaver in his voice—that couldn't be blamed on the connection. Suddenly I remembered him—*saw* him—sitting alone on that London park bench on a winter day, just after his release from Ally Pally, while we were waiting be deported. Sitting alone and staring at nothing.

"Billy, what do you think I should do?"

Don't call me at work, I thought. For three years I'd enjoyed the righteous pleasure of a salary. By then—I have statement slips from the *Pensionskasse* and could double-check, but don't need to—I was earning one hundred seventy marks per week, more than double what I'd started at. I never knew what salary my father earned at Walden, but I doubt it was as much, though he also had a share of race winnings.

Even after what they'd done to Dr. Ziegler, even with Ducky Krebs throwing his weight around at the office, I was still proud to be an IG Farben man, as dismaying as that may sound. I wasn't about to pin an NSDAP badge to my lapel, but I wasn't going to rock the boat, either. And here was my worried father wishing to discuss a socialist chauffeur's disappearance over a telephone connection that could be eavesdropped upon at any time by switchboard girls, by Dr. Winnacker, by Dr. Schiller, by my colleagues wearing lapel badges. All my instincts screamed, *Here is a nest of trouble. Stay away. Here is a poison cup. Here is a threat possibly fatal to everything you have ever wanted in your life.*

I was aware that in the preceding forty-eight hours, all over Frankfurt and possibly all over Germany, dozens—perhaps hundreds—of leftists had been rounded up into impromptu *Konzentrationslager,* the wild camps the policeman had referred to. On the radio they were calling it *Schutzhaft,* "protective custody."

Solomon was a Reichsbanner, a loudmouth, and a Jew employed by the Jewish traitor baron. Any one of those was enough to make him a target for the auxiliary police turned loose in our fair city. I'd seen their trucks speeding down narrow streets in the medieval center, ignoring traffic laws, and I wanted to tell Buck to take the tram back across the river, go home, close the Walden gates behind him, and forget what he'd heard or hadn't heard, seen or hadn't seen.

Then I had a brainstorm. It wasn't the time to be emotional or irrational. The Solomonic problem had to be dealt with crisply and efficiently, in executive style. In other words, by passing it along to someone else.

"What we must do," I said, "is contact Kaufman. Let Kaufman deal with it. Herr Kaufman's a lawyer and can make inquiries through the proper channels. Stay away from Klinger School, Dad. Let's not go looking for trouble."

"But I'm not far off. I could walk there in ten minutes."

"I'm going to ring Herr Kaufman. Go home, Dad."

"Kaufman is, likewise, a Jew," my father remarked. "What's going to happen to him if he goes up there?"

"He's a lawyer. An officer of the courts. They won't trifle with him."

"Well, I can't go home without some news. Can't face that wailing woman."

"I'm going to telephone Herr Kaufman right now."

"I believe I'm going to walk up there and—"

"No! Definitely not! Go home!"

I hung up and glanced around to see who had been listening. The other fellows seemed absorbed by their work but probably had caught every word. At least four others in our office apart from the absent Krebs were sporting NSDAP lapel pins. My father and I had been speaking English, but this was the Translation Department. Everyone within earshot knew the language perfectly.

They kept their heads down. No one met my eyes.

My generation knew the smart thing was to stay away from other people's trouble. But my father, in his mild way, could be relentless. I thought he'd probably head for the Klinger-Oberrealschule despite my advice.

I rang Kaufman. It was a violation of protocol to use an office phone for personal business, and I figured Dr. Winnacker would give me his cold version of hell if he found out, but there wasn't time to go to the tobacco shop across the street.

Frau Fleck, the lawyer's indomitable secretary, demanded to know exactly why I was calling. She'd never liked me, and she had no intention of putting me through to the great man.

I let her know I was calling from IG Farben headquarters and insisted on speaking directly to Kaufman about a matter of urgent personal importance to the Baron von Weinbrenner, a supervisory director of the company. Her default German subservience kicked in. Kaufman came on the line.

"All right, my dear Billy, what mess has our Karin gone and gotten herself into now?"

It startled me, his assumption that I was calling on Karin's behalf. His doing so gave me a little thrill of pleasure, but quickly I explained that Solomon had been taken into custody, probably by a band of SA, and probably was being held in the basement at the Klinger-Oberrealschule.

"You can't be serious! A high school! A basement!"

I explained that my father was on his way to the school to make inquiries.

"Your father shouldn't interfere." Kaufman sounded annoyed. "He has absolutely no standing in the matter. He won't get anywhere and may be exposing himself and the baron to unforeseen consequences. In short, he is putting his nose where it doesn't belong. The authorities are under no obligation to tell him anything."

We were speaking German. Kaufman's English was limited. I had never cared for him. When I worked in his office I found him fussy and overcritical. He preened himself on his familiarity with the constitution of the German republic, by then the deadest of dead letters. Like the baron, he had been a front soldier, in his case in the artillery of the Grand Ducal Hessian (Twenty-fifth) Division. He also kept his *Eisenkreuz* in a leather box on his desk. And just like Eddy Morrison, the proprietor of Frankie's English Bar, Kaufman had been wounded in the neck during the Battle of the Somme. The visible portion of his scar looked like a claw mark.

"Perhaps you can make inquiries," I suggested.

"You ask me to go up there?" he said.

Silence.

I had not really grasped the significance of what I was asking, which was that he, a well-to-do, powerful, respected Frankfurt lawyer—but a Jew—poke a stick into a nest of vipers. I had always thought of Kaufman as a thoroughly establishment figure, a friend of Lord Mayor Landmann, whom I'd met in his office. Someone even the SA would treat with wariness. Deference, even. What did Herr Kaufman have to worry about?

Buck, on the other hand, with his English clothes and the very slight English intonation that lingered in his German when he was tired—my father was vulnerable. My father could be a target once again.

"Well," Kaufman said, "I could telephone one or two *Schupos* whom I know, but I doubt they would appreciate such a call. This whole business of protective custody—the law is very unclear. There's certainly no doubt the Reds were planning a conflagration."

"I doubt Solomon was planning anything except getting drunk."

He chuckled. "Always been a loudmouth, that fellow. I have no idea why the baron keeps him on. But for Weinbrenner's sake I suppose I shall have to go myself and reconnoiter the situation."

Now I was beginning to have second thoughts. "It's SA who is holding him, you know, not regular police—"

"Of course it is, they've been turned loose by their masters, the swine."

"I don't want anything happening to my father."

"Very foolish of him to get involved." He paused, then started speaking in a different tone, formal and succinct, the same tone I'd heard him use when dictating correspondence to Heidi, buxom Heidi who married the pig farmer.

"I am going to pay a visit to the Klinger-Oberrealschule. I'm informing you as a matter of record, do you understand? If you do not hear from me within a few hours, say by fifteen *Uhr*, go directly to the Schutzpolizei offices in the Römer. Insist on seeing Oberleutnant Schwamborn. Do you hear that? Oberleutnant Hermann Schwamborn. Inform him that Lawyer Kaufman, whom he well knows, has paid a visit to the Klinger-Oberrealschule and has not been heard from. They have a good deal of respect for me, these *Schupos*. Understand?"

"Yes."

"Your father has more courage than sense, do you know that?"

He hung up.

Shame, that was what I felt. I had asked of Kaufman what I was afraid to do myself. And it was my bloody alma mater they'd dragged Solomon to.

I'd followed my instinct to stay clear of trouble. Like any rat, after sniffing a threat, I had slipped into the nearest available hole.

I was hating more and more the loudmouth of a chauffeur for forcing this confrontation with my own cowardliness. And I resented these two oldsters, my father and the Jewish lawyer, for their damn courage.

Me, the bodyguard. *Quelle blague.*

For the next hour, I tried to work but was unable to concentrate. I kept getting up and pacing around like a sick dog. The report on my desk, a detailed analysis of the pulp and paper industry of Quebec, our largest North American market for bleaching chemicals (chlorine and caustic soda), had come to me in inadequate, practically incomprehensible English. Paragraphs swam before my eyes. I was expected to summarize them in a few paragraphs of flawless German.

I could tell that Kaufman, despite his bluff manner, was aware that auxiliary policemen were a dangerous unknown. Imagining my father in their clutches gradually became unbearable. Grabbing my hat and overcoat, walking fast, I approached Dr. Winnacker's office. I didn't wish to make eye contact with the other fellows. I trusted my two pals, Ernst Mack and Robert Briesewitz, but no one else.

Dr. Winnacker's door was shut, of course. I ignored the pretty secretary, Fräulein Reppe. She was still looking rather shattered—she had worshipped Dr. Ziegler. I wondered how long she, as a Jew, would last at IG. Ducky Krebs had always treated her respectfully. Perhaps that counted for something, perhaps a lot.

I rapped on our new chief's door. Very unusual behavior—at IG Farben, subordinates didn't disturb the chief; it was always the other way around. Fräulein Reppe, mouth agape, was too startled to say anything.

"Yes, what is it?" came from within.

As I entered he had his feet up on his desk. Dr. Winnacker was a heavy man, big boned, with broad shoulders. He looked tired. All we knew about him was that he had lived in Buenos Aires and helped organize Anilinas Alemanas, IG Farben's Argentine subsidiary. There had already been gossip that his wife was an Argentine Jew.

He was a stylish dresser, Dr. Winnacker. In the middle of winter he was wearing two-toned shoes. Later he told me that he had his suits made by a famous old firm of English tailors in Buenos Aires.

"You have some trouble," he said calmly.

He, or Fräulein Reppe, must have listened in on the telephone conversation with my father. I started to speak, but Winnacker held up his hand.

"I really don't need to hear about it, but if you have personal matters to attend to, you may go. There's nothing on your desk that's pressing, is there? Go. We'll see you tomorrow. We'll have a talk. I want to get to know each of my men. *Ich wünsche Ihnen viel Glück.*"

><>-0-<><

I stepped into a paternoster cubicle and rode it down to the lobby. Those cubicles were just big enough for one person: you stepped in alone and stepped out alone; you rode in perfect silence.

The paternoster lifts were like my career at IG Farben: silent, narrow, and self-enclosed. Riding up—or down—in my own private space.

Outside it was gray and cold. Scattered lines of rain mixed with snow pattered very quickly, like cats' feet, then swept away on gusts of wind. Leaving headquarters and looking back I always was a little intimidated by our building's size. It was like sailing near an ocean liner in a small sailboat or a skiff. Awe and primal fear. If the big ship foundered, the small one would be sucked down, too.

I caught a tram. Somewhere near the Eschenheimer Tower I jumped down and started walking. It was raining hard by then, cold crisp rain.

I was a few blocks from my alma mater when I saw them coming without at first being able to identify what the disturbance was about: a parade, a march? A squad of stormtroopers, military rifles slung on shoulders, was walking down the middle of the road. They weren't marching; they were sauntering. As they came near I saw they had a prisoner. The stormtroopers were smiling and joking with one another and the prisoner was stumbling to keep up, and I saw to my horror this was Herr Kaufman. Around his neck hung a placard ICH WERDE MICH NIE MEHR BEI DER POLIZEI BESCHWEREN.

I will never again complain to the police.

He was without trousers or shoes, had on only a brown mackintosh over his winter long underwear. There was normal traffic on the road, and it was pulling over to give the SA men right-of-way. It was raining normal rain, and workmen were passing on normal bicycles. People on the sidewalk glanced at Kaufman and kept walking. It was a stunning experience. The new regime in action. What one felt right away: here was where the power was. Boys in brown shirts, Mausers slung on their shoulders, they had it now.

And I'd finagled Kaufman into that horrid situation. If I'd not telephoned him—because I didn't want to take responsibility myself—he would be in his office, sitting at his desk, not stumbling down the road in the rain.

Kaufman, in this setting designed for humiliation, did not appear humiliated. He did not even look frightened. His face wore the same expression I had seen it wear when he was examining a piece of work imperfectly done. A respected lawyer, law degree from Marburg University, fifty-four years old, being marched through the streets in the rain in his underwear—and still he managed to look disdainful. As if already composing in his mind the official complaint that he would lodge with the authentic police. The damages he would demand. The jail sentences he would insist on for these mutineers, who would need to be punished harshly and quickly, so that order might be restored to Germany, the precious Germany which Herr Philipp Kaufman (Iron Cross Second Class and First Class; wounded in the neck on the Somme) believed in so devoutly.

After they had passed, I ducked into the Bethmann garden and threw up, vomiting in the rain, among dripping bushes. Fear and self-loathing. Of course I'd been too afraid to confront them. "Afraid" actually doesn't begin to do it justice. It was terror, complete panic that had locked me up, made my legs stiff, arms heavy, stomach loose.

I kept walking toward the Klinger-Oberrealschule. That took all the courage I had. I figured my father was in there, and I couldn't imagine what they had done with him.

That school had been a benevolent place. I'd had some good friends there, some brilliant teachers.

There was a small crowd lurking across the street from the main entrance. Dressed like workmen, they wore cloth caps and were getting soaked. No one carried an umbrella. Some trucks were parked haphazardly. A pair of SS men in black were posted at the door to the school. That was a surprise—most auxiliary police were SA, in their tawny-yellow outfits. The SS men wore rubber capes and were keeping under the overhang to stay out of the wet.

"What is going on?" I asked. "What's happened? This is my old school."

A young worker in blue overalls glanced at me. "There's no school today, it's a KZ now."

"A what?"

"*Konzentrationslager.* They have prisoners in the basement."

He turned abruptly and walked off. No one else said a word. We all stared at the SS in their black outfits. People kept breaking off and walking away. The pack of onlookers was shrinking.

Then I saw Günter Krebs step out of the building, holding two steaming mugs, which he handed to the men on guard. Günter Krebs, Ducky, in full SS regalia: black boots, black uniform, leather belt with cross-strap and holster, necktie, cap with chin strap. The SS was much sharper looking and better tailored than the SA.

"Krebs!" I called.

The guards scowled, but Günter looked up, saw me, smiled, and waved.

I approached. "I'm looking for my father. Have you seen him?"

"Come here, come here, we're not going to bite. Ah, Billy, old fellow, I was going to telephone you, only I supposed you wouldn't like receiving such a call over the line at work. Your old man's inside. Come fetch him, take him home, we've no interest in detaining the old gentleman. Stand aside, you fellows," he ordered the guards. "Here is Billy der Engländer, can't make up his mind if he's a proper German or not. Come on inside, dear Billy, let's get out of the rain."

I followed him inside. Electric lights blazed in the corridor of our old school, but the classrooms were dark.

"We've sent the schoolboys home, given them a holiday," said Günter.

"What are you fellows doing here?"

"Come along, Billy, where have you been sleeping? My crew has been ordered to concentrate prisoners."

"Why? Who?"

"The bloody Reds, of course. The town is being swept for Reds. There wasn't enough space in the jail to hold them so we have made a concentration camp here."

"Günter, my father isn't a Red."

"No, of course not. He does work for the rich Jews, though, doesn't he? Turned up here with a Jew lawyer. Your father should know better. We sent that fellow packing pretty fast with a squad of SA bumpkins we didn't want around. He won't be back, I assure you."

I could hear screams and thumping from the bowels of the building.

Günter Krebs, my office colleague, my old schoolmate, seemed weirdly calm in his manner, but also thrilled. His uniform was well tailored. He had a pistol in his buttoned holster. His boots shone.

I felt disoriented. Old schools are packed with the smoke of extinguished feelings, and I felt again young and very vulnerable. Was this a dream we were both inhabiting, Günter Krebs and I?

Maybe it was Ducky who was dreaming, and somehow I was snared in his dream. My stomach was raw; my throat sore; my mouth tasted of burn.

In the basement a man was screaming.

"Oh, they are a pack of hyenas," Günter said. "But we're teaching them a thing or two. Your father's all right. I've got him safe in a coal scuttle. Come along. Best to collect the old gentleman and get him out of here. How did you get off work anyway? Does Dr. Winnacker know you're here?"

"I didn't tell him anything."

"I have many new responsibilities," Günter said. "Winnacker had better adopt a more flexible attitude than Ziegler, or there will be difficulties."

He escorted me along a corridor. The floor had recently been polished, the acrid odor of the wax was intensely familiar from school days. There was loud shouting from the basement.

"The man my father was looking for is the chauffeur for the Weinbrenners—"

Günter stopped abruptly and seized my shoulders. His gray eyes under blond eyebrows looked straight into mine. I think this was a proud hour for him. He had resolved himself as a personality. At *Grundschule* he'd been unpopular. Once or twice he had persuaded a few of the others to gang up on one or another of the Jewish students. Once Kracauer had been their victim—they'd thrown his books and his boots over the wall. Günter had been the ringleader, but when the pogrom moment in the school yard passed, the other boys kept their distance from him. In the last months before matriculation, boys began telling one another that Krebs had terrible personal odor. Whether he actually smelled worse than the rest of us, I don't know, but it became a legend. In the morning when our classroom was unlocked there were sometimes a dozen bars of Nivea soap stacked on Krebs's desk. Maybe it was a conspiracy of some Jewish boys. Probably Kracauer was behind it. It happened every couple of weeks. Everyone was amused except Krebs. Glowering with fury, he'd shoulder his way into the classroom and seize the soap bars and chuck them into his desk.

After the war Krebs had a career as a salesman at BASF, one of the IG Farben successor firms. He died on a photo safari in South Africa in 1979.

"Take some advice from an old school friend, Billy."

He was jovial. Maybe he and his mates had already blown off enough pressure down in their dungeon that he could allow himself a sweet pause, basking in his own *Freundlichkeit*, friendliness. The screaming in the basement was a chamber concert with Günter's SS men playing the instruments. Everything in their lives was at last in tune.

"Make no further inquiries regarding the Communist Dietz. Leave him to the authorities, do you understand? His case will be properly dealt with, I promise you. Do you understand? And don't go around boasting how that disgusting Jew Weinbrenner got you your place at the IG. Such talk won't win you any friends."

This all happened before I or anyone else had watched half a century's worth of films about secret police and Nazis and the brutality of ordinary "decent" men in uniforms, so I didn't recognize the situation, I didn't know the story line. I couldn't put it together fast enough to tell myself what was happening. What had started as an ordinary day kept getting darker and crazier. I was reeling.

Ducky resumed his splayfooted stride, boot heels making a crisp squeak on the linoleum. He pushed through a set of fire doors, and I followed him down a white stairwell to the basement, which had always seemed more ancient and grimier than upstairs: a warren of storerooms, furnace rooms, steam pipes, coal cellars. Briesewitz and I used to sneak down there to smoke cigarettes in the furnace room.

Two SS men came stomping along the narrow corridor with pistols and wolfish grins. They seemed in the best of humor. An inebriated atmosphere. Not drunken, but hysterical somehow. I felt like Alice in Wonderland, fallen down a very dark rabbit hole.

The storerooms we passed were shut. I heard shouts, wails. Then another scream, lasting three or four seconds before it was cut off. Ducky didn't pause.

When I later heard a scream like that in the Florida Everglades, the guide said it was a panther caught in a leg trap.

Ducky and I squeezed past four or five middle-aged workers in blue smocks, kneeling on the floor, groaning, faces pressed against the cement wall. The SS guards had placed broom handles on the floor and were forcing the men to kneel on them.

Steam pipes seethed. The guards must have been coaling the furnaces; the boilers were going full blast. We came to the metal door of the coal scuttle. A towering SS guard snapped to attention and saluted Krebs, who returned it nonchalantly. The guard shoved open the door.

"Here you are, Lange!" Ducky called. "Stand up! Let's go! Your time is up."

Lange, not *Herr Lange*. For a classmate to address my father with such informality, this was like the ground giving way. Even after the brutality I had witnessed, it shocked me.

My father stumbled out into the corridor, blinking. His suit was filthy, his hands were black, his face was grimed with soot.

"Your good son has come to take you home. Please inform your dear *Judenbaron* he needs to be more careful employing dirty little kikes like this Bolshevik Dietz. And if I were you, Lange, I would be thinking about looking for a different job. It doesn't pay any longer to work for the Jews."

Clutching his hat and English raincoat, my father nodded, warily. As far as I could tell they hadn't beaten him up, but he was trembling. He grasped my arm tightly as we walked the corridors of the dungeon. Somewhere a Strauss waltz was playing on a gramophone, and as we climbed the stairs the music came chortling after us. Never since have I been able to hear a Viennese waltz without a feeling of fury and something like seasickness. Through my sleeve I felt my father's grip on my arm. By the front door I stopped and helped him put on his coat.

The little knot of proletarian onlookers had been shooed away. There were only the SS men, the shining street, and the rain. We walked away as quickly as we could.

"Billy, do you know what they did with Kaufman?"

"Yes, I saw it."

There were tears on his face; he rubbed them with the back of his hand. "Vipers they are. We must do something, Billy. This can't be allowed to continue—"

"I'm going to telephone the police, the real police."

I ducked into a cigar shop, pulling my father along with me. With trembling hands he lit a cigarette while I used the public telephone to ring the number Kaufman had given me. A man answered and I asked to speak to Oberleutnant Hermann Schwamborn.

"The *Oberleutnant* hasn't time to talk to everyone. What are you calling him about?"

The proprietor of the shop was eyeing us warily.

"I was instructed by Lawyer Kaufman to report his disappearance. Kaufman has disappeared."

"What do you mean 'disappeared'? If he's disappeared, how did he give you instructions?"

"Before he went to the Klinger-Oberrealschule—look, he hasn't actually disappeared. Half an hour ago he was being frog-marched along the Eschenheimer by a squad of SA."

There was silence on the other end of the line.

"Will you please connect me with the *Oberleutnant*?" I asked.

"Can't. He's not here."

"Well, may I speak with whoever's in charge, please? I need to make a report."

"They are all busy. You can try tomorrow or the day after. No more calls today. Good day."

The line went dead.

I tried ringing Kaufman's office—Frau Fleck must start getting in touch with people who might be able to help.

No one answered the phone.

My father gripped my arm. "I must send a wire to the baron, he'll know what to do."

We left the shop and walked to the post office, where I watched him print the message in English and hand it over to the telegraph clerk.

We caught our tram across the bridge. I asked if he'd seen Solomon Dietz.

"Didn't see him, heard him. They were giving him a beating. Terrible."

We were almost whispering.

It was like the London buses during the war, when people forgot themselves and lapsed into German, and my mother and I felt so vulnerable.

"You know it was him? For certain?"

"Undoubtedly. But please don't say anything to your mother. It would only cause alarm."

"You're joking. What are you going to tell her? That you fell down a coal scuttle? Look at you, it's written on you, you're covered in soot."

"The Lord Mayor Landmann, he's a Jew. For Christ's sake he'd better start cracking down on this lawlessness."

We walked through the Walden gates. My father was determined to see Herta immediately. My mother caught sight of us walking down the drive and hurried out.

"Wherever have you been?" she cried.

"There's been a set of mistakes," Buck said. "From one end of the day to the other. Foolishness everywhere. But things are calming down."

"Calming down? That is not the impression I have. Dr. Goebbels was screaming on the wireless. There's no other word for it. Screaming."

"Well, there's nothing for it but keeping one's head down, staying out of trouble."

"Is that what you call paying a visit to a Reichsbanner club?" she said. "On this of all days? That's a funny way to keep out of trouble, if you ask me."

We continued down the graveled avenue to the coach house. The rain had paused. Branches were coated with gray ice. Mist moved like smoke through the woods.

The forest couldn't hide us. An Apache bow or even a Browning automatic pistol could not protect us. We were living in yet another new country.

We climbed the icy wooden steps. Herta must have heard us; she opened the door before my father had a chance to knock.

"He is dead. You needn't tell me." Her face was white.

"Frau Dietz, what I know is that your husband is in custody of the SS. I was unable to see him myself, but I know he was being questioned. I have sent a cable to the baron."

"They won't allow my man to live. He hates them too much. He's too strong. He hates them." Herta sounded drowsy, like a person having trouble staying awake. Possibly she'd been drinking. "They'll kill him."

Was my old classmate Günter Krebs really prepared to soak his hands with a man's blood? What was I going to say when Krebs showed up at the office?

We had nothing more to tell Herta. We walked back to Newport. It was raining again, and the rain was freezing and forming cuticles of ice on bare branches.

"I'm chilled," my mother said. Buck tried placing his arm around her shoulders, but she moved away.

As soon as we were in the house, he once more tried Kaufman's office. This time the call was answered. I could hear Frau Fleck on the line, screaming at my father; she held me responsible. She finally admitted Kaufman was safe at his apartment. The SA goons had turned him loose.

My father then telephoned Kaufman's home. His wife answered. Frau Kaufman was much younger than her husband, who used to complain about her dressmakers' bills, which came directly to his office.

Buck asked to have a word with Kaufman, but she said he was in bed and not speaking to anyone.

"Frau Kaufman, if you please, it's very important. Terribly sorry we are for having involved your husband in this terrible business. But something must be done and quickly for poor Solomon Dietz. Herr Kaufman and I need to discuss—"

She hung up on him.

Buck sighed, and fretted. He couldn't think what else to do about Solomon that might not make the situation, whatever it was, even worse. Finally my father said he was going out to the stables to check on the mares in foal, but my mother insisted he go upstairs and lie down. And finally he did. She went up with him.

Then I got on the telephone and had the operator ring up the main number for Universum Film Studios, outside Potsdam.

I'd never tried telephoning her. I'd not seen her since that storytelling dawn on the Eschenheimer the year before.

What was I thinking?

Fear and guilt jangled my blood, and she was the one I turned to.

She was her father's daughter. She must know important people in Berlin, people who could intervene, rescue the chauffeur.

I was scared. I was pretty good at not showing it, but, really, I was scared as hell.

I reached the main switchboard at UFA. A minute later Karin was on the line. *"Hallo? Wer spricht?"*

I was struck by the sound of her voice buzzing across Germany on that one electric thread connecting us.

"Wer spricht?" Who is speaking?

"It's me—Billy."

"Who?"

"Billy Lange."

"Ah so. Billy. What—is my mother all right?"

"Your mother's in England."

Pause.

"Whatever is she doing in England in bloody March? My uncle's house is bloody cold and damp. She shouldn't be traveling, it wears her so. How does she look?"

"All right. Thin."

"Your mother has written. All right, tell her I shall come to Frankfurt soon, it's time. Yes. Are they going off this summer? Is an expedition planned?"

"Styria, I think."

"I don't want her falling ill in some horrid Austrian village."

"Karin, I must tell you what has happened."

I spoke too fast, spilling the dismal events. She kept asking me to slow down, but my burden of guilt was chasing me like a runaway cart horse.

"Those swine!" she said. "It's bad enough here in Berlin, but I didn't suppose they would be so bold in Frankfurt. They're trying to get at my father, do you see?"

"I'm worried my father will do something foolish, go back to Klingerschule in the morning, something like that."

"Longo!" she exclaimed. "Good old Longo works at Prinz-Albrechtstraße, the Ministry of Justice; I shall telephone him."

I'd never mentioned my conversation with good old Longo the year before. There was no point mentioning it now. Perhaps he could be prevailed upon to do some good.

"We'll get to the bottom of this. Kaufman, Kaufman . . . oh Lord, and we must do something for him—when do my parents get back?"

"Don't know."

"Tell your mother she must send to Kaufman's office a bunch of roses, yellow roses. A really big bunch, massive. The man probably hates flowers. Tell your mother, on the card, no names, but write this: Pour le Mérite. Understood?"

Every German schoolboy knew Pour le Mérite was the highest order of merit awarded by the kingdom of Prussia for extraordinary personal achievement.

"I'm going to ring up Longo right now," she said.

⊱┄┅⊙┅┄⊰

Next morning most of the wreckage was cleared up. Brownshirt squads were no longer tearing about the town. At IG headquarters no one mentioned them or the SS or the impromptu KZs. It was as if a resolution had been passed enjoining us not to discuss such things, so discordant they were, outside the chorus of everyday life. Even my friend Robert Briesewitz, who had taken up Kracauer's role as Günter Krebs's chief tormentor, kept his nose buried in work during the days following.

Günter Krebs didn't show up at the office. Would I have confronted him if he had? Probably not.

Our former colleague Kracauer might have had something bitter and funny to say about brownshirt bumpkins running wild in a sophisticated, urbane city like Frankfurt—but Kracauer was headed for Uruguay.

Our new chief, Dr. Winnacker, spent the rest of the week going around the department on an informal inspection, introducing himself personally to everyone, perching on the desks and chatting, mostly about nothing.

Hold on, gentlemen! Attention please! By any chance did you happen to see four drunken louts in brown frog-marching a respected Frankfurt lawyer down the Eschenheimer yesterday afternoon in freezing rain?

But I didn't say anything, and there was nothing in the newspapers.

Günter Krebs never did report for work in Dr. Winnacker's department. Two weeks after the Reichstag fire, we learned he had been promoted to a management-level job with special responsibility for labor relations in the plant at Hoechst.

Kracauer never made it to Montevideo. He was en route to Bremerhafen and South America when a pack of brownshirts accosted him on the platform at Hannover. He was traveling with a set of expensive leather luggage given him by his parents. When a brownshirt pitched one of the suitcases down onto the track, Kracauer had to scramble down to fetch it. He was trying to hoist himself back onto the platform when he was kicked in the face and fell backward, hitting his head on a steel rail. The stationmaster halted the train before it could run him over, but Kracauer never regained consciousness.

By the time we heard he was dead he'd already been buried. We weren't told details, only that he'd died in an unfortunate accident. Weeks later I ran into Rothbart, another Klingerschule old boy and former member of the Niederrad Winnetou tribe, who told me the real story.

Karin's parents returned from England one week after the Reichstag fire. Lady Maire's arm was in a sling; she'd had a fall while hunting with her brother in Northamptonshire. The baron had purchased a mare, Mountain Pass, at the Doncaster sales. From London he'd telephoned and fired telegrams to Germany, seeking the whereabouts of his chauffeur. In those days Weinbrenner still thought of himself as a powerful person. That was his habit, like thinking he belonged to Germany and Germany to him. As soon as he was home, he hurried up to Berlin where he learned through an old Uhlanen comrade at the Interior Ministry that Solomon Dietz was being held at the new *Konzentrationslager* at Dachau in Bavaria.

Unable to reach the camp commandant by telephone, the baron decided to show up in person, though everyone warned him against it. My father wanted to accompany him, but the baron wouldn't allow it. Stepping off the train at Munich, he had difficulty persuading a taxi driver to bring him out to the KZ at Dachau. In the end he had to pay four times the meter fare to get there. He was wearing his Iron Crosses (First and Second Class) pinned to his overcoat.

I don't know what happened exactly, but they humiliated him in some way. Perhaps they roughed him up. He was lucky not to be arrested, my father said, but in those days they were still a bit wary of people like the baron, though it wouldn't take them long to overcome their inhibitions.

The baron was never the same afterward. He never again got on a horse, for one thing.

That summer, while my mother and Lady Maire were driving around Austria, *Dietz, Solomon* would appear on a list of prisoners "killed while trying to escape" printed in the newspapers.

> ⊱────•◦•────⊰

In the last week of March 1933, the young motorcycle salesman, Meyer, had rung me up at work to say that a shipment of new machines had been delivered, the latest models, and I must stop by and have a look.

"Undoubtedly the finest road machines in the world," he enthused. "Real touring bikes. What you must do, Lange, is learn to ride. This is a feeling like no other, all that horsepower between your legs."

I said I'd stop by. Meyer and I were on friendly terms. We'd had a few evenings together drinking *Apfelwien* and going to films. He shared with Günter Krebs a taste for the strongest Hessian apple wine and for cowboy films—though Meyer definitely approved of Gary Cooper. He had hopes of emigrating to the United States. His uncle was in Delaware, an industrial chemist.

Saturday was dark and wet, certainly not motorcycle weather. All week the Nazi newspapers had been proclaiming a nationwide boycott of Jewish stores to start on Saturday, but I didn't figure it would amount to anything. People always needed to shop. I caught the tram across the bridge and got off near the Zeil. Packs of stormtroopers in tawny uniforms were patrolling outside the big department stores, strutting back and forth, yelping insults at the few who dared to go inside, but not actually preventing them. In front of Wronker's, a crowd had gathered, many of the women holding shopping bags. More and more people were ignoring the stormtroopers and dashing into the store—why not, Wronker's always had the best selection of clothing and goods at reasonable prices. The boycott was turning out a failure.

I turned down the street where the motorcycle showroom was and noticed a crowd in the road. Weird. It was a dismal Saturday morning, and an ordinary, second-rate commercial street with no big stores or glamorous cafés, only the motorcycle showroom, some car-repair garages, and a commercial printer's shop.

Unlike the shoppers on the Zeil, this crowd was a mob. They gave off almost a steam, as though they were one big, wet, breathing beast. People were guffawing, and I heard someone yell, "Let's kill him! Let's string him up!"

I caught a glimpse of poor Meyer with a couple of *Schupos* standing on either side of him, holding him up. He'd been roughed up. One sleeve was torn right off his blue suit. Brownshirts were arguing with the regular policemen.

There was a mood of camaraderie. People were offering cigarettes to strangers, lighting up in the rain. I recognized a couple of men from my office in weekend clothes. They stayed at the edge of the crowd, but they looked quite relaxed, as though this were a normal Saturday and they'd happened across an amateur football match on the sports field. One of them held a beautiful Irish setter on a leash.

Brownshirts were at their apogee. They were no longer necessary now that Hitler had the army, and a year later he had their leaders shot, and that was the end of them. But that Saturday, April 1, 1933, they were allowed to rule the streets.

I touched the sleeve of a well-dressed gentleman my father's age. "What's going on?"

He studied me for a moment before replying. "They want to hang the fellow."

"What's he done?"

"They say he was messing with an Aryan girl. Riding about with her on a motorcycle in the rain. They had a spill. She's in hospital. Stupid to go riding in the rain. He's a Jew, they want to string him up, but the police have him now. Ridiculous. I don't know what's happened to this city."

After that he turned and walked away. He probably decided he'd said too much. A few moments later I left, too, and stood waiting for a tram that carried me across the river and almost to the Walden gates.

On Monday I chose not to walk down that street where the showroom was located—why should I go that way? It certainly wasn't the most direct route between my tram stop and IG Farben headquarters. And I was a young man in a hurry. I had serious work to perform.

I didn't want to know what had become of Meyer. There'd been nothing in the newspaper. Insane things could happen, and they were ignored. We weren't living in the real world anymore.

I didn't pass that way on Tuesday, either. On Tuesday night I lay in bed thinking about warriors and blood brothers on the Staked Plain. I couldn't find sleep, I tossed and turned for hours, sheets damp with sweat.

I couldn't be such a miserable coward and live with myself. I had to struggle against my own nature.

Wednesday morning I forced myself to walk past the showroom. The plate glass had been replaced, a motorcycle was gleaming on display, but the place hadn't opened yet. It was too early. I was glad.

But after work I forced myself to go by again. Peering through the window, I saw two salespeople on the floor. I didn't recognize either of them. One was polishing a bike. There were no customers.

I stepped inside. The fellow polishing looked up. He was a husky blond. "Good afternoon."

"Good afternoon. I'm looking for Meyer."

"Meyer?" He seemed puzzled.

"Yes, Meyer. He was helping me choose a machine."

The two of them looked at each other. They both shrugged at the same time.

"Meyer doesn't work here anymore," the blond fellow said.

"Really?"

"Meyer's resigned."

He looked at me, and I saw a version of myself, a young fellow coated with ambition, with eagerness to get on. Ambition and a tincture of fear.

"Do you know where I might find him?"

Yes, we'd been out on the town together a couple of times, but in those days you had to know people awfully well before exchanging details of personal lives. I hadn't a clue where Meyer lived or if he had any family.

"Well, no. But may I help you? Were you looking at a particular machine?"

"I should like to contact Meyer."

The blond fellow opened his hands, a helpless gesture. "Meyer's resigned."

The other salesman, black haired, spoke for the first time. "Too many questions here! What does it matter? Ask us about motorcycles, not about Jews."

"Do you know where Meyer lives?" I asked the blond fellow.

"Not a clue. I can demonstrate any machine on the floor. Which were you looking at? Are you an experienced rider?"

"I don't have time now." I was trembling. Maybe they noticed; I don't know.

"Well, stop in again, we'll show you whatever you like."

I left the showroom and never went back, and never saw Meyer again.

Frankie's English Bar was shut down in the aftermath of the Reichstag fire, with a couple of auxiliary police posted outside, ostentatiously taking down names of anyone foolish enough to inquire when the bar might reopen. No one saw Eddy Morrison. People said he'd left for London or Paris or New York. I heard that the Polish bookie, Willie Chopdelau, had been arrested and deported.

No one expected Frankie's to reopen until, after six weeks, it did. By then light had crept back in the sky, the last hunks of snow had melted in the Walden woods, and suddenly the neon sign was glowing on the street near Goethe's house, and there was Eddy Morrison in his dinner jacket, greeting customers. Willie Chopdelau was at his regular table with his telephone and money box, telling everyone he'd been on a holiday in the south of France, and Brutus the White Russian doorman was selling hashish to his coterie of regulars and elegant wristwatches to anyone else.

In July, while our mothers were touring through Styria, Karin rang me at the office to say she was just getting on a train in Berlin and coming to see her father about "some business matters." We arranged to meet for drinks at Frankie's in a few hours. I changed into a fresh shirt kept in my desk drawer, shaved with a razor also kept in my desk, burnished my shoes to a gleam, and spent a good five minutes brushing my hair, wielding a brush in each hand.

I was at the club when she arrived straight from the *Hauptbahnhof*.

She wore a skirt, a peasant blouse, sandals, and a leather jacket. I couldn't forget watching the rising dawn with her the year before, and her casual remark about sleeping with me—or, more accurately, *not* sleeping with me.

She said she'd had to let go of her Eschenheimer flat. "Couldn't afford it. Don't know how much longer I'll have a job. The regime presses. The big men at UFA wobble. Future uncertain. Such— *Fragwürdigkeit*—how would you say?"

"Shiftiness. Opposite of trustworthy."

"Do you know, Billy, when you telephoned with the news of poor Dietz, I did try to get Longo's help."

"You know Dietz is dead?"

"I didn't like him, but they are much worse, who killed him. Bloody Longo—four telephone messages I left with his bloody secretary. Not a word did he answer, the cad. At last I took a cab out to Potsdam where I knew he was living with some Ministry of Justice boys in a Palladian mansion, by the lake.

"The servant said he wasn't at home, but his Mercedes was there. I'm sure he had a woman with him, but he ought to have known I don't give a damn whom he's fucking, I only wanted his help calling off the dogs who attacked my father's lawyer and kidnapped his chauffeur. I left a note on the windshield, telling him to ring me, but he didn't.

"Next morning, old Billy, I show up at the Ministry of Justice. Prinz-Albrechtstraße. Wait in the lobby, but he does not appear. I think someone recognized me, tipped him off, and he crept in another door. I tried to go up in the elevator, but the gendarmes threw me out of the building.

"That week I was trying to write a scene but struggling with it. I keep a pair of brilliant scissors in my desk drawer for cutting and pasting, and suddenly the scene in my head was me riding out to Longo's mansion in a taxi with scissors in my purse. I'd get out of the cab, send the driver on his way, cut my wrists open with my scissors, and scrawl TRAITORS! MURDERERS! SWINE! in blood all over the Palladian front of his house, then lie down on the marble doorstep, so that everyone could see what crimes are being committed in Germany."

"But you didn't."

"No, I didn't."

"You shouldn't even imagine such scenes. It's not good."

"Oh, Billy, dear Billy—always sound advice. You're so good about good."

She was shivering. I took her hand, and it was cold. She wanted another drink, and I ordered for both of us. There was music, but we didn't dance. We shared a taxi out to Walden, not saying a word. We got out under the porte cochere, and she kissed me on the cheek and ran inside carrying her train case.

The next afternoon she returned to Berlin, and I didn't meet her again until the following summer.

✸   1938

Herr kaufman was telephoning every morning to receive a summary of the baron's condition. Yet the lawyer wouldn't come out to Walden. He believed stormtroopers were watching him. He didn't wish to incite them to pay another visit to the estate.

But I don't think it was *Sturmtruppen* Kaufman feared. I think he could not bear to see his old friend as helpless as he was.

Dr. Lewin had left for Cuba without having been able to enlist another surgeon, and Karin kept trying to develop a plan to somehow get her father to a hospital in Zurich.

When she asked Herr Kaufman about releasing funds to take her father to Switzerland, the lawyer immediately poured cold water on the idea. If she even attempted to apply for an exit permit for her father, he'd have to forfeit everything he had left to the *Finanzamt*. And the Swiss would never grant a visa anyway.

"As you ought to know better than most," Kaufman remarked, "the dear Swiss aren't exactly open to the idea of indigent Jewish refugees. In short, Zürich is a fantasy."

That afternoon I walked across the bridge and through a city that resembled its normal self. Glass had been swept up. Shopwindows had been replaced. A certain number of Jews had disappeared. Old Frankfurt was almost cheerful under a bit of rare, pallid November sun. The streets near the Römer, lined with timbered houses, positively bustled. An early tang of Christmas was in the air.

I was headed for the travel bureau to see about exchanging our tickets for a later sailing. I'd warned Karin we couldn't postpone too long or we'd run out of money because I no longer had a salary. She had no savings, and what was left of her father's capital was locked up in *Reichsfluchtsteuer* bonds.

"I'll gladly refund you," the brisk young travel agent said. "These tickets I can resell in about five seconds. However, finding two berths on another vessel from Rotterdam: not possible. Nor from Le Havre, nor Southampton. Not this season, my friend. All the Americans are returning home in time for Christmas, and every Jew in Germany tries to get to New York, and they're paying through the nose for passage on a Dutch ship. But I can offer you two berths tourist class on TS *Bremen*. She sails from Bremerhafen the seventh of January, handsome ship, fast, Norddeutscher Lloyd, five days to New York. You couldn't do better, my friend."

Jews were given unequal treatment on German-flagged ships. She would never agree to a German ship.

"No, that won't do."

The young man looked at me quizzically. "Are you sure?"

"Definitely not. We'll keep the booking we have."

"*Ich verstehe,*" he said coldly. I see. "Well, then, too bad. I'm afraid I can be of no assistance. Good day."

>─◆◇◆─<

My parents came to check up on the baron. He was comatose and didn't stir the whole time they were there. After they'd left the room with Karin, Otto the taxi driver lingered behind and shot me a look.

"Situation's not good, eh?" he said.

"No, it certainly isn't."

"My old man? Got smacked on the head at work. In the rail yard at Krupp's, they were loading steel beams with a crane, one swung loose— well, you can imagine. Knocked him cold. They kept him in the works hospital for a month, couldn't do a thing. For six weeks afterward he lay at home gasping like a fish, shitting and puking whenever my ma tried to feed him. Couldn't say a damn word. Rolling his eyes. Priests sprinkling holy water—it was pretty awful. Finally he dies. Broke my mother in half. Too late I realized what I ought to have done. I ought to have put him out of it. Spared everyone those last weeks. I was the eldest son, for Christ's sake, who else to do it? He could be a bastard sometimes, but I owed him that much. I owed my mother. Only I was a punk of fifteen, and I didn't have the nerve."

Otto nodded toward the baron. "The old boy, he's not going anywhere, right? Life ain't worth shit, right? And it's very rough for the Fräulein. Listen, mate, say the word, and I'll do for him what I couldn't for my old man. I'd use that pillow, easy as pie. He'll never wake up. He's most of the way gone already, isn't he? Listen, I'd do it for a dog, wouldn't you?"

I was on the point of saying *Yes, by all means, let's do it.* Because he was right, it would have been better for everyone, certainly for her. But just then Herta bustled into the library with a tray and a bowl of that damn yellow soup of hers, the smell of which was beginning to nauseate everyone. My father called for Otto. My parents had to get back to their duties at the hotel.

"Time someone did the right thing," the cabdriver told me, pulling on his cap.

 CHARLOTTENBURG

Letter. Addressed *Herr Billy Lange, Übersetzung Abteilung IG Farben Hauptsitz Frankfurt A. M.*, postmarked *Berlin 17.9.1934.* Lange Family Archive, 11 C-09-1934. Special Collections, McGill Library, McGill University, Montreal.

—

KVW
Geisebrechtstraße 5, Berlin

17.9.34

Billy dear,

All right, time you came up please. I am just off the K'damm, driving me crazy. September too crazy warm in Berlin for September too much light in the flat in this summer. Always I have told myself Karin what you will always seek and always want more and can never get enough is: time & light Zeit und Licht

Zeit und Licht

but I find too much of both in Berlin this horrid September stink, come here Liebster Billy we shall go off to Wannsee with a picnic basket of grapes and wine. Here is Greengrocer Egeler not a bad chap actually from the Breisgau and speaks his Schwäbisch which the Berliners with their Schnauze pretend not to understand, but always he has been to me friendly & cheerful. One hour past I stopped at his shop to buy peaches and a bunch of grapes lovely in such hot weather I eat only

372 — Peter Behrens

fruits and a scrap of cheese. Arranging a beautiful crescendo of peaches and strawberries on the table outside is young Herbert Egeler the son, who performs deliveries on a black bicycle and a nice boy. He is wearing today: Hitler-Jugend outfit. And on his delivery bicycle are attached 3 small Hakenkreuzflagge with the sickly cross. I feel most ill. "May I please assist you Fräulein Weinbrenner?"

"Herbert really are you pleased with Mr. Hitler?"

"Oh yes. I suppose so."

"What is it that pleases you?"

"Well he is manly. He will make Germany clean and strong. He will get rid of the idiots."

You best had come to Berlin dear Billy.

From Anhalter Bahnhof, U-Bahn to Uhlandstrasse, from there 10 min. walk.

Your old friend,
K

Letter. Addressed *Herr Billy Lange, Übersetzung Abteilung IG Farben Hauptsitz Frankfurt A. M.*, postmarked *Berlin 17.3.1935*. Lange Family Archive, 11 C-03-1935. Special Collections, McGill Library, McGill University, Montreal.

＞

KVW
Geisebrechtstraße 5, Berlin

17.3.35

Dear Billy,

I cannot explain about my mother as I am rather in torment. Yes I ought to visit more often but am very afraid of her actually. In pain she'll always say something bitter. Bitter and banal. Which makes it worse. 'Whatever have you done with your hair!'

She knows how to suffer so well.

As to my quitting Germany, can't see it, yes perhaps in a year or two if things get awful, but—not now. My skill with the system of permits and Reichsfluchtsteuer (if you may call it a system) is NEEDED here BADLY and I've no right to withdraw. Good old Kop has excellent contacts at the South Americans so we are pushing Jews that way.

I will ask you: come up to Berlin as soon as you can. I realize you have your own affairs. Only you must know what you are to me. I am a crazy old woman. In short: I need you. Talk. Bed.

Dance and sleep in your arms Buffalo Bill. If you drive the Wanderer instead of the train we might go for a jaunt. Oh my honorable brother.

Yours,

K

In the summer of 1934 my father and the baron entered horses in the Grand Prix de Paris, the Grand International d'Ostende, and the Deutsche Derby. My mother and Lady Maire were on a motor trip through Poland, where roads were supposed to be terrible.

In June I had transferred from the Translation Department at IG Farben to export sales. The new job came with a substantial raise. My pal Robert Briesewitz made the jump with me. We were glad to leave nervous Dr. Winnacker behind and move up to the fifth floor. Our new boss, Dr. Anton Best, was an old hand at IG's overseas operations, and had recently been summoned back to headquarters after five years in Peru.

Wishing to look the part of the sophisticated international business-man, I invested most of my salary increase in new suits, a blue wor-sted and a gray flannel, ordered from the British tailor in Hamburg. I wore English striped shirts, my wonderful Paris neckties, and, briefly, an experimental mustache. I became a regular at Frankie's, spending more time and money there than I could afford. I told myself Frankie's English Bar was the only place in town I felt at home. In July we read of a crackdown on the brownshirts, the suicides of their leaders. The newspapers said they'd been plotting a putsch. No one quite knew what it meant. Was it possible things now might start getting back to normal, whatever normal was in postwar Germany?

I told myself I needed the cosmopolitan atmosphere at Frankie's, the jazz, the clear-cold martinis I sipped in honor of Karin. She'd vis-ited her parents very briefly in the spring, but I'd been in Belgium on a business trip.

I'd been keeping an eye out for her all summer, not realizing she was immersed in affairs at UFA, which was undergoing a putsch of its own.

On a very warm August night Robert Briesewitz and I stopped in at Frankie's after working late at the office. Robert had his trumpet, which he kept in a drawer in his desk. He was a fan of the New Orleans trumpeters, especially King Oliver and Louis Armstrong, but Bix Beiderbecke was in his opinion the greatest horn player who'd ever lived.

Out of habit, I checked the room for Karin. She wasn't there. We had a couple of drinks, then Robert was invited to sit in with the house band, the Louisiana Seven. Robert's talking endlessly about various jazz styles could be a bore, but his solos were a discourse that lit up the room. Hearing his trumpet on "Singing the Blues" or "I'm Coming Virginia," I always felt perforated by the music. Its wryness and jauntiness were so much more humane than the ersatz emotionalism of mawky ballads like the "Horst Wessel Lied." My friend Robert Briesewitz blowing his horn that summer was the opposite of everything officially sanctioned. His solos were statements about the real world, and at the same time they *were* the real world.

Robert—he went missing at Stalingrad.

What a small room it seemed, at Frankie's, what a band of outsiders, what a lit-up haven in a frightened city. Listeners' faces wore human expressions of delight and wonder. Maybe people always looked like that on the streets of New Orleans or Kansas City, but on the streets of Frankfurt, they never did.

We were due back at our desks in a few hours. I lacked Robert's musician's aptitude for late nights. Around one o'clock I caught one of the last trams across the river.

I had passed through the iron gates at Walden and was headed for our Newport cottage when I heard music, splashing, and loud Berlin voices coming from the swimming pool.

Jazz was playing from a record player set up outside the pool cabana. I recognized the sound: Sid Kay's Fellows, a Berlin big band. Robert disapproved of them—too commercial—but I thought they were all right.

Glasses and champagne bottles were strewn on the grass. A whiff of hashish flavored the night air.

Some of those thrashing about in the swimming pool wore evening clothes—men in white ties and tailcoats, girls in gowns. Others seemed to be without any clothes at all.

A short, buxom girl pulled herself out of the pool, quite naked, and I recognized the famous film actress Rosy Barsony. She waved as though she recognized me, then dived back in.

I felt ridiculous standing on the grass in my English worsted suit, clutching my leather attaché. I'd had three or four drinks at Frankie's, and Robert's trumpet had stimulated, as it often did, a state of inchoate yearning. Riding the nearly empty tram across the river Main, I'd been thinking of the cases one heard of, or read about in the *F-Zeit*, lost souls who had thrown themselves into the swirling brown river. What could a person feel, or not feel, that would make them want to do such a thing?

Watching Karin's friends cavorting in the pool, I felt a scrap of wild lonesomeness, like a piece of shrapnel piercing my skin. This was her world, and I certainly was no part of it.

"Billy! Take the plunge!"

At first I couldn't make her out in the boisterous crowd of splashers; it wasn't until she swam to the side and began dragging herself out of the water that I recognized her. She was naked as Rosie Barsony.

Our mothers were touring the east that summer, hunting down golden icons and astounding images of suffering. The baron was in residence at the main house. My father was in bed in the Newport cottage. The poolside jazz and the braying Berlin voices were probably keeping him awake, but he wouldn't complain, not unless he thought his mares and yearlings were being disturbed.

Karin wrapped a towel around herself. "I've lost me job, old Billy."

"What?"

"All of us. Ditched, thrown off, fired, kaput. The UFA is now a Jew-free zone. Only good Germans making good German films."

She had a small, lithe, strong body. She had a quality of fineness. I mean strength and delicacy all at once. Powerful, womanly . . . oh, I don't like to describe her in such terms; I sound like Longo describing a racehorse. Poor taste. Immoral. Worse, a violation.

None of your damn business or anyone else's what her naked body was like.

What a hypocrite's affair this memory business is.

They would all be dead by now, wouldn't they? Rosy Barsony, I read her obituary years ago. Most of the people in the swimming pool would be dead soon enough. Murdered in Dachau, Theresienstadt, or Auschwitz if they were Jews or politicals. Killed on the steppes if they weren't. Or roasted by incendiaries in the cities, or smothered under heaps of rubble.

Anna Rabou wasn't one of the party that night. The Jews had all been fired from UFA, and Anna had chosen to stay on, in the end to serve Dr. Goebbels, Hitler's propaganda chief, who longed to be the film impresario of Germany.

"Where's your motorcycle, Billy? You're not exactly dressed like a demon of speed."

It startled me, in the midst of all that was going on.

"Motorcycle?" I replied. "No, I haven't a motorcycle. The shop was smashed up during the boycott last year. My friend Meyer disappeared. I don't go there anymore. I have a new position at IG, Karin."

"Do you? I dream of *el llano*."

She wasn't drunk, or not like some of the others splashing in the pool, shouting and being so "carefree." Her voice was clear and distinct, and I could hear every word under all the tumult.

Carrying her in my arms that long-ago afternoon had been like participating in a ritual, or performing a play. I don't know which play, but we'd known our roles.

"They're going after my father now, you know," she said.

"Aren't you cold?"

"Bloody cold. Put your arms around me."

I did. She was warm and damp and smelled of chlorine. I didn't give a damn my beautiful suit was getting wet.

"This bunch you see here, last of the Yids," she said. "I should not have stayed at UFA so long. Ought to have left that sewer months ago."

"I'm sorry."

"Ah, Buffalo Billy, let me know when you're going to Texas. I'll be coming along."

All right, a ridiculous scene: film people (*former* film people) splashing and yelping in wet finery, a few of them—mostly directors and technicians—soon to depart for glamorous Hollywood. But Karin Weinbrenner had her own dignity, small body wrapped in a towel, hair damp and tangled, face shining, legs dripping, and I felt the old powerful connection between us reasserting, like players after their solos coming together again, horns, drums, and bass, 4/4 tempo, swinging.

A reed arrow stinging across my path, an Apache bow, an introduction to Winnetou and to Germany. We'd been born in the same room in the house called Carefree, and suddenly I was aware that, notwithstanding her friends, her colleagues, the talented pack of midnight swimmers and soon-to-be exiles, I was the one closest to her. With all she had achieved, some part of her still counted on me.

She took a step back and smiled. "Your poor father. I hope we are not keeping him up with our racket."

"He'll manage."

"Your father, Buck, born a thousand miles out at sea."

"Yes."

The crowd in the pool was thrashing wildly, like a school of fish caught up in a purse net.

"Good night, Karin. Good night to you all."

"Good night, Buffalo Billy."

I started across the lawn for Newport cottage. She still counted on me. I felt thrilled, relieved, and terribly responsible.

>-+-o-+-<

A few weeks later, Günter Krebs suddenly reappeared at headquarters. Our chief in export sales, Dr. Best, crept away into his office without saying a word. Rumor had it our Dr. Best was another who'd been unwise enough to marry a South American Jew, in his case a Brazilian.

Ducky stayed clear of my desk, at least. I watched him conferring with other fellows. Robert had said Ducky spent his time at the Hoechst plant delivering idiotic harangues to the workers. "They've got him as the plant cheerleader. Spends all his day spewing absolute dreck. Perfect job for him."

Krebs stood at my colleague Willy Frey's desk, chatting. Willy handled dyestuffs and bleaching agents for the Indian market. I was relieved Ducky was keeping away from me. I wondered if it was because he had a bad conscience. After all, he was a killer, with Solomon Dietz's blood on his hands, and he knew that I knew. I certainly didn't want to have a fake-normal chat with him.

Was I more wary of Ducky Krebs, or he of me? Probably he wasn't afraid of anyone by then except his SS superiors. The black uniform was designed to give men like him a supine power. There was nothing more they needed. The uniform was a radiant piece of power.

Just then one of the office boys came hurrying through the department with a blue basket of mail. "Something for you, Herr Billy, and it smells kind of sweet!" he cried, tossing a sheaf of letters on my desk. At the top was a small linen envelope, with her KvW engraved in a Bauhaus font. No Fraktur typeface for Karin.

Her letter inviting me to Berlin was startling. It had been a couple of months since our encounter by the swimming pool, and now she was asking me to come up to Berlin as soon as possible. My head spun. Everything else in my life immediately became of secondary importance. Down at the other end of the office Krebs in his black outfit was enjoying a joke with Willy Frey, who'd heretofore seemed a decent type. Well, I didn't give a damn about those two.

I checked the railway timetables. The last FD-Zug *nach* Anhalter Bahnhof, Berlin, was departing Frankfurt Hauptbahnhof that evening at 18 *Uhr* and arriving after midnight. I didn't notice Ducky Krebs slipping away. After work I took the tram out to Walden, where I packed a knapsack and informed my parents I was off to the Taunus for a hiking weekend with Robert and Ernst. I would have preferred to carry a valise to Berlin—more sophisticated—but the knapsack fit my hiking story. A natural-born liar, apparently.

I just made the Berlin express. I splurged to buy myself dinner. A pack of rowdy businessmen in the dining car was enjoying a supper of roast pork with plenty of wine and loud talk. Possibly they were IG Farben higher-ups, *Prokuristen*, sales chiefs, research scientists, but I didn't recognize their faces. Thousands of serious, accomplished, well-educated men worked for IG. As the train smashed its way across Thuringia they had their brandy and lit their cigars. Then one of them started to sing. He had a decent voice, too.

> *Clear the streets for the brown battalions!*
> *Clear the streets for the stormtrooper!*
> *Millions are looking upon the swastika full of hope,*
> *The day of freedom and of bread dawns!*

At first I assumed they were singing in mockery, a well-fed business-men's joke—defiant, subversive, even dangerous if there happened to be any SD plainclothesmen or party fanatics aboard, because this was that awful NSDAP anthem, the "Horst Wessel Lied," and SD men were known for helping themselves to seats in first-class express trains, whether or not they had paid the fare.

In another moment people at tables up and down the length of the dining car had joined in. Businessmen and well-dressed women, sing-ing with full throats, earnestly, and actually more or less in harmony. A gangsters' song sung by a chorus of diners on a first-class express. While white-jacketed waiters stood rigidly at attention.

After the last verse there was stillness within the dining car. The racketing of steel wheels, but human silence. The truck wheels groaning a bit as the carriage leaned through a curve. Cigarette smoke drifting, blue.

Then the waiters went back to work, and slowly the murmur of con-versation resumed. And I drifted out of the scene because I was think-ing about Karin and what waited for me in Berlin. I was nervous as hell. Would she be awake when I arrived, probably not before 2:00 a.m.? Had the *Hausmeister* been informed of my arrival? If not, who would let me into the building? Never had I spent the night with a woman.

In this type of situation, was it customary to wear pajamas to bed?

I thought not, but had packed mine. Just in case.

Karin Weinbrenner was shy in bed, as if needing detachment from what we were doing. I was not expected to speak. She preferred that I did not. I had to hold her. She seemed terrified, but at the same time wanting this act to be done. Maybe the violence of the breeding sheds at Walden had stayed with her—I don't know. It's not great fun to see a thoroughbred stallion being put to a mare.

No doubt Lady Maire's stern manners and physical remoteness had something to do with Karin's withholding of herself. Because I was the first and I believe the only man she ever slept with. The defiant daugh-ter, the Berlin flapper, the bohemian—yet she told me she'd never been intimate with another man.

"What about Longo?"

"Certainly not!"

Had she slept with Anna? I never asked her. Possibly.

When we were in bed I was aware there was something off, only I did not want to put my finger on it because she was beautiful, her body delicate, her skin lustrous and heated. Intimacy was fascinating, though a part of me could sense something that was withheld. I expected sex with her to be like flame—burning, flickering, illuminating. For her, I'd say the sex was like dodging down a rabbit hole, or a fox going to earth. In bed with me, I think, became somewhere safe she could hide. Inexperienced as I was, jejeune, immature, and in many ways stupid— a hobbledehoy—I sensed that quite soon. For me sex was an alternate universe, where everything was turned on its head, sex was the opposite of everything I did at IG Farben. For her, sex was a ritual that allowed her to feel grounded, earthbound. Sex was refuge.

That first night in the Charlottenburg flat, I seemed to be operating from a different region of myself, as if my body were an airplane my mind was trying to fly and barely succeeding. About to crash-land at any moment. To delay climax I made myself think of those burning avia- tors popping like sparks in the black sky over north London. Afterward I slept hard, and in the dawn we made this wordless, strenuous love again, then Karin had a bath. When she came out of the bathroom, I went in and shaved, bathed, dressed. Returning to the bedroom I found her dressed in a summer frock, holding a black straw hat to match.

"I hope that was all right," she said.

"The bath? Fine. Plenty of hot water."

"The bed, I mean."

"Oh."

"Do you have much experience in that area?"

"No, not really."

"But it was all right, yes?"

"Yes, of course. More than all right."

She gave my cheek a peck. "Now what shall we do with our day, Billy? Would you like to go to the zoo?"

"As you like."

"Oh no, we must go out, you'll want to feel the city. There's nowhere like Berlin."

We rode the lift down and had breakfast at the café across the street, at a table shaded by plane trees. It was cool enough so early.

She said, "You mustn't think whatever's wrong with me is wrong with you. It's just these damned Germans sometimes I can't bear."

"Well, you're German."

"Light me a cigarette, would you? Let's go to the zoo."

Headed for Kurfürstendamm we passed a greengrocer's shop. I saw the delivery bicycle bedecked with swastika flags and a young man in a grocer's smock setting out pears on a table who smiled and wished us a friendly *Guten Morgen.* Karin returned the greeting and squeezed my arm.

"It's hard when they pretend to be such decent chaps," she said.

By then she was working at the Zionist Federation, but she was not happy there.

"The Zions consider they have made a deal, a bargain, with the *Finanzamt*, who says, *Ja*, we are all in favor of Jews for Palestine, good riddance, so long as they hand over money, property. It's like the mouse bargains with the cat, Billy, where does it end? Badly for the mouses, I think."

She said the Zionists hoped for support from her rich father but doubted they'd get any. "He hates to hear of people leaving Germany. Anyway he's not so rich anymore."

On the Kurfürstendamm a weekend mob, carrying rolled-up towels, knapsacks, picnic baskets, was headed for the parks and lakes that surround Berlin. She suddenly seemed in a brighter mood.

"Everybody in Berlin wishes to be out on the lakes," she said. "Everyone wants a little boat to sail, shiny green with a black transom and white sails."

"We could hire a boat."

"Are you a sailor, Billy?"

"Not so you'd notice."

"And your father was born a thousand miles from anywhere." She slipped her arm through mine. "No, I don't think sailing is quite the ticket. Some other time, perhaps. Today, the zoo. Listen to the monkey chatter. Perhaps take a nap. Things are always happy at the Tiergarten. Unless you're an inmate, I suppose."

I began hearing loud electric squawking. A loudspeaker truck. Looking over my shoulder I saw the ponderous gray beast slowly grinding down the boulevard. It was packed with drunken SA men. They were out hunting—I'd heard of them doing it in Frankfurt, though I'd not experienced it. The truck geared down and slowed to a crawl as it came up behind us. A schoolmasterly voice crackled from the loudspeaker.

"*Nicht korrekt!*"

Her arm was linked through mine. Without looking I could hear hoots and jeers from men standing in the back of the truck. I resisted an impulse to walk faster.

"Not correct to wear Frenchy clothes!" the loudspeaker railed. "*Röter Lippenstift!* Frenchy lipstick! It is not in keeping with the German Frau of today! *Es is nicht richtig für deutsche Mädchen wie französisch Prostituierte aussehen! Nicht korrekt!* Offensive!"

I turned us both about. She hung on to my arm. We started walking quickly in the opposite direction. The loudspeaker truck rumbled on, searching out fresh targets. A flow of faces streamed past us, normal faces of people hurrying, shopping, strolling on the K'damm.

That was always disorienting, the normalcy of the world. Berlin faces preoccupied with the business of living, shopping, eating.

The electric snarl broke out again; they'd found another target.

At the zoo we looked at the gorillas, the swimming hippos, the brooding yellow lions, then established ourselves on a bench in a corner shaded by plane trees, where she removed her shoes, lay down, put her head in my lap, and fell asleep.

>─•⊙•─<

Of all our weekends in Berlin—really not so many—a good deal of our time we spent in bed. Sleeping, yes; lovemaking, yes; but also hours of reading or talking. Often we wouldn't go to sleep until dawn. We'd sleep through the morning, awaken early in the afternoon. I usually was out of bed first, made coffee, brought it in to her. She'd be scribbling in her *Kinds of Light* notebook or reading poetry, always German, or a novel, often American, or working on office files, calculating the *Reichsfluchtsteuer* her clients would have to pay before they'd be allowed to escape.

I sometimes brought office work to Berlin, which I did in bed, feeling quite important. She didn't mind; she had her own work. She quit the Zionists for the small agency Stefan Koplin started. I was sending German dyestuffs around the world. She and Kop were sending German Jews.

Her bedroom in Charlottenburg with afternoon light slanting through the French doors and the subtle rumble of the afternoon city was a wonderful place for us: safe, quiet, cool. She owned sets of beautiful sheets, Irish linen from flax fields and mills Lady Maire's family owned in Belfast and Derry.

We were in bed when she told me it was Anna Rabou who had delivered the news she was fired from UFA.

"Poor Anna, it was her job to inform us. Such a difficult assignment! She expects us to feel sorry for her! Of course we all knew it must go that way. Only the famous, the bountiful Anna Rabou had been disguising reality to fool herself. She'd inhaled Nazi mist in her lungs. 'One day you'll be invited back'—that's what she told me."

"She's a rat," I said.

We both relished the fast, hard lingo of pictures like *Public Enemy*, *Scarface*. In gangster films, turncoats and informers were *rats*. By then we knew we were living in a gangster world.

"Well, the rats run the UFA now. I ought to have said, 'Why then, my dear bloody woman, if this policy is disgusting, then resign! The rodent Dr. Goebbels is going to be running the shop any day!' But, you know, I didn't say a thing. They'd summoned a herd of taxis. Cars lined up to take Jews away so Germans could get on with the business of making pictures. I ought to have told Anna what's what, in front of everyone. But I did not. I just got into my taxi. Such was the last scene, dénouement, of my career at UFA. Not very effective dramatically, I agree."

>─+◆>─◦─<◦+─<

During those months while Lady Maire was dying, soft-spoken people from the Städel Museum crept around Haus-Walden preparing an inventory of her art collection for the tax authorities.

Eilín loathed the assistant curator, Herr Speck, in his brown suit and gray shoes, tiptoeing about with a notebook and magnifying glass while the baroness lay upstairs, bedsores rupturing and leaking blood, ruining featherbeds and mattresses. When he dared poke his nose into Lady Maire's bedroom, my mother hurled a silver hairbrush at him, and he scurried away. That evening at Newport Eilín told us the story, trying to make it sound funny, but ending up in tears.

Had I seen her cry before? I can't remember.

My mother and the baron took turns reading Somerville and Ross stories aloud to the dying woman. Herta and my mother bathed her with soft sponges and rubbed ointments into her yellow skin, and all the while meticulous preparations for the looting of the Walden estate went forward.

Karin made a few quick visits home in those months, never staying more than a night or two. I might catch a glimpse of her, but she came and went very quietly, like a leaf on the wind. My mother told us Lady Maire had asked Karin to fetch clothes from her dressing room, and Karin collected armfuls of gowns and laid them on the bed where her mother could touch them, handle them.

⤞⬩◦⬩⤝

Whenever I was up in Berlin we generally avoided any mention of Walden. I felt guilty about lying to my parents. I think Karin felt frustrated, helpless, and angry about the fact her mother was dying, knowing now they would never enjoy a closer, sweeter relationship.

Berlin, even after three years of the regime, still had the flash that sleepy old Frankfurt lacked. Berlin still was a neon town.

A Saturday afternoon. April 1936.

I came in on the train, met Karin at her dingy office, and took her to lunch at a café on Unter den Linden. We had just finished lunch when Anna von Rabou came onto the terrace. I recognized her at once from all the stories in the illustrated papers. She was tall, powerful—stately, I would say. Handsome, not pretty. A bit horse-faced but distinguished looking. In age, halfway between Karin and her mother. She was still publishing books and writing films while other writers were being cut off or forced into exile. Her husband, Fred Scheps, had fled to Hollywood and wasn't coming back.

Anna was with a group of people, very fashionably dressed and jolly. They were just sitting down when she caught sight of Karin and immediately left her friends to approach our table.

I rose to meet her; Karin sank lower in her chair. Anna shook my hand, then bent over to brush Karin's cheek with her lips. Karin sat slumped, staring straight ahead, like a sculpture made of wax.

Anna had a lot of self-assurance. She could put on a pretty good show. She sat down. Taking a pack of English cigarettes from her purse, she offered them to us, and I accepted one to be polite. Karin shook her head.

Anna turned her attention to me. She seemed to know all about my family, our relationship with the Weinbrenners.

"Such an interesting background you have, Herr Lange. Lange is a good German name, but then you are not really a German are you? And not really an Englishman, either. Is this what it means to be Irish, so will-o'-the-wisp?"

"Ich bin ich." *I am who I am.*

"Well!" She smiled. "That means nothing whatsoever, does it? A man these days ought to be able to state exactly who he is and what he's about."

"What are you about, Frau von Rabou?"

I'd had a couple of aperitifs, and her challenging manner provoked me. She was like a battleship sailing into our quiet harbor and leveling her guns.

"Very simply, Herr Lange, I'm a storyteller. I am working to make sense of this country of ours in its difficult time. I am part of a machine. I struggle; I do my bit; I hold out for the same values I've always held dear."

It was startling how much she resembled Karin's mother—same height, same calm, same severity. They were both from old-fashioned military families, so perhaps the resemblance wasn't so surprising.

"Our Karin, I know—I feel—she still burns with anger that I chose to keep on with work at the studio. The unjustice of it, pogroms against innocent Jews, betrayal of artistic values, etcetera. She thinks it is a pack of ruffians I'm thrown in with, I have traded virtue for a little tag of fame.

"I wish, Herr Lange, you would explain to the child, since she won't listen to me, and has returned all letters I've written over the past two years, that her Anna doesn't know where fame lies. Doesn't know or care where the riches are to be found, or praise—doesn't have a clue about any of that. Her Anna remains the same person she was, an artist who does her work and hopes to contribute something to the nation.

"Do assure our little friend, Herr Lange, that her Anna disapproves of treatment the Jews have received. On this subject my position is crystal clear. Foreigners are one thing, but Jews who are good Germans, it's shameful. There are many who share my feelings.

"But perhaps the will of the *Volk* has displaced the Jews for just a little while so that new hands might steer the ship. Once these hands are more confident, things will relax, and the chosen people will be welcomed back. The best Jews are good Germans."

Karin stood up without a word and disappeared inside the café.

"Ah so," said Anna. "She's not doing herself any good by the high-handed way she's behaving."

She put out her cigarette and stood up. She never showed the slightest discomfort or unease. I stood, and she offered me her hand.

"Give her my most sincere love. Tell her no matter how she behaves, her Anna holds her dear."

We shook hands. I watched her rejoin her friends. She spoke, and they all started putting on hats and coats, though their drinks hadn't arrived yet. Anna Rabou put some money on the table and they left. She didn't look back.

Karin must have been watching from inside. As soon as Anna was gone, she came back out on the terrace.

"All right?" I asked.

"Billy, I was in love with this woman. Like a mother she was. Much more, actually."

I didn't know what to say.

"It's finished, however. She's spoiled it. Even the memory. Don't you ever do anything to spoil it, Billy. Don't you dare."

>⊶⊷—○—⊶⊷⊰

Later that Olympic summer, 1936.

Lady Maire was close to death. A telegram was sent to Charlottenburg, summoning Karin, and I was dispatched to meet her train. By then I was the owner of a small secondhand car, a model called a Wanderer. Not much of a car, really, but sturdy, cheap, and practical.

I drove out through the iron gates and across the river. Cold breezy night for summer. It was late, but the *Hauptbahnhof* was busy: serious trains had just arrived; others were just pulling out. The *Hauptbahnhof* aroma of steel, of cinders, electric brakes. Dust and rubbish and old newspaper pages swirled along the platforms.

The express from Berlin slid in on schedule. Stepping from a second-class carriage, she saw me and waved.

We greeted each other on the platform with our customary awkwardness and hesitation. It was always there, at first, whatever it was. Wariness. Being in Frankfurt made things even more awkward, somehow, and we kissed clumsily, like dutiful second cousins. I took her suitcase and we walked out to my old car.

I started driving for the bridge, and she took a cigarette from her purse.

"Do you want to go somewhere and have a drink?" I asked.

"No, I'd best get there. My mother's going to die tonight, isn't she?"

"They are certainly worried at the house."

"Your mother will feel the loss, she's such a devoted friend."

"How is Berlin?"

She was lighting the cigarette. "I've been a terrible daughter, Billy. A fiend, I've been."

"I don't think that's the case."

"Yes, well, what do you know of it?"

We crossed the river, passed through a dreary bit of Niederrad, sped down the road to Walden, where I'd left the iron gates swung open. There was no porter anymore. As we drove through, she caught her breath sharply; it sounded like someone taking a blow.

"Are you all right, Karin?"

"Of course not."

I stopped the car and got out to close the gates. When I got back in, she was sitting so stiffly, like a woman holding a clenched fist to her past.

"I'm sorry you have to go through this," I said.

She snorted. "One's mother dying—nothing out of the ordinary, is it? I see twenty people a day with far more difficult things to manage."

"Maybe your mother's death isn't something you manage. It just happens, and you rely on your friends."

"Oh, don't talk nonsense, Billy, just get me to the house."

I stopped the car under the porte cochere and pulled her suitcase out from the backseat.

"I'm sorry," she said. "Don't mind me, Billy. You're the one I count on, old man."

She pecked my cheek, then grabbed her suitcase and hurried inside. I knew my mother would be standing guard at Lady Maire's bedside. Eilín would see to everything that needed seeing to.

I parked beside Newport cottage. The house was dark, except the kitchen, where Buck and my grandmother were sitting up, each with a schnapps in a small crystal goblet.

"Any news?" my father asked.

"None that I know."

My parents had been warned they would have to vacate Newport once the city took over the estate. Internment, deportation, hyperinflation, and, finally, a stock-market crash had repeatedly wiped out their savings, so where would they—and my grandmother—live? There wasn't a plan yet. Con's brother's farm in Africa, perhaps they could go there.

Buck offered me a schnapps, but I was tired and had to go to work in the morning, so I went upstairs to bed. My Conoco road maps, stiff with age, were still pinned to the walls, but had become invisible, I no longer saw them.

It took a long time to fall asleep. Lady Maire had offered us a home when we were refugees coming into a fierce country. Now she was dying, and everything was flying apart. Nothing really lasted, it seemed.

The baron happened to be asleep when Lady Maire died early the next morning, but Karin and my mother were with her.

▷—◁▷—◦—◁▷—◁

They had hoped to bury her at Walden alongside her son, but the Catholic bishop wouldn't permit burial in unconsecrated ground, so plans were hastily made to lower her coffin into a crypt at the dowdy little parish church at Niederrad, Our Lady of Good Counsel, which she had endowed.

My parents, my grandmother Con, and I made the formal call at the house to pay our respects. I noticed a stack of yellow lumber on a pallet under the porte cochere. Carpenters from the Städel had been building crates for the artwork the museum was commandeering for itself. Work was suspended for the moment, but they would be back after the funeral.

Lady Maire's coffin was in the main hall. Weinbrenner and Karin sat in stiff chairs brought in from the dining room. They stood up as we entered, and everyone shook hands formally. The German rituals of a death. The baron looked old and small. He wore his medals. Karin looked tired and pale. She had on the same black dress she'd worn the first time I'd seen her at Frankie's with a black cashmere cardigan over her shoulders. Ungainly floral wreaths from Lady Maire's family in England and Ireland were arranged on either side of the altarpiece, *The Lamentation*. The flowers gave off a cold, unnatural scent. The baron had asked my grandmother to find Irish shamrocks to be placed on the coffin along with a handful of blue German cornflowers, and Con had picked a small bunch of cornflowers, then dug and potted a clump of trefoil clover, which she insisted was certainly shamrock, even if it wasn't Irish.

There'd not been many visitors judging from names in the condolence book, which were mostly Jewish. Weinbrenner was the traitor baron, and people were afraid.

If I'd had a moment to speak to her alone, I'd have asked Karin to meet me across the river at Frankie's. Martinis, music, dancing—that was what the situation demanded. But another set of solemn people arrived to pay their respects, and Karin and her father had to greet them, and we had to leave, and I never got the chance.

><+>+O+<+>+<

Word got around the office that old Weinbrenner's wife had passed away. The day before the funeral, Dr. Best stopped at my desk.

"That poor old gentleman, they're peeling everything from him, aren't they?" Best sounded regretful. "They're not leaving him much. Kicking him off the supervisory board of directors, really disgraceful. Not right! That old man was one of Germany's most brilliant colorists. Where is the funeral being held? What time? I'll certainly be there."

⊱━◈━○━◈━⊰

Karin announced that she was walking to the church. My grandmother Con asked to walk along with her, and Karin agreed.

I squeezed into the Ford's backseat with my father. The baron sat in front, and Eilín drove. On the way we passed Karin and Con walking along the roadside, Karin leading her mother's old hunter, Paddy.

There were perhaps thirty people at the funeral Mass, most of them Jews from old Frankfurt families. The others were loyal people who'd worked at Walden: domestic staff, trainers, grooms, stable hands. Dr. Best never showed up.

Anna Rabou did, however. She stood in the back of the small church, very tall, dressed in her elegant, severely tailored style. She might have been an actor placed onstage in an expressionist play, speaking no lines but carrying heavy dramatic weight.

After the coffin was lowered into its granite tomb and last benedictions said, Karin and her father left the church arm in arm. The rest of us followed. My mother was crying. The day had cleared. There was sunlight, and traffic hurtling up the road. The air smelled of gasoline. Lady Maire's old Irish hunter stood tethered to the iron fence, waiting patiently. Lady Maire had often ridden him to Mass. Traffic and passersby didn't fluster him.

I watched Anna Rabou shake hands with the baron. Did he know who she was? Probably. He kept track of everyone and everything.

I saw Anna offer Karin her hand. They briefly shook hands. Anna said something. Karin nodded, but she was already looking past Anna to the next person in line.

There was a car with a uniformed driver waiting, and I watched Anna get into it and be driven away.

I was going to stick with Karin whether she wanted me to or not. I approached as she was untying her mother's hunter from the gate. She didn't say anything. She took up the reins, and we started walking down the road, with traffic spinning past us.

"Why don't you get aboard?" I said. "You must be tired. I'll give you a leg up."

"I'm wearing a dress."

"It won't be elegant, but we could manage."

She kept on walking. After a while she said, "Billy, my mother would *not* approve."

"No, probably not."

Abruptly she stopped, and tossed me the reins. "You first. He can carry us both."

No saddle, no stirrups. I flung myself up on Paddy's back. He was a good sixteen hands, and I had to struggle to get a leg over. It wasn't graceful, but I managed at last. I grasped Karin's arm and pulled her up behind me, and we clip-clopped down the road, keeping to the side as trucks and cars sped past, her dress hiked up, her hands resting on my shoulders.

><+>-·O-·<+><

A few days later, three lorries belonging to the museum came through the Walden gates and grumbled up the gravel drive to the main house.

Paintings and artifacts the old Jew's wife collected rightfully belonged to the Volk, did they not? What right had the old Jew to possess such priceless expressions of Christian faith? And the fellow owed money, taxes, didn't he? Typical! He'd no doubt been cheating and chiseling the taxman for years. It's how they are, that tribe. Whatever happens to him now is only justice, isn't it?

My godfather was the *verräterischen Judenbaron*, and they intended to leave him nothing.

He remained mostly in his library that day. After helping themselves to what they wanted of his books, they left him alone in there.

When I came home from the office that afternoon there was still one fat gray truck parked under the porte cochere and Karin standing beside it, conferring with a young man who wore a blue museum smock over his white shirt and tie.

"Don't you see what you're doing?" she was saying as I approached.

"I understand your feelings, miss, believe me, I'm not without respect for your family." He wore spectacles. He looked sensitive, intelligent. In his twenties, with thinning hair. An assistant curator. "However, honestly, such pieces really do belong in a proper museum like ours."

She saw me. "They are crating up *The Lamentation*," she said in a flat voice. She turned back to the curator. "This is theft. Stealing. Looting."

"That statement I must correct," he said. "It's a matter for the proper auth—"

"How can you let yourself be part of it? Haven't you any self-respect?"

She turned away before he could respond and I followed her into the house. In the front hall, where her mother's coffin had been, two carpenters were on their knees, building a crate for *The Lamentation* altarpiece: three mourning women with the dead body of Christ. The scent of sawed boards was pungent. The carpenters had a heap of clean straw and sacks of cotton rags for careful packing. It was a massive thing, probably quite frail, although somehow my mother and Lady Maire in 1927 had brought it all the way from Spain in the backseat of the Ford.

The carpenters avoided looking at us.

"We're being taken to pieces," she said.

⊱ ⊰

She asked me to accompany her back to Berlin; she didn't want to be alone. So I asked Dr. Best for a couple of days against vacation time, and he let me have them. I informed my parents I was off to Breslau on business.

During most of that train journey Karin sat gazing out at green countryside. When the train halted at Leipzig, we were briefly alone in the compartment. She was staring at a horde of travelers out on the platform when suddenly she spoke.

"All the times I wanted to be held by her. And when she needed me, where was I? Trying to keep four hundred kilometers always between us. I should have been closer, I should have forgiven her, yes?"

"Yes."

"I forgive her now, I forgive you, my dear mother. I hope you forgive me."

We took a taxi to Charlottenburg.

Whenever I was with her, I always needed cash on hand to pay for taxis.

As soon as we reached the flat, we went to bed. With the French doors open wide to the little iron balcony and the rumble of Berlin at dusk, I asked if she would miss Walden once the city forced her father to leave, which my father said was inevitable.

"Berlin is home to me, old man. Walden was my parents' museum of themselves."

She was silent for a while before she spoke again.

"Do you think my poor old mama's somewhere out there, Billy? Is she watching me now?"

"Do you feel she's watching?"

"Can't be sure, old man. Can't be sure."

━━━◆━○━◆━━

Another Berlin visit. The following summer, I think. So 1937. I drove up to the city in my Wanderer car so that we could make an excursion out into the countryside.

An August afternoon in my little car with her, our windows cranked down, salt-scented air—that tasted like freedom.

We both liked to *move*.

There weren't so many cars on the roads then, especially to the northeast. The regime was planning *Autobahnen*, even starting to construct them, but you couldn't travel them yet. The existing roads weren't much good but were often empty, and we could go as fast as we liked, though the Wanderer had nothing like the feline power of Longo's Mercedes. She might clock a top speed of ninety kilometers per hour but only on a smooth road and with a tailwind. Still, that seemed fast enough, breezing down empty roads in Mecklenberg. Whenever there were lakes accessible we always made a point to stop and swim. She disliked bathing costumes, said they were pornographic, and refused to wear them. So I had to swim naked, too.

We stop to go birding in a marsh.

That world is closed off now, behind the Iron Curtain, rearranged, many villages smashed in the war. Maybe the marsh is still there.

We're on a walkway across the wetlands. Silver-gray planks strung together to make a narrow wooden path perhaps a kilometer in length, so narrow that if we meet anyone coming from the opposite directions, passing by will be tricky. This is a well-known birding locale. Hunters come up here, too, in season, but in summer it's people like us up from

Berlin, or down from Rostock, armed only with binoculars, hoping to spot whooper swans, egrets, night herons. She's ahead of me, wearing a summer frock, white-and-brown checks, sewn in Berlin by her expatriate Parisienne dressmaker. Her shoulders are bare, sunburned, peeling a little bit. On her feet a pair of green sandals, and around her neck a strap from my father's old naval binoculars, the pair he used for watching sailboats out in the English Channel.

In Charlottenburg we use the binoculars to play a game she calls Who's a Rotter? Zeroing in on patrons at café tables across the street we have ten seconds to decide if they are (a) full-blooded Nazis, (b) halfhearted Nazis, or (c) not Nazis at all. She claims to be Olympics caliber at the sport, but there is no way of independently confirming our scores.

In the wide, fragrant marsh it's not party members, but egrets and herons, black storks and whooper swans, we're looking for. We've left behind the city and its seas of rippling flags, red and white with the jagged black cross in the center, making hideous use of the breeze.

But the marsh is a separate world. The wide sky is hazy, a gray-silver sky with rain possible, but if so, it'll be warm rain. I'm following her along duckboards. The planks are silvery and squeak and bend underfoot as we tread upon them. The marsh is a sea of silver-green grasses, and the wind ripples the grass with a sibilant sound, like bedsheets tearing. There's no one else in sight, not a single person. It's a marsh, so you wouldn't expect a crowd, but it still seems extraordinarily empty from the point of view of city folk like us. And my nose has picked up a first tangy scent of the sea.

She stops so abruptly I almost bump into her.

"Egret," she says, raising the glasses.

The bird is stalking its next meal, frogs or whatever it is egrets feed on in a marsh. Its stride is awkward, hesitant. And while she peers through the binoculars, I place my hands on her hips.

It is the first time I have touched her in such an intimate and possessive way outside the bedroom, touch her as only a lover would.

"Jolly good luck to see an egret," she says.

Two young people breezing through the wide countryside in an open car, walking on duckboards across a marsh, breathing the sifting fragrance of the sea—it sounds a charming romance. Was it? I don't know. I never had any perspective from which to analyze the relationship. It didn't occur to me to try. Most people in those days were confused and startled by relationships. Young men, anyway—we never imagined or predicted the depth and complexity of our feelings about young women until such feelings overwhelmed us. No one warned us.

We believed in privacy. Our feelings were our own. Words? Words were facile things, superficial, limited. One only spoiled one's feelings by talking of them.

Following Karin Weinbrenner along duckboards set across marsh mud and sea brine, I didn't own language to discuss my feelings. To "put them out there," in the jargon everyone seems able to wield today. To put myself out there. No.

Perhaps if I had been able to put things in plain language, it might have been plain that things between us were so damnably unequal, that I loved her as I would never love anyone else and that she loved me as a young woman might love a devoted brother, a trusted bodyguard, or a horse that never stumbles, never shies, but takes all fences willingly, and carries her safely across.

When we were apart and I thought of her, I left words out of it. What came to mind instead were flashes of bold color in sunlight. And always an impression of wide-open country and the pair of us traveling, alone together, great distance at great speed.

>⊶─○─⊷⊰

The regime had been in power four years, and the medieval city seemed harder and brighter, a city now trying to march in step, ferocity and declension unmistakable. Here was the street where Meyer had been mobbed, here the sidewalks where *Sturmtruppen* swaggered; here shop-windows were smashed; along here a lawyer was frog-marched; here loudspeakers sputtered inchoate rage; here drunks howled insults at women getting into taxicabs.

With the proclamation of the Nürnberger Gesetze, Herr Kauffman as a Jew could no longer practice law, so he put the baron's affairs in the hands of a decent "Aryan" lawyer, who persuaded the city of Frankfurt that instead of kicking Weinbrenner out it might be profitable to let him remain in his own house for now while extracting an enormous rent. The city did require that we clear out of Newport, however, and my parents went to the hotel at Bad Homburg, and I found my rooms near the Römer.

My grandmother decided to go to her brother in Africa. After nearly ten years in Germany Con said goodbye to us, to Willy Chopdelau, Eddy Morrison, Count Istvan and all her friends at Frankie's English Bar. She traveled first to Ireland, where she spent a few weeks with Aunt Kate at Sligo, before sailing from Southampton for Mombasa, via Suez.

In Kenya, sometime around the middle of the war, my grandmother fell from her horse and broke her neck. She died instantly—so we were told. You never know if that's true, but I hope it was. Killed in action. Exactly the sort of death she would have wanted.

✠ 1938

KAUFMAN HAD TELEPHONED AGAIN TO CHECK ON THE BARON'S CONDItion. Then he asked that I stop by his office.

"I've my schedule in front of me. Be here at four o'clock, please. I can see you at four o'clock."

I doubted he was as busy as this sounded. The baron had been Kaufman's principal client, and the baron no longer had much property to administer and very few legal rights left to defend. And Kaufman was no longer permitted to call himself a lawyer—but still kept his office, the drowsy rooms where I used to work. Grouchy Frau Fleck was still his secretary, though I can't imagine what there was for her to do.

And Kaufman kept me waiting half an hour, for no reason I can think of other than that he did not wish me to forget I'd once been his lowly part-time office boy.

When I was at last admitted to his presence, he didn't invite me to sit down. I sat down anyway. He arched his eyebrows.

Kaufman always was a difficult man to like. He had courage, all right, but he was also an old-fashioned Prussian *Rechtsanwalt* with several pins up his ass.

"I must warn you there is to be a criminal investigation of this incident at Walden," Kaufman said without preamble. "The police are quite serious about it, apparently."

"The police are actually going to do something? I must say I'm surprised."

"The target of their investigation is, of course, the baron."

"How do you mean?"

"A matter of criminal trespass," Kaufman said calmly.

"More than that, surely. It's at least a case of attempted murder."

Kaufman steepled his fingers and stared at me. "You don't hear me, sir," he said softly. "The individual under investigation is the Baron von Weinbrenner. They are indeed weighing whether this is a case of criminal trespass. If they conclude it is, then Weinbrenner will be charged as the trespasser. They've served him a notice of eviction, which, against my advice, he completely disregarded."

"But he's paying enormous rent—"

"He is no longer in a position to do so. And the city of Frankfurt has chosen to terminate the arrangement. The authorities emphasize he has no legal right to remain in occupancy. They consider it a serious matter, and there will be fines, though God knows what they think they can squeeze from him. In short: he'll have to vacate Haus-Walden."

There was nothing to do with that sort of news except swallow it and try not to choke.

In the silence I became aware of the sound of city traffic, never so violent as Berlin's, but the hum of an active city all the same. It sounded so healthy and normal.

"I pray he dies," Kaufman said. "Because the alternative is not good. I pray my old patron dies in his own bed and very soon."

When I left, he shook hands with me, for the first time ever. Frau Fleck offered only her usual scowl.

>–•◦–◦–•–◦–◦•–◄

My parents came out again that afternoon and acted overjoyed when the baron seemed to swim up out of his morphia haze and utter a few sounds that might have been words. Their jubilation irritated me. They were fooling themselves. It was another edition of what was happening all over Frankfurt: denial of reality.

Then the snake uncoiled, and the old man began twisting and writhing. It took my father and me to hold him down while Karin delivered another injection, and during those shocking moments while the baron writhed and screeched and shat himself, my parents could no longer ignore the reality of the situation.

They rode back to Bad Homburg in Otto's taxi. My parents normally never took taxis, but they had only a few hours free, and there was no easy way to travel by tram. He probably gave them a break on the fare.

"In Zürich," Karin said, "it should be possible to find the right doctor."

We were in the kitchen, with Herta, warming by the stove, drinking coffee. Outside there was a lacquer of early snow on the ground. The kitchen was warmer than the library, smelled better, too.

"Well," I said, "I believe Swiss doctors like to be paid."

"Listen, you can't tell me anything I don't know about Swiss doctors. When I was at school in Lausanne there was one fellow, very good at setting bones, but all he wanted was to get a hand up your skirt. But they know their broken bones, the Swiss."

I told her she wasn't facing facts, and facts had to be faced, because the SS *Volendam* was scheduled to sail from Rotterdam for New York in fewer than five days. I'm sure I spoke brutally. I felt trapped. Sixty milliliters. Pushed in *quickly*. That was what Dr. Lewin had said.

She telephoned Kaufman once more, and he must have drenched even more cold water over the Zurich idea, because she did not mention it again.

It was getting colder. Winter was on the way. I scoured the house for extra rugs and blankets and a set of moth-eaten curtains and brought what I found down to the library for us to sleep on or under. I built up the fire so it would burn a couple of hours without being tended.

"Your father is dying." I was working on the fire and looked around to see her lean over the baron, tucking in his blankets. He was asleep, if you could call it sleep. Really it was just the opiate.

"We're all dying," she said.

We arranged our pallet bed near the fire and lay spooned together. I put my arm around her. She was shivering that night. Winter was definitely moving in, and the fire wasn't enough. Every time a branch rattled a window or knocked against the roof tiles, or a truck hooted out on the road, I could feel her flinch. Sometime in the middle of the night we awakened and made love, rather roughly. I don't know why these things come as they do—the poison gas of fear spills out as passion. Maybe I was trying to cover my fear with excitement. Maybe she was, too. Perhaps death hovering in the room, breathing down our necks, was an aphrodisiac. We made this strenuous love and fell back asleep glued to each other, but just before sleep I felt wholly aware and wholly conscious of my attachment to her and my responsibility for her safety, and this awareness filled my body like an active thing.

A couple of hours later I woke with a start. Heart pounding. In my dream I had been falling down a well. I sat up suddenly, the gorge of panic in my throat.

Ever since the assault we'd shared a mostly unspoken fear that the stormtroopers would return, though it was difficult to imagine what they could possibly want, because there was so little left at Walden. Pleasure in desecration—maybe that was motive enough. Fantasies of buried Hebrew treasure. Setting woods on fire, burning out the Jewish ghosts, Irish ghosts, ghosts of famous racehorses.

Karin was kneeling in front of the fireplace. The fire was nearly out and she had on her tweed overcoat over a nightdress and was trying to get a blaze going.

Her father was snoring. Deep opiate snores. He sounded like a clown pretending to snore, exaggerating for laughs, but it was no joke. He was still insensible on the last injection she had given him before turning in. I glanced at my watch. Four o'clock in the morning. Dark outside. Sudden, violent whips of rain slashed on the windows.

The decision had made itself while we slept. Maybe our bodies' entanglement made things plain. Bodies have crying needs.

The bearish smell in the library was grim. A November storm was definitely blowing in, rain beginning to clatter at the windows. I got up, pulled on clothes, and went to the bookshelf where we kept the morphine. Assembling a hypodermic I tried to concentrate on what my hands were doing, and nothing else, as I filled the syringe.

It's how such things are done: methodically, step-by-step; pay attention to procedure, keep the mind as cold and clear as the bleb of an icicle.

Her father lay snoring in his morphine catacomb.

I was prepared to do it, but at the last moment she took the hypodermic from my hands. And I let her.

She'd been delivering four or five or six injections every day. She was practiced at it; she had the technique. Even when the snake was writhing and striking she was expert at finding a vein.

With him asleep it was much easier.

We didn't speak. Nothing to say. She punched in the needle and pushed the dose through quickly. And he never made a sound. Afterward we sat at opposite ends of the window seat, only our feet touching, leafing through her old Winnetous, which the monsters had left behind.

⚜ | BEST WESTERN

In the fall of 1977 I had a new book out and was invited to deliver a talk at Texas Tech, in Lubbock. No wine or liquor of any sort was provided at lunch at the faculty club, and this made me grumpy. A graduate student drove me back to my perfectly adequate but dispiriting Best Western motel. I wasn't flying until the next morning, and I found myself in the middle of El Llano Estacado with an afternoon to spare.

The desk clerk was able to have a rental car delivered right to the motel. I set off, driving somewhat aimlessly but in general heading for New Mexico.

By then I'd experienced *el llano* on countless visits, but those had always been purposeful quests, research trips, often with graduate students. I'd usually have a rigorous schedule of interviews set up with Apache, old XIT cowboys, oilmen, cotton farmers, academics. Once I'd tagged along with a vanload of doctoral candidates on a field trip: we set up camp near the Clovis Man site in New Mexico, and we hiked every trail in Palo Duro Canyon State Park.

El Llano Estacado was in many ways a distressed, even broken, country. Within a few decades of the Comanche's defeat, it had been fatally overgrazed. During World War I, with prices high, the land was planted in wheat and, after wheat prices collapsed, in cotton. During the thirties there was terrible drought: *el llano* was close to ground zero of the Dust Bowl. After the Second World War the Ogallala Aquifer was plumbed, and then the land was overirrigated and fed massive doses of chemical fertilizers. The conurbations of Amarillo and Lubbock with their shopping malls, airbases, and interstate highways sprawled out over the ex-grassland.

Of course *el llano* was never "untouched." Like any landscape, it had always been changing. In the eighteenth century Spanish horses caused a massive shift in the ecosystem and jump-started the Comanche empire. But by the middle of the twentieth century, with metastasizing cities and subsidized, unsustainable agriculture, *el llano* was being treated like a machine whose owners were determined to squeeze the last bit of work from it before tossing it on the junk heap.

That was the real *llano*, which for decades I had visited, mapped, photographed, interrogated, written about. The place my life's work centered on. But there was always *el llano* constructed in our minds— a dream of bareness, boundlessness, and light.

For the rest of the afternoon I did nothing but drive. There's no better way to take on that landscape than with a car or, better yet, one of those rugged Comanche ponies that nourished themselves on cacti.

Heading west, I put nearly two hundred miles on my rental Chevrolet, past dirty gray cotton fields and thousands of acres of once-pasture with not a whisker of grass on it, only crumbly gray soil and taut barbed wire.

I knew the country so well by then that even at seventy miles per hour I could see it, feel it, and derive solace from it, without really looking at anything but the blacktop straight ahead.

Plenty of travelers have left their bones on *el llano*. It can seem endless, but of course it isn't. If you can keep going, you'll find water, food, shade, on the other side.

I drove in a kind of numbness that day. I felt her presence, especially as I came nearer the New Mexico state line. The clutter of oil derricks, irrigation gear, and cotton fluff thinned out, and the land became stark.

El llano is perfectly level to the eye but in fact slopes upward to the west, though not by much. A meter or so per mile. It seems higher out that way because it's even more bare and empty; it feels closer to the sky. There's not much there but wind, barbed wire, sunlight. *Featureless*, you might say. It's the sort of country where pilgrims lose their way.

With her I was always in someone else's film. I wasn't writing the screenplay, wasn't the star, wasn't the Llano Kid. Maybe I was Gary Cooper's horse, or the western wind. Maybe the light. Maybe the red bluffs. Maybe the horizontal yellow, maybe the distance, maybe emptiness, maybe the no-place-to-hide.

In the hamlet marked as Grady, New Mexico, on my Avis road map, there was a tiny post office and an elementary school. Some crumbling adobe walls were all that remained of the tourist court where we'd spent our last night.

I had crossed and recrossed *el llano* many times since then but never had revisited those particular ruins. No good reason to.

And still there wasn't. I had planned to take a walk across the fields, but I didn't even get out of the car. I peered at the stumps of adobe walls for a few moments, then powered the window shut, swung the car around, and headed back to Lubbock. The next morning I boarded my flight for Chicago, and home to Toronto.

Next to the bleak grandeur of its emptiness, nothing installed by human hands has ever amounted to much on *el llano*.

❧ 1938

Holograph on paper fragment. Signed *"K,"* undated, no envelope, no postmark. Lange Family Archive, 11 C-12-1938. Special Collections, McGill Library, McGill University, Montreal.

Mein lieber William!

I'm sorry sorry but really I cannot stay.
Don't feel correct.
What there is to come and don't have strength for it.
Just not myself.
Very tired.
Take good care of yourself, my dear brother.

Your love,
K

Our first night out of germany, in a hotel room almost on the Holland-America quay at Rotterdam, I remember her mixing martinis with Dutch genever gin and talking about a plot she'd heard of back in UFA days. An actor's plan to assassinate Hitler, Goebbels, and Göring at a movie premiere.

"Be careful what you say, Karin. Who knows, maybe the walls are listening."

"This is a free city."

"Yes, well, I don't know about that. My parents are still in Germany."

"Give me a cigarette, damn you. I won't smoke these German weeds anymore. I wish you'd go out and get us some Dutch cigarettes. I can't smoke this Nazi tobacco."

The instant freedom and safety we'd won by crossing the Dutch frontier felt dishonorable to her, a swank and phony pose. We were safe merely because we carried the right passports. All we'd needed to get ourselves clear of dear old Germany was a ticket on a fast, comfortable train.

Genever packs more of a punch than English gin. She kicked off her shoes and lay on the bed, lighting a cigarette and gazing at the ceiling. "Damn cold in here, William Cody."

"I shall run you a bath."

"Baths cost extra."

"Hot bath, two guilders, we can manage it."

"No. Go fetch us some Dutch cigarettes."

"Let's get you into a bath first."

The bathroom was down the hallway. I paid our landlady two guilders, and she ran the hot bath. In our room Karin was dozing, cigarette smoldering between her fingers. I led her to the bath, and while I was scrubbing her back she read aloud extracts from narratives written by people who'd traveled across El Llano Estacado, dire warnings mostly.

⊳⊶⊷◦⊶⊷⊲

A contingent of American college boys was sailing for home on the SS *Volendam*. Amherst College, Williams College, the University of Virginia. Six boys who'd been studying together at Heidelberg had formed a jazz band; they called themselves the Calamitous Collegians, and they knew how to swing. There was a very hot trumpet player, a short fat fellow from the state of Maine, who could blow a solo or two that reached with fingers into the heart and made life seem round, not flat. And their drummer was superb. He could get the stolid Dutch deck officers jitterbugging. Another boy, slight, dark Italian American, could sing rather well; he had a supple bluesy growl and a sort of phrasing I'd never heard before that brought the song close. One afternoon at a tea dance in the tourist-class lounge he gave us a version of "Here and Now," the first time I heard what became a standard:

> *This night's a chance I'm taking*
> *A long-lost dream,*
> *I'm waking*
> *Only to offer myself to you*

It was unexpected, and extraordinarily moving, to hear such a blues in the middle of the ocean. It seemed a bittersweet promise from America: life was risky, life was tough, but at least it was life, not death, that was on offer now.

The Calamitous Collegians were fans of Ellington, you could tell, and Benny Goodman. A lively and accomplished dance band. It was hard to imagine anyone jitterbugging in Heidelberg, which hadn't struck me as a swinging town. But my associations with the place were unpleasant, excepting the moments with Lily on the hillside above the Neckar, which had retained their vivacity.

There weren't so many young women aboard the ship, and all the college boys wanted to dance with Karin. She loved it.

Young people drank a lot in those days. Some of it was in competition with one another, a kind of race, also considered a test of character. You were supposed to put away a lot of booze without showing it so much. You might show it a little bit, that was acceptable, it was "grace under pressure." It was quite okay to be "tight," to be "a couple of sheets to the wind"; it made people looser, more relaxed, sometimes even a bit wiser.

Karin had her clear-cold martinis at Frankie's English Bar, but she'd sipped them very slowly, two drinks to last the whole evening. Liquor was never a focus for her. But those days at sea, there was a great deal of stress. That's what it's called now—stress. Then it didn't have a name, or not one I knew. Then it was just a powerful, uncomfortable—even shameful—set of feelings. Unspeakable, literally. It felt a lot like being a coward. It felt a lot like being a bore.

When we experienced such feelings, our instinct was to hide. To get rid of ourselves, at least temporarily. Music helped. What do you think swing was all about but shucking off gloom? The best dancers and musicians were never normal people. I remember lying in my berth, near dawn, wide-awake, with my cabinmates snoring—three strangers, sharing a cabin in the bowels of the ship. Deep inside, the ship always smelled of warm paint. My stomach felt as if it had been packed with wet cement, and I seemed to be whirling, faster, faster. Maybe this was a new version of what my father had experienced, what he and my mother called his barbed-wire disease. It wasn't just lethargy or passivity. It was curdling, discomposing fear deep in the belly.

If I remained in my berth, my outlook only grew more bleak, but once I forced myself to get up—no matter how pointless that seemed—things eventually got better. So I began getting up earlier and earlier. The same with her. We'd meet in the ship's galley, a cavern, bright, warm, and bustling where the Javanese cooks were busy preparing breakfast for three hundred and fifty. Cheerfully they'd offer mugs of coffee with delicious cream.

We were at sea in more ways than one. She was pregnant and of course oughtn't have been drinking any alcohol, but we didn't think that way then.

Am I trying to apologize on her behalf? Idiot. She owes no one any apology.

Our third night at sea, there was a supper dance in the second-class saloon. First class and tourist class invited. Music courtesy of the Calamitous Collegians.

Karin wore a green frock. I'd not seen it on her before, but she must have rescued it from the heap on the sidewalk in Charlottenburg.

After all that time on the illicit dance floors in Berlin, we were good together, familiar with each other's moods and rhythms. Her mood that evening was buoyant, I would say. Carefree. *Sans souci*. Three days out from Europe, three more to New York. We were headed directly for the future.

"Billy, old thing, give me a cigarette."

She'd been dancing with one of the college boys, and he had brought her back to our table. We'd all had a lot to drink. It turned out my cigarette case was empty.

"I'll fetch some from my cabin," I told her. Cigarettes were sold duty-free on board, we each had a couple of cartons of Chesterfields stashed away.

"No," she said, "I'll fetch mine. I want a bit of fresh air."

Throwing on her wrap, she headed off. She could have followed the stairways and passageways inside the ship, but I saw her head out on the boat deck instead, where it was cold and icy, but also magical in a certain way. We were in the middle of the Atlantic, in winter, between two worlds. American jazz was spooky and true and making our bones jump. All evening people had been stepping out on the deck to peer at the cold stars and remind themselves of the size of the universe.

A few minutes later the trumpeter from Maine was just biting into one of his hard solos when a deck officer approached my table and leaning down to speak in my ear said there had been an accident, and might I follow him, please?

While the music jumped and wailed, I trailed him out into a white passageway where he informed me that Mevrouw von Weinbrenner was in the ship's infirmary. A pair of stewards had carried her there after finding her in a heap at the bottom of an icy ladderway between the saloon deck and boat deck.

I followed the Dutchman and his squeaky rubber soles along the passageway. The smell of warm paint was nauseating, and I could feel the ship beginning to twist and roll in a heavy sea.

Karin was being examined in a small surgery room. The Dutch head nurse sternly ordered me to sit down and wait. So I sat in one of the blond wooden chairs screwed to the floor. Nurses and doctors were authority figures.

It's not easy for me to connect myself to the obedient young man I was then. That midwinter passage marks one of my divides. Then and now. Europe and America. Before *el llano*, after. Prewar, postwar.

There was never a time in my life before Karin. She's in me from the beginning. We're born in the same room, after all. Different years, same season. Same sea, same quality of light. Curtains flopping and bouncing in the same afternoon onshore breeze. She's always there, always an element in my thinking, my construct of the world.

Sanssouci.

I used to wonder if we'd been born two parts of the same person, neither of us complete without the other; something always missing. Yet the only photographs of us together are a couple taken by the ship's photographer. I haven't seen them in a while; they're tucked in an envelope stuck in a shoe box along with a sheaf of old passports. Black-and-white images not much bigger than a good-sized postage stamp. We're lying on deck chairs, wearing overcoats, under blankets, basking in the sun.

When Mijnheer Dokter stepped out of the surgery room his smock was soaked in bright red blood. He was lighting a cigarette when he noticed me. He had eyes like poached eggs. "Well, well."

"How is she?"

"Not so good. Your friend was pregnant, yes? Well, that is over, unfortunately."

They only let me see her after the sedative had taken effect. There were six beds in the little ward, but Karin was the only patient. Her face was white, haggard. Everything was white, even the floor. The SS *Volendam* was really being tossed about by then, and in the surgery I could overhear Mijnheer Dokter at work on another patient, a college boy with a broken arm, consequence of high jinks out on the icy saloon deck.

Another nurse, prim and young, sat by Karin's bed, movie magazine open in her lap. Karin was asleep. When I looked down at her, I saw her father in his bed, and it made me queasy. Or that might have been the ship tossing about.

I found my way back to the second-class saloon—I needed the music, needed the company. But the party was over. Stewards were cleaning up the detritus. So I bundled up in my overcoat and scarf and went out on deck and managed one complete turn around the ship. I was remembering the Irish Sea and my mother about to throw herself overboard. Perhaps I'd been wrong about that. Perhaps it had been my delirium, scarlet fever coming on, my brain on fire. Perhaps it was all in my mind, along with my great fear of losing her.

>─+◆>─0─<◆+─<

After drawing the sheet over her father's face, Karin had telephoned his lawyer with the news.

"Herr Kaufman says there must be a proper Jewish funeral," she reported. "Only I'm going to bury him here, which is what my father wanted. Poor old Kaufman is not going to like it."

"How are you feeling?"

"I'm living a new life," she said. "I'm not the same person I was, not at all."

"It'll come back."

"What will?"

"You'll get through this. You'll get over it. Everything will pass."

She looked at me for a moment. "I'm going to take a bath. I want to get death off my hands."

An hour later Kaufman and my parents arrived together in Otto Stahl's taxi. As soon as he'd offered condolences Kaufman began arguing for burial in the Jewish cemetery on the Fischerfeld.

"But my father wished to be buried here," Karin told him. "Here at Walden, Herr Kaufman, next to his son."

"Your father was a good Jew. He was always in his heart a Jew. He was persecuted as a Jew. He must be buried as a Jew."

"As a Jew, yes, but here in his own ground."

"But they've stolen it from him, haven't they? If you bury him here, God knows the swine will disrespect his grave."

"Walden was my father's ground," she said firmly. "He never gave it up. We'll bury him here."

Kaufman groaned and sat down heavily in the baron's leather desk chair. I wonder what had happened to Weinbrenner's Iron Cross (First

Class and Second Class) which used to be displayed on the desk. Maybe it was stolen. Maybe he'd thrown it away.

"He must be buried by tomorrow," Kaufman said. "This is the custom. Will you respect this, at least?"

"Yes, of course."

Kaufman said he knew a young rabbi who might agree to perform funeral rites at Walden as long as a car could be sent for him; it wasn't safe for Jews to travel on trams. And a proper Jewish coffin had to be ordered immediately.

My father, Otto, and I carried the baron's body upstairs, bundled up in a bedsheet, like a collection of dirty laundry. He weighed almost nothing. There was a mood of excitement, disruption, upendedness. My mother and Herta must have washed the body—I don't remember, but there was no one else to do it. Maybe Karin helped, but I doubt my mother would have allowed that.

I remember Karin in the kitchen, sitting in a chair near the range, holding a cup of coffee with whiskey in it. That's a scene I still have, half a century later, a few frames of mental footage: a young woman, thick messy chestnut hair and a winter-pale face, sitting in a chair close to the warm stove and lighting one cigarette from the butt of another. She's inward, swimming in her own thoughts. Herta meanwhile is upset, nonstop tears—poor woman, she doesn't know what's to become of her; she expected a pension from the baron, but the money's gone. Nonetheless she's hard at work, making cauliflower soup, cutting sandwiches.

Me, I'm excited. I'm trying to contain the exuberance and confidence I can feel welling up inside. The door has suddenly swung wide open, and in a couple of days we'll be sailing for New York.

And Kaufman—I see him sitting in the baron's chair in the library with an old Hebrew volume, one of the few spared from the fire, open on Admiral Spee's desk, and his index finger skimming the page, right to left, right to left, like a Talmud scholar.

In the autumn of 1942 they arrested the old lawyer and dragged him aboard a train for Theresienstadt where he died the following winter after an operation for gallstones performed in abysmal conditions.

After searching the stables, Otto and I located a pair of spades. The stables still had a lingering scent of horse. It was cold, getting dark, probably four o'clock in the afternoon. Rain was beginning to freeze on bare birches. The woods were still autumnal, still smelled of ground, but soon the ground would be locked under a freeze.

As we walked along the narrow, quite overgrown bridle path, Buck said, "It is hard to think now what a refuge the old place was for us thanks to that man, who made it so."

And Otto Stahl remarked, "If you'd seen the behavior I have seen on the streets of our Frankfurt!"

That remark struck me, for I'd had my hand in this pogrom, urging the death of an old man so I could scamper safely out of Germany. I suddenly felt like throwing up. But I didn't. Otto had his spade sloped on his shoulder like an infantryman. Rain ticked on trees and spattered crisply on the ground. Brown burrs stuck to our clothes.

In the clearing the taxi driver and I started by shoveling through a mat of dead leaves, then a stringy layer of black soil, then brown earth and gray-blue clay mixed with sand. Buck stood watching us, the brim of his homburg tipped forward, coat collar turned up against the rain. Eventually he went back to the house and returned with a flask of tea and a flashlight, and we kept on digging until it was done.

Her father's death surprised no one; it was his fierce clinging to life that had been the surprise.

Out in the stables Otto and my father located a couple of fir planks, and some lumber, from which they knocked together a pair of trestles. They assembled a sort of rough bier in a cold upstairs bedroom, and the baron's body, wrapped in a linen bedsheet, was laid out.

"A shroud without pockets," Kaufman intoned. "We take nothing with us when we leave this world."

And the body must not be left alone. Someone had to sit with it at all times, Kaufman insisted. A watchman, a *shomer*. So during the night each of us, including Otto the taxi driver, took a turn. Otherwise we stayed in the library where my father and I kept a good blaze crackling. We had cups of tea, cigarettes, tiny crystal glasses of Irish whiskey from a bottle Buck had brought. Karin dozed on our pallet of rugs near the fire, and I told myself we'd given her father his death, which under the circumstances was the best gift possible.

I pictured us crossing *el llano* under wide blue sky. I wanted us both to become new people.

Early the next morning Otto Stahl drove into Frankfurt to collect the rabbi and a proper Jewish coffin, which Kaufman had ordered from a carpenter in Sachsenhausen.

I went for a last walk in the woods with my parents. These were the woods, possibly this was the path, where they had courted, where Buck proposed marriage and where Eilín bolted like a startled deer.

I was still in my twenties, still carrying almost everything and everyone important along with me. Life so far had been a process of accumulation, people and experiences, layer by layer. Everything held on to; nothing lost.

"Well, I don't know what's to become of it all," my father said.

We didn't go near our old Newport cottage, too painful. The paddocks were shaggy; the white fences needed paint; pigeons roosted in horse stalls. Bushes and saplings had sprouted on the yearling track that once cut through the woods; you couldn't gallop young horses down there anymore.

We were on our way back to the big house when we met the taxicab coming up the drive with a pine coffin strapped on its roof and a rabbi in the backseat.

The rabbi, in his tailored overcoat and pearl-gray homburg, looked like any brisk Frankfurt businessman. The Jewish coffin had no screws or nails, no metal whatsoever, no handles. Kaufman looked it over carefully, then nodded his approval.

My father and I brought the coffin upstairs, lifted the body in, and closed it. With the help of Kaufman and the taxi driver, we carried the coffin downstairs and started along the bridle path. Without handles it was awkward to carry; we had to bear it on our shoulders. A gray, blowy morning with a whiff of snow. Seething clouds, not one scrap of blue sky. Poor old Kaufman was panting and stumbling, and my father made us pause, set the coffin down, take a breather.

Karin wore a mourning ribbon, a scrap of some black material, pinned to the sleeve of her Harris Tweed overcoat.

"'O thou that lives in the covert of the most high and in the shadow of the almighty.'"

While the rabbi recited psalms, we gently slipped the coffin down into the grave using two leather longe lines Buck found in what had been the tack room. The rabbi had a thin voice that was hard to hear with the wind buffeting the tops of the spruce trees and trying to sweep his words away.

Karin stood between my mother and Herta, staring down into the grave. The wild wind was scuffling dead leaves. I could feel how isolated she was. Her aloneness, orphanhood, were like a fog around her.

As soon as the rabbi indicated it was time to start filling the grave, my father and I reached for the spades, but Kaufman protested.

"Rabbi! It is for the Jews to bury Jewish dead!"

My father held out his spade for Kaufman, but the lawyer wouldn't take it from him directly. Buck had to place it on the ground, then Kaufman allowed himself to pick it up, and while the rabbi recited psalms in German and Hebrew, the old lawyer began weakly scraping soil into the grave. It took him a long time to fill it, but no one dared interfere.

▸·◂▸·◦·◂▸·◂

A very cold December noon, bright sunshine, and here was the Statue of Liberty and a wild traffic of ferries, shipping, tugboats, etcetera. Passengers lined the boat deck. Silent. Impressed, awed. Intimidated, actually.

"Wow!" said Karin.

"*Wow?*" I said.

She'd never "wowed" before.

But we'd not been in America before, either. She laughed, pleased with herself.

A launch slewed alongside the ship, and customs and immigration men scampered up the gangway. From the Fifth Street pier at Hoboken our taxi charged through the Holland Tunnel. Speeding up Broadway, Karin wept. Emotional overload. Too much to handle.

The Commodore Hotel, beside Grand Central Terminal. Six dollars per night. Pretty expensive, but no one at the desk inquired whether we were married. I tipped the freckle-faced bellhop a whole dollar— "Thank you, sir!"—because I couldn't sort out the American coins.

"Yippee!" Karin cried.

Yippee.

Two enormous beds and an enormous bathtub.

"Pretty damn plush," I growled, trying to sound hard-boiled.

We wanted to sound American, put ourselves in the American picture.

That evening, drinks in the bar. Old-fashioneds. Filet mignon, wonderful. More drinks. A kiss in the elevator.

Tears before bed.

Next morning, breakfast in bed, coffee in cups—"As big as birdbaths!" she declared. Bread, despicable—steerage class. Butter, not so very good, tourist class. Marmalade rather too sweet—second class. Orange juice, first class all the way.

How did I track Mick McClintock down? I'd not heard from him since his stay at Walden eleven years before. My aunt Kate, writing with the news from Sligo, had once mentioned that Mick McClintock was making a great success of his career with the New York police and had married an Irish girl.

There were a dozen M. and Michael McClintocks listed in the Manhattan phone directory. And if he were still in New York, and if he had a telephone—not everyone did, in those days—it seemed just as likely he could be living in Brooklyn, Queens, or the Bronx.

I went down to the lobby and located a Brooklyn phone directory with an array of M. McClintocks listed, but only two Jeremiah McClintocks, one on Ditmas Avenue, which a bellhop assured me was in Flatbush.

When I rang the number, a girl answered. It turned out she was Mick's cousin and gave me the telephone number of the apartment on Linden Avenue, also in Flatbush, where Mick and his wife lived.

It was ten o'clock in the morning. A woman answered the phone. I introduced myself and told her I was in New York on a very brief visit. Mick was asleep—he'd been working a night patrol—but she went to awaken him.

A minute later, a male voice came over the line. "Who is it?"

" 'Down goes the pony,' " I said.

Pause.

"Billy?"

I told him that I had left Germany, probably for good, and was emigrating to Canada. When I told him Karin was with me and we were about to buy a car and strike off across America, Mick insisted we meet for lunch and named a French restaurant on Lexington Avenue he said was not far from our hotel.

After getting off the phone, I told Karin of the plan. I was surprised that she didn't seem interested in joining us.

"But Mick would love to see you. You must remember him well enough, don't you?"

"Do give him my regrets."

"He brought over that Irish mare, Lovely Morn. You used to sit on his bed in the room above the stable, he was worried your mama would find out. Don't you remember? We all went off together to see Hitler."

"I've only one day in New York, and I'm going to spend it in the shops along Fifth Avenue."

"Shopping? Really? You'd rather?"

After the last horrid weeks in Germany, maybe the pull of those brilliant shopwindows was irresistible. We'd seen enough on our cab ride the day before to be dazzled by New York's fabulous display of goods.

"Karin, we ought to get married here in New York, don't you think?"

"Why?"

"The obvious reasons," I said. "Love and devotion, etcetera. Making an honest woman of you. And getting hotel rooms will be easier."

"We had no trouble getting this one."

"Yes, well, not everywhere's like New York."

"I'll marry you when we get to the other side," she said.

"Of the continent, you mean?"

"Yes."

She was still in bed when I left, sipping coffee that had cooled and reading a *New York Herald-Tribune* story about trainloads of Jewish children leaving Berlin and Vienna bound for foster homes in England.

I walked uptown. Mick had arranged to meet at Café Martin, on Lexington Avenue in the Seventies. There was a reservation for three, under the name McClintock.

Linen tablecloths, a French headwaiter, wine list on parchment, crystal goblets—I found the place much fancier than I'd expected or, really, could afford. I didn't know why Mick had chosen it. An Irish bar—and there were a dozen within a short walk of the hotel—might have suited both of us better.

Probably he'd imagined an elegant French restaurant would suit Karin better, his idea of Karin.

I was sitting down when he arrived. He seemed taller than ever, filled out, even a bit jowly, but pink, vibrant, and handsome. His sandy hair was thinner. He wore a brown suit and a Brooks Brothers shirt with a rolled button-down collar. A green-and-blue-striped silk tie. On his finger a gold wedding band.

He didn't try to hide his disappointment when I told him I was alone. He ordered manhattans for us and insisted I ring the hotel and persuade Karin to come.

"Billy, man, tell her to hop in a cab. The woman needs to eat."

There was no answer when the hotel switchboard rang our room, and I told Mick she was out exploring the famous shops along Fifth Avenue.

He shrugged and ordered us a second round of cocktails. We looked at the menu. He chose an expensive bottle of wine. He had two children in Brooklyn, he said, both daughters, and a baby on the way. His wife, Kathleen, was from Louisburgh, county Mayo.

When first he arrived in America, he'd found work as an exercise rider at Belmont. Then for a couple of years he was head groom at a stable in the Berkshires. At last he'd been permitted to take the civil-service exam and join the New York police. He was now a patrolman attached to a precinct on the Lower East Side; also he worked two shifts each week as doorman in an apartment building on Central Park West.

We finished the bottle of French wine and shared another. I can't remember the food, whether it was any good. I tried to describe our last weeks in Germany. Every time a customer entered the restaurant Mick looked over his shoulder as if he still hoped Karin would show up. I said she'd agreed to come out only after learning she was pregnant, and she had lost the baby on the crossing. My original idea had been to marry once we reached New York, but now I was not sure it was going to happen, even after we reached the West Coast.

"But you love the woman, Billy, do you not?" Mick said. "There's nothing in the way of that."

"I do. Always have. Always will. Not sure how she feels. Not sure I understand her. I know she needs me."

"You give each other a good life and let go of old Germany. That's my word on the subject, Billy. Welcome to America." He raised his glass. "*Slainté.*"

He insisted on picking up the check. I invited him back to our hotel—we could station ourselves in the hotel bar and wait for Karin to return from her shopping expedition.

I was actually worried that in her weak, ungrounded state she might have spent far too much of our limited hoard of cash in the shops on Fifth Avenue.

Mick and I started walking south on Lexington, but at Sixty-third Street he suddenly changed his mind, saying he had to report for duty at his station house on the Lower East Side. We said a very hurried goodbye at Sixty-third and Lexington, and he disappeared down the steps of the subway entrance.

When I reached the Commodore, instead of going into the bar I took an elevator upstairs and found a DO NOT DISTURB sign hanging on the door of our room.

Karin was in bed, wearing her nightgown. The maids hadn't been allowed to organize things or make up the beds. Our breakfast trays were still on the floor. I realized she had never left the room.

She held out her arms and smiled. "Ah, Billy, I've been feeling awfully dozy."

"No Fifth Avenue?"

"We really must watch the funds, Billy, mustn't we? Not the time for silly shopping. How did you find your old Mick?"

"You ought to have joined us."

"Not up for it, old man. How is Mick?"

"Married, with two little girls and a baby on the way."

"Good for him."

I helped her out of bed. There were small blots of blood on the bottom sheet and on her nightgown.

"We should see a doctor."

"No, no, I'm getting better, Billy. I'm miles better. Just ring for the maid."

"I shall run you a bath."

"Excellent."

After her bath she seemed in high spirits. "Let's go to Fifth Avenue, old Billy."

"It's bloody cold out there, you know."

"I don't care."

Wrapped up in overcoats and scarves we rode the elevator to the lobby. Lexington Avenue was hurling with fierce traffic, and the light had gone; the air was black and freezing. We walked one block, then had to turn back. It was just too cold. In the hotel bar I ordered manhattans. The barman was from Roscommon and had seven children. We had more cocktails. Then I was hungry and wanted to order us steak sandwiches from the bar menu, but she insisted everything was much too expensive, and anyway we really ought to see more of New York.

So we bundled up again and headed out to the Horn & Hardart Automat on West Fifty-seventh Street, recommended by the barman, where we had hamburger steaks for fifteen cents, slices of cherry pie for a nickel, then a long, bitter walk back to the hotel. Long before we got there she was weeping from the cold—we both were. Tears sticky on our eyelids, and yellow cabs flashing past, and the cut of the wind.

⊱─·◈·─◈─·◈·─⊰

In June 1968—Bobby Kennedy had just been assassinated—I was leafing through *Time* magazine in a dentist's office in Toronto when I learned that the Metropolitan Museum had acquired what was left of the Weinbrenner Collection, including *The Lamentation*, from an Irish great-nephew of Lady Maire who'd spent decades tracking pieces down.

A few months later I was delivering an academic talk at Columbia. I skipped the faculty lunch afterward, met Mick McClintock in an Irish bar on Amsterdam Avenue, and we hopped in a cab and headed for the Cloisters, where the Weinbrenner pieces were on display.

We had stayed in touch after '38. Exchanged Christmas cards. He'd just retired from the NYPD. He and Kathleen were about to move to Florida.

Mick had never seen *The Lamentation*—he had never set foot inside the main house at Walden. In the cab heading uptown I told him how my mother and Lady Maire had discovered the altarpiece. Lost on a back road on the Castilian *meseta* in the blaze of summer, they had offered a ride to an old man who turned out to be a monk. The next morning he brought them to the ruined manor house where *The Lamentation* had been stored in a hayloft for twenty-nine years.

As we stood before it at the Cloisters, I remarked that Karin had always connected the piece with the death of the young soldier Frölisch, who died at Walden in his mother's arms.

Afterward, strolling through the wonderful Cloisters gardens, Mick told me that Karin had come to his room above the horse stalls on his last night in Germany. They had spent the night together.

"Only talking, Billy—that's all we did. Lay there talking about everything under the sun, but we didn't do anything. Maybe I thought it too soon. I don't know. Maybe I was thinking we'd have plenty of time. You see, we'd made up our minds she was coming with me to New York. It was her notion. It seemed crazy, but then I began to believe we might pull it off. Because we both wanted to so badly. You remember what she was like—the power she had.

"She slipped off to get her passport and pack a few things without disturbing the big house. I met her on the lawn. It was drizzling. She had what we used to call a train case—do you remember, girls had them, not much more than a handbag? She traveled light. Jesus, Billy, all I had meself was a grip, a ticket on the SS *New York*, and fifty-one dollars. She'd lifted some marks from her father's desk.

"Whatever I was feeling then, Billy—whatever it was, I was prepared to live on it. Sure and it made no sense. It was the only time in my life, I'm telling you, that I've stepped out on thin air. There was no real plan. Nothing sensible. Ireland I'd left, America was coming at me like—like I don't know what. Like a storm."

The baron still had influence in 1927. He wouldn't for much longer, but he did then. Mick and Karin got as far as the Hamburg-America ticket office at Bremerhafen before they were stopped by detectives. He was taken into custody, and she was put into a taxi and disappeared.

"That must have been when they sent her away to the Burghölzli," I told him.

"The what?"

"A clinic, a sanatorium. At the University of Zurich. Lady Maire told my mother Karin had a nervous breakdown."

"Ah, Jesus."

Mick said he'd struggled with the detectives until he was knocked on the head and put aboard wearing handcuffs, which were not removed until the ship was under way.

He and his Kathleen had six children, three before the war, three after. He'd served in the air force. Coming home, he made sergeant in the NYPD, then lieutenant, then captain. He bought a house in Queens and another farther out on Long Island. Now they were retiring to Florida. Clearwater.

"What the hell did I ever have to offer a girl like your Karin von! A few days in Flatbush would have worn it pretty thin, I suppose."

He stopped on the path. Grasping my arm, he spoke in a choked whisper. "We should have gone for Rotterdam, Billy, or Liverpool! I could have cashed my ticket, got us to England somehow, we could have found another ship!"

He let go my arm and brushed his cheeks with the back of his hand. "What the hell, Billy, what the hell."

Mick flew as tail-gunner on a B-17 during the war. In March 1944 his group was on the raids that wrecked Frankfurt. It could have been his squadron, he said, even his airplane, that dropped the incendiaries that finally destroyed Walden.

But Walden had been poisoned and ruined by then, I reminded him, so it was just as well. Sometimes it is better, cleaner, when things burn right down to the ground.

><++<·O·<+><

Karin and I were both in better spirits in the morning. The day was even colder, but very bright, and we struck out along West Forty-second, heading for Ninth Avenue where used cars were sold, according to the barman at the Commodore.

Our fortune amounted to seven hundred dollars in American Express traveler's checks and four hundred dollars in cash. I'd left the traveler's checks in the hotel safe and brought along the cash.

A shining, fierce Manhattan day. Brute of American wind that only sharpened as we got nearer the river. Crossing Eighth Avenue we were nearly knocked down by a taxi. By then we were exhausted from our crosstown trek: I felt weightless, and Karin was limping—her feet were frozen numb, she said. We entered a coffee shop, sat on stools at a "counter," and ate a hot dog each. For a nickel, as much coffee as we could swallow. Not very good coffee but hot. Her feet hurt terribly as blood rushed back in.

Up and down the cold corridor of Ninth Avenue we wandered, strings of electric lights that marked the used-car lots swaying in the howling wind. Our salesman was crude and flippant. We tried to bargain; weren't much good at it. I paid three hundred ten dollars for a Plymouth coupe, battleship gray, 1935 model.

"A sweet machine," the salesman kept repeating. "A very sweet machine."

Karin named the Plymouth "Sweetie."

Next morning, crossing the George Washington Bridge: *Sweetie, get us to the other side!*

That night, on the outskirts of Harrisburg, Pennsylvania, in a snowstorm: *Sweetie, keep going!*

Next day, down the slippery length of Virginia. *Sweetie, don't fail us!*

The coffee shop of the Peabody Hotel, Memphis. Black waiters wearing starched white jackets served white customers. *"Ich will meinen Vater,"* she said, looking up from her scrambled eggs and grits. I want my father.

"I'm sorry." I reached across the table to touch her arm.

"Ich bin fast leer." I am just about empty.

"I'm going to get you there."

"Wohin?" Where?

"Wherever you need to go."

"Bring mich nach Hause." Take me home.

⊳⋅◇⋅⊴

When I reached Vancouver, I made a point of keeping very busy. Plenty of colleagues and customers to meet. And everyone had to take the measure of me. I found a room in a boardinghouse and a few weeks later a small apartment. Because of the difficulty of importing a vehicle into Canada, I had sold the Plymouth in Blaine, Washington, before crossing the border. But I soon acquired another car, a secondhand Buick, which I kept until after the war.

I probably put two thousand miles a month on that car at a time when most roads in western Canada were unpaved. I was an ambitious young salesman, selling chemicals by the tank-car load to paper mills and lumber mills in the remote interior of the province.

The Canadians took me for an Englishman, and being English carried a certain social prestige in Vancouver. After six months I was able to afford a larger apartment, on English Bay, with a maid. I joined a canoe club. Joined the yacht club. Developed a circle of companions who passed for friends.

Then the war came, and millions of lives broke open, mine being one. I didn't hear from my parents after one letter via the Red Cross in 1940. I joined the Canadian army, did my officer training in Ontario, went overseas as a second lieutenant in an infantry battalion, was trained in England as a POW interrogator. Wounded in Holland, shrapnel in both legs from a German tank that blew up in a street in Nijmegen. Ended up in Germany in 1945. Saw Bergen-Belsen, saw the ruin of everything. Found my mother, still alive, in Frankfurt. My father had been caught in the center of Frankfurt during an American daylight raid in January 1944. Eilín happened to be out in the countryside that day, bartering Buck's last pair of English shoes and some silver picture frames for potatoes. When he didn't show up at the hotel that evening, she knew he'd been killed. Next morning she went to a temporary morgue set up in the old guardhouse, the Hauptwache, and found him laid out on the floor with a couple hundred other victims. She wanted to bury him at Walden, but the place was a Luftwaffe hospital until it burned down, and they buried only fliers there, no one else.

Buck was buried in one of the municipal cemeteries but never had a gravestone. When Eilín and I tried finding his grave after the war, we were unable to.

After 1945 the life I'd begun in Vancouver no longer made sense to me. I couldn't believe in it anymore. I'd lost its thread. While still overseas I'd started planning an academic career. I made up my mind to study geography and literature together. I wanted to investigate in a rigorous way the hold particular regions have on the imaginations of artists.

I enrolled as an undergraduate at McGill. There were plenty of veterans on campus, so I didn't feel too odd or too old. Later, at Harvard, Bernie DeVoto and Stegner were among my teachers. In 1950 I was the oldest person ever awarded a Ph.D. in history by Harvard University. My dissertation, "Stolen Girls: Comanches and Baptists in Texas," was nominated for the Pulitzer Prize in History.

I met Elizabeth in Cambridge. We are very different people, but our relationship from the start has been based on mutual respect and affection and, later, love of our children, and I think it has given us both satisfaction. The marriage certainly anchors my life. Without it, I'd probably still be out wandering *el llano*.

In 1945 I found myself alive on the other side of history and slowly began accumulating what I needed. Academic credentials. A profession. Marriage. A family.

Even before the war ended, my mother was hired to manage the U.S. Army Officers' Club in Frankfurt. During that first postwar winter, when thousands were starving, she was paid in dollars and had all the food she needed. Eighteen months later she received her first Irish passport and left for Sligo, where she was able to buy her cottage on Rosses Point with funds I sent.

When I began traveling to Europe regularly for academic conferences, I always tried to add on a few extra days to visit her at Sligo, or she'd meet me in Dublin or London. She came to Rome when I was delivering a talk. After transatlantic airfares became affordable she would visit Canada every couple of years. Her grandchildren knew her well. She enjoyed excellent health right up until a few days before her death, at ninety.

━━━◦━━━

Of course there really is no country of dreams that also exists outside the dreams.

Crossing *el llano* that afternoon, heading west from Canyon, Texas, toward New Mexico, we soon left the last irrigated fields and the wild green of winter wheat. The real soul of *el llano* had always been hard as bone. Those Comanche ponies really did live on scrub.

The road was straight and level. She wore a pair of sunglasses bought in a pharmacy in Oklahoma City, and a yellow silk scarf.

Half a century later I'm in the clutches of the same colon cancer that killed Lady Maire. Stage 4, the oncologist announced. During these days I am supposed to be making my peace with this quite-rotten world.

I shouldn't say that. As worlds go, maybe this one isn't so bad.

The yellow scarf is tied over her hair, knotted under her chin. The sunglasses were bought at the drugstore where we sat at the lunch counter and ate hamburgers and she dared order something called a malt—we presumed it was beer, but it wasn't.

Had she been able to keep going a little while longer, we'd both have made it. This seems to me true. She might have found what she needed on the other side. As I did.

What strikes me now is her youth. She was younger than my children are.

So many have left their bones on El Llano Estacado.

><+>∙O∙<+>∙<

Altitude, not latitude, often determines climate in the West. Sometimes on *el llano* it snows.

When I awoke that morning in a tourist cabin in the hamlet of Grady, New Mexico, I looked out and saw the ground covered with an inch of gleaming snow.

Karin was nowhere to be seen. I assumed she must be in the rather primitive outhouse.

Sun had just snapped over the horizon. The snow was already dripping and melting. The highway would burn clear and dry before very long.

I blew at embers in the stove, added kindling and a couple of piñon logs. I was always good at fires. With the blaze roaring and the stove creaking I filled the kettle from a pail of well water and set it to boil for coffee. We had coffee and milk and a few groceries we'd bought the day before at the Piggly Wiggly store in Amarillo, Texas.

I must have made coffee. Still she did not return. When I looked out, in all directions I saw as pure an emptiness as ever I'd imagined. It would be easy to track her across the fresh snow, but if she wanted solitude in which to savor the uncanny joy of *el llano*, then I wouldn't disturb her. I figured she must already be feeling the flavor and warmth of the rising sun.

El llano was never a blank page. Those southern plains have as active and bloody a history as any piece of this earth, but it wasn't my history, wasn't hers.

I finished my coffee. I was probably starting to worry.

Still am worrying. *Did I let you down?* I think about it all the time.

I'm carrying you still.

The sun was up, blazing. In shirtsleeves I walked outside, sniffed the piñon smoke flowing from the metal pipe chimney, heard snow dripping off the eaves. There was a faint, fresh breeze. Her footsteps were imprinted in snow, which was melting fast to red earth.

It was easy to follow her trace across the highway. She'd skipped over the road ditch, slipped underneath the barbed-wire fence, left a scrap of tweed cloth caught on a barb.

There was a cattle gate nearby; she must not have noticed it. I swung it open and started across the pasture. New Mexico sun on snow was so bright, nearly blinding. I could feel the sun's strength but also a cold wind pushing at my back.

Half a mile in from the highway was an irrigation ditch. It was only a couple of feet deep, but deep enough to give a bit of shelter from the wind, deep enough so that I didn't see her until I had nearly stumbled over her.

She had taken off her coat and spread it out. She lay on her back, looking up at the sky, like someone daydreaming on a picnic blanket by one of the summer lakes outside Berlin. Her eyes were open.

She had on one of her chic Berlin dresses and a pair of rubber overshoes bought at Gimbels in New York.

She'd pushed up a sleeve and punched the needle into a vein on her left arm. On a patch of melting snow I saw the empty glass bottle and the needle and syringe with its pink plunger pushed all the way in.

I lost track of time for a while. Eventually I decided I couldn't leave her out there. From Karl May I knew *el llano* was a country of bears and coyotes, of scavengers.

So I picked her up. She didn't weigh very much. I began carrying her in my arms across the fields. The snow had mostly disappeared. Red soil glued to my shoes.

I crossed the highway and kicked open the door of our tourist cabin and laid her on our noisy, squeaky bedsprings. I covered her with my jacket. I was shivering. I added wood to the stove before going back outside. I was approaching the old woman's cabin when her door creaked open. She stood holding a Winchester rifle in both hands. I recognized the rifle from so many western films.

"There's been an accident," I said. I spoke in German—it just came out that way. I repeated myself in English.

I was trying to warn my feelings away. I did not want feelings at that time. The ground I remember: red and wet. The blue sky, the violent sunlight.

"*Está muerta?* She dead?"

Like a lot of people out that way, she might have had Comanche or Apache blood. Her brown eyes were almond shaped and her steel-gray hair was in a thick braid. Fear seemed no part of her. She lived so far from anyone's help maybe fear was no use, fear had atrophied.

"You go to Clovis." She motioned at the Plymouth with the rifle barrel. "Find the sheriff. Get out of here. Go."

On the driver's seat of the Plymouth I found the note Karin had scrawled on a sheet of paper torn from her notebook. The woman stood watching while I cranked the starter, punched the gas pedal too hard, and flooded the carburetor. I reset the choke, counted to thirty, and stabbed the starter button with my foot. The engine caught, and the car began to growl and shake like an animal. The highway was clear and dry. It took an hour to reach Clovis, with nothing on the way, no traffic, no animals, only the surreal emptiness of *el llano*. The sheriff's office was in the courthouse at the center of town. There was no one in. The clerk in the tax office sent me to a café across the street where the waitress pointed at a man in a gray suit, white shirt, and black necktie, alone in a booth eating his lunch. He stared at me while I described what had happened, then he picked up his hat and I followed him back to his office. An hour later we started for Grady. I sat in the backseat of the sheriff's Pontiac, a deputy in a mackinaw jacket sitting beside me. Someone had snapped handcuffs on my wrists. Two more deputies followed in a wheezing truck.

When we got there I wasn't allowed to get out of the car. The woman stood in her doorway watching the sheriff go into our cabin. He came out after a while and disappeared into the old woman's cabin for what seemed a long time. I watched the deputies carry out Karin's body wrapped in a sheet and place her in the back of their truck. It was nearly dark when we started back to Clovis.

I was the only prisoner in the Curry County jail until Christmas Eve, when they locked up a young cowboy who'd been fighting. He was sick all night, and in the morning the deputy made him scrub out his cell before turning him loose.

The day after Christmas we buried her. The cemetery was mostly dirt, very little grass. The sheriff stood alongside me. There was a warm, pleasant wind. The pine coffin was like her father's, except with metal nails. The nearest rabbi was in Santa Fe, two hundred miles away. A New Mexican priest read Old Testament psalms.

The coroner ruled the death a suicide, and I was handed the keys to the Plymouth, which had been driven to the courthouse. Her things were in her suitcase in the trunk, except her overshoes, her purse, her British passport, and the *Kinds of Light* notebook, which were in a grocery sack on the passenger seat. Nothing was missing as far as I could tell.

It took three days, driving all day and most of the night, to reach the Canadian border. I sold the Plymouth, crossed the border, started life in a new country.

I didn't know what to do with her things, so I had the clothes laundered and cleaned and packed them in a cedar chest. I should have given them away, but that seemed impossible at the time. After the war they no longer had the same power over me, but I held on to the chest, as my wife and children are perfectly aware. I still have it. It's in the attic of this house. After my death I've asked my son to see to it that everything is burned. He'll manage that. It's too much for me. I've asked him to hold on to these pages for twenty-five years, and after that he may do with them what he likes.

Arten von Licht Buch [Kinds of Light Book], *Karin v Weinbrenner*. Unpaginated. In English and occ. German. Lange Family Archive, 11 C-12-1988. Special Collections, McGill Library, McGill University, Montreal.

———

Although I traveled over the plains for more than three hundred leagues, there were no more landmarks than if we had been swallowed up by the sea.

—Francisco Vázquez de Coronado to the king of
Spain Oct 20 1541

In oklahoma we had encountered bitter weather, a norther, with a horde of freezing droplets of dust and rain rattling and banging against the passenger side of the Plymouth. I turned south at Guymon, Oklahoma. Soon we crossed into Texas, and soon after that were across the Canadian River, very weak and thin in those drought years, hardly a trickle showing.

South of the river we could see the red-rock bluffs of *el llano* rising up from the desert floor. The highway was built on a rubble incline, and as we started climbing, our speed began dropping. I could feel the motor straining, and downshifted.

Then suddenly we were at the top of the bluffs, and the blacktop shot before us like an arrow, perfectly level, perfectly straight. This was the great high plain, *el llano*. And almost immediately the black clouds cracked and the sun pitched down a rainbow. It lit the country up so quickly it took us by surprise.

"Pull over!" she cried.

We had not passed another car since crossing the state line of Texas. There was no traffic in sight, and I could see a long, long way ahead. I pulled over. She flung open her door and was out almost before the car stopped. I happened to notice a small dark stain on the back of her skirt and saw a spot the size of a quarter left on her car seat. Ever since the miscarriage there had been cramps and bleeding, sometimes heavy.

She had left her door hanging open and was walking along the highway.

I shut off the motor and climbed out. There was a scent of sage, of rain on dry ground. The rain had stopped by then. Little ghosts of steam fluttered from hot asphalt.

To the east I could see the silver-blue column of rain walking away across the country. Sunlight spread over fields the color of lion skin, fragrant with wet. There was a tick of hot metal from our car. Barbed-wire fence flanked the highway on both sides; wind had piled up tumbleweeds along the western fence. The highway ran perfectly level as far as I could see, pointing like a needle to the level horizon. The sky kept opening up. A tumbleweed broke free from the mash and went skittering across the road.

One feels vulnerable, certainly. Humans are small out there. But the sun shone with power, and El Llano Estacado just then spread out before us like a promise we could believe in.

A young man wearing a silk necktie bought in Paris. A young woman with a blot of blood on her skirt. A Plymouth car with blue NEW YORK WORLD'S FAIR license plates, pulled over on the highway shoulder, passenger door hanging open.

"Billy!"

She was pointing to the west. When I looked that way I saw a small herd of pronghorns moving across a wide pasture.

My blood hummed. So we'd been right after all! *El llano* was a powerful place, and its magic was occurring for us. The past was behind us. Sweetie the Plymouth was taking us in the right direction, toward the future. Sage smelled like incense, and small, hasty, finely tuned animals were moving like our best dreams across open country.

I'll leave you here, beside a highway in Texas, just come up on *el llano*. It's not where our story ends, but it's where I'll leave you, your right hand shading your eyes as you watch those antelope flicker across a yellow field—alert, sensitive, tuned to one another. Moving in unison, like a darting flock of birds.

Why you've done it, Billy Lange. You've brought her to the open country.

That's what I was thinking.

It's rare to recognize happiness for what it is, but I did then. It was like that morning on the Eschenheimer Anlage, your pied-à-terre—French doors flung open, rain just past, and the fragrance of trees floating from the palm garden across the road. I held it in my hands, I knew it for what it was.

ACKNOWLEDGMENTS

Jenny Mayher of Newcastle, Maine, was, once again, my earliest reader. Her suggestions and insights were invaluable. I learned a lot about Llano Estacado from *Horizontal Yellow: Nature and History in the Near Southwest* by Dan Louie Flores, from John Miller Morris's *El Llano Estacado: Exploration and Imagination on the High Plains of Texas and New Mexico, 1536–1860*, and also from Meredith McClain's Web site, www .meredithmcclainphd.com. I owe huge debts to NIAS-Netherlands Institute for Advanced Study, to the Dutch Foundation for Literature, and to the Canada Council for the Arts for their generous support.

A NOTE ABOUT THE AUTHOR

Peter Behrens's first novel, *The Law of Dreams*, won the Governor General's Literary Award, Canada's most prestigious book prize, and has been published in nine languages. His second novel, *The O'Briens*, appeared in 2012 and was hailed as "a major accomplishment" by *The New York Times*. The author of two short-story collections, *Night Driving* (1987) and *Travelling Light* (2013), Behrens held a Wallace Stegner Fellowship in Creative Writing at Stanford University and is a Fellow of the Radcliffe Institute for Advanced Study at Harvard University. Born in Montreal, he lives in Maine.

A NOTE ON THE TYPE

This book was set in Janson, a typeface long thought to have been made by the Dutchman Anton Janson, who was a practicing typefounder in Leipzig during the years 1668–1687. However, it has been conclusively demonstrated that these types are actually the work of Nicholas Kis (1650–1702), a Hungarian, who most probably learned his trade from the master Dutch typefounder Dirk Voskens. The type is an excellent example of the influential and sturdy Dutch types that prevailed in England up to the time William Caslon (1692–1766) developed his own incomparable designs from them.

Typeset by North Market Street Graphics,
Lancaster, Pennsylvania

Printed and bound by Berryville Graphics,
Berryville, Virginia

Designed by Betty Lew